PENGU
ADAM
Vo

David Fraser, author of *The Hardrow Chronicles*, of which *Adam Hardrow* is the first volume, is also a biographer and a military historian. He has previously published six novels, including the *Treason in Arms* series which spans two world wars. He was once one of Britain's most senior generals, is married, has five children and lives in Hampshire.

DAVID FRASER

ADAM HARDROW

VOLUME I
OF
The Hardrow Chronicles

PENGUIN BOOKS

PENGUIN BOOKS

Published by the Penguin Group
Penguin Books Ltd, 27 Wrights Lane, London W8 5TZ, England
Viking Penguin, a division of Penguin Books USA Inc.
375 Hudson Street, New York, New York 10014, USA
Penguin Books Australia Ltd, Ringwood, Victoria, Australia
Penguin Books Canada Ltd, 2801 John Street, Markham, Ontario, Canada L3R 1B4
Penguin Books (NZ) Ltd, 182–190 Wairau Road, Auckland 10, New Zealand

Penguin Books Ltd, Registered Offices: Harmondsworth, Middlesex, England

First published 1990
1 3 5 7 9 10 8 6 4 2

The moral right of the author has been asserted

Filmset in Ehrhardt [Linotron 202] by CentraCet Cambridge

Printed and bound in Great Britain by
Cox & Wyman Ltd, Reading

CHAPTER 1

'What I have got to decide,' said Colonel Dauncy, 'is whether
or not to initiate the procedures which would lead to your
trial by court martial. For a serious offence. You realize that,
I suppose?'

'Yes, sir,' said Adam Hardrow. He would have preferred
to say nothing, the question appearing essentially rhetorical,
but his commanding officer had paused after the interrogative
note he had given to 'I suppose', and had then barked 'Well?'
– a habit of his.

'Yes, sir.'

Behind the colonel's chair was standing Captain Benedict
Jameson, Adam's company commander and immediate
superior. At a small table set at right angles to the colonel's,
the battalion adjutant, Lieutenant Tom Stubbs, sat, pen
poised in the right hand, apparently absorbed in an open
exercise book. He had a separate office immediately outside,
adjoining the colonel's, but this was his station when justice
was being dispensed.

Colonel Dauncy grunted. Then he gave something which
sounded like a sigh.

'I wonder if you realize, young man, what a deplorable
lapse of discipline this is? You, an officer in this regiment
whose duty it is to set an example at all times – *at all times* –'

Adam reckoned that this wasn't going to be too serious.
The colonel, perfectly capable of administering a scathing

reprimand, of reducing officers and men before him to ashes with the scorching of his tongue, had called him 'young man'. He had uttered the words angrily but they were inconsistent with the cold correctitude which would have presaged real trouble. He made a mistake there, a tiny part of Adam's mind registered; whatever he's decided he should have kept me guessing a bit longer. The fleeting thought came to him with more affection than concern.

'– decided to disobey my explicit and very important orders, given out two days ago. Do you remember exactly what they were?'

'Yes, sir.'

'Well?'

'You ordered, sir, that all ranks living in barracks were to remain in barracks until further orders. And that married personnel, if not parading or on duty, were to remain in their quarters or home, immediately available if recalled.'

'And you are in no doubt as to why I gave those orders?'

'You expected the official order for the battalion to mobilize at any moment, sir.'

'Exactly.' Colonel Dauncy looked at Adam with a particularly stern, indeed menacing countenance. Behind his eyes, however, misgivings were in play. From the BBC news, two days earlier, he had drawn his own very definite conclusions. Soviet Russia and Nazi Germany had signed a pact and every experienced commentator was taking the view that this gave Hitler a free hand against Poland. Britain and France had guaranteed Poland. From brigade headquarters, above him, Colonel Dauncy had gathered that nothing was official yet but that mobilization must now be only a matter of days away. Hours perhaps. How not? On his own initiative Colonel Dauncy had decided that everything must be absolutely ready, doubly, trebly ready; so that when the button was pressed the 2nd Battalion, Westmorland Regiment, would be ahead of the whole division in its mobilization. Reservists would return to find the battalion machine wound up and prepared. Mobilization stores would be methodically issued, cleared, accounted for while other battalions were, metaphorically speaking, rubbing the sleep out of their eyes. He had stridden into his office in a grim, businesslike way, sweeping Tom Stubbs into his wake.

'I want all ranks confined to barracks and quarters when not on parade. The word will come at any moment now. I talked to Brigade from my house.'

The adjutant had demurred.

'You don't think that this might go on quite a while, Colonel?'

'It can't.'

'We can't really keep the whole battalion locked up for days on end. After all, we –'

'Who's talking about locking them up? I merely wish to have them instantly available. It takes too long if men are all over the town. To say nothing of officers.'

'Right, sir. Of course, sir, the War Book gives us quite a lot of time, and everyone knows what –'

'Get that order out,' Colonel Dauncy had said curtly. His mind, within minutes, had turned uneasy. It was true that the mobilization instructions allowed for a period of warning. He knew that Tom Stubbs, as he started to write a message for all companies and departments of the battalion, as he rang for the regimental sergeant-major, was saying to himself that the colonel was being edgy and unbalanced, and was mucking the battalion about unnecessarily. The old man's jumping the gun, the adjutant was thinking; if he bobs like this sitting in Aldershot what's he going to be like when we go to war? He's past it, that's the trouble, he's over the hill. At forty-five. Colonel Dauncy, a sensitive and perceptive man, understood very clearly, and his face had assumed an even more determined expression. He had spent too much of that day looking at the telephone, willing it to ring with the dramatic order

3

which would justify his prudent anticipation. It hadn't. Through the thin wall separating Tom Stubbs's office from his own he could hear the adjutant's telephone. That hadn't rung either.

All that had been two days ago, since when the 2nd Westmorlands, at first excited and alert, then sensing anticlimax, ultimately bored and questioning, had been confined to their red-brick Aldershot barrack blocks. Colonel Dauncy had started this morning by saying to Tom Stubbs, 'Companies have got all the preliminaries well out of the way now. Once the official word comes it'll take no time, no time at all.'

'Quite, sir.'

'I think we'll relax the orders, Tom. Making certain things clear. No leave of any kind, of course –'

'Of course, sir.'

'Walking out can be permitted after duties today, provided all office telephones are manned at all times –'

'Right, sir.'

Then Tom Stubbs had told him about Second-Lieutenant Adam Hardrow. And two hours later Second-Lieutenant Adam Hardrow was standing stiffly to attention in front of Colonel Dauncy's desk, and Colonel Dauncy was looking at him very sternly.

He was looking at a tall young officer with very dark, wavy hair, rather a pale face, blue eyes, and mobile, sensitive features. It was a face difficult to imagine in sleep, a face which looked as if thoughts and emotions and intentions were perpetually forming and re-forming behind the eyes. The nose was slightly beaked and the lips generous and full. Adam Hardrow was broad-shouldered but slender, with the slenderness of youth. A whitened scar about two inches long, the mark of a fall from his pony when six years old, slightly disfigured the right temple of his forehead.

Colonel Dauncy said again, 'Exactly. At any moment this

battalion is likely to be ordered to mobilize for war, *for war*, you understand! And soon thereafter to move to France, as part of one of the leading divisions! Regular divisions, of an expeditionary force! And if an officer of this battalion is to remain in it, fight with it, he must demonstrate responsibility. And discipline.' Colonel Dauncy took a deep breath.

'You, on the other hand, not only went off somewhere, illegally and against orders, last night. You then, behaving not like an officer but like a naughty schoolboy, chose to climb back into barracks over the barrack wall. Where, having fallen from the top of that wall, you were found by the battalion orderly corporal. By *the battalion orderly corporal*! Do you think it's good for the discipline of this battalion that a corporal finds it his duty to report a young officer, in a dinner-jacket, found lying between the barrack wall and the kitchen door of the officers' mess?'

'No, sir.'

'Where had you been?'

'To a party, sir.'

'*To a party!* In spite of my orders! In spite of the gravity of the – the international situation!'

Adam said nothing to this. He liked the colonel, and did not fear him. He wanted to make his face indicate respectful contrition, recognition of the heavy burden of responsibility his commanding officer bore, regret that his own criminality might have made it heavier. He had, however, never been good at controlling his own very expressive features or simulating mood at will. He did his best but only succeeded in looking sulky. There was a long silence during which Adam fixed his eyes on a colour print hanging on the wall above the colonel's head: it depicted a battle during the Sikh wars, the regiment, red-coated, engaged heroically, the Sikhs (of extraordinarily ferocious appearance) seeming to be getting the worst of it. Beneath the picture Benedict Jameson's eyes looked straight past Adam, straight ahead.

Adam heard Colonel Dauncy say, 'Were you drunk?'

'No, sir.'

'You were lying on the ground –'

'I'd twisted my ankle, sir.' He added, and knew it was foolish, 'It's all right now.'

'I don't care a damn how it is now. You say you weren't drunk.'

'Not in the least, sir.'

'Why should I believe that?'

'I assure you, sir,' Adam said, 'that it is true.'

Tom Stubbs looked up sharply. Something in Adam Hardrow's tone had introduced into the room a note, a flavour, perhaps even a tension, which had not been there before. Benedict Jameson, with enjoyment, recognized it. Getting on his high horse, he thought, prepared to take punishment, to take the rap for breaking the rules, for being an ass, but not prepared to have his word questioned!

Colonel Dauncy also felt it. He snorted. Then he said, 'You have set a disgraceful example. You will find it hard to retain the respect of your men. How can you demand instant obedience from soldiers who know that you, yourself, are disobedient? Supposing one of your men had broken out of barracks –'

Adam was well aware of this line of reprimand. He deserved it. He gazed at the embattled Westmorlands and Sikhs.

'– would now be in the guardroom, and on a very serious charge –'

Adam knew the answer, of course: I'd do my job, the man would do his punishment.

'– indiscipline, immature and irresponsible –'

And so will I.

'– you will be confined to barracks and will do the duties of orderly officer for one month –'

And no mobilization?

'– your personal appearance could also do with smartening up. The adjutant will arrange for you to drill with the potential non-commissioned officers' squad when not parading with your company. That's all.'

Adam saluted, turned about and marched out of the room, the door being opened as if with automatic machinery by an orderly who, in theory, acted upon the sound of boot striking floor as Second-Lieutenant Hardrow turned about, but whose ear, in practice, had been attached to the gap between wall and ill-fitting orderly-room door. Benedict Jameson moved to the front of Colonel Dauncy's desk and saluted before his own departure.

'That young man is lucky, Captain Jameson.'

'Certainly, sir.'

'I hope he'll live it down.'

'If you mean with his platoon, sir, there'll be no problem. He's very popular. They love him.'

'They do, do they?'

'Yes, sir, and I'm afraid they're likely to do so now more rather than less.' Benedict Jameson could get away with this sort of thing. Handsome, relaxed, quick-witted, an ironic smile on his face more often than not, he could imply without open impertinence that nobody was likely to withdraw respect from a high-spirited young officer who had chosen to ignore a manifestly foolish and premature order, given out in a fit of the jitters by a commanding officer who was past it. All that and more was conveyed by Captain Jameson's informative phrase – '. . . more rather than less.'

Colonel Dauncy muttered, 'He's very like his father.'

Jameson said nothing, and after a second or two, during which his commanding officer seemed about to speak and to think better of it, he saluted again and left the room. With some shuffling of papers Tom Stubbs, too, got up to go.

'Just a minute, Tom.'

7

Colonel Dauncy was gazing out of the window in the right-hand wall of his small office. Through it he could see a squad of young soldiers, potential NCOs, drawn up for drill. They were, he could see and hear through the closed window, being put through it by Company Sergeant-Major Turvey, a warrant officer surplus to establishment who was under orders to move north to the depot but who, with the authorities' agreement, was remaining with the battalion for a further month to supervise this course. It didn't look as if the course would continue to its ordained end but, with some reluctance, the commanding officer had agreed to its starting as planned, despite his continuing certainty that war was imminent. The regimental sergeant-major had stressed the importance of this routine measure. And life had to go on. Soon young Adam Hardrow would be standing in those ranks, put through it more than any by Turvey, a hard man.

'I've just had this letter, Tom.'

Tom Stubbs had remarked the envelope, without particular inquisitiveness. He was not inquisitive by nature. The envelope had been marked 'Personal, Confidential'.

'You can read it, Tom.'

The letter, signed by somebody describing himself as an assistant military secretary, said that Lieutenant-Colonel John Dauncy, MC, Westmorland Regiment, was to hand over command of the 2nd Battalion Westmorland Regiment, and proceed immediately to take up the duty of assistant district commander of a newly formed Appleby Home Defence District, Northern Command, in the rank of lieutenant-colonel. Lieutenant-Colonel Francis Fosdike had been selected to assume command of 2nd Battalion, Westmorland Regiment, from 27 August 1939. Both officers would report in writing through command channels when change of command had been effected. The letter added that particular numbered paragraphs of King's Regulations applied. Colonel Dauncy guessed, correctly, that these explained that he would

8

not be entitled to certain perquisites once his time at the head of his battalion was concluded.

'Good Lord, sir, that's tomorrow. Sunday.'

'Bit of a rush, Tom. Of course Frank Fosdike knows it all well –'

'He doesn't know this battalion well, sir.'

'No, mostly with 1st Battalion recently. And Staff, of course. Anyway I'd better ring him up. He's been at the War Office for the last two years, as you know.'

'This will be a shock to the battalion, sir. They'll be upset. When will you tell them?'

It was true. Tom Stubbs's words were sincerely meant. He was painfully alive to John Dauncy's shortcomings. The colonel was slow, he seemed to have slowed down even more in the last three months. He took time to make up his mind, particularly in small things. He was liable to sudden fitful decisions, made almost on impulse – alarming if anticipated as possible in the atmosphere of the battlefield, an atmosphere Tom Stubbs, aged twenty-seven, could barely visualize. But the men of the battalion liked Colonel Dauncy. They grumbled about his moods and his sometimes erratic orders, and they mimicked his voice and his rather waddling walk (for he had always looked the part of commander better when sitting his horse, and the horses had been given up a year or two back). Yet they liked him. They trusted him. They referred to him as Johnnie. They thought he was fair. They reckoned that he cared about them. Had they considered the matter, which few, if any, had done, they would have decided that he had no ambition beyond serving his regiment and commanding them, all of them; and when their wives met him he was beautifully mannered, courteous. Orderly-room Sergeant Vokes's notoriously formidable and outspoken wife had said, 'The Colonel treats every woman like a duchess,' and the word had stuck. They were going to miss Colonel Dauncy, Tom Stubbs decided.

And what about him? The colonel was a widower, and childless.

'Where will you live, sir? Up there?'

'No idea, Tom. It'll soon be wartime, or so I still believe, as you know well. In wartime, if it's anything like the last show, people live all over the place. Requisitioned houses. Barracks put to odd uses. Local authority buildings – the lot. I remember it all well. I imagine this so-called District has plenty of accommodation, or will have. There'll be a mess. I'll take Higgins, of course.' Lance-Corporal Higgins was Colonel Dauncy's batman.

Colonel Dauncy said that the brigadier had rung him up the evening before and been very nice, 'surprised as I was'. Then they talked about how and when to tell the battalion that they were soon to be in new hands and Colonel Dauncy said that he must now have a talk to the regimental sergeant-major, arrange for a few words to the sergeants' mess, that sort of thing. He'd tell all officers in the ante-room after lunch today. And the battalion had better be paraded –

'Like to tell them myself, rather than let it get around as a rumour.'

'I expect, sir,' said Tom Stubbs, 'that they know already.' It always amazed him that so shrewd and experienced an old hand as the colonel could still appear ignorant of how instantly the best-kept confidences became the stuff of barrack-room gossip and embroidery. Colonel Dauncy gave one of his grunts. Before the adjutant left the room he said abruptly, 'Young Hardrow's very like his father.'

'So you said, sir.'

'Same devil in him. Same pride, too. Same sort of – er – suppressed force.'

Colonel Dauncy didn't make a habit of discussing subaltern officers with this sort of psychological insight and interest. Tom Stubbs said, 'It's certainly true that the men like him.'

'They liked his father very much. His father was my company commander. Badly wounded in March '18. Huns' last big push. He – Adam Hardrow, Adam senior – never really recovered. Health very poor. Died in '25. Wife was Russian, of course.'

'So I believe, sir. A very regimental family.'

'Very. Well, mind you keep chasing and chivvying this one, regimental family or not.'

'Of course, sir.' After a moment, and diffidently, Tom Stubbs said, 'Do you suppose I can ring up Colonel Frank now, sir? Colonel Frank Fosdike? I imagine he'll want to discuss the arrangements – and I suppose we may all be in a bit of a rush –'

But Colonel Dauncy was gazing out of the window again and didn't appear to have heard. His mind was not on his successor. Nor was it on his own future and his own pain, excusable though that would have been. It was on his Westmorlands. Now that he was leaving them his anxieties, never far from the surface, were, perversely, stronger than ever. Were the battalion good enough? How would they do in the greatest test of all, which couldn't be more than weeks away? What more could have been done?

Colonel Dauncy's mental image of war had been formed twenty-five years earlier and his absolute faith in his regiment and in the British military system was of equal vintage. He had been a very young man in the Ypres trenches – young, nervous, cheerful in spite of the nerves, quick to respond to friendship. He'd joined just after First Ypres, that savage, disorganized scrap in which historians later wrote that the old British regular army died. Well, his battalion hadn't died, but when he joined it, raw from Sandhurst, there'd been just under a hundred Westmorlands left. All ranks. He'd never forget the atmosphere – a sort of uncomplaining, almost gentle, fortitude. You could tell that every man you spoke to had lost one, two, three friends. Dear friends. The sort of friends the army gave you, and nothing else in life could produce. He'd been wounded, but very slightly, at the beginning of 1915 and was back with his battalion within three months.

Then there'd been the Somme. Thank God, they'd been pushed in during the later stages, not in July, not on the first days. It had been grim, but the battalion had taken it well – a mass of new recruits had made up the numbers, but all volunteers still and almost all north-country men, their own sort of men. And then several more battles, which always seemed to take the same form – optimistic forecasts from on high, promising beginnings, then too much mud, too many damned German machine-guns, too many German reinforcements, moving so much more easily than us it always seemed – moving over clean ground, of course, instead of ours churned by our own artillery. But in the end had come 1918 – and that extraordinary German push in March. Astonishing! Fog – then six hours' bombardment, no more; and then, slipping through the fog like ghosts, the leading *Sturmtruppen*. Suddenly materializing, darting, dropping. No tanks or that sort of stuff, just brilliant infantry work and a short, very short, devilish storm of gunfire so you couldn't hear, couldn't think. Then back. Back and back again.

But we'd held. The old Westmorlands had held – that was when Adam Hardrow had been hit; just after his marriage too. What a great chap! And then, miraculously, the battalion going forward, in the summer months, forward at last, skirmishing in open order, clean ground, green fields, trees with leaves on the branches. And the Germans going back – going back fast in some places. And then the end. Anticlimax. Relief, but the rather uncomfortable relief of life returning to limbs in which feeling had for some time been numbed. But we'd won. We'd won, and we'd won because, in the last resort, we were better. Unbeatable, the British soldier. Specially the north-country man.

Then the 1st Battalion and India. Colonel Dauncy had enjoyed India – the occasional excitement, the periodic 'internal unrest' operation in the twenties and thirties, the long marches, the sport, the sense that at least the damned war was over, it was peacetime in spite of India's problems and life was meant to be enjoyed. Then, unexpectedly – two fellows just senior to him had sent in their papers, retired unusually early – England and the 2nd Battalion and command. Command remarkably early – just approaching forty-two. The battalion had been at home for those fifteen years, most of the time pitifully under strength. But this year they'd been reinforced.

And the battalion were good, had always been good. They shot well, they marched decently, they looked well on parade. Discipline – Colonel Dauncy was unshakeably convinced that discipline and discipline alone had won the war – wasn't, of course, what it had been when he'd been young. Free and easy, some of the young NCOs were in their ways. Needed a sharp touch of the whip more often than not. That was true of the whole army, the whole country. Field training? Colonel Dauncy supposed that there'd been too little – the men always seemed to be taken away for duties of one kind or another, and there were these enormous jamborees arranged by Command, tattoos, celebratory parades and the like – but he was unsure what he'd want to teach them even if he had the opportunity. They knew how to dig a trench, and they knew how to handle their rifles. It was unlikely the next show would resemble the open warfare of 1918 – Colonel Dauncy knew enough of the high command's concepts to realize that it would be trenches, damned trenches once again. Digging. Caring for the men's feet and health. Insistence on minor routine – that was where precision and discipline saved lives. The large-scale exercises – and there hadn't been one for ages – didn't teach the soldiers much. He supposed the staffs knew their business. Colonel Dauncy didn't really know any generals, except the one who had inspected them last year and asked a lot of questions whose drift was rather hard to understand.

Yes, he thought they'd do all right. Awful to think of it all happening again – the last war only seemed to have finished a very few years ago. John Dauncy's life had somehow slipped away, a brief interval of quiet between the last German gun of November 1918 and now.

And now the 2nd Westmorlands were again, just as in 1914, part of a regular brigade in one of Britain's very few regular divisions; and, as such, were due, when the balloon went up, to take their place in the line alongside the French. In the British Expeditionary Force – just four divisions, anyway to start with. Pathetic, Colonel Dauncy supposed and doubtfully articulated to himself, although such matters were not for him.

It had been a good party.

Adam had started the evening at his mother's house. Willie Vincent, a friend in another battalion in the brigade, a Sandhurst contemporary, had got him to the mess telephone the previous evening.

'Adam, you're coming to this party at the Beamishes, aren't you?'

'I can't.'

They had both been entertained to dinner a few weeks earlier by Mr and Mrs Beamish who had a pretty house in Richmond, three daughters and no sons. Adam forgot exactly how Mrs Beamish had got to know of him but she had. She had said, 'I used to know your father. *Years* ago.'

It must have been, Adam thought. He remembered his father very clearly but had been only six years old when he died. Mrs Beamish had indicated that her own memories of Major Hardrow were entirely favourable. She had said, when Adam and Willie Vincent were leaving, 'You'll get a card about our little party on 25 August. Everybody's so on edge that I'm sure it's essential to keep going as usual. We're having a few young people to dinner and perhaps dance, it'll be so good for the girls, so many people haven't gone away this August, all so worrying, no point in being got down, mind you two make a note of the date, Aldershot doesn't take you young things long, I know, I worry terribly when I think of the way you all drive, I suppose you could come together –'

'Willie's got a car, Mrs Beamish. I haven't.'

'I'll be chauffeur,' Willie said. 'It's awfully kind of you.' And as they drove homeward they agreed the Beamish girls weren't too bad, food and wine had been first-class, old Beamish had been in the army in the war and then obviously made a lot of money (in insurance, a fellow guest had told them) and Mrs B never stopped talking but was kind. No reason not to accept. And three weeks later had come Colonel Dauncy's order followed by Willie's telephone call.

Adam had said, 'I can't. I'll write a line to Mrs Beamish.'

'Why can't you?'

Adam had explained. Willie had said it sounded extraordinary. Everybody knew the situation was serious, everybody would jump to it if the balloon went up but meanwhile what the hell? Willie's own commanding officer had just caught the night train to Scotland, saying he'd come back if the army mobilized but meanwhile he wasn't letting Hitler interfere with his shooting, and this week had been arranged long ago. 'What's so special about the Westmorlands?'

Adam, on most occasions, would have told him, and they'd have ragged each other, each fiercely proud of his regiment behind the banter, the good-natured insults, the mockery. This time, however, he'd felt irritated. It was an absurd order. Everyone knew that after mobilization was ordered there would be plenty of time. Furthermore Adam had undertaken to see his mother who lived in London, in Elm Park Gardens.

The plan had been that he should go up by train, change and have a talk at home, and then be collected by Willie *en route* to the Beamish festivities. Mrs Hardrow was in a rather nervous condition. She would be disappointed.

Willie had pushed. He'd said, 'Nobody will know. Get someone to say you're in bed with flu. If you need to say anything. I can't believe you'll be missed. You're not having evening parades or anything, are you?'

'No. Just sitting about, frankly. Nothing left to do.'

'Can you get to the station without trouble?'

Adam said he could think of something. By now he'd decided to flout authority and was enjoying himself. He knew the particular place in the barrack wall where an active young man could get over, for the return journey in darkness. Thus he caught an evening train to London, having arranged with a friend to say, 'I *think* Adam's in bed with a touch of flu,' if anybody asked after him during the evening. (He later discovered nobody had.)

Adam took a taxi from Waterloo to Elm Park Gardens.

'Darling,' his mother said, 'I was so worried you'd not come. Dreadful news on the wireless all the time.'

'Well, here I am, Mama. Going to a party. I must change in a minute.'

'Adam, is there really going to be a war?'

'My commanding officer certainly thinks so. He's surprised it hasn't started yet.'

'I can't believe we should go through all this for the Poles. If it is for the Poles.'

Adam avoided political discussion with his mother. She lived, very vividly, in the past and he found it difficult to talk without discord. For Natasha Hardrow the most terrible event in the history of the world had been the Russian Revolution of 1917. It had driven her, aged nineteen and an only child, from the home she loved a hundred and fifty miles south of Moscow. It had deprived her of parents, for although her mother had escaped with her it was only to die from broken health in 1920, and Natasha's father had disappeared – presumed murdered – in the chaos of Russia in 1918. The Revolution had driven Natasha to exile and to England, supported by little except her courage and a handful of rather distant English relations.

And there, two months after reaching London, she had met the young and enormously handsome Major Adam Hardrow, on leave from the army in France. She had been introduced to him at a party given to raise money for refugees. Many were much worse off than Natasha, whose mother was quarter-English and was able to assemble a few (very few) financial assets in England. The party, following a concert, had been attended by a number of Russians, all stunned by recent events, all assuming that the turning upside-down of their world must be temporary, all talking of the imminent day of return, all exchanging snippets of news, all – without exception – haunted by some memory of terror. All resolutely refusing to contemplate the reality of permanent exile. All laughing and embracing and, here and there, weeping a little. All indomitably brave. And Adam Hardrow had been there, bored, brought along 'by someone', resenting the waste of an afternoon of his precious leave, but curious too, eyes restless, penetrating. Those eyes had met Natasha's. A moment later he had walked confidently across the room and obtained an introduction to her mother.

And they had, instantly, fallen in love. Two months later, in the first week in March 1918, he had again secured a week's leave and they had married, a rapidly arranged, delightful, wartime London marriage, Adam immaculate in gleaming field boots and perfectly cut khaki tunic, Natasha as prettily dressed as her mother could manage amid the exigencies of wartime London.

Three days later he had returned to France. And a fortnight after that the telegram had arrived – 'severely wounded but doing as well as can be expected'; something of that kind, bringing tears of gratitude for his survival and anguish lest the severity of the wounds might have savaged Adam's body or mind or personality beyond recognition, might have destroyed his life. And hers. Within weeks Natasha knew for certain that she was pregnant.

Adam had returned, military service over for him, thank God, but with the future twisted and foreshortened. The German shell splinter had found his lung, and another had almost simultaneously smashed his left leg above the knee. They had built a life of a sort together, and Natasha had found to her indescribable relief that nothing had impaired her love for him; but Adam had been living on borrowed time, and in 1925 a sudden bout of pneumonia killed him. Young Adam had been born a week before Christmas 1918, his father still convalescent. The twins, Nicholas and Saskia, had arrived in 1922. They had all lived frugally, in London, convenient for the medical attention Major Hardrow required too frequently; but had also acquired a remote farmhouse on the borders of Yorkshire and Westmorland, not far from the regimental depot at Kendal; not far, either, from the village which, according to family tradition, had given them their name.

'No great status or any nonsense of that sort,' Adam Hardrow senior had said on that subject, 'but in the old days a man, as often as not, was known by the village or hamlet he came from: "John of Borstal", that kind of thing.' He'd smiled at his own little joke, made more than once, but Natasha knew that it gave him pleasure to feel that his roots tapped deep. Great-grandfather Hardrow had made a modest – by now very modest – fortune in textiles, during the Napoleonic Wars, but the family's pride was to have come of north-country stock, hardy yeomen with inherited determination and pugnacity. And good looks, Natasha often said to herself fiercely; I've married into a family with natural beauty, how not? And then, in 1925, he was gone.

The only close Hardrow relative was her husband's cousin Beatrice, a spinster of about his own age, who was permanently lame from a riding accident in childhood. Natasha had only met Beatrice twice and neither time could be described as a success – there had been a visit soon after young Adam's birth to the remote stone-built house, half farm, half manor, where Beatrice lived her rather solitary, reclusive life. Beatrice had been gruff, rather formal, obviously eaten by shyness and by no means forthcoming to her cousin Adam's young, strange, Russian wife. After Adam's death, when young Adam was at school in the north country, Natasha had supposed she should visit Beatrice and suggest making her home a base for a half-term visit to her son. It hadn't worked in the least well. Surprisingly, after the experiment, young Adam had said, 'I rather like Cousin Beatrice.'

'My God,' Natasha had countered, 'she never speaks! Did you get one word from her?'

'Not really. But she gave us an awfully good tea. And I like the house. I like the way it sort of grows out of the hill.'

'The rain! . . .'

'I liked the rain.'

Natasha had the sense to recognize incompatibility when she met it, and the visit had not been repeated. Cousin Beatrice was never mentioned at Elm Park Gardens and Natasha was untroubled by the thought that her son Adam's nearest Hardrow connection – for Beatrice, only daughter of an elder son was, Natasha supposed, the head of their family in some undefined and unimportant way – was almost wholly a stranger to him. His father, Natasha knew without pleasure, had been rather fond of Beatrice, but there it was.

And painfully like his father young Adam had become, sitting on an upright chair in her little drawing-room, frowning at some inward thought, raising his eyebrows when Natasha said, 'If it is for the Poles . . .'

'I suppose, Mama, it's time to say to Hitler, "Stop! No further!" It happens to be the Poles because that's where he's made clear his eyes are fixed. Danzig.'

'Oh dear, you're too young to remember how it all happened! Why should the Poles have Danzig? That corridor cuts Prussia in half. *We* wouldn't like that!'

'Of course not. But Poland would have no outlet to the sea unless –'

'Lots of nations have no outlet to the sea. And Poland has only just become a nation, anyway. Before 1914 it –'

'Mama, Poland is one of the most ancient nations of Europe. It was reborn in 1918, after the Versailles Treaty, because it had been destroyed by –' They had had this conversation before. Adam said 'by events', aware that he needed to change soon if he was to get to the Beamishes without keeping Willie Vincent waiting. Conversation with his mother about previous partitions of Poland and the historic map of Europe tended to go on a bit.

Natasha sighed sadly. She said, 'I don't see that it's *our* business. The Poles are a quarrelsome people, there was always trouble with the Poles.'

'There was always – !' Really, Adam thought, Mama still talks as if she were sitting in Moscow or Petrograd as she invariably calls it. She hates the Soviet Union like poison, but with part of her mind she reckons that the Poles are still tiresome subjects of the tsar who mustn't be allowed to get out of control. He decided there wasn't time to remind his mother that a Nazi–Soviet pact had just been concluded, that at least all her enemies had lined up together on the same evil side of the line. And on the near side of the line, whatever their faults, were the Poles. He said, 'I must go and change, Mama darling.' His mother moved her face sharply away from him and he knew that her eyes were full of tears.

'Oh, Adam! I feel I've seen it all before! Young men going to war! Uniforms! Railway stations! Telegrams!'

'I know you feel like that, Mama. Of course you do.'

'I just *can't* feel it's necessary. And you're –'

'Only a child, Mama! I know!' Adam smiled at her, and she turned her face back to him and said 'Darling!', and he moved across and kissed her. Bother the Beamishes. And Willie Vincent could be given a glass of sherry if he arrived early.

Natasha said, 'Darling, I know I see the whole thing very personally. Mothers do.'

'Of course they do.'

Natasha looked more cheerful suddenly. Her moods always changed rapidly.

'An old friend called on me yesterday – somebody in your regiment. In your father's regiment. I suppose I should call it "the Regiment" but I was never really an army wife, as you know, it was all so short and then Adam was invalided out and so forth. I knew some of them of course, his brother officers, in the early days, but then, somehow –'

'Mama, who was this old friend?'

'Frank Fosdike. He was in the same battalion as Adam, as your father. He's a most charming, intelligent man. I don't think I'd seen him since – oh, probably since your father died. Then I met him out to lunch, extraordinary, last week. And yesterday he telephoned and asked if he could call on me. Very unexpected, really quite embarrassing! I hadn't time to ask anybody else round –'

'It sounds most improper, Mama!' Adam's voice had a chuckle in it, but he had noted the uncertain, almost flirtatious note in his mother's voice when she had said 'very unexpected'. His mother, Adam said to himself, was forty-one or forty-two. Pretty old, of course, but still lovely with her black, black hair untouched by grey, her white, white skin and her figure which was astoundingly slim. And her clothes, her style were always perfect, Adam thought, although, God knew, she managed on remarkably little money, and there was as yet no way in which he could help her. He looked at her, as he said 'most improper, Mama!', and realized, with gratitude, that he was lucky to have a mother he could talk to and love without affection, without sense of obligation. He also realized that he had not greatly relished the touch of near-excited uncertainty in her voice as she'd said 'Frank Fosdike'.

Now she said, 'He lost his wife, poor man. Two years ago.'

'Ah! I've never met Major Fosdike. I've heard him talked about of course. I suppose he knew Dad well.'

'Oh yes, it was so lovely being able to talk about him, about your father. He – Frank – was much younger. He was only twenty when the war ended, but he had the last year, that awful March 1918 German attack when Adam was wounded, all that. Frank greatly admired him, admired Adam.'

Adam nodded, without great display of interest. As a senior major of the regiment, currently serving on the Staff, Frank Fosdike moved in a sphere remote from Second-Lieutenant Hardrow.

'He's in the War Office,' Natasha said.

'Does he think war's inevitable?'

Natasha sighed. Not answering directly, she said, 'He – Frank – was saying how much he wished he knew you. Knowing Dad, and so forth. And he said, which was rather nice for me, "I hear he's outstanding. I look forward to seeing plenty of him."'

'He said that? "Seeing plenty of him"?'

'Yes. And wasn't it splendid that he'd heard so well of you?'

'I can't understand it. Any of it. I'm far too young and junior and unimportant for someone like that even to have heard my name.'

'Nonsense, Adam. Of course he knows your name. I think he's about to leave the War Office, do something else, he hinted it, he was rather – well, animated.'

'I see.'

'And he knows your name, of course he does, you're your father's son.' Natasha added, 'And mine.'

With a sudden switch of subjects she said, 'And do you know who's arrived, first visit to London in five years? Uncle Alex!'

Uncle Alex, Alexei Alexeivitch Kastron, was the much younger brother of Natasha's mother, her youngest uncle. Alexei lived in Paris, an existence suspected by Adam of being pretty threadbare. He had only met Uncle Alex twice, since it was clear that funds did not extend to frequent cross-channel trips; and Adam had never visited France, although his French – insisted on by wise, trilingual Natasha – was reasonably fluent.

Adam's mother adored Uncle Alex, despite his poverty a figure of some glamour. Uncle Alex was a widower, with one son about Adam's age although of Natasha's generation.

'Poor Uncle Alex,' Natasha said, 'he won't know what to do with himself if there's a war. Do you know he was the youngest colonel in the Imperial Army? The *youngest colonel*! He was only about thirty, think of it! Everybody told us he was an absolute byword for bravery.'

'Yes, so you've told me, Mama. Now I really must go and change.'

'He was in the cavalry. Fighting the Germans in Galicia, in Poland. Beating them too, until, until –' Natasha sighed. Adam kissed her.

'I must run, Mama. A friend's picking me up.'

'Uncle Alex would love to see you. He telephoned me from what sounded an awful little hotel, near Paddington somewhere. I'll try to get hold of him when you come up next. If you do.' But Adam was already bounding up the stairs to the bedroom which had always been his.

*

It was only a little later in his career that Adam came to appreciate how much life imitates fiction in the use of coincidence. Hear a name for the first time for ages and it will be spoken to you again twice before nightfall. Meet a person, and the same person turns up as if by appointment several times within the week. Learn of some bizarre circumstance overtaking another, and you will meet it yourself next day. And so forth. It was almost as if acknowledging an inevitability that Adam was introduced by Mrs Beamish to a tall girl in a white dress with rose-coloured silk at the neck and on the sleeves, a pretty girl with long, brown hair bound with a ribbon of the same rose colour, and a rather large nose. Her eyes – Adam thought afterwards that they were grey but he was unobservant about the colour of eyes – were friendly, full of laughter.

'Now Caroline, this is Adam Hardrow. Adam, this is Caroline, Caroline Fosdike.'

Caroline was particularly easy to talk to. She said she lived with her father, in London, and was learning about flower arrangement. Then she intended to arrange flowers for parties and functions, working from home.

'One can make quite a lot of money. But I expect it'll come to an end any minute now, don't you? My little world must be about to crash, I feel. I can't see people arranging flowers, or paying for it, during a war.'

'I suppose not,' Adam said, 'and I suppose that a war's inevitable.'

'Daddy certainly thinks so. He's in the army, in the War Office.'

'Frank Fosdike?'

'Yes, that's right. Why – do you know him?'

'He's in my regiment. He's about the senior officer in it, I should think, bar our colonel, our commanding officer. And I'm about the junior officer in it. So I certainly don't know him. But I know of him.'

The Beamish radiogram was blaring out 'Music, Maestro, Please', and Adam steered Caroline Fosdike into the Beamish dining-room, parquet floor now cleared for action. Adam, unlike the great majority of his contemporaries, danced well and with enjoyment. Caroline was not only pretty, he thought, but was restful to be with. When she spoke it was to say something sensible, and when they were both silent their bodies responded harmoniously to the music and to each other. Adam decided that apart from an obligatory dance with each of the Beamish girls, necessary tariff for the evening, he'd spend all of it that could be managed with Caroline Fosdike. It had been worthwhile secretly flouting Colonel Dauncy's orders. It was a good party. Somebody, amid laughter and a mild but unforceful protest from Mrs Beamish, turned several lights out. The dining-room was now only dimly lit. The radiogram was fed 'The Way You Look Tonight', followed by 'Smoke Gets in Your Eyes'. They circled slowly. Records were piled on an automatic dispenser and turned over or changed after seven or so had been played. The Beamish girls obviously had quite a collection, with the bands of Ambrose and of Artie Shaw predominant.

Caroline said, 'So you're in the Westmorlands. Does that mean you're at Aldershot?'

'It does.' Adam's arm tightened round her waist and his cheek brushed hers. I suppose, he thought, war is going to mean not often smelling a girl's scented skin near, like this. Well, there it is! He touched her cheek with his lips and her hand on his shoulder moved a little, a very distant caress.

'I shouldn't say this, Adam –'

'Say it!'

'I think you're going to see my father quite a bit. I'm not allowed to say more.'

'You needn't!' So old Fosdike was returning to the regiment! As second-in-command, presumably. Adam murmured, 'Cheek to ask, but I suppose your father's about forty, isn't he?'

'Forty-one.'

'My mother knows him. My father died years ago.'

'And my mother,' Caroline said, 'died last year.'

Lights went on and Mr Beamish called out some instructions about supper. They'd already dined, and well; but midnight was thought to bring the absolute obligation for more, and Adam was of an age when food and drink should be taken whenever on offer. He steered Caroline towards a glass of champagne, and murmured 'Later?' It had to be a Beamish girl next.

'Later?'

'Hope so!'

And much, much later Willie Vincent had set him down in the appropriate avenue running eastward from the Queen's Parade at Aldershot. And Adam had missed his foothold descending from the top of the wall. And Orderly Corporal Janson, respectful but aware of his duty, had found him; and made the appropriate entry on the report.

'When was the regiment formed? Jackson?'

'1804.'

'1804, what?'

'1804, SIR.'

'I should bloody well think so. And next time you come to attention take less than ten minutes about it. And close your heels. Hear me?'

'Yes, sir.'

'Well, bloody well close them now, then! Why anybody thought some of you would ever make non-commissioned officers in this regiment Christ only knows. Who formed the regiment? Bates?'

'The Earl of Appleby, sir.'

'That's right, Bates. The third Earl of Appleby. The regiment's first colonel. What was his full name, Bates? Well, COME TO ATTENTION, BATES! God Almighty, if Hitler

26

could see some of you he wouldn't be able to start a war, he'd die of laughing. Now – the first colonel's full name? I've told you. You was told in your first regimental history lecture when you joined the depot. Wasn't you?'

'Yes, sir.'

'Well, what is it?'

'Forgotten, sir.'

'FORGOTTEN! Some of you'll forget your own names every morning. But I WON'T! NO, I WON'T! Full name of first colonel of the regiment, Herries.'

'Don't know, sir.'

'Tell him, Mr Hardrow.'

The sweat was coursing down inside their shirts and the tightly wound puttees itched their calves. This was their first stand-easy for twenty minutes. Company Sergeant-Major Turvey had gazed at them as he had first called them to attention, given them 'open order march' and 'right dress' for his inspection. Turvey could have been a great actor, Adam decided; he was an artist at registering emotions with movement in the somewhat coarse features of his mottled face, with the set of his shoulders and the gestures of his right arm. Under the left arm a cane was tucked which could also be used with immense dramatic power.

Turvey had completed his inspection, finding some fault with each one. When he had come to Adam, standing in the ranks with the rest, he had paused and his voice had assumed a note of appropriate respect. It was, Adam knew, entirely insincere, intended to fool no one.

'You should have a word with your batman, Mr Hardrow, sir. He has not done his work properly on your belt.'

There was no correct response to this. Turvey had continued in his voice of mock-embarrassment at having to utter such criticisms to an officer.

'When standing to attention, sir, the toes should be pointed outwards at an angle of – no sir, no sir, not too much. That's

27

all wrong! I thought they really got that right at Sandhurst, but I'm afraid the place isn't what it was.'

And so on. Then they had started foot drill, squad drill. Up and down, up and down, up and down, faster, faster, faster –

'Squad will advance, LEFT TURN. LEFT – RIGHT – LEFT – RIGHT, RIGHT TURN. Move to the left, ABOUT TURN. Squad, HALT. Herries, are you bloody deaf or something? Step off sharp now. Quick MARCH. LEFT, RIGHT, LEFT, RIGHT. Watch it now. Salute to the right. SALUTE, ONE, TWO, THREE, FOUR –'

This was the preliminary 'chasing', the penal hour before the potential NCOs would undergo other instruction. The duties of a lance-corporal in the barrack-room. The duties of corporal of the guard. The duties of orderly corporal. The organization of the platoon and the routine duties of a section commander. And so on. Adam would leave them to Turvey's mercies and resume the duties of orderly officer, parading with his company when not so engaged. At night he would sleep by the orderly-room telephone and twice during the night would go round barracks, visiting sentries, peering into remote corners for intruders or malefactors, permanently alert and permanently available.

'Full name of the first colonel of the regiment. Tell him Mr Hardrow, sir.'

'John Jameson, third Earl of Appleby,' said Adam conversationally. Although not invited, he decided that a little more time could be spun out of this stand-easy. It was likely that Turvey's next torment for them would be drill at the double, mark time at the double, knees up, up, up, up –

'He – the Earl of Appleby – raised us as a regiment of volunteers during the Napoleonic wars. Then, after those wars, after the Peace of Paris, we were made a regular regiment, on the regular establishment.'

'That's RIGHT,' shouted Turvey, as if personally responsible for this development. 'That's right, sir. On the regular establishment. And under what title, Price?'

Price was in the same company as Adam, B Company. A large, gentle, phlegmatic man, he was devoid of even the smallest tinge of ambition and had not in the least desired promotion. His company sergeant-major had said to him, 'You're for the next corporals' course, Price.'

'Me, sir?'

'You. Captain Jameson's named you. Now don't you let me down.'

'But, sir –'

'Don't "but" me. And blow your nose.'

Price did his best to look intelligently at Company Sergeant-Major Turvey. Turvey disliked B Company sergeant-major and looked forward with pleasure to the chance to say to him in the sergeants' mess, 'Pretty dim men from B, I have to say it. Pretty dim, not up to the standard. That oaf Price for instance –'

Turvey put his face very near Price's chin and looked up into his eyes with his own small, pale, bloodshot orbs.

'Under what title, Price?'

'The, the –'

'The 115th, you blockhead! Why d'you think there's a "115" on your cap badge? Why –'

'Company Sergeant-Major,' said Adam suddenly, 'I expect Price was wondering whether you wished him to say the 115th which we became, but which was not, of course, the original number under which we were incorporated. Price knew, because he attended my regimental history lecture last Thursday and we talked about it, that our first number was the 114th. Only after 1835, with the formation of the regiment now named the North Yorkshires, were we slipped to 115th. Shall I explain to the squad why?'

'Thank you, sir,' said Turvey. 'Most interesting!' He had

lost the initiative and resented what he suspected were a few well-concealed smiles here and there among the squad. He looked at his watch. One more question and then there'd be time for seven minutes of sheer hell for them before the duty bugler blew 'Disperse'. He fixed Price with his eye again, pointing his cane with menace.

'Now, Price, you've heard that the first colonel was John Jameson, third Earl of Appleby. Has he had any relations in the regiment recently?'

'Yes, sir.'

'Can you name one, Price?'

'Yes, sir.'

'THEN DO SO, PRICE!' Turvey roared. His prey was near to eluding him.

A vacuous smile spread over Price's large, florid face as he said simply, 'Me company commander, sir.'

'Captain Jameson, that's right,' Turvey said shortly. 'Some sort of relation of the first colonel, I know. Now you lot had better sharpen up the way you answer and your general ways. The new CO, Colonel Fosdike, is going to inspect the squad before you pass out on Saturday week. Colonel Fosdike is very, very particular. Colonel Fosdike knows me well, he knew me in the 1st Battalion, where not one of you lot would have lasted five minutes. Before parade today he said to me, he said, "Company Sergeant-Major," he said, "how's that squad of po-tential NCOs of yours doing?" Colonel Fosdike's only been here two days but he'd marked you already, see? "Not too bad, sir," I said, "but not too good either." "Right, Sergeant-Major," he said, "I'll inspect them myself! On Saturday week." So God help you if you let me down! Now, properly at ease –'

At that moment an orderly, who had marched across the parade-ground, moved up to Company Sergeant-Major Turvey and stamped to attention.

'Excuse me, sir.'

Turvey swung round and looked at him with a frown.

'Well, young fella – ?'

'Message for Mr Hardrow, sir.'

'Well, there's Mr Hardrow, in the ranks,' said Turvey irritably. 'Report to him.'

Adam watched as the young soldier marched up to him, uncertain exactly where to position himself to deliver his communication. Officers generally stood somewhere where it was possible to identify and isolate them. This one was standing at ease, with a private soldier on each side.

'Excuse me, sir –'

'Yes?' said Adam.

'Commanding officer's compliments, sir, and would you report to him in his office, right away?'

CHAPTER 2

Although they had both spent the last forty-eight hours in the same barracks Adam had not yet spoken to Colonel Frank Fosdike nor seen him at close quarters. With the rest of the battalion he had heard with sadness Colonel Dauncy tell them that he had been ordered to hand over, but Adam had been carrying out his duties as orderly officer when the new battalion commander spoke to all officers before lunch on his first day, and since then, as far as he could observe, Colonel Fosdike had spent much time in his office. There had, as yet, been no personal contact with Mama's friend, with Caroline's father. It was probably just as well. Commanding officers were, Adam knew, best avoided; the less they saw of one the better.

Now Adam had been summoned. Tom Stubbs's door was open; he got up as Adam passed in the passage, said 'wait there' and went into the colonel's office. A moment later he emerged and said, 'Report to the commanding officer now.'

The colonel's door was ajar and Tom Stubbs gestured Adam inside but didn't accompany him, closing the door behind him. Adam marched up to the table and saluted.

'Second-Lieutenant Hardrow, sir.'

'Yes,' said Frank Fosdike, 'you couldn't be anyone else.' His voice was soft, almost caressing, and held a smile in it. Adam knew that this was not going to be a reprimand, but he felt wary. He retained the wariness but found it mixed with perplexity at Colonel Fosdike's next words.

'I knew your father well, Adam. I admired him very much. I'm delighted that his son is serving in the regiment and in this battalion.'

'Thank you, sir,' said Adam. It was all very odd. There must be more to a summons to the CO's office than this genial family reminiscence.

'You're awfully like your father. I suppose you were very young when he died, you probably hardly remember him.'

'I was six, sir. I remember him very well.'

'Good. Good. I saw you drilling with the young potential NCOs just now.' Frank Fosdike's tone was now unmistakably humorous.

'Yes, sir.'

'And you've hardly been in the mess since I've arrived. Permanent orderly officer or something.'

'For four weeks, sir.'

'Pretty tough sentence, Adam.'

'I deserved it, sir.'

'Probably. Probably. Anyway, I think you'd be better employed with your company than drilling with prospective lance-corporals. You passed off the square months ago, I take it. So I've told the adjutant that that part of – of your punishment is over. You'll be orderly officer tomorrow, Friday, but after that Tom is restoring the previous roster and as far as you're concerned that's that.'

'Thank you, sir.'

'I'm told you've got a good platoon. I expect you – and it – will be tested pretty soon now. Do you know what's very probably going to happen tomorrow morning – on your last orderly officer day, in fact?'

'No, sir.'

'Keep it under your hat. Unless there's a change of heart by the government between now and bedtime, reservists will

33

be recalled tomorrow.' These were men who had finished their active service but had a commitment to recall in emergency.

'Mobilization, sir?'

'That's it. That's it, Adam. And plenty to do. By the way, how's your mother?'

'She's perfectly well, sir.'

'Saw her the other day. You're very important to her, Adam.'

Adam said nothing to this. Deep inside him irritation was stirring at this insidious, agreeable battalion commander who so easily passed to a favoured second-lieutenant expectations about mobilization, about dramatic events, which as far as Adam knew, had not yet been communicated to company commanders or anyone else; who remitted so lightly the penalties of Adam's acknowledged wrongdoing; and who spoke with such intrusive familiarity of Adam's mother and her love for her son. But 'Steady on,' another bit of his mind tried to say, 'he's the colonel, after all, and he's being pretty decent to you!'

'All right, Adam, that'll be all. As I say – it's good to have you in the battalion.'

Something made Adam pause before saluting and turning. Something made him say, 'Excuse me, sir –'

'Yes?'

'I'd like to say that Colonel Dauncy was perfectly fair in his punishment of me. Perfectly fair.' He supposed, a moment later, that he sounded priggish.

'So you implied just now. Very right and proper of you to say it, Adam.' Frank Fosdike nodded dismissal. After the door closed behind Adam Hardrow he remained looking at it for a few seconds before reaching with his left hand for the next document in the in-tray. Well, the battalion would undoubtedly be ready to receive reservists and issue mobilization stores with the minimum of stir and disruption. That old ass John Dauncy and his fussing had ensured that, at least; and when the brigadier, using oblique language earlier this morning, had warned him of the next day's likely activities Frank Fosdike had been able to say, 'I understand you, sir. No problems that I can see,' with a satisfying show of nonchalance.

Benedict Jameson said, 'So you're out on remission!'

They were in B Company office, Benedict sitting on a folding wooden chair which he tilted precariously backwards every now and then. His cap was pushed to the back of his head, the peak crowning his broad, slightly tanned forehead like a halo. They wore caps in company office when company orders were being taken and formal business done. This was just concluded.

'Out on remission! And after tomorrow, I gather, back at full-time duty with the company!'

Adam nodded. Ben Jameson was friendly and generous with his platoon commanders, treated them almost as equals, confided in them when discussing the men of the company, chuckled at their peccadilloes, pretended to commiserate with them if in trouble with CO or adjutant, enjoyed occasionally dispensing the hospitality of his home to them, and attracted from them a good deal of affection as well as respect. This respect was accorded to a very alert, intelligent officer who taught them a lot in an apparently effortless way. Ben set a certain 'tone' in his company, a tone of unfussiness, of high standards achieved without too much straining, of style. Imperceptibly young officers joining the company were touched by the same style. Imperceptibly non-commissioned officers adapted to it, even the more rigid and unimaginative among them realizing that in B Company a particular sort of manner, quiet rather than noisy, sensible rather than ostentatious, was the accepted thing.

But despite the atmosphere of relaxation which Ben Jameson generated – sometimes with some contrivance – and despite the admiration he awakened in his subordinates, that admiration was mixed with more than a little fear, although none would have admitted to it. His mind worked fast and his tongue could be cutting. His voice was never raised, but it seldom needed to be. His frequent half-smile and his somewhat languid manner masked a strong, decisive character and no man in B Company mistook the fact. His young officers – warmed by his smile, watchful of the movement of his eyes, enjoying with the sense of privileged observers his minor affectations – were, nevertheless, in awe of him.

The awe was undiminished by Ben's human weaknesses. One afternoon, a few months after joining the company, Adam had found himself walking back from the garrison hospital to barracks with the senior platoon commander in the company, Bobby Forrest. Both had been visiting men of their platoons in hospital – Bobby Forrest had been three years in the battalion, all of them in B Company. As they reached the main road a car drove past them, rather fast, the driver hooting cheerfully; a woman was sitting beside the driver.

Bobby chuckled, 'Ben in his new car!'

'And his wife with him,' Adam remarked, for something to say. He had not yet met Felicity Jameson. She was spoken of, cautiously and with respect, as a beauty.

Bobby said, with another chuckle, 'Or somebody else's!' Then he said, 'Ben's incorrigible, you know! A great man, our company commander, but incorrigible when it comes to the pursuit of ladies.' He said it quietly, with no hint of criticism. As far as he was concerned, Adam well knew, Ben Jameson could do no wrong.

Adam had said, conversationally, 'How long's he been married?'

'Ben? About five years, I think.' Bobby had sighed. Then

he'd said, rather sententiously, 'My God, we're lucky to be in B Company! With Ben! He's by far the best company commander in the battalion – the men have got absolute faith in him.' Bobby might have felt, Adam decided, that he had been improper, even disloyal, in hinting at his hero's failings, and to so junior an officer. They'd walked on in silence.

Now Ben Jameson said, 'Unless we're actually fighting the Germans on Saturday would you like to come to dinner?'

'I'd love to.'

'You've not met Felicity. If the rumours are right, and I expect they are, we may be in the middle of mobilization by then, but one's got to eat. You'd better come at about eight. Not a party or anything. You know where we live.'

Adam did – the Jamesons had taken a house in a small village five miles from barracks. On that Friday the German army invaded Poland. And on the Saturday the regular reservists earmarked for the 2nd Battalion, the Westmorland Regiment, began to arrive in Aldershot, to be smoothly absorbed by the battalion's administration and the arrangements Colonel Dauncy had meticulously, if prematurely, ordained.

Felicity Jameson poured herself a drink and said, 'You never told me your youngest officer was such a stunning looker!'

'Is he?'

'He is. And although he's so young, he's got a lot of character. I liked him.'

Felicity wore a short, dark blue dress, cut to a very low V at the neck and leaving her arms and shoulders bare. She was not particularly tall, but had considerable presence, and her entry into any room brought a momentary hush. Felicity had very dark hair; dark, rather definite, eyebrows above brown eyes. Her skin, very smooth, was the colour of honey. She had a somewhat deep voice and a trick of looking for a silent second or two and very steadily at a person before addressing

37

a remark. Shapely, and with slender wrists and ankles, Felicity was a little plump. Agreeably so, Adam had thought.

Ben Jameson stretched himself on the sofa and yawned. It had been an exhausting day but he'd been glad that he'd invited young Adam Hardrow to supper; he should have had him to the house long ago but there'd been one thing and another and it hadn't worked out. Felicity had clearly been rather taken with the boy, so the evening had slipped by agreeably, and when Adam had left – tactfully and mercifully early – it sounded as if his expressions of gratitude had been sincere.

Ben looked without particular pleasure at the only oil painting in their small drawing-room. It was a copy of a portrait owned by his third cousin, the head of his family, and it represented John Jameson, third Earl of Appleby, first colonel of the regiment. Ben's great-great grandfather had been younger brother of that Earl and his own forebears had served, more often than not, in the Westmorlands. They'd had, on the whole, little money, although ('Thank God one of us had the sense not to go into the army,' Ben would comment lazily) Grandfather Jameson had achieved a modest career at the Bar and had married quite a rich woman from a Nottinghamshire business family. Ben's own father, however, had spent most of this inheritance and had certainly not added to it.

Ben had indicated the portrait to Adam. 'First colonel.'

'What relation exactly, Ben?'

Ben had explained, and rather liked the frowning absorption in Adam Hardrow's face. He really loves this regiment of ours, Ben thought, he's adopted it as his very own family. He minds, though God knows why he minds quite so much. He had already observed that young Adam Hardrow's knowledge of their regimental history went far beyond the modest requirements of duty.

'What about your cousin – the present Lord Appleby?'

'Cavalry. Thinks it smarter. That's the way these things go.'

Adam's gaze had gone back to the indifferent portrait copy and Ben had given him a glass of sherry.

'Your own family's a regimental one, too, Adam?'

'My father, you mean. Yes. And my grandfather for a short while only. In India.'

'Well, there we are. It doesn't seem to me particularly important.' Then Felicity had come in, and they'd talked of little but 'the situation'. And at nine o'clock they'd listened together to the news on the wireless. There had been scenes in the House of Commons. The prime minister had made a statement about the German offensive, an offensive which seemed to have been accompanied by a massive air onslaught, but which, the newsreader said, was being held by the Poles at all points. At Westminster members had shouted questions as to why no British ultimatum had yet been sent to Germany. 'It is understood,' the smooth voice of the newsreader had added, 'that the Cabinet will meet later this evening.'

Ben switched the set off and the three of them sat in silence for a while. Soon Adam said, 'I'd better be going.' He had borrowed a friend's small car.

'See you in the morning, Adam.'

'By which time I imagine we'll be at war!' Adam's eyes were bright. Felicity said to herself, 'He's utterly overjoyed!' She was uncertain what she herself felt.

'Doubt if we'll be actually at war,' Ben said calmly, 'but there'll be an ultimatum. Withdraw from Poland or else.'

'Which I presume will be rejected?' But Ben just said, 'Goodnight, Adam. Nice seeing you here.'

Next morning was Sunday. At half-past eleven the men of 2nd Battalion, Westmorland Regiment, were gathered in the mess room round an improvised wireless loudspeaker system, listening to the melancholy tones of Neville Chamberlain. There had been no church parade. The Westmorlands heard

39

the prime minister tell them that no answer had been received to a British ultimatum. Britain was therefore at war with Germany. The struggle was against evil. Right would prevail. Colonel Fosdike felt particular satisfaction that every Westmorland reservist had returned. Companies were at war establishment. Within weeks the advance party would be off to France.

'Mr Hardrow, sir.'

'Yes, Sergeant Pew?'

Sergeant Pew, Adam's platoon sergeant, was a short, broad-shouldered man from Barrow-in-Furness, with strong, very regular features.

'Could I have a word about Crowe, sir?'

Crowe was a reservist, a man who had joined the platoon on the previous Sunday, travelling on his railway warrant to London from Barrow and to Aldershot from London according to his instructions. There had been a large party on the same train, eleven of them had come to B Company, and three of the eleven to Adam's platoon. Despite the distance, they had been some of the first arrivals. Adam had interviewed each man, asked about the personal circumstances of each, tried to assess whether the man was the sort who would remember his soldiering, slot easily back into the army, put on his new uniform (the entire battalion were in the process of being issued with a fresh set of kit from the mobilization stores) with a certain wry satisfaction well concealed by jocular profanities; or the reverse, mind twisted by uncomprehending resentment, personal anxieties, family troubles. Most of them were between five and ten years older than Adam.

Adam had marked Crowe. Crowe was an exceptionally smart man who had immediately and instinctively adopted the position of attention when interviewed, while still in his civilian clothes. Crowe wore a very worn but tidy brown suit, soon to be dispatched to his home address, postage by courtesy of the army. Crowe had looked a useful addition to the platoon, tall, obviously strong, alert in his manner, somewhat silent and reserved without any appearance of sulkiness. Adam had noted, however, that Crowe had not smiled when Adam had tried a small joke as he had done with each. Crowe had been very serious.

'What about Crowe, Sergeant Pew?'

'He's gone absent, sir.'

'Did he say anything to you about any trouble at home, anything of that sort?'

'No, sir. Not a word. He must have walked out after parade on Wednesday, last night. Only here three days. He's on the morning report. They'll be getting on to the police, of course.'

'He looked a good chap to me, Sergeant Pew.'

Sergeant Pew said nothing to this. It was early days yet, he reckoned, to say whether individuals in the platoon were or were not to be relied on. Crowe came from Ulverston, not far from Pew's own home. So did several of them. If he'd gone home it was an expensive trip. The journey back would be in handcuffs, most likely.

Adam said, 'Well, he was prompt and punctual in obeying the original order of recall.'

Three days later, on 10 September, Crowe returned – not in handcuffs but of his own volition, walking into barracks in mid-morning after travelling from the north overnight. Adam was informed, after B Company's morning parades were over, that Crowe was a prisoner in the guardroom, and due to appear at company orders shortly. He marched into Ben Jameson's company office.

'There's a man of my platoon, sir, Crowe, who's about to come before you.' Company commanders were addressed as 'sir' on parade or in the company office.

'Well?' said Ben, 'I gather he went absent, we've got to stamp on short absences, the CO has made that clear, and he's right. Orders for the advance party's move are expected

41

any moment – they're at forty-eight hours' notice, you know that. And the main body of the battalion won't be more than a week after that. We can't have men hopping off to Westmorland when they feel like it, even if they aren't away very long.'

'I think he's a good man, sir. I was hoping, as it's a short absence, that he won't have to go before the CO.'

'That,' said Ben coldly, 'is my business. Anything else?'

'May I speak to him before you see him, sir?'

Ben nodded. Company orders were due in twenty minutes and Crowe, an escort beside him, was already standing at ease in the passage when Adam saluted and moved from the room. The company sergeant-major was busying himself marshalling other applicants and malefactors. Adam said to him, 'Captain Jameson wishes me to see Crowe for a minute, Sergeant-Major. Before orders. Alone.'

'Right, sir,' said the company sergeant-major, by name Darwin, doubt in his voice. He didn't care for platoon commanders who tried to interpose themselves like grit in the moving wheels of justice. A small side office was used to house company stationery and indeterminate impedimenta not to be taken to France. Opening the door to it, the company sergeant-major snapped, 'Crowe. In here!' To the soldier escorting Crowe he barked, 'Not you, Smithers!' and Adam found himself confronting Crowe at very close quarters.

'Stand at ease and easy, Crowe. I wanted to ask whether there's anything you'd like to tell me, before going before Captain Jameson.'

Crowe took a little time to say, 'No, sir.' Adam was studying him carefully. Crowe was a handsome, well-set-up man of, Adam judged, about twenty-eight. He looked deeply unhappy.

'Are you sure, Crowe? The company commander will, of

course, ask you if you've got anything to say. I take it you admit you went absent?'

'Yes, sir. I went home.'

'To Ulverston.'

'Yes, sir.'

'According to my platoon record you're married. Is your wife ill, perhaps? Or expecting? If there's real trouble at home I know Captain Jameson will do his best to help you.'

'It's not like that, sir.'

'Well, what is it like?'

Crowe said, 'The wife, sir –' Then he seemed stuck.

'Yes?'

Very slowly, very painfully, Crowe said that his wife had sometimes – it had happened twice, he couldn't say why it was – left home. Disappeared. Gone off. Then, two days later, she'd come back. Said she'd been with friends.

'Why?'

Crowe couldn't say. He said, in a very soft voice, 'I didn't go for her, like,' and he seemed to be half pleading and half apologizing for the fact that he'd not beaten his straying wife. What other decent course of action was open to a man, his voice seemed to suggest. Adam, not yet twenty-one and inexperienced in the world, suddenly felt quite certain that Crowe loved his wife. Perhaps very much.

'And your wife went off the day of your recall, is that it?'

Crowe said, almost inaudibly, 'The very day.' Then he said, 'I'd not dodge me recall, but then I'd got to go back, sir, to see. There's nobody –' No relations to speak of. No neighbours of particular closeness to reserved, silent Crowe. Just an unstable, erratic girl. The Crowes had no children.

'Do you think your wife will be all right now, Crowe?' It transpired that Mrs Crowe had been back at home, penitent and overjoyed to see her husband, when Crowe had made his illicit journey.

43

'Yes, sir. She'll be all right. Her mum lives in Barrow. She'll keep in touch.'

Adam knew that there was no certainty at all in Crowe's voice. He said, 'Well, you'll have to do your punishment, Crowe, of course. But in future – no matter where the battalion is, here, or in France or wherever – for Heavens' sake ask to see me if you're worried, and talk about it. Understand? There's nothing much people can generally do, but at least *talk* about it. And we'll be running quite a – a sort of regimental contact organization, a welfare organization as it were, from the depot, you know. Sometimes there are things that can be done to help, even if it's just a matter of a friendly visit.'

Crowe said, 'Yes, sir.' Then, unexpectedly, he said, 'I like the army, sir. It's not that.'

At that moment Company Sergeant-Major Darwin threw open the door of the little cubby-hole in which they'd been talking and said, sharply, 'Out here, Crowe!' Formal proceedings were about to begin.

Adam told his company commander that Crowe had an unreliable wife and had been unhappy, but that he, Adam, was sure Crowe was at heart an excellent man. Crowe had returned to duty of his own accord and crime of this sort was, Adam believed, wholly out of character. Adam felt gratified by the award to Crowe of the lightest sentence Ben Jameson could with propriety inflict.

Afterwards Adam said to Sergeant Pew, 'He's a decent man, Crowe.'

'Yes, sir.'

'But with a difficult wife.'

'That may be, sir,' said Sergeant Pew. Privately he reckoned that if the British army's fighting strength were to be dependent on the incidence of difficult wives we didn't stand a chance. He also reckoned, however, that his platoon commander was a decent bloke, no question.

*

The 2nd Westmorland's advance party left Aldershot for France twelve days after the battalion reservists had begun to arrive. In that time of feverish activity not only was new personal equipment issued to every man, but new and unfamiliar weapons were taken into service for the first time. They had, of course, been told about these, but only a few officers and men had carried out courses on them or even seen them. To each platoon a large and extremely heavy anti-tank rifle was entrusted, a two-man load with a monster clip of cartridges. And so on. Battalion transport arrived – much of it civilian vehicles requisitioned and overpainted. Adam's 'platoon truck', instead of an army fifteen-hundredweight, was a baker's van with the previous owner's name still decipherable. The men of B Company worked a full and hard day, mastering new equipment as well as time allowed, shooting on the thirty-yard range, and marching several hours a day to harden the soft feet of men from civil life; seeking also to bind newcomers and old hands together with the bonds which only the unison of a marching body of men can provide.

Sometimes the whole battalion marched together. Returning to barracks they marched past Colonel Fosdike. It was curious how seldom they seemed to see him. He appeared to move in a somewhat remote and elevated world, referring to international politics with easy familiarity, mentioning generals by name and nickname when talking in the mess before lunch to a circle of seniors, mentioning them in a casual sort of way. He clearly found it of use to call often at brigade headquarters, and at divisional headquarters on some pretext more than once. 'Our commanding officer,' Ben Jameson observed to anybody within earshot, 'is a man of influence, clearly. How privileged we are!' There was what Adam inwardly described as 'that certain something' in Ben's voice.

Other battalions of the division, they knew, had moved to

other parts of England on mobilization. They, the Westmorlands, were to travel to the port of embarkation direct from Aldershot. It was rumoured that forty-eight-hour passes 'to say goodbye' might be granted if they didn't travel for another fortnight. In general they remained in barracks or quarters, instantly available. They saw the advance party go with a sense of heightened tension. Then, on 16 September, Ben Jameson told them the orders.

'Passes until midnight, the 18th, all ranks except the rear party.' A rear party of men unfit for service abroad was to remain in barracks and clear up after they'd gone.

'When are we to go, Ben?' They were in the officers' mess, just about to lunch.

'Looks like the 21st.'

'So we'll just have two days here –'

'And Christ knows it's all we need! The whole battalion's bored stiff by now with hanging about.'

But, bored or not, there was considerable excitement in the air as Ben harangued the company in his easy, rather offhand way about the necessity of being back on time, absolutely on time, even if it gave a man twenty hours of rail travel for only an hour or two at home. Everybody had been surprised by the absence of the bombing which all England had expected as the instant accompaniment of war. Rail travel, despite the blackout and troop movements, was still proving possible. And now London theatres and cinemas, closed on the outbreak of war in anticipation of an immediate rain of destruction from the sky, were one by one opening again.

Adam telephoned Elm Park Gardens.

'Mama, it looks as if I've got tonight and tomorrow night off, back here Monday evening.'

'Oh, darling! I thought you must have gone already! Frank told me he hoped you'd get a few hours off but then I heard nothing –'

'Colonel Frank? Have you seen him?'

'Yes, he called in here, he had some sort of business in London, I suppose at the War Office –'

Rum! Then – 'So, Mama, I'll catch a train at about tea-time.'

'Lovely, darling. Are you going out somewhere this evening? If there's anywhere open!'

Adam had tried to contact Caroline Fosdike, but with some diffidence. He thought that to take Caroline out would be, or should be, delightful. On the other hand, unless she were already away doing war work of some kind, he knew that she kept house for her father at what she'd described as their little house in London, so that if Colonel Fosdike gave himself leave with the rest of his men Caroline might have domestic duties. Adam certainly didn't want to intrude on the Fosdike ménage. Tentatively, however, he'd dialled the number from the mess telephone. No reply. He'd tried twice more. Still no reply.

'Don't think I'm going anywhere, Mama. Shall we go out together? You and me?' The twins were back at their respective schools, term having just begun.

'Darling, I can give you dinner here. I don't know that it will be very grand, but we'll manage. And tomorrow I've got Uncle Alex coming and I *so* want you to meet him, so it will be perfect.' It would, Adam knew, be very good even if not perfect. His mother had a gift amounting to genius for producing excellent food at no notice at all and for unexpected numbers. Natasha had no sense of time or punctuality but she could make any meal an occasion, a celebration. Parties were in her blood, and two people or more made a party. Even the work and alarm and irritation caused by the compulsory air-raid precautions (strips of adhesive paper across windows to minimize blast; dark material lining curtains to prevent the escape of light) could not destroy her short-lived happiness as she bustled about her house that

47

afternoon, planning and contriving the entertainment of Adam in a few hours and of Uncle Alex and Adam on the following evening.

'My dear, dear Adam,' said Uncle Alex, 'I wish, I wish with my whole heart that I was twenty-two and not fifty-two. One feels useless, absolutely useless!' Uncle Alex spoke English with a slight and charming accent, stressing the consonants at the ends of words in a 'foreign' sort of way but as at home with the language as he was with French, the language of home and nursery, or with Russian, the nostalgic Russian of distant, alienated homeland. Or, for that matter, with German or Polish. Uncle Alex had had to adapt to many and various and taxing circumstances since getting away from the Revolutionary Kiev Soviet by the skin of his teeth in 1917. Colonel Alexei Kastron, youngest of his rank in the tsar's armies. Wartime promotions, and all of them earned. But nowadays Uncle Alex worked in Paris for a small travel-agency business and it didn't look as if travel agents were likely to be needed much for a while.

'Useless!' said Uncle Alex. 'Although now that the Sovs have lined up with Hitler's *canaille* one might suppose that somebody like myself could have some sort of value. I have been to the French Ministère, where I know several people. Very polite but absolutely nothing doing!' Uncle Alex obviously rather enjoyed this colloquialism and he said again 'Nothing doing! Nothing at all!' He was a slim, neat man, with grey, receding hair, a cavalryman's figure still, and a tiny moustache.

'I even have a friend, a very good friend at GQG – that's Grand Quartier General, you know. They're very busy, but I managed to see him, I'd better not name him, and told him I was very, very happy to serve *in any capacity*! France has been good to me.'

48

Natasha asked if anything had come of this and received from Uncle Alex a shrug and a gesture with spreading palms.

'Not yet, my dear. But I shall keep trying. And you, my dear Adam,' Uncle Alex said, turning on Adam his particularly charming smile, 'it is good to see you in uniform. Of course your mother is distressed – that is the way of women in war. We wouldn't have them otherwise. But for me it is good to see a relation dressed as a soldier.' Since the declaration of war Adam, and every member of the armed services, had worn uniform whether on duty or off, at all times.

Natasha was looking puzzled. 'Uncle Alex, you have been trying your luck with your friends in the Ministry in Paris, on the staff –'

'That is so, my dear.'

'But you came here in the last week of August. Before war broke out.'

'Indeed I did, Natasha. And I don't know when ordinary civilian passengers will be allowed back. I am, so to speak, stuck in London! However, from my business I have good contacts. I think it will be quite easy to travel by the end of the month.'

By which time, thought Adam, I imagine most of the British army will have reached France. He smiled at Uncle Alex and said, 'So you were quite sure war was coming, sure enough to try to get into it!'

'After Hitler agreed with Stalin, wasn't everybody sure? Of course I was sure. All France was sure. We heard there was uncertainty here in London but there was none in Paris. When I had my first rebuff I decided to come here as planned, but when travel to France is permitted I shall return and try again.

'And now, have you heard? The Bolsheviks have crossed the Polish border and are joining in devouring the Polish carcass. Poor Poles. Poor, poor Poles!'

Natasha looked impatient and unrepentant. She was

49

frowning during Uncle Alex's declamation and now she said, 'Uncle Alex, why didn't the Poles do a deal with the Germans? They had no real right to Danzig. It's German, we all knew that. As it is, they've provoked Germany and now the Bolsheviks are taking their opportunity. And we, the British, the French, have done nothing to help, nothing at all.'

'My dear Natasha, so far from helping, it is the British and French who have encouraged the Poles to be stiff-necked. They guaranteed to Poland that they would go to war if Germany attacked. That meant, to Hitler, a challenge; and to the Poles a – a blank cheque, you would say, to be as intransigent as they wished.'

Adam was not prepared to let this pass without comment. He said, 'I don't see what else we could do, Uncle Alex, frankly. If Hitler wasn't confronted sooner or later by us saying "No further", what would ever stop him? It happened to be Poland.'

'"It happened to be Poland,"' said Uncle Alex, a touch of irony in his voice.

'We're at war anyway,' said Adam. 'We may not have been able to defend Poland –'

'Nobody can defend Poland against both Germany and Russia. Nobody ever has.'

'All right. But we've gone to war. We've honoured our guarantee. And we'll win in the end. The point, surely, is that Germany isn't simply going to get away with it.'

Uncle Alex sighed. Before his eyes, evidently, there appeared a continent engulfed by barbarians, with the British and French chirruping futility from somewhere west of the Rhine. And the greatest barbarians, for Uncle Alex, stood east of the Vistula. He said, 'Germany should have been instantly attacked. Instantly. While the Wehrmacht was in Poland.'

Adam's mind went at once to Colonel Fosdike's most

recent lecture to all officers. In this, speaking fluently and often amusingly, he had drawn on his experiences of the Great War, only twenty-one years ago. 'I don't imagine,' Colonel Fosdike had said, 'that our high command – the Anglo-French high command – is likely to show complete indifference to the lessons of the last show! In fact they're very, very well aware of them. And the great thing is to make the other fellow attack you, not walk over the top at him. That's why, when we get out there, we're going to work on and improve the finest military defence system ever devised by man. Sooner or later the Huns *must* attack it – I know they're doing pretty well just now, opposed to Polish lancers, poor devils! But when they attack in the west, *as they must*, they'll find out what a garden path Mr Hitler's led them down,' and so on.

'Uncle Alex, do you gather from your French friends that they would have been keen to attack? I thought – certainly we've all been told for years – that French strategy is defensive. Why should they suddenly leave their marvellous Maginot fortifications and attack the Germans, surrender all the benefits of the defender?'

'Because,' said Uncle Alex, suddenly very solemn, 'Germany will soon be able to concentrate all her forces on one front. It was worth great risks to engage her before that became possible. Great risks. I fear –' But at that moment Natasha told them, briskly, that she was tired of strategy; and Uncle Alex laughed and started to amuse her with stories of questionable propriety about some of the émigré Russian population in Paris.

'You're wanted on the telephone, sir,' said Sergeant Tullett, officers' mess sergeant. Adam had returned in time for supper. Protracted farewells with Natasha had threatened, and he'd decided that it was best to cut matters off at Elm Park Gardens at tea-time and to get under way. Officers were drifting into the mess, the young ones noisy and excited, the older ones talking quietly in corners. Nothing now between them and France.

It was Caroline Fosdike. Adam said, 'Caroline, I've been trying to reach you, but it seemed difficult. I was going to ask you to have dinner. Oh dear! Oh dear, oh dear!'

'Never mind. I expect you'll all get leave from you-know-where.'

'I expect so.'

'Adam, I might write to you sometimes. If you'd like.'

'I certainly would like. Tell me what's going on here. What are you intending to do? Still flowers?' A ghastly facetious observation about a likely boom in wreath requirements if German bombers started operations came to his mind but he suppressed it. What inappropriate dreadfulnesses sometimes bubbled up!

Caroline was saying that she hoped to be taken on as a driver by a government car service. 'Rather a smart uniform!'

'You'll look terrific in it, Caroline. And you'll write.'

'And *you'll* write.'

'I promise. And, as you say, they'll probably start leave soon. There was pretty regular leave last time, I believe. Goodbye, Caroline.'

'Goodbye, Adam.'

'Any absences, Sergeant-Major?'

'None, sir. And some of the lads spent most of the time travelling. But they made it. Good deal of beer drunk on the train, I'm afraid, sir. But no trouble.'

Ben Jameson nodded. Company Sergeant-Major Darwin was, he reflected, too good a man to be left for long in his present position, and it would be a great pity when he left B Company. Darwin would be put in for a commission soon, Ben expected. Darwin was young – he'd been promoted extremely fast, was still in his twenties. Darwin was fit and quick-witted. And the war would bring plenty of opportunities to men like Darwin. If it went on long enough. There had been a huge expansion of the army – on paper at least. A few months ago they'd doubled the size of the Territorial Army with a stroke of the pen, and then found they'd have to milk Regular regiments dry to find a few officers to look after the wretched Terriers, who had virtually no equipment as yet! Yes, the war would foster promotion all right. And in a lot of places, for quite a while, the blind would be leading the blind.

Ben settled a few details with the company sergeant-major, who then saluted, turned to his right, and left the room. Ben tipped his chair back dangerously, as he so often did, yawned and fingered the lapels of his battledress jacket. The new battledress was far from popular with everyone, although the absence of buttons to polish had found a good deal of favour in the ranks. Adam moved round the desk to salute and take his leave.

'Have a good break, Adam?'

'Yes, thank you.'

'I suppose you're leaving a broken heart or two behind you.'

Adam smiled politely. The only times he felt less than enthusiastic devotion to his company commander was when the latter's mood was suggestive.

Ben smiled at him thoughtfully. He said, 'You really love it, don't you?'

'Love it?'

'All this business. Going to war. The regiment. The sniff of battle. Most people take it as it comes, long for it to be over, resent it a bit. Not you. It's what you've been longing for all your life. Right?'

There was a long silence. Adam wanted to be honest. One didn't admit to this sort of thing. War was the greatest calamity yet dreamed up by man. War was wicked. War had

53

only come because the Germans, God-defying, inhuman, insatiable, had inflicted it on the world. The only moral response must be one of deeply unhappy acceptance, coupled with prayer that it would all be over as soon and as bloodlessly as possible.

Ben repeated, with his lazy, mocking smile, 'Yes, longing for all your life. Right?'

'Right,' said Adam. He suddenly felt defiant and free. Ben seemed disposed to talk.

'You're an oddity, you see. It's probably something to do with losing your father, and having a father who fought in the regiment. We want to endure as much as our fathers – it helps make us their equals, which we all long for. True?'

'Perhaps.'

'Then there's the regiment. I've watched you when you've lectured about it. You've really felt what you've told the men, you haven't recited it parrot-wise. As a result you've interested them. Just as you manage to interest them on the few occasions we've been able to get out to do some little tactical run-abouts. I watched you the other day when the company marched to Chobham Common. I listened to you when we got there, when I gave the three of you an hour with your platoons. You didn't see me.'

'No, I didn't.'

'You were making them move in small packets, the bren-gunners, the riflemen – in twos and threes. We've not been teaching that. You were telling them why. You'd worked it out.'

'I thought,' said Adam, feeling very junior and very young, 'that it would be good for everyone to think about it, to work out some system of moving forward under, under –'

'Well?'

'Under fire. It was, well, sort of experimental.'

'It was bloody sensible. But who says we're ever going to move forward – or sideways, or backwards for that matter –

under fire? You've heard our revered CO – only lunatics attack in modern war. The Germans are cast for the part of lunatics, you see, Adam! You and I are going to improve the defences if they need improving, and then wait for the lunatics to show themselves when the shooting season opens!' His voice had its familiar, sceptical note. He said, 'Anyway, I like your enthusiasms. And your regimental connections for that matter.'

'Not as strong as yours, sir,' said Adam boldly.

'True. And how outdated that sort of reverence is! If I possess it, which I generally doubt. I certainly don't share your zeal for battle. And yet, and yet – I find most soldiers stupid, and many boring, but I prefer them as types to the *commerciants*, however prosperous. Absurd, isn't it?'

'Not entirely, perhaps,' said Adam. It was getting difficult.

'Of course it's absurd. A particularly futile form of snobbery! Futile snobbery!' He smiled, with the little twist at one end of the mouth Adam knew well, and said, 'But we both have it, my dear Adam Hardrow!

'Enough introspection. The company office isn't the place for it. Anyway, this time next week we'll be in France. At the front. Ah, that word fingers your heart, doesn't it, young Adam! The front! And perhaps we'll find whether we're as good as we're always telling ourselves we are.'

Adam stood still and looked a question at him, and Ben Jameson said, very suddenly, 'We've been asleep for too long, Adam, and we've not known it! We've supposed ourselves awake! Army! Country! We've been resting on our laurels, you see. The laurels of 1918. And, of course, we've been told that 1918 settled it all for ever as far as the British army was concerned. No more continental adventures! Leave war to the Royal Air Force and the anti-aircraft people! Leave it to the navy! But now, quite suddenly, Adam, we find the old record's being put on again, the old song sung. I suppose I'm wrong but I have the feeling that the record's scratched a bit and the spirit's rather gone out of the singing.'

CHAPTER 3

Before movement to France Adam had had few dealings with the battalion second-in-command, Major George Wainwright, known throughout the regiment – and, indeed, though he barely acknowledged its existence, the rest of the army – as Whisky Wainwright. Whisky Wainwright had acquired his soubriquet at an early age, not from alcoholic excess but, from the accident of euphony. An older officer, in an era when nicknames tended to be almost universal, struggling for a prefix to go with the W, had noticed Wainwright's already luxuriant and spreading moustache and called out, 'Hey, you, Whiskers over there, you, Whisky –', and 'Whisky' he had become.

Whisky Wainwright was an abstemious man, as it happened; but as men sometimes, often unconsciously, cultivate the image others have formed of them, imitating the caricature. Whisky seldom drank anything but Scotch. He drank three fingers of neat Scotch at seven o'clock in the evening, brushing away the offer of soda or water with curt disgust. The only wine he ever took was the ritual glass of port at mess dinners, and he often left even some of that in his glass. Very occasionally, after such dinners, he would order another three fingers of Scotch. He was a gruff, monosyllabic bachelor, who struck considerable alarm into the young. It took time to discern that behind Whisky's terse, dismissive sentences, behind his frowning look of disapproval of most things, there was an extremely kind heart.

Whisky had seldom served away from the regiment, but had spent time in both 1st and 2nd Battalions. He had never been to the staff college or any other place of higher military instruction and the very idea would have aroused ribaldry. He was so singularly without personal ambition that in any other profession – and in most other armies – he would have been regarded as some sort of freak. What, it would have been asked, does this man *want*? What is his purpose? What are his motives? Such questions could never have been addressed to Whisky, but had some such interrogation penetrated, and some sort of language been found to express both question and answer, Whisky would have replied that he enjoyed serving in his regiment, that it was the best one in the army, that it had, by and large, the most decent fellows in it, and that nobody but a crank or a shit would want to leave it to go and sit in some ghastly little office with a bunch of staff pen-pushers, absorbed in licking arses and calculating their promotion chances. The army paid you next to nothing but it didn't expect you to clock in and clock out like a bloody factory hand. It expected you to do your own job; look after everyone under you, even if (especially if) they had fallen foul of authority; and enjoy yourself – and see that others enjoyed themselves too.

Whisky was a large man, tall, broad, burly and heavy. His own enjoyments were sporting rather than intellectual and nobody in the 2nd Westmorlands could boast of having observed him reading a book. In the days when the battalion's field officers had been mounted on government chargers he had been able to hunt cheaply and a good deal; and he had been a bruising if unlucky point-to-point rider, breaking his collar-bone with a frequency which led even Whisky to acknowledge that he'd better slow up a bit. He loved shooting, preferably wildfowling – he relished the solitude, the testing weather, the dawn or near-darkness, the total absence of softness or distraction. It was said that Whisky owned some

57

sort of cottage in a remote part of the Lake District where he occasionally spent a few hermit-like days, but this might well have been fantasy. Whisky had played Rugby football for the battalion until he was nearing forty, massive, pugnacious, a battering ram of a man. When he was sighted, striding through Aldershot barracks or, now, French billets, head thrust forward, hips rolling in an almost nautical manner, soldiers tended to look up and give each other understanding grins. A man would say to another, quietly, simply, 'Major Wainwright!'

'Yeah.'

In some way none could describe, a sort of phenomenon had passed by.

In England Adam had never been given evidence on which to form any estimate of Whisky's military skill. Adam was no prig and had no particular taste for judging his seniors, but he found that it was impossible to avoid hearing certain opinions, discreetly and not very disloyally exchanged among subalterns, or some of them. Thus Colonel Frank Fosdike was 'clever'; 'shrewd'; 'amusing'. Ben Jameson was, quite simply, the best company commander in the battalion. Tom Stubbs, the adjutant (now a captain under the easier wartime dispensation of temporary rank) was 'Old Tom', respected and steady. Captain Roger Braid, commander of A Company, was fussy, a nit-picker, nagged his subordinates, but would take infinite trouble over the personal problems of his men. And so forth. But Major Whisky Wainwright? No man knew. His grunting derision of anything resembling military theory or study was notorious.

On the other hand there was no detail of battalion life, organization or system which Whisky didn't know backwards. Did this expertise at domestic routine extend to the infantry task in battle? Adam hadn't the faintest idea. Once, however, Whisky had barged into the small room in a requisitioned farmhouse which served as B Company headquarters, exchanged a few words with Ben Jameson and stridden out again, passing Adam, who happened to be at the farmhouse door, with an indifferent nod. Adam had reported to Ben and found the latter smiling with a certain enjoyment.

'Good old Whisky!' Ben had said, and added enigmatically, 'Whisky's no Napoleon! But when the time comes he won't duck!'

One November day, about six weeks after their arrival at the battalion's home in France, the second-in-command suddenly and alarmingly appeared, unheralded, in Adam's own platoon area. They were digging trenches, digging, digging; filling and laying sandbags; constructing defensive positions along the Franco-Belgian frontier. Beyond that frontier lay neutral Belgium. The enemy was the other side of Belgium or far to the south-east – in either case many, many miles away. There was nothing resembling battle, no gunfire, no clouds of attacking Germans, no onrush of tanks to be halted by the anti-tank rifle (the Boys 5.5 anti-tank rifle, an unpopular weapon, heavy on the march and with a vicious recoil). There was nothing here which could make Adam feel that he was in some way carrying on the work for which his father had been wounded. There was cold, mud and a good deal of boredom. The trenches slowly took shape, and the authorities had seemed surprised that they tended to fill with water whenever it rained. Drainage had been, somewhat belatedly, devised. Nights were spent in billets behind the line.

Sergeant Pew had approached Adam at mid-morning. The platoon had already been working with shovel and wheel-barrow for two and a half hours.

'DR just come, sir. Message.'

It was odd that a message should, perhaps mistakenly, have reached this particular platoon rather than being delivered to B Company, and even odder that it had been thought sufficiently important to be sent out to the platoon at work rather than await their return to billets and the usual evening assembly of officers at the company office. The written message, from the orderly room, was, however, clearly addressed 'OC 5 Platoon'. As it happened Adam's was the only platoon of the company working on the trenches that morning. He read that Second-Lieutenant A. Hardrow had been selected to attend a course of instruction for infantry regimental officers in field engineering, at Aldershot. The course would last two weeks and was due to start on 12 November.

'I've got to go on a course, Sergeant Pew, to learn how to dig trenches! Twelfth November – Good God, that's the day after tomorrow! It'll mean leaving the battalion this afternoon, I should think!'

'There'll be a movement order, sir,' said Sergeant Pew. 'May have gone to the company office.'

'Well, this has been delivered to me here. Why –'

'Orderly room may have bogged it, sir. Sent that to you out here and movement details to the office in the village, sir.'

'I think I'd better go back and find out. It looks as if I ought to be getting ready – as if I've got no time at all. Although company headquarters would surely send word out to me if –'

'Might not, sir! The captain and the sergeant-major are on the range and there's only Bliss there.' The rest of B Company had marched to an improvised rifle range. Bliss was Ben Jameson's orderly and runner, who occasionally minded the field telephone. Bliss would certainly not initiate an urgent recall of Second-Lieutenant Hardrow in response to unexpected instructions. Sergeant Pew added, 'He's a bit slow, is Bliss.'

'I'd better get off back to company HQ and see what's going on.' Billets were a half-hour's march along a muddy farm road.

'I think you had, sir.'

'I might not be back.'

'Right, sir. The lads are all right.'

Adam put on his jacket, cap and belt, and set off. When he had walked about twenty yards he heard a bellow, as loud as anything he had heard since reaching France.

'MR HARDROW!'

'It's the second-in-command, sir,' said Sergeant Pew, softly and unnecessarily. Nobody had heard Whisky's arrival and nobody could say by what means he had materialized. Adam turned and saluted. Whisky glared at him. They were about five yards apart.

'Mr Hardrow, why the hell are you wearing your jacket?'

'Sir, I was about to –'

'Don't you know that in this regiment officers take off their coats and work with their men?'

'Yes, sir. I've been digging. I've just had a message –'

'Where's your shovel?'

'Over there, sir.'

'Never let me catch you again with your coat on if your men are working. *If* they're working! Why aren't their shirts off? It's a lovely day.'

'Sir, we've had shirts off about half the days, but after last night's frost and in today's wind I thought –'

'Has your shirt been off?'

'When the platoon's been stripped down, yes, sir.'

'Now what the hell were you saying about having a message?'

'I've just had one, sir. Addressed to me, personally, from the orderly room. I've got to go on a course in England. It starts the day after tomorrow. I imagine I may have to leave the battalion area this afternoon, and since my company commander is on the range I thought I'd better go back to billets as quick as possible to see if there are any movement orders for me.'

Whisky stood without gesture or word and stared at Adam. Adam stood still and stared back at Whisky.

'I came out here from battalion HQ. I've got news for you, as it happens.'

'Sir?'

'That message should have been sent last night. There was a sudden vacancy on the course at Aldershot. Brigade allocated it to us. CO nominated you. Orderly room made a balls-up and didn't act till this morning.'

'I see, sir.'

'And five minutes after that DR was sent out to you the telephone rang from Brigade. Whole bloody course has been cancelled. Don't ask me why. Probably be laid on again in the spring. Happened to hear it just before I came out to see what you were up to. Coming anyway.'

'Right, sir.'

'Suppose you're disappointed.'

'Not in the least, sir.' Whisky was still glaring at him and something made Adam decide that he was not prepared to be intimidated. Subordination was one thing, acceptance of hectoring was a little different. He said, 'Well, I'd better get my coat off again, sir.' And he smiled. To his astonishment Whisky gave something not wholly unlike a smile back.

'Don't rush it. Now I've come out to see your platoon you'd better show me round. And for that you may as well keep your jacket on. Come on. Hey there, Sergeant Pew,' shouted Whisky, 'I'm going round the platoon!'

'Yes, sir.'

'Come with Mr Hardrow. Come with us.'

They moved from trench to trench and section to section. The men were working hard, and a little self-consciously harder for Whisky's presence. They were digging soakage pits to help clear the waterlogging. So far the day was dry.

As he moved from place to place Whisky addressed a brief, gruff comment or question to almost every man. Sometimes the comment took the form of a primitive joke and invariably the man receiving it laughed. Here and there Whisky found fault and said so in memorable language. Eventually he completed his tour. He drew Adam a little away from the working soldiers.

'You'd think, Adam, wouldn't you,' said Whisky, 'that the British would know about the water-table in this bit of France? Christ knows the army was hereabouts for long enough twenty odd years ago!'

'Yes, sir,' said Adam, 'you would!' The same sentiment had been on all their lips since soon after arrival. Adam felt warmed by Whisky's use of his first name. It was customary, but from Whisky it was noteworthy. He seldom called anybody anything. And now his voice was serious and interested.

'Don't you find it bloody astonishing that we were told fortifications on this border would be pretty well organized, whereas we found almost nothing? A few miserable pillboxes which we're in the process of scrapping and replacing –'

'Quite, sir.'

'A strand of wire which wouldn't keep a donkey in, let alone a Hun army out, or even slow it down –'

'Right, sir.'

'So we dig and dig. And there's apparently plenty of time. No hurry. No urgency. Think we'll fight from these positions?'

'I hope so, sir.'

'Well, I don't believe it. Look at the map.'

'Sir?'

'It's a hell of a frontage. Long and thin and weak. If the Huns pierce it, Christ knows what would happen.'

'Surely, sir,' said Adam, 'the Maginot Line, on the Franco-German border, isn't weak? It's immensely strong. Or so one supposes.'

Whisky grunted.

'That may be. But that's only half the front. About.'

'You think, sir, that they'll come through Belgium –'

'How should I know where they'll come? Or whether they'll come? All I know is that the French and British armies are manning one hell of a long front, and the Huns can pick their place and their time. We're just sitting on our arses waiting for them. And people seem to think they'll oblige, and walk towards us in a replay of last time. I don't think it'll be like that.'

'I suppose, sir,' said Adam, 'that the line, the Franco-British line I mean, is no longer than last time, in '14–'18? And we held then. Even in March 1918, when the Huns could concentrate everything against us.' He thought of his father. It was in that great onslaught that Adam senior had been wounded, never really to recover.

To his complete astonishment at the range of the other's knowledge he heard Whisky Wainwright say, 'Even in March 1918, you say. When the line ultimately held. And when your father was hit, eh? There were more of us then, Adam.' He added, perplexingly and disturbingly, *'And we were better!'* Then – *'And the French were better!'*

His inspection over, Whisky stumped off as suddenly as he had originally materialized. Sergeant Pew's eyes followed him appreciatively. 'In good form, sir,' said Sergeant Pew, 'the second-in-command!'

'The German,' said Colonel Fosdike, 'is a repetitive animal, a creature of habit. Thorough. Tenacious. But fundamentally unimaginative.' All officers had been assembled in a barn on the edge of the village which housed battalion headquarters. On the floor was a rough cloth model map of Belgium and northern France, with the main cities and rivers indicated by tape and name-cards, but little else marked except a cluster of stones and moss which the battalion intelligence officer, with some artistic talent, had constructed to represent the Ardennes. It looked formidable.

'As you all know,' Frank Fosdike told them, 'the Hun may violate Belgian neutrality. He did last time. He probably will again. He will – or he may – try to turn the allied left flank, just as he did last time, through Belgium. But those of you familiar with your military history will be aware that in 1914 he ran out of steam, that he wheeled inwards too early with his right wing, and that we smashed him – the French and we smashed him – on the Marne. Battle of the Marne. September 1914. And this battalion was there.'

It was bitterly cold in the barn. Officers were wearing sleeveless leather jerkins over their battledress jackets but the damp cold was particularly penetrating to the feet. Adam wiggled his toes inside his ammunition boots and faced the gloomy certainty that a very nasty cold in the head was coming on. He wished he was with the platoon, digging. At least they were warm. He surreptitiously rubbed his hands together.

'But the Marne,' said Frank Fosdike, 'was a damn close thing. An encounter battle, if you like. A surprise to both sides. If the Hun comes through Belgium again, *our* object is to see that there are absolutely no surprises at all. That's one of the reasons you've all been digging. When the last show settled into trenches, in November 1914, after First Ypres, trenches were improvised. Dug pretty well where people found themselves. Hasty. Only improved later. It's been your job to see that if it happens like that again our positions *won't* be hastily improvised. They'll be deliberately prepared, carefully sited, strong. And they'll hold!'

He paused. He had given a touch of stern theatricality to 'they'll hold!', and there had to be a slightly difficult transition of mood to the next bit. The next bit would imply a rather more adventurous strategy.

'Some of you – some of us – may well say, "Why sit and wait for them, if they come through Belgium? Why give them a clear run? Why not do them maximum damage as they come – not only with attack from the air, as would of course happen, but by engaging them earlier? We've now got our firm base, our thoroughly prepared positions behind us, so why not give them some hard knocks *before* they close up to us? Even stop them in their tracks, who knows?" Some of us might think like that. Well –' Frank Fosdike's voice took on an amused, slightly mystifying timbre, 'well, gentlemen, believe it or not but I have an idea such thoughts may conceivably have struck our high command as well!' Several of his audience tittered. Frank Fosdike paused again. Certain decisions had been made very recently at an elevated level, the orders were not yet detailed or definite, and the whole matter was certainly not for open discussion. Soon things would be different. He gestured towards the map on the floor. One could put it carefully, intriguingly.

'As you can see there are a number of rivers in Belgium. Dyle –' (the intelligence officer, Harry Venables, indicated it with a long pointer), 'Senne, running through Brussels, Dendre, Schelde – or Escaut as those Belgians who prefer to speak French call it. Roughly parallel to each other. And each one, in effect, giving a shorter front than our present one. I don't know what the map suggests to you but I know what it suggests to me.' Most officers did their best to look wise.

'I know what you'll say – or at least think,' Colonel Fosdike continued. '"What about the Belgians?" *Well* – what about the Belgians? For their own good reasons they're neutral, which is why none of us are allowed to go poking our sharp little noses across the border. But again, I've got a feeling that the Belgians know something about recent history, that they know a good deal about geography, and that they can make an appreciation, a military appreciation, just as shrewdly as you or I. I've also got a feeling that they've not wasted their time since our friend Adolf Hitler came to power. And my final feeling is that I suppose it's just possible – *just* possible

66

– that they have discreetly shared a few of their thoughts with our people over these last months!' He smiled encouragingly. He had, without breach of security, set the stage for some of the battalion's forthcoming activity over Christmas and beyond. They were to practise long moves in motor transport, and they were to practise taking up and then withdrawing from new positions in the field. Apart from these tactical exercises, digging, revetment and improvement of the main line on the Franco-Belgian frontier would, of course, continue.

Ben and Adam walked back together the two kilometres which separated the battalion-headquarters village from the billets of B Company.

'You'll be my senior subaltern officer from next week, Adam. There's a new grub joining the company.' Second-lieutenants in the Westmorlands were known as 'grubs'. Bobby Forrest, commander of 6 Platoon, had been nominated for a long course in England preparatory to becoming battalion signals officer – and was already studying for it under the battalion signals sergeant. The third platoon in B Company, 4, was commanded by Platoon Sergeant-Major Merrow, a warrant officer class 3 and thus junior to the company sergeant-major; Merrow's platoon were by no means unanimous that this recent innovation was a welcome arrangement. Merrow could not directly seek Ben Jameson's ear as could, for instance, Adam Hardrow. Merrow wanted to be a company sergeant-major himself one day. He kept his head down and his platoon knew it.

There was no second-in-command of the company, although in some battalions second captains were available to fill this post, now established. Adam asked the new grub's name.

'Brett, I gather,' Ben said in his indifferent way, 'John Brett. Or Jack Brett perhaps. Supplementary reserve, and has been for the last three months at the depot. Must be of age,

67

anyway.' Officers were not supposed to be sent to France if under twenty-one. By some wonderful lapse on the part of the authorities Adam – whose twenty-first birthday was in this month, December 1939 – had beaten the ban and stayed with his platoon.

'I know Jack Brett,' Adam said.

'You do?'

'Yes. He's a nice chap. He was attached to the battalion for a fortnight last May. You were on leave.'

'Ah! Well, you'll have to indoctrinate him into B Company ways. Talking of which,' said Ben, with apparent irrelevance, 'you've not been into Vevers recently. Don't get stale.'

Vevers was the nearest sizeable town. Adam said, 'Bobby and I plan to go in this evening. If that's all right.' Transport was run into Vevers on particular evenings for each company.

'Quite all right. I'll be going myself.'

'It'll only leave –'

'PSM Merrow will do company duty. If the policy is to have only three officers in a company, instead of the five which in my view it should have, warrant officers must take their turn. Anyway, why not? The CO agrees.'

'Thanks,' said Adam. Vevers wasn't a thrilling place but there were several passable restaurants. Ben looked at him with a smile as they walked along in the gathering dusk and said, 'Mind you're careful!'

The reference was perfectly clear. Vevers boasted other pleasures as well as restaurants and at least a half dozen of B Company had suffered in health from contact with the ladies of that town. Adam nodded without amusement. A number of his brother officers had but one idea for evening entertainment but he couldn't discard a certain fastidiousness. That sort of thing was – well, surely it should be inseparable from at least an element of genuine emotion? Or was that priggish? Less than manly? He knew that something in him rejected a purely commercial transaction. He had experimented several times in London and although it had provided a certain relief, satisfied a certain curiosity, it was – well, devastatingly less than he was sure it could be. Absurd it might be, and immature, but didn't sex demand at least the illusion of a certain particularity, of a person being special to another person? And what could be less special than a customer?

Yet he certainly missed what he dreamed that a girl could provide. The sort of girl one wanted. Perhaps the sort of girl he'd meet on leave to England – for home leave had been started and Adam could look forward to appearing on the leave roster during the first months of 1940. Perhaps someone like Caroline. Perhaps Caroline herself.

Ben asked if Bobby and he planned to dine at the Lion d'Or, and Adam said that they did. But at eight o'clock that evening, at the imperfectly blacked-out door of the Lion d'Or, they found that there was no available table. Some half-hearted expressions of regret came from the *patron*.

Adam, not for the first time, exploited his competent French. Natasha had been uncompromising with her children about language and as a result Adam – owing little in that respect to his formal schooling – spoke both French and German easily. He knew that his colloquial skill with the language could take a Frenchman by surprise and sometimes open unaccustomed doors – on the whole the English were tongue-tied. Adam asked if the *patron* could make any particular alternative suggestion. They knew the Duc de Bourgogne, of course; but it was always crowded. And now, so sadly, the Lion d'Or was impossible. Perhaps some less well-known place, less well-known to the majority –

It worked. The *patron* told them to try no. 59 rue de Peronne. There were only a few tables, it was very select, Madame did not necessarily wish that the whole British army, they would understand –

'*Bien sûr!*'

The *patron* of the Lion d'Or was an unusually good-natured man.

'*Je telephonerai moi-même!*'

And he did so. Seven minutes later Adam and Bobby found themselves sitting in a small room set with only eight tables, tucked away behind an ordinary-looking café, and ordering what might be the best dinner either had had since landing in France. '*Ça coûte cher!*' The *patron* of the Lion d'Or had hissed as a warning as they left him, but who cared? There was nothing else to spend money on except women and this. And this promised to be good.

Bobby said, 'This'll set us back a bit.'

'Looks like it,' said Adam, sniffing with appreciation. He had an allowance of £100 a year from the trust of his father's will, and his pay was eleven shillings a day, but he had few extravagances. Bobby, paid as a lieutenant, must be slightly better off.

'Looks like it.' Adam scanned the wine list without comprehension. It didn't matter.

It was nearly eight thirty, and they were both attacking the *boeuf bourgignon*, when the door from café to restaurant opened to admit Ben Jameson. With him was a tall, remarkably beautiful girl, with fair hair and very fair skin. Both were laughing as they came into the room and moved towards a table in the corner furthest from where Bobby and Adam were sitting. They had a brief word with the waiter, still laughing, and he bustled off to fetch them an aperitif. They settled at their table, murmuring a little to each other. Then Ben looked up. It was too dark to see his expression, but he raised his hand and Adam saw his head nod forward towards the girl's. A moment later they stood up and moved across the room together. Even in that short distance the girl had slid her hand round Ben's upper arm.

'Well, Bobby and Adam! Doing yourselves well, I hope!

Angélique, these are two brother officers of mine, Lieutenants Forrest and Hardrow.'

Ben seldom made the attempt to speak French. Bobby and Adam stood up and Angélique extended her right hand prettily, while keeping the left on Ben's arm. She smiled at them, and then smiled up into Ben's face. She said nothing.

'You're clever to have found no. 59,' said Ben. 'It's a favourite haunt of Angélique's!' He chuckled and returned with Angélique to their table.

'Quite something!' Adam said in a low voice. The impact of Angélique had certainly been remarkable. It was impossible to express to anybody but himself how much he disliked the intimate gesture with which her hand had found Ben's arm. He supposed it was jealousy. It would be marvellous to find an Angélique. Bobby looked wistful and at the same time dog-like in his devotion to Ben. He said, 'I'd heard old Ben had fixed himself up pretty well.'

'He has, has he?'

'So it seems. So it seems.'

'Darling Adam,' Natasha's letter ran,

At least it doesn't seem from the newspapers as if you're in the midst of battle. Just at the moment we aren't having what we had from the start last time, lists of casualties in every morning paper, friends, friends, friends! It was worse in Russia because they didn't get the lists together for a while and then published them all at once, so that they were *enormous*. I know that's a depressing way to write, darling, but I can't help feeling as I do, and naturally, therefore, I thank God that all is at the moment apparently so quiet.

And over here, no air raids, no real difficulties. We all carry gas masks and the streets are full of uniforms but otherwise life's pretty normal except for the *damned* blackout! I hate it! It depresses me! and I don't believe it's of the slightest use. Don't tell me the Germans don't know where London is and couldn't find it if they wanted, in these days of compasses and so forth! But there we are, I suppose I'm just a stupid woman who knows nothing.

Uncle Alex, as you know, got back to Paris at last – about the first week in October. I've had one letter from him, which took ages. I imagine it's the censorship which makes them particularly slow (and I hope they read this!) as people can never resist other people's business and really Uncle Alex writes such scandal that I should think they pass it round the censorship bureau for a week before sending it on its way to me! Anyway, Uncle Alex says the French think it's quite possible there'll soon be peace – or some of the French, some of his friends. Now the Germans have beaten the Poles they've got what they want in that direction. And the Bolsheviks have gobbled up the Baltic States, those wretched Balts, pretending it's just giving them assistance, and are busy shooting all the so-called bourgeoisie there, poor creatures. So that keeps *them* busy! Not to speak of this dreadful Soviet attack on Finland! What a world!

And so, according to Uncle Alex, there really isn't much point for the Germans in carrying on a dreary struggle in the west against France and England. What has Germany to gain? And what have *we* to gain? So he thinks there may soon be some sort of peace formula.

I certainly hope so, my darling! I know you'll be disappointed, of course. You're just like your father. All he wanted was to get back to the front – he really did! He was unhappy away from it, somehow. And what did it do for him? It killed him in the end.

I know I shouldn't write in this sad way, darling. Frank said, 'Write cheerfully, for God's sake!' and I certainly haven't, have I! Frank came to see me when he was in

London on leave, and I dined with him – he was *very* charming. He always says such nice things about you it makes me proud, proud, proud – even though I wish to Heaven it was all over –

Natasha ended with brief news of the twins and Adam opened his other letter. It was from Caroline.

Dear Adam,

I've got quite a good idea of where you are and what you're doing because Daddy was home on leave and spent most of it in London. I didn't actually mention you to him but he brought the subject up in a way because he talked about your mother. In fact he went round to see her at least once and he took her out, also at least once.

Perhaps I shouldn't say this, in fact I know I shouldn't, but I think he's really rather smitten with her – Daddy, I mean, with your mother. He said, 'You must meet Natasha,' in a meaning sort of way, and he's bright as anything when he's going to see her. I can't help wondering whether he's got serious ideas about giving me a stepmother, and you a stepfather for that matter! Of course there's no word spoken here, Daddy can be rather forbidding and I still get nervous with him and after all it's his business (and hers of course). It would be rather funny if you and I became stepbrother and sister suddenly, wouldn't it! Without being consulted, so to speak! I think I might withhold my consent!

Caroline gave news of her driving. She was, it appeared, driving a 'very important government scientist', and she enclosed, 'a *really* hideous snapshot of me in uniform, just to make you laugh!' Unsurprisingly, it was far from hideous. Caroline looked very fetching – Adam thought that the uniform was green, but he wasn't sure. The photograph showed Caroline, skirt rather short, legs excellent, jacket very waisted, standing by the open door of a smallish saloon car. A fore-and-aft cap was perched jauntily on one side of her luxuriant curls. She appeared to be laughing.

Caroline's letter ended by hoping that perhaps Adam himself would be getting leave in the New Year. 'Look after yourself and don't get into trouble,' she ended, 'Love from Caroline.'

Adam read her letter several times. She had promised to write, and this was her second. Adam had also written two letters – rather stilted and uncommunicative, he admitted to himself. He inspected the snapshot of Caroline again, and thought he'd put it in his wallet rather than tuck it into the small frame of the photograph of Natasha which decorated his billet. Colonel Fosdike was not in the habit of inspecting officers' billets on his periodic tours but it might produce complications if he unexpectedly came on a snapshot of his daughter.

Adam reread, thoughtfully, Caroline's sentences about Natasha; 'I think he's really rather smitten': 'bright as anything when he's going to see her'. He was unsure what emotion these passages aroused in him. Not joy, certainly. He put the letters into the small attaché case he had brought in his kit to France and started to make himself ready for the night exercise they were about to undertake. Withdrawal in the line.

Jack Brett was older than Adam. Born in 1917, he had joined the supplementary reserve of the Westmorlands, serving attachments with them and obtaining a provisional commission, during his first year after leaving Durham University. Jack had secured a job in an auctioneer's office – the idea had been to 'see whether it suited him', with the possibility of studying for the appropriate qualifications if it did. A quiet, thoughtful young man, he found the army alarming. To his great credit he had not hesitated to join, well before it became

74

obligatory; to seek a commission; to offer himself. Jack had a high sense of duty.

But asserting himself did not come easily. He saw others' points of view with too much facility, and although the modesty this induced was attractive, it sometimes led to a lack of self-confidence of which he was unhappily aware. Ben Jameson attached him to Adam's platoon, 'for a bit. Adam will help you find your feet. Then you'll have 6 Platoon.' Ben was kind. Secretly he felt dubious about Jack Brett.

Jack, also secretly, found Adam himself somewhat intimidating. He told himself that this was absurd. Hardrow was senior, of course, but he was appreciably younger. He wasn't a university graduate or anything like that. Why, Jack asked himself, should he, Jack Brett, feel a certain nervous tremor when Adam Hardrow, in his quiet, unemphatic voice, told him what he should do or asked him, with perfect politeness, whether he had done some particular task. Jack felt that he was on approval, and that he might, without much difficulty, find himself returned to the makers. Ben Jameson's lazy assurance terrified him, and it was clear that Adam was made in Ben's image, that they created between them a charmed circle into which it would be hard for Jack to break. He had not supposed that war would be so difficult in this sort of way.

'Mr Brett.' It was Adam's voice in the darkness. The platoon had occupied an area spread over two hundred yards during the latter part of the cold winter afternoon. Symbolic trenches had been scraped – it had been decreed that these should only be sufficient to mark the position. Withdrawal was to be effected within each of the three sections on a man-by-man basis, carefully laid down. Men would be counted past a section check-point after quitting their trenches. Section commanders would then report the section complete at a platoon check-point, and the platoon be shepherded back through a company rendezvous. And so on.

Sequence was important. Contact with the man in front was important – it was a particularly dark night. Numbers, above all, were important. It was easy to lose a man in the darkness. Individuals, sections and platoons all needed to be scrupulously counted through.

'Mr Brett, you will remain with Corporal Egan's section, and report to me at the platoon check-point when the section's clear. Count them out yourself, so that you'll see exactly what a section commander must do. Then stay with me.'

'Right, sir.'

'You know the timings.'

'Yes, sir.' It came perfectly natural to Jack to call Adam 'sir' when on duty. Military protocol in the Westmorlands demanded it, but instinct didn't quarrel.

Forty-five minutes later there was movement within B Company. Silence, absolute silence, had been enjoined by Ben, and no man wanted Company Sergeant-Major Darwin to nail him for swearing under his breath just because the edge of his neighbour's shovel had caught him in a nasty place. There was shuffling, a hissed word from section commanders here and there, the inevitable clank of equipment as men shuffled, peering, through the darkness and squelched cautiously through the mud of the fields Colonel Fosdike had secured for the exercise. But, on the whole, the movement was commendably quiet. Adam, at the platoon check-point, was conscious of heavy breathing beside him. The steel helmet etched against the night sky was slightly higher than his own. Jack Brett was a tall young man.

'Eleven section complete, sir,' muttered Jack.

'You're sure?' Adam's voice was severe, although he had no real reason for the question. He supposed that, having been given the task of looking after Jack Brett, he wanted to impress on him the importance of accuracy. Darkness could be hell.

'Yes, sir.'

'Then stay with me.'

The exercise continued, drills carried out methodically. It was at the company check-point that Sergeant Pew hissed through the darkness, 'Mr Hardrow, sir!'

'Well?'

'Pratt, sir. Corporal Egan says he's missing.'

'When did he see him last?'

'In the trench, sir. At stand-to.'

'But he was counted out. Mr Brett reported all nine men out.'

'Couldn't be, sir.'

They were murmuring, shapes communicating facelessly.

'Mr Brett,' said Adam, very softly and very coldly, 'did you hear what Sergeant Pew has just said?'

'Yes, sir.'

'Well? I told you to make yourself personally responsible for counting the men out.'

'Corporal Egan said –'

'Don't tell me what Corporal Egan said. If Pratt isn't here he wasn't counted through. How many men did you count?'

'Nine, sir.'

'Which included yourself?'

'Yes, sir. Nine in all from the section. Corporal Egan's section.'

'Which is nine, and ten with yourself. So you missed one and Pratt is asleep in a trench. If the Germans were opposite us he'd be dead or in their hands by now. Because a section commander had made an idle mistake.'

'Yes, sir.'

'You personally are negligent and irresponsible.'

'Yes, sir.'

'Now, Mr Brett, you will go back. You will take Corporal Egan with you. You will find Pratt and return with him.'

'Yes, sir. The section –'

'Never mind the section. Go now. And return through this check-point.'

'Right, sir.'

Three minutes later Adam reported to Ben Jameson.

'Five platoon complete less three men, sir.'

'What three men?'

'One man was left in the trenches, sir. I didn't count him out. I've sent Mr Brett and Corporal Egan back to find him.'

'Why,' asked Ben, 'didn't you become aware of that at your own platoon check-point? You've come the whole way back here a man short.' His voice was deadly.

'I made a mistake, sir.'

'We'll discuss that tomorrow. And so you've sent the wretched Brett off in the darkness, have you?'

'Yes, sir. With Corporal Egan.'

Ben turned away. It was only next morning that he was accosted at battalion headquarters by Whisky Wainwright. Whisky was grinning.

'Hear you lost a man last night, Ben.'

'Yes,' said Ben coldly, 'I did. But not for long.'

Whisky had been standing in the darkness, unperceived, near B Company's check-point. Now he said, 'That new grub, young Brett, couldn't count. Young Adam Hardrow told him off good and proper. I heard 'em. Good and proper!'

Ben smiled rather grimly. He was thinking fast. Later, in B Company office, he sat down at the trestle table and told Company Sergeant-Major Darwin that he wished to speak to Mr Hardrow. When Adam marched into the office, prepared to do bitter penance for losing a man on a night exercise, Ben smiled at him in his usual ironic way and told him that the Aldershot field engineering course was now on again, and that Adam's name was definitely down for it. 'In February,' Ben said, 'late February, I think. And you can take your week's leave immediately before it, so you'll get a month at home. I spoke to Tom. I'm perfectly happy about it. Sergeant

Pew can command your platoon on his head. Young Brett will be all right, I've no doubt, no doubt at all. And we're getting a company second captain, Geoffrey Purvis from the 1st Battalion.' Adam looked as interested as he could. He didn't know Geoffrey Purvis. He rather disliked the idea of another captain in the company, an intimate of Ben far senior to him, to Second-Lieutenant Adam Hardrow. To Geoffrey Purvis Adam would be just another platoon commander, just another grub.

Ben was talking away in his somewhat mocking voice: 'Geoffrey had to come back from Egypt with some ghastly complaint and now that he's better he's coming out here instead of going back to the fleshpots of the Nile. Poor devil! So B Company will be awash with officers. Colonel Frank asked me if I could spare you – unusually civil gesture by a CO I must say – and I said I could.' Ben's expression was, Adam thought, not censorious in the least. The mishap of the previous evening was, it seemed, to be overlooked. In fact Ben's mind was on Angélique; and as Adam saluted and left the cold little makeshift office he found that Angélique's face and figure suddenly came, very clearly, to his mind also.

'Why did your parents christen you Ivan?'

'Why did yours call you Adam? I'm not Russian and you're not the first man.'

Adam laughed, 'My father was Adam. *My* mother really was Russian, and she probably imagined sons in England always took their father's first name. Adam Adamovitch.' Luckier than Adam and Bobby Forrest on a previous occasion, they had secured a table for two at the Lion d'Or.

Ivan Perry said, 'My mother was in love with a character in Tolstoy –'

'Which one?'

'Prince Andrew Bolkonski. Calling me Ivan brought him

79

nearer. My father was wholly uninterested. He survived the war and he remained uninterested.'

'And, like mine, died soon after the Armistice.'

'That's right, from flu.' Ivan Perry, a subaltern in A Company was a very fair young man, with a pink and white complexion which made him look even younger than his twenty-two years. He had been two terms ahead of Adam at Sandhurst, but right from the beginning they had warmed to each other, finding an instant rapport which defied any particular rationalization. Temperamentally they appeared very different, with Adam serious, even a touch grim at times, and Ivan giving an impression of something not far from a rather charming frivolity. But Adam found that with Ivan he could talk – talk about their contemporaries, talk about their elders, talk about the army in a way which was uninhibited by a trifling difference in seniority. Then, after a few long conversations in the mess and a few somewhat hectic evenings together in London, they had increasingly found that they could talk about everything – about books, about the music both were discovering with amateur but passionate enthusiasm, about what really moved them, about what they believed. They found that they could nearly always laugh together, catch each other's eye. They found, stumbling a little, unsure but disguising from the other the unsureness, that they could talk about girls. And as September 1939 had approached they had talked and talked about the imminence of war. For Adam it was always a heart-lifting moment if the chance of battalion life threw him for a precious hour together with Ivan; companies were separated by some distance and there was no battalion mess. They had dined together twice previously in Vevers – magic evenings of talk both light and serious, exchanges of discovery and laughter.

In one respect they differed sharply. Ivan's background was wholly unmilitary. He had drifted to Sandhurst, propelled by a strong-minded widowed mother who was sure that war was coming and believed her son had better find his niche before it began. He affected to find the regiment and its ways endearing but a little absurd. Adam, austere and dedicated at least in this respect, tolerated and even enjoyed Ivan's ironic detachment. He was pretty sure it didn't go deep. For his part, Ivan smiled with pleasure at Adam's simple-minded devotion to the Westmorlands. It gave him the chance now and then to dig the Hardrow ribs in a way which neither found disagreeable.

Ivan now said, 'You've never really told me whether your mother has still got Russian relations alive. Or were they all shot by the Bolshies?'

'Some were. Yes, she's got a few surviving relatives. An uncle – he lives in Paris; and he's got a son, that sort of thing.'

'You know them?'

'I know them – not well. They're charming. They're obsessed, of course, with the Revolution. Twenty-two years ago now, but they're sure it'll all collapse, it's so wicked and lunatic and unpopular – that's what they think.'

'And then they'll go home.'

'I don't,' said Adam, 'really believe they believe it. I'm sure my mother doesn't. But there's no doubt that for them the world ended in 1917. I quite understand it.'

'So do I.'

'I'd like you to meet my mother, Ivan. After all, if your mother called you Ivan because she was in love with Prince Andrew you'd better meet a real Russian.'

'My mother,' said Ivan, 'got over Prince Andrew Bolkonski quite soon after I was born, I fancy. She took up other things. She's a strong-minded lady, with one idea at a time. In the last few years it's been the German menace. That's why she was utterly determined I should be a soldier. Most unsuitable. But one would have been called up anyway.'

'Talking of mothers –'

'Yes, Adam? Talking of mothers?'

'There's something very, very personal I'm going to say to you now.'

Ivan Perry looked politely interrogative. He said, 'If you choose.'

'It's odd. It's about my mother. She thinks the CO is – well, he was a friend of my father's. He's been in touch with my mother recently.' Adam seemed stuck.

Ivan said, helpfully, 'And he's talked about you?'

'Probably. But that would be natural. No – the thing is he's – well, he went to see her when he was on leave.'

'Why not?'

'Took her out to dinner.'

'Again, why not?'

'Why not!' said Adam. Ivan recognized the set of his mouth. It was stubborn and hostile, an expression with which Ivan was familiar. The scar on Adam's temple suddenly looked very prominent. Ivan said, 'Are you trying to tell me that our very own, revered Colonel Frank Fosdike, has ambitions to become your stepfather?'

'No idea. Not impossible.'

'Oh, Adam!'

'Exactly!'

They sat in silence for a little and Ivan ordered two cognacs. Adam Hardrow was dear to him by now and he recognized that this had been no easy business to mention to an outsider. He said that perhaps the matter would become clearer to Adam when he went on leave in February, and Adam grunted and nodded. Then they talked of other things.

CHAPTER 4

It was usual in the Westmorlands for officers and NCOs attending courses of instruction away from the battalion to appear before their commanding officer before departure. They would do the same, for congratulation or admonition, after return, when a report on their performance from the course commander would be read out. Due to leave for Calais in the back of an icy truck at 3 p.m., Adam duly presented himself that Thursday morning in February to Colonel Fosdike after the latter's daily orderly room. The adjutant, Adam recognized with gratitude, had been particularly kind in arranging his movement two days earlier than strictly necessary. The course was to assemble the following Monday week at Aldershot. In addition to his regulation week's leave, taken before, he would have a long weekend in London. It would have been possible to fix his travel for Saturday, but Tom Stubbs had done the decent thing.

Colonel Fosdike seemed in a particularly good mood. His temper, it was judged in the battalion, went up and down. There were bad mornings. This didn't seem to be one of them.

'Important course, this.'

'Yes, sir.'

'I know some of you think there's nothing left to learn about entrenchment after the last four months' work. The fact is that everybody, *everybody*, can learn a great deal. In the last war I think it can be said that the British army had hardly learned how to build a *really* decent system of trenches before 1916! No proper instruction, you see.'

'Yes, sir.'

'I shall probably expect you to run a series of short field-engineering courses within the battalion when you get back.'

'Right, sir.'

Colonel Fosdike smiled affably. He said, 'You're going on leave immediately before the course, the adjutant tells me.'

'Yes, sir.'

'Well, have a good time. My – my regards to your family.'

'Yes, sir.'

Adam returned to B Company for lunch and to collect his kit. There wasn't much to do but hang about and wait for the Calais truck which was due to collect leave parties from all companies including his own. The men were already gathering, their battledresses well-pressed, their greatcoat buttons gleaming. Spirits were high. Sergeant Pew materialized. Company dinners were already over.

'Well, I'm off to change after I've had some lunch, Sergeant Pew. Then you won't see me for nearly a month!'

'Right, sir. Enjoy your time in England, sir.'

'I've got to run some courses, the CO says, when I return. Never mind, the platoon's in good form and you've got everything well in hand, Sergeant Pew.'

Sergeant Pew didn't smile. He said, 'Pity about Wilkins, sir.'

'What about Wilkins?'

'Got twenty-one days from the CO this morning, sir.'

'*Twenty-one days!*' Adam took a firm grip on himself. There could be no question of implying the smallest criticism of Colonel Fosdike's justice. No comment whatsoever could be made. Wilkins, however, was a quiet, industrious soldier. A Barrow man, like Sergeant Pew, he had missed a connection, arrived late at the London reporting centre for men returning from home leave or courses, and consequently had been put on a boat forty-eight hours after the one he had been due to catch. All soldiers had had impressed on them that it was the individual's responsibility to report punctually, no matter the difficulty. However, trains from the north were known to be unreliable in the conditions of wartime; Wilkins had probably tried less than very, very hard to get to London before the proper hour; but twenty-one days! Twenty-one days field punishment! It meant reporting at all hours, parading with full kit at all hours, confinement in the company guardroom. It meant, above all, forfeiture of all pay. Wilkins had a young family. He had a good record. He was not a man to try it on, to evade duty. It had, Adam had supposed, been a case for a short punishment. Perhaps even for admonition alone.

Twenty-one days! Sergeant Pew said, 'He's a bit down, sir.'

'I expect so.'

'Wife's expecting.'

This seemed near-universal in the platoon. Adam said, 'Well, get him over it when his time's done. Cheer him up. He's a good man, really.'

'Yes, sir.'

'But of course they've all got to realize how important it is to get back in time. If there were large-scale absence, home leave would be stopped. We've all had that rubbed into us.'

'Yes, sir.'

'And so has Wilkins.'

Sergeant Pew said nothing to this for a moment. Then he observed, somewhat enigmatically, 'Maybe he was unlucky.'

Adam said, 'Maybe he was.' He spoke frankly, his tone implying that the British railway system had let Wilkins down. He knew perfectly well that Sergeant Pew's words had contained the improper suggestion that Wilkins had appeared before Colonel Fosdike on one of the CO's bad mornings.

Sergeant Pew seemed reluctant to salute and depart. The

platoon would not be parading for work for another thirty minutes.

'Wright's taken it just about as bad as Wilkins, sir. Wilkins's punishment, I mean.'

Wright and Wilkins were particularly close. Within the platoon certain pairs of men were joined by especial bonds, everybody knew it and respected it. Sometimes they came from the same town or village. Sometimes – more often – they had first joined up together, been squad mates at the depot, discovered the strange, intimidating new world of the army alongside each other. Sometimes they simply recognized in each other an affinity which seldom found much expression in conversation. Thus, when Sergeant Pew had occasion to call out, 'Hey, two of you, over here!' and Wright sheepishly ambled over, it was automatic that Wilkins would join him. Wright and Wilkins. Of course, Adam appreciated, Wright would feel Wilkins's sentence as if every day of it were being undergone by himself as well. As for the forfeited pay, Adam guessed that each week a few shillings' worth of something or other would find its way from Wright to Wilkins. They shared all things. They would certainly share pain.

Caroline was looking delicious and she knew it. New clothes were already a rare luxury, and a good many lectures were being read by government spokesmen on how belts must be tightened 'for the duration' and how every need which required imported stuff to satisfy it – and it seemed most nice clothes came into that category, unfortunately – must be firmly suppressed or at least only gratified to a very meagre degree. Until Hitler was beaten, or called the whole tiresome adventure off.

So that to Caroline the war spelt a certain privation. She recognized, however, that so far she had little to grumble about. Driving her scientist was, on the whole, more entertaining than arranging flowers, and she had quite effectively put him in his place on an early occasion when he had said that he preferred to sit in front. She had soon found his right hand resting on her left knee, and then moving stealthily upwards towards her left thigh. Caroline had trodden hard on the brake, stopped the car and turned to look her Very Important Scientist full in the face. He had smiled, a little uneasily. It had been after lunch.

'Dr Merryman, I think you'd better sit in the back.'

'But Caroline, as I told you, I prefer to sit in front. I feel pompous if I sit in the back. It's more companionable in front.'

'Well, I,' said Caroline, 'don't like you sitting in the front. I don't like you putting your hand on my knee. In fact I very much dislike it. It rather repels me. I'm sure you'd prefer me to tell you that quite frankly.' She had kept her voice very cool and polite, and Dr Merryman had said that as it happened he'd prefer her to put him down, he felt like a bit of air and would walk the remaining half mile to the Ministry. Next morning Caroline stood smartly by the open back door and Dr Merryman got in without a murmur. She had had no more little difficulties of that kind.

And in the evening, wartime, in spite of the blackout and the fact that a lot of places were only running at what might be called half-speed, was a good deal more amusing for Caroline than peace had been. Caroline had arranged for two girlfriends to move into her father's house to keep her company. Colonel Fosdike's room was ready for him if he were ever to turn up on leave unexpectedly and he entirely approved of the arrangement. The girls had a lively time. So far, remarkably few young men (except for those in the navy), seemed to have gone to 'the war' overseas, and none of them were getting killed. A great many, of course, were training or something equally dreary in various parts of England or Scotland, but more often than not the telephone would ring and a voice would announce that some more or less agreeable dancing partner from a year ago had managed to get a weekend's leave and had turned up in London. What about Caroline coming out and dining somewhere?

Caroline mentioned her father in her somewhat infrequent prayers, but was confident Daddy would be all right. She was having a lovely war.

And here was Adam Hardrow sitting opposite her in the blue uniform of the Westmorlands, 'undress' in former times but now worn more often than not instead of the evening clothes which had largely been put away 'for the duration'. Adam was sitting there, with his eager, serious face which she had tried to picture on the three occasions she had written letters to him, but not always with much success since so many other faces, some also eager and some serious (but many very much not) had interposed.

Adam for his part, studied Caroline's face. He also looked with a lot of pleasure at Caroline's neck and shoulders. She was wearing a green dress and it showed off the cream-coloured skin of her slender shoulders particularly well. Adam nevertheless wished that Caroline would contrive to avoid emphasizing that she knew the place in which they were dining, knew London by night, and the ways of the world in general, so much better than he did. She had already told him that it was her favourite table.

'They've put me here twice already this month! I love it here!'

But Adam soon found that he was enjoying being with Caroline, very much indeed. And Caroline decided, about half-way through dinner, that Adam Hardrow had a certain something, a quality – almost a *hardness* she said to herself with a touch of surprise, it sounded so unsympathetic – which was different from most of the other young or not so young men who took her out. A quality which intrigued. His somewhat sulky looks were definitely fascinating, there was no doubt about that. Even that scar was rather terrific in its way. And he was so, so *concentrated*. No, hardness was quite the wrong word, Caroline said to herself; he's not hard, but by God he's not soft! She felt a tiny tremor of excitement at this somewhat banal discovery. Adam had told her that her letters had meant a lot to him.

'And yours to me, Adam.'

'They're deadly. My letters. We can't write about what we do. And it would be even more boring if we did!'

'Why?'

'Because what we do is soul-destroyingly dull.'

'I thought –'

'You thought that because we're "over there" it has to be exciting. The front line. Trenches. Guns. Germans. It's not the front line, it's opposite neutral Belgium. The trenches are dug by us again and again and again and are much less exciting than digging a vegetable garden. The guns don't fire and the Germans are almost as far away from us as they are from you here.'

'But I suppose that will change, Adam.'

'Perhaps. Anyway it's an odd way to fight a war. Don't let's talk about it.'

'Your letters aren't dull, Adam. You write about what you read, and what you think. I love them. Please go on writing them.'

They got up to dance and Caroline seemed to melt into his arms in a very satisfying way. Adam knew that he danced well, by the modest standards of his race and generation. He had natural rhythm. The band's vocalist grinned at them engagingly as they passed, and thought about his journey home in the small hours. Bloody blackout! Farcical, the whole ruddy thing! Not a bomber seen or heard since the ruddy war began! Government scare-mongering!

They danced for a long time. The music, strident at first, turned dreamy, hotted up again and then turned back to dreamy and stayed that way. The lights went very low.

Caroline's cheek brushed Adam's and then rested against it. Adam's right hand moved gently at the base of Caroline's spine. She stroked his wrist with her right hand.

'Sit?'

'All right.'

They returned to their table and sat side by side in the subdued light on the banquette, Adam's arm firmly round Caroline's shoulders, her head turned to him, her eyes serious. After a little Caroline gave a small sigh and drew herself very slightly away.

'Could I have a glass of water?'

Adam made signals. He was having a good evening. Trench revetment and 5 Platoon seemed a very long way away.

'Daddy seemed really very well when he was home on leave.'

'Good,' said Adam.

'He's very funny about all of you.'

'Ah!'

'He's a marvellous mimic, you know. You've probably never seen that side of him.'

'I don't think I have.'

'He imitates voices and so on, I almost feel I know the people. Hysterical!'

'It is, is it?'

'He makes me laugh so much. I hope he doesn't get too lonely over there. Nobody much to talk to, I gather.'

'Being the CO is probably rather a lonely job. Inevitably. Like being the captain of a ship.'

'Mm-m.'

'He's got a second-in-command, though. I imagine that helps.'

'Is that Major Wainwright?'

'That's it. Whisky Wainwright.'

'He sounds deadly.'

'I wouldn't exactly say that.'

'Not Daddy's type at all.'

'Perhaps not. But a wonderful man, I promise you.'

'I doubt if Daddy would agree. But never mind, Adam – darling Adam –'

Adam felt a slight pricking at the back of the neck as Caroline said this. It was the first endearment.

'– darling Adam, *you* are absolutely the blue-eyed boy, I can tell you that.'

When Adam said nothing Caroline murmured, 'You know what I wrote about – about Daddy and your mother –'

'Yes.'

'You didn't mention the subject in the letter you wrote back.'

'No.'

'I wondered why.'

'Well, I didn't know what to say. I didn't know what to think.'

'Has your mother mentioned it?'

'Not really.'

'I'd love to meet her, Adam.'

'And I hope you will, Caroline. On my next leave, perhaps. You see I've got to go to Aldershot on Sunday. For this course.'

Their evening together, near the end of Adam's precious week's leave, had been the first on which Caroline was free. Afterwards Adam took her back to the Fosdike house, embracing her warmly in the privacy of the taxi. At her door, however, Caroline explained that both her lodgers had been out as well, 'and I can see from the lights they're still up, making coffee or something. You'd better not come in, Adam.' He had kept the taxi, and the grumbling driver took him back to Elm Park Gardens. In spite of the caresses in the taxi, the evening had not ended as well as it had promised. Why hadn't he been asked into the Fosdike house? Why did

Caroline want to keep him from meeting her lodgers, or her lodgers from seeing him? It didn't matter but it somehow irked, it was ridiculous, it spoiled things. And things had been going rather nicely. He had assured Caroline that he would telephone from Aldershot if he possibly could. It seemed unlikely that another evening in London could be managed.

Natasha, on the whole a tactful and uninquisitive mother, had learned that Adam had taken Caroline Fosdike out to dine and dance. She had observed that Caroline 'always sounded a charming girl'.

'Yes, Mama. Charming.'

'And pretty, no doubt.'

'Certainly. And amusing.'

'She couldn't fail to be that. Frank is such *very* good company! Rather sardonic, but always entertaining! I think you're all very lucky to have him with you in France.'

'Mama –'

'Yes, darling?'

'I don't like Colonel Frank.'

'Adam!'

'I thought I'd mention it. Naturally my feelings are totally unimportant and anyway I keep them to myself. I'm only a second-lieutenant, the lowest form of animal life. But since you've mentioned him I thought I'd tell you. Just between you and me.'

'Don't you feel a little uncomfortable, in that case, taking his daughter out?'

Adam said, truthfully, that his opinion had been slow in the forming and yes, it did make him feel a bit uneasy with Caroline in a way, but after all he'd only taken her out once, they didn't spend the evening talking about her father, it was really quite unimportant and anyway Adam was probably talking nonsense, he shouldn't have said it, forget it, Mama.

92

'I don't think I can. Forget it.' Natasha said it slowly. Looking at his mother Adam thought there must be a good deal in Caroline's speculations. It was, perhaps, just as well that he had spoken up with such bluntness. It was no doubt best that Natasha should know his feelings early rather than late.

Natasha began talking about the twins. Adam had had one letter – at Christmas – from each of them and had written twice to each himself from France. Letter-writing was not a habit to which any of the Hardrows took with much zeal, although Natasha was assiduous and Adam did his duty by her. He asked how Nicholas was getting on. Nicholas was in the last year of his time at the same northern public school that Adam had attended. He was, Adam knew, often in a certain amount of trouble. Saskia, at a boarding-school near Salisbury, had the reputation of being an exemplary pupil. Twin-like, the two tended to confide only in each other.

'Darling, Nick thinks he wants to go into the air force.'

'Well, why not? But I thought he was hoping to go to university? Or does that still stand, and the RAF come later, if the war's still going strong?'

'He's turned against going up to university. John Edgcombe is furious. He wrote a sensible letter to me – furious.' John Edgcombe was Nicholas's housemaster, and had once been Adam's. The Hardrows approved of him.

'If he really wants to fly, Mama, you can't stop him. And I can quite understand him wanting to get on with it. He's afraid the war's going to end before he gets into it.'

'Oh Adam, I wish to God it would! Is it a very long training? For the RAF, I mean?'

'I expect it's quite long. But Nicky's only just reaching his eighteenth birthday, next month, isn't it? They won't take him yet. Anyway he's got another two terms at school.'

Adam said that he didn't know the RAF regulations and policy but he was sure it would be some time before Nick could be eligible for flying duty. After all he, Adam, had not really been meant to go to France, because he was under twenty-one. His mother sighed, as she often did in their conversations, a sigh of irritation at the follies of the world, of incomprehension about how it would all end, of anxiety, above all, for her sons. This particular sigh also contained annoyance that her elder son had so emphatically announced his dislike for an attractive man who was being assiduous in his pursuit of her, Natasha. In so far as one could be assiduous from the other side of the Channel. Really, Natasha thought, it's crazy, the whole thing's crazy. Why can't human beings simply love and laugh and live? What a century! What a world!

Adam's Aldershot course started on a Monday morning. The telephone in the officers' mess, a penny-in-the-slot machine, was in constant use and there was often a small queue outside the booth door. An unfriendly notice on the mess notice-board announced that the mess staff had been instructed not to produce small change for the telephone in response to officers' requests, as this had caused 'administrative difficult-ies'. Despite this the mess corporal, an easy-going soul, could sometimes be persuaded to oblige. Adam had rung Natasha once, and tried Caroline twice without success. Caroline had, however, written a very sweet note, posted to Aldershot and reaching him on the Thursday, to thank him for 'a lovely evening'.

Incoming telephone messages were sometimes received by the mess staff, with ill grace, and notes for student officers placed on the notice-board. A week after Adam received Caroline's letter he found a message at lunchtime. Would he ring a local number. No name was given. Adam sought Mess Corporal Fisher.

'Corporal Fisher, I've had this message. You don't happen to know who sent it?'

'No, sir. It's Sergeant Bayliss's writing. He took it, most probably. On the office line.'

'Is Sergeant Bayliss there?'

'He's off till this evening, sir.'

Adam, pennies in hand, got a place in the booth. This was mysterious! A woman's voice answered and he pressed the appropriate button and heard his coins clank into the Post Office's keeping.

'This is Adam Hardrow. I had a message to ring.'

'And this is Felicity Jameson, Adam. You had dinner with us.'

'Of course!'

'And I wondered whether you'd like to come to supper here tomorrow? As you know, it's quite near. Ben told me in a letter that you were at Aldershot for two weeks. It'd be lovely to see you if you're not doing something else.'

'Good Lord, absolutely nothing else. Nothing at all. I –'

'So will you come?'

'I'd love to. I'm not sure how.'

'I'll pick you up. I've got some petrol.'

'That would be marvellous – er – Felicity.' He explained the whereabouts of the barracks which housed the course and Felicity sounded very cool and practical about finding it. Capable. She said, easily and unfussily, 'and I'll take you back, of course. No distance. No problem.' At eight o'clock the next evening Adam found himself sitting on a sofa in the Jameson house, a brandy and ginger ale in his hand, while Felicity moved in and out between sitting-room and kitchen talking a little, asking practically nothing about France and the Westmorlands, inviting Adam's opinions about how things were going with the world and the war in a way which was extraordinarily *sensible*, he said to himself. Sensible, thoughtful, and somehow flattering in its maturity; and in the maturity it implied in him. Adam thought that he had never talked to a woman quite like this. There seemed no barriers of understanding at all. Felicity never seemed to be 'putting him on his manners' as he inwardly expressed it. She was quick, intelligent and entirely natural.

She was also entrancing to look at, as Adam acknowledged to himself with a certain uneasiness. The last time he'd seen her had been that evening when it had become clear that war was about to break out, and Adam remembered her deep voice, the atmosphere she conveyed of stillness and control; how every movement was deliberate – as deliberate as it was graceful. He also remembered her dark beauty, but it hit him on this Friday evening with even more power. She'd been wearing blue before, he remembered. Now she was wearing black. On both occasions her skirt was slightly shorter than was usual at that time, and Adam was very aware of how slender and shapely were her legs. Felicity didn't smile a great deal. Her eyes, beneath her rather full dark brows, were very expressive. When she says something, Adam thought, she puts her full force behind it. She gives one her full attention. She's incapable of silliness or superficiality.

After giving him a simple but deliciously cooked supper, Felicity said that Ben, as he knew, had had leave over Christmas. She understood that it wouldn't be again for a good many months.

'I suppose that's right.'

'What do you do over there, Adam, when you're not working?'

'Not much. We sometimes go into the nearest town, Vevers, and have dinner or something.'

'Or something,' Felicity smiled gently. There was nothing tiresomely suggestive or arch in the smile.

Adam smiled back. He said, 'It's not much of a place.' He couldn't dismiss the picture of Angélique from before his eyes. Angélique had no business here. It was all wrong.

'Would you like some music?'

'Yes, please.' She played several dance records. Then she

said, 'You like Mozart, don't you.' It was a statement, not a question.

'How do you know, Felicity?' They'd not spoken of music. Nor, as far as he remembered, had he ever talked about it to Ben. One didn't talk to Ben about things like that.

'I just know. Perhaps just from looking at you.' She put on one of the later symphonies. When she changed the record for the second time she said, 'I think this side's a bit scratched.'

'No matter.'

Felicity paused as if listening or thinking hard, said, 'No, I think it's all right,' and then joined him on the sofa. The backs of their hands were touching. They sat very still, the music linking them. The last movement of the symphony reached its joyous conclusion. Adam said, 'I'll stop it.' His breath was a little short.

'Leave it. It turns itself off. One of the last extravagances we indulged in before the war started.'

Felicity's skirt had rucked up a good deal as she sat down. Adam's eyes found themselves drawn to the glimpse of her thighs which showed above the black stocking tops. Her face and neck had the tint of honey. There was a click as the gramophone appeared to do whatever it was meant to do.

The tips of Felicity's fingers were now moving gently over the back of Adam's hand. Then she said, very quietly, 'You're a very sweet person.'

'Felicity, I –' Adam made a choking sound. He felt, rather than saw, that Felicity was smiling.

'You're telling yourself that I'm Ben Jameson's wife. That he's your brother officer, your company commander. Your friend.'

Adam said nothing.

'Ben and I have a tolerant marriage, you know. It's better for both of us. If we constrained each other much the bonds would break. With a bit of give the bonds hold. I don't expect you can understand that. You're very young. But very sweet.'

Adam didn't trust himself to say anything. The only certainty he knew was that he wanted Felicity in his arms quite dreadfully. It was as if the air around the two of them was crackling with electricity, and the charge would become uncontainable unless he could hold her close and feel the unimaginable smoothness of that skin against his. He was breathing heavily and unevenly.

'I know Ben amuses himself when he can in France. It doesn't upset me. He is what he is. So am I.'

Adam found his voice. It sounded high-pitched and idiotic, a sort of tremulous squeak. He said, 'But I suppose you love each other, Felicity?'

'That word can cover a whole range of emotions and relationships. Yes, the answer is yes, of course. But, as I've said, we – Ben and I – love best and understand best if we're not censorious. I don't think you find that easy to accept – yet. Never mind. Take life as it comes, Adam.'

Adam turned his head and looked hard at her. Felicity was looking at him with what appeared to be enormous seriousness. Three seconds later, with a strong, violent movement, Felicity was sitting on Adam's knees, her arm round his neck, her mouth pressed to his lips and her tongue probing and twisting in search of his. Adam collapsed back on the sofa under the force of Felicity's attack. One hand, half resisting, half responding, found her left thigh and the other arm clutched her shoulders as the two of them slid from sofa to floor.

'Time I was driving you back to your dear old barracks, darling boy.'

Adam looked at his wrist-watch. It was on a small table which he remembered had been knocked over at one point but had suffered no damage. It was half-past two in the morning.

'Felicity, you're – you're –'

'Wonderful?'

'Wonderful.'

'Now, my sweetest boy, this has to be just a little something between you and me, see? I know I said I've got a tolerant marriage and I have, but appearances still have to matter. And in the army more than in most places, right?'

'Maybe. Felicity, nobody will ever, ever –'

'Good. I don't want to become notorious in the Westmorlands! I'm not a very regimentally minded regimental wife I'm afraid, but all the same –'

Adam's mind felt numbed. He had the sensation of a man recovering from a general anaesthetic. He didn't know what he thought or felt. Or if he thought or felt. He kissed Felicity when she dropped him at the barracks, and knew without any very clear emotion that what had happened had been important for him and not in the least for her. As he went to bed in his bleak room – which by an extraordinary and happy fluke was one of the few unshared ones – he knew that life and conscience were going to be more complicated henceforth. He couldn't face thinking of the moment when he would next encounter Ben Jameson's sceptical, mocking eyes – Ben Jameson, his commander, in many ways his idol; Ben Jameson, who had from his first days in the battalion shown him friendship, shared jokes with him, encouraged him; Ben Jameson whose wife's naked body had, for three incredible hours –

Oh dear, oh dear! Adam put out the light. Next morning before breakfast he found two messages had been received for him the previous evening, both recorded by Corporal Fisher in his round, rather childish hand. One said that Miss Fosdike had telephoned and would Mr Hardrow ring if he came in before midnight, she was at home. The other was from Mr Nicholas Hardrow and said that he had left school unexpectedly, was joining the RAF and would ring Mr Hardrow again at one o'clock the following afternoon.

'There's a call for you, Mr Hardrow. As a matter of fact, sir, student officers are not permitted to take calls on the office telephone. Mess president's orders.'

'Thank you, Sergeant Bayliss. I'll tell my caller to ring off, and I'll call back from the call-box.'

Sergeant Bayliss softened. The office was not being used at the moment, he had marked young Mr Hardrow as a nice-mannered young gentleman, always ready with a 'Good morning, Sergeant Bayliss' and a smile, not like some of them these days, God knew where they came from! Officers! Sergeant Bayliss was a regular. Bad feet had consigned him to this reasonably cushy billet in Aldershot. He disliked the mess president.

'Won't matter this once, sir. Just carry on.'

'Thank you.' Adam marched to the mess office telephone and Sergeant Bayliss closed the door.

'Adam Hardrow here.'

'Adam, it's Nick.'

'Where the hell are you?'

'Adam, I'm just joining the air force. The thing is this –'

'What d'you mean you're just joining the air force? You're still at school.'

'I've left.'

'Since when?'

'Since yesterday afternoon. I walked out. You see I've got this friend, you don't know him, he's a great chap, he's joining the RAF and his father is very high up in it. And he, the father, can get me in, to start flying training pretty well straight away, and then when I'm eighteen and a half –'

'Nick!'

'– every chance of a commission, apparently, after the full training, and I've got good exam results, you know –'

'Nick!'

'– apparently the earlier one starts the better, it's really absurd to sit at school when I'm already eighteen, which is the age you're allowed to start training –'

'Nick!'

'– and all it needs is your parent's or guardian's permission. Then you report for selection. My friend's father says he's sure I'll sail through selection. There are all sorts of tests but he's sure I'll pass them.'

'Nick, shut up. And listen. I think *all* that you've said is rot. All of it. And there will be no question whatsoever of Mama's permission. She'll be most upset.'

'Well, that's it, you see, I've given your name. I've said that my father's dead so it's your permission that's necessary. They're writing to you. Or rather they will write to you.'

'If anybody writes to me,' said Adam, 'I'll tell them that you have absolutely no permission of any kind and that you're a runaway from school.'

'I've also given them Cousin Beatrice's name.'

'*Cousin Beatrice!* You must be mad!'

'Well, she's sort of head of the family. I thought –'

'Listen,' said Adam grimly. 'Listen, Nick. Where are you now?'

'In a hotel in Lancaster. That's another thing –'

'What's another thing?'

'I'm a bit short of money, Adam. I wondered if you could just send, say three quid? I'll pay it back. When you start training you get paid something.'

'Now listen, Nick,' said Adam, very clearly and slowly and emphatically, 'just listen to me. This is what you've got to do. Can you pay the bill at the hotel?'

'Just.'

'Pay it. Have you got enough for the fare and the taxi to get back to school?'

'But I'm not going back to school.'

'Answer my question.'

'Just.'

'Then you will, at once, catch a train and go back. You will, before leaving Lancaster, telephone Edgcombe and tell him that you have been a fool and are on your way. And when you get back I hope you will be beaten black and blue. If you *don't* do that, right away – are you listening?'

'Yes, Adam.' Nick sounded furious.

'– if you don't promise to do exactly that, I shall, straight away, tell the police here to see that you're apprehended by their colleagues in Lancaster.' Adam had no idea if this threat was enforceable. Probably not. It was ordinary practice with absentee soldiers but schoolboys might be different. He put a lot of confidence into his voice, however. He also said, 'And I'll tell Mama.'

'Why?' Nick's voice was bitter and sulky, but Adam knew he was finished, that at heart he'd been undecided.

'Because school will get on to her, of course. Presumably have. She's no doubt worried sick. You're so selfish and irresponsible that it's hard to find words for it. Now put the telephone down and do exactly what I've said. Will you promise me?'

'I suppose so.'

'And Nick –'

'Well?'

'I know you'll join the air force one day. And it won't be long. But for God's sake, old boy, don't wreck things by smashing the rules to pieces and jumping the gun.'

Adam put the telephone down and found that he was shaking. His mother would be in a fearful state if she'd heard and he supposed that she had. Another telephone call to be made this evening. And one to Caroline, he supposed, which made him very uneasy indeed. And surely there must be a call to Felicity? Or perhaps not. The night before must be as if it had never been, she'd implied. Perhaps that barred even telephone conversation. The extraordinary thing was that Adam wasn't sure if he longed or dreaded to hear her voice. All he knew without question was that he was extremely glad that the course was dispersing, and he, Adam Hardrow, had a movement order which would take him to London, Dover and then Calais, and back to the 2nd Battalion, the Westmorland Regiment, the following morning. England was too much to handle, just at the moment.

Eventually he decided that a letter to Felicity and a letter to Caroline would be better than telephone calls. Adam was not particularly skilled with the pen but he mistrusted his ability to carry out ambivalent telephone conversations even more.

To Caroline he wrote next morning that it was rotten they'd not had another evening together. He enormously hoped there'd be regular leave and if so he'd be in early touch. Good luck with the driving. He made no further reference to letters – somehow he felt incapable of doing so with sincerity.

To Felicity he wrote – a letter that went through several drafts – that she was, as he'd said, wonderful. That he'd never forget what she'd given him. That he couldn't, he feared, get the picture of her – '*all* of you' he wrote, boldly – out of his mind. That of course he promised everything would simply be a heavenly memory between them, with very much love, Adam.

And Adam thought that perhaps another letter was due. Writing it made him feel uneasy and obtrusive, but he supposed he'd better make utterly sure that Nick was stopped at all points.

Dear Cousin Beatrice,
I believe it possible you might get a letter from some authority in the RAF saying your name has been given by

my brother Nicholas as some sort of reference. Nicholas told me he'd given your name, which he had no right to do, and I apologize.

He's trying to join the RAF while still under age and my mother would be furious – he's still at school. I think I've made him see he's being stupid, but I thought I'd better write to you and explain, in case you get a letter. If you do, please ignore it.

I remember very well what fun it was visiting you once at half-term, and what a superb tea you gave us, and how lovely your house is. I do hope you're well. I'm in the Westmorlands now (2nd Battalion), but I've been doing a course at home. I'm very well, though life is often rather boring. I'm so sorry to bother you.

Love from your affectionate cousin,
Adam Hardrow

'Your transport's here, Mr Hardrow,' said Sergeant Bayliss, appearing suddenly in the emptying mess ante-room. Goodbyes had been said, mess bills paid.

'The driver's got to pick up another officer, sir. You need to be off.'

'Oh, good lord, right, Sergeant Bayliss. I've just got two letters to get into the post –'

'Need to hurry, sir. And mess bills are closed and paid as you know, if you were after stamps.'

'Oh dear –'

'Give them to me, sir,' said Sergeant Bayliss, his soft spot for Mr Hardrow persisting as he took the letters and three-pence, 'give them to me. I'll see they catch the post. And good luck, sir.'

'Don't expect you feel you've been away at all, sir.'

'No, that's about right, Sergeant Pew. All well here?'

'Be a bit better now the weather's drying out, sir. It's been chronic these last weeks.'

'I'm sure.'

'Still, April's almost here now, sir. The lads will be glad to see you back, I wouldn't wonder.' It was, Adam thought, extraordinarily nice of Sergeant Pew to say that, in his loyal, detached, grumbly sort of voice. Sergeant Pew was one of the old school of NCOs who didn't believe in letting officers get too good an opinion of themselves or their reputations. They might stop trying.

Adam said conversationally, 'Any excitements in the company?'

'Various flaps, sir, now and then. Same old thing. German attack due. Top French brass planning a big offensive in the spring, that sort of thing. Comes and goes. Lads treat it all without much attention by now. All they ask is how long it's all going on, sir. Don't seem to make much sense just sitting here.' Adam was about to deliver one of the stock correctives to this line of thinking – apathy and complacency were, they were all told often, the army's chief enemies, ready to do the Germans' work for them. Sergeant Pew seemed, however, to feel that he had said enough to deflate any enthusiasm which Mr Hardrow had brought back from England. He said, 'Corporal Andrews – Andrews has been made up, sir.'

Andrews was an exceptionally intelligent and able young man in another platoon of the company. Adam knew that Ben Jameson thought highly of him, had marked him early. Adam, for some reason he could not analyse, never felt entirely easy about Andrews. Andrews was undoubtedly alert and impressive; on any sort of training he tended to shine. He was an excellent shot, very smart, very articulate – almost glib, Adam said to himself uncharitably. Of course Andrews had been promoted. It was altogether just. The army couldn't possibly waste material like Andrews. Adam was unsurprised when Sergeant Pew said, 'It's said he's being put in for officer training. For a commission.'

'I don't know how old Andrews – Corporal Andrews – is.'

'He's nineteen, sir.'

'Well, I expect he'll get it. Get recommended for an officer cadet training unit.'

'He's not,' said Sergeant Pew, 'been before the CO yet. But I expect the CO will put him up for it. He's got plenty to say for himself, has Andrews.' No 'Corporal Andrews', Adam noted. Sergeant Pew's tone was non-committal.

Ben Jameson welcomed Adam back in his usual rather languorous way. It was, Adam realized, inevitable that he imagined he felt Ben's eyes on him with a certain speculative intensity. He supposed he should feel the worst sort of treacherous swine, but somehow he didn't exactly, although he knew that his unease would take a long time to dissolve; perhaps would never dissolve. He felt inexperienced, immature, over-serious, hagridden with a guilt surely no man of the world would find other than absurd. Felicity had made it clear that she and Ben were 'tolerant' of each other's lives, provided matters were kept unobtrusive. Adam reminded himself fiercely of Angélique. He needed to do that pretty often. It was, from their first encounter on Adam's return, necessary to mention Felicity to Ben – anything else would have seemed fishy, surely? But the mention wasn't easy.

'I saw Felicity when I was at Aldershot, Ben.'

'So I've heard.'

'She asked me to supper. Terribly kind of her.'

'I'm sure it gave her pleasure.'

'Don't know about that –'

'Do you not?' But Ben, smiling, turned away at that moment, and Adam found himself talking to Ivan Perry. Ivan Perry had found some excuse to call on B Company and was lunching with them.

It was Adam's first full day back in France. Ben was now deep in conversation with the company second captain, Geoffrey Purvis – Geoffrey Purvis from the 1st Battalion, from Egypt. Geoffrey Purvis was a slender, dark-haired man of about thirty, with a well-tended black moustache. He seemed affable in a shy sort of way, although Adam suspected that they would all become familiar and perhaps excessively familiar with Geoffrey Purvis's anecdotes of life in Cairo – there had been several of these before lunch. Ben, however, was so far treating him very much as a kindred spirit. Adam grinned at Ivan. Ivan winked back.

'A happy leave?'

'Oh, yes.'

'Emotionally complicated?'

'Why on earth do you say that, Ivan?' It had been softly said, but even so!

'You look rather buttoned up. Seething within. Never mind – are you about to give us all little talks about new ways of digging trench latrines?'

'I expect so. I've not had any directions of that sort from Colonel Frank, yet. I dread it – with luck he'll forget about it and just leave me peacefully here with the platoon!'

'I doubt it. I doubt it. In fact if what rumour says is true, your days with your platoon are numbered anyway.'

'Ivan, what the hell –' But Ivan was at that moment claimed by Ben Jameson for some bit of business which was the ostensible reason for his visit to B Company, and Adam had no opportunity to question further his unwelcome and obscure speculations. He said nothing to Ben, and Ben said nothing to him beyond observing later that the CO was away for a week and 'wants to see you himself on his return. To talk about how you've done on your course and what use he wants to make of your knowledge, for the edification of us all.'

'Where's Colonel Frank gone?'

'To the Maginot Line. Some of us British amateurs are being sent there, brigade or battalion at a time, to see what real war is like.'

Adam knew this. If Colonel Fosdike was away on this duty

it could be presumed that the Westmorlands would them- selves see the Maginot Line soon. It would at least make a change. There was even some sort of patrolling going on, and the odd encounter with small bodies of German troops who seemed as inactive as their enemies.

'It'll soon be spring,' Adam said. 'Do you believe in this spring offensive the French are said to be planning?' He was forcing himself to talk naturally, with the old familiarity, to Ben. Ben had always treated one as an equal, conver- sationally, genially. Well now one was rather more an equal, wasn't one, Adam's mind disagreeably suggested.

'I don't believe the French are up to it,' Ben replied. 'Not if what I've heard is true.'

'You mean –'

'The French are fed up with the war. They don't see the point. Nobody can help the Poles by now. The Huns and the Russkies have carved them up – put the clock back.'

'Not good, surely!'

'Not good in the least. But why does it make necessary a war between Germany and France, yet again?'

'To –'

'Or Germany and England?'

'To –'

'To teach Hitler he's gone too far. All right. Is he learning? Will he learn, unless somebody attacks Germany – and successfully?'

'I suppose there'll be bombing,' said Adam. There were so many conversations on these lines, and it didn't seem that the drift of argument had changed noticeably during his time away from the battalion. Next day they heard that Colonel Fosdike had contracted a very nasty bout of flu when visiting the Maginot Line and was in a base hospital near Le Mans. Later the battalion learned that their commanding officer wouldn't be back until about the end of April. There had been 'complications' and sick leave had been granted.

Adam attended Whisky Wainwright's orders to hear Whisky read out his report from the Aldershot course. Whisky read it aloud stumblingly. Then he glared at Adam.

'Learn anything?'

'A bit, sir.'

'Interesting?'

'No, sir.'

Whisky gave one of his snorts. He said, 'CO may have some ideas of getting you to run field-engineering cadres for young officers. Got two more joining next week. Some sergeants, too. Don't know exactly what CO has in mind. You'd better get a week's course planned, but Colonel Frank will be back at the end of April and we won't start anything before then.'

'Right, sir.' This was odd. Whisky was in command – why on earth not set Adam's knowledge to work right away, if it had been worth sending him to Aldershot at all? Why delay so routine and unimportant a point of detail for Colonel Fosdike's decision on return? Adam concluded that the expertise he had acquired in field engineering was not regarded as of urgent value, at least by Whisky Wainwright. He also concluded, perhaps unfairly, that it was another example of the CO's liking to keep even the smallest and most detailed decisions of battalion life in his own hands. Anyway, it suits me, Adam said to himself. Ben had already set him to work in the company, lecturing on trench planning, drainage and fortifications. Experience had taught them all a good deal, but Adam could convey, he supposed, some useful tips.

But during the following week they all heard, with a good deal of excitement, that the German army had invaded Denmark and that an amphibious force had set German troops ashore at various points in Norway. The war, it seemed, was at last hotting up. In the ensuing weeks they watched, at first with a thrill of release that Britain was at last actively engaged, then with grim dismay, how attempts by British expeditionary forces to land in Norway and dislodge the Germans either foundered and ended in evacuation, or were apparently making progress so slow as to be invisible. Whisky Wainwright said that the bloody Huns had stolen a march. Ben Jameson said lazily that they seemed to be rather quicker on their feet, snow or no snow. The Norwegian forces had apparently played little or no part in the defence of their land. And from Denmark came stories of an almost entirely peaceful occupation of a country which seemed disposed, if not to welcome, at least to tolerate the Wehrmacht. In France the pace quickened – the Germans had surely demonstrated that this was war, after all. But of course, on the Western Front, if those Germans tried anything, they'd find a totally prepared and first-class enemy. After the comparative walk-over they seemed to be having in Norway, it should be a salutary shock. Or would it? Adam pushed away recollections of the disturbing scepticism of Whisky Wainwright, of Ben Jameson.

On a day when the news from Norway was particularly depressing, Adam received a letter in unfamiliar handwriting, difficult to read. He looked at the signature – 'Your loving cousin, Beatrice Hardrow'.

So at least old Cousin Beatrice was 'his loving cousin', remembered his existence and wasn't too fed up with the family in spite of Nick's impertinence! He read the short letter. What an odd old girl, he thought as he read.

Dear Adam,
Thank you for your letter. It took some time to reach me and I deferred replying until sure that no communication of the sort suggested was in the post. None has arrived, and I expect none will now.

I don't know what the RAF authorities would have asked me or what I would have replied. I would, of course, have made it clear that my relationship to your brother in no way constitutes guardianship or carries responsibility. As to the general principle, however, I have every sympathy with Nicholas wishing to fly. I also have every sympathy with his desire to leave school and involve himself in the war. War is for young men and at his age he is a young man. Any spirited – indeed any sensible – human being would wish to do what he wishes or something like it. I expect, however, that you feel the responsibilities of an elder brother acutely, and I can't criticize that, I suppose.

I am so glad you are in your father's regiment – *our* regiment. And I hope that it will bring you happiness and pride, to accompany what I suppose will inevitably be the suffering and fear and the bad things as well.

Your loving cousin,
Beatrice Hardrow.

Colonel Fosdike returned to duty, looking rather frail, on 2 May. Two days later Adam marched in after battalion orders. His presence had been commanded. Colonel Fosdike looked at him with his usual agreeable smile.

'Well, Adam, I've not seen you for a long time. Course go well?'

'I think so, sir.'

'You got a glowing report. Naturally. And now I want to talk about your future.'

'Yes, sir. The second-in-command told me to get a course plan ready. I can start it whenever you say, sir.'

'Ah, maybe, yes, quite right, later that might be very useful. But just now I've got something rather different in mind for you. There are going to be some changes. Tom's giving up being adjutant.'

Tom Stubbs had seemed a permanency. He personified battalion headquarters, was impossible to imagine elsewhere.

Imperturbable, he knew everything that was going on. And he was efficient. Adam stood still. What was all this leading to?

'Going to A Company, second captain. Harry's taking over as adjutant.'

Harry Venables. Intelligence officer. Bright but rather mercurial.

'I want you to take over as intelligence officer. There's a new boy arriving on Monday. He'll take over your platoon in B, Ben suggests. I want you to start taking over from Harry on the same day. Monday.'

'I feel I don't know much about it, sir.'

'IO? You'll pick it up. The intelligence sergeant, Cobb, is first class. Knows it all. We'll send you on a long course some time this summer, if conditions permit – the Hun won't start anything till this Norway show's out of the way but it may not be long now. Your course might have to wait.'

'I understand, sir.'

'Meanwhile Harry will show you the ropes, and you're lucky he'll still be around. As adjutant, I mean.'

'Yes, sir. I have to say that I don't feel very – er – that I don't know much about it. As I said.' Adam knew that he sounded futile and unconvincing.

'No matter, no matter at all. You're bright. You'll read yourself in very quickly. You're a linguist, too, which is a wonderful bonus. You speak French *and* German!'

'More or less, sir.'

'You'll find yourself interrogating our prisoners!'

Adam smiled politely. He saluted and left the room, head awhirl. His overwhelming sense was of misery at leaving the platoon. Leaving Sergeant Pew. Leaving Wilkins. And Wright. And Crowe. And Pratt. And Corporal Egan. It was unthinkable, but it had to be thought.

The 'new boy' taking over Adam's platoon was called

George Garthwaite. Adam had a few words. He didn't take to Garthwaite.

From Monday morning, 6 May, Adam started trying to master the duties of battalion intelligence officer. 'There's an awful lot of bumf,' said Harry Venables, 'a lot of it is unimportant. The ISUMs matter, although more often than not there's nothing in them, and although in theory you then brief the CO, in practice he likes reading them himself. Why –'

'What's an ISUM?'

'Intelligence summary. Comes down from on high. German activity, latest titbits gleaned from Berlin, German units opposite various parts of the front, long-term forecasts. Everything you can imagine.' Harry Venables talked on, knowingly. He enjoyed showing off a little.

'It's hotting up quite a bit, actually. Lot of activity in the Rhineland. Later in the week I'll take you to Brigade. You'd better know the people there. You'll find most of your opposite numbers quite a bit senior to you, of course. Not that it matters,' Harry said kindly.

Sergeant Cobb, no substitute for Sergeant Pew as friend and counsellor, hardly tried to conceal his scepticism about Adam's competence to perform his duties. He clearly enjoyed asking the occasional question he was tolerably sure would flummox him.

'Would you like me to continue the Wehrmacht ORBAT updating index, sir? Or would you prefer it done in a different way?'

Adam knew that there would come a time when he and Sergeant Cobb would have to understand each other more clearly. The time was not yet. The ground was not yet firm beneath his feet.

'Go on doing it as you have been, Sergeant Cobb. And go

on doing everything in the same way as for Mr Venables. If I want to change anything, I'll tell you.'

'Right, sir. I simply wondered –'

'Quite.'

Adam never remembered a week in which he read more. He had never worked harder at trying to assimilate both fact and conjecture. His task was made the more difficult for having only a young regimental officer's sketchy knowledge of the British Expeditionary Force's composition. He knew his own company, his own battalion. The brigade in which the battalion, one of three, was serving was more or less familiar ground. Above that, Adam knew that his touch must be unsure.

Once Colonel Fosdike looked into the small farmhouse kitchen which did duty as intelligence office.

'Getting the hang of it, Adam?'

'Doing my best, sir!'

'Make sure Harry introduces you to the I boys at Division as well as Brigade, won't you. They ought to know the faces of all the battalion IOs.'

'I see, sir.'

'Anyway, make sure they know the face of *my* IO.' Colonel Fosdike smiled as he said it. Adam reflected, without enthusiasm, that one of the duties of a battalion intelligence officer in battle was to accompany the CO on most occasions when the latter was away from battalion headquarters. They'd be seeing a good deal of each other. Assuming, of course, that there would one day be a battle – Norway, and the persistent descriptions of unusual German activity in the western districts of the Reich, had somewhat quickened the British army's collective pulse.

On the Thursday Ivan Perry put his head round the door.

'If they wanted an intellectual at headquarters why didn't they choose me?'

'Why not indeed, Ivan? I'd swap tomorrow.'

'Weekend's coming up, Adam. Don't kill yourself.' The battalion attempted to maintain something like a normal weekly routine. Saturday afternoons were devoted to football, a game pursued by the Westmorlands like a religious cult. Saturday evenings were usually clear and as many men as could be transported generally 'walked out' in Vevers. On Sundays there was a church parade, by companies, the padre travelling to each by rotation.

'I think,' said Adam dolefully, 'that I'll be reading paper the whole weekend. And on Saturday morning Harry's got to take me to meet these terribly important intelligence people at divisional headquarters. I'm going to be briefed, imagine!'

'You probably know much more than me already.'

'I probably do.'

'Come and dine at no.59 on Saturday. I'll try to telephone Madame.'

'It would be fun, Ivan. I suspect I ought to be working but –'

'Or we could try to get there this evening. I'm on duty tomorrow.'

'No, I'm duty officer tonight. Sleeping here by the telephone.'

'Saturday then. And relax a bit. You've got the rest of the war before you.'

There was a good deal of unaccustomed noise that Thursday as Adam lay down on a camp-bed by the orderly-room telephone. What sounded like explosions from both north and south were too frequent for comfort. 'Air raids, sir,' Sergeant Cobb said, appearing at midnight with a cup of tea. He was on duty too. 'Air raids, no question. German bombers active. There'll be a good deal in tomorrow's ISUM. French civvies will all be running round in circles, wouldn't wonder! It's a new pattern of activity, new pattern altogether.' Sergeant Cobb liked the jargon of intelligence. It was, however, not until half-past six on Friday morning, 10 May, that Adam found himself in Colonel Fosdike's billet, having knocked at the door of the room where the colonel slept, entered, found a light switch, and turned it on. Colonel Fosdike blinked at him.

'What is it?' he asked.

'We've just had confirmation, sir. The Germans have invaded Holland and Belgium. Plan D has been ordered.' And as Colonel Fosdike, mind still torpid, swung his legs out of bed and yelled for his batman, he registered that he had seldom seen an expression of such beatific happiness as that on young Adam Hardrow's face. Adam, as intelligence officer, had been privileged to read the top-secret orders, orders to be activated by codewords of which the first had now been received. Adam knew what Plan D meant. The British Expeditionary Force was to march into Belgium and advance to the Dyle, to Brussels and beyond. And to meet the Wehrmacht at long last. And whatever Ben Jameson's scepticism and Whisky Wainwright's grunts about us being less than what we'd been; whatever the whispers about equipment not being up to that of the Germans, about the powers and numbers of the Luftwaffe, the efficiency of the panzers who'd stunned the Poles; whatever, whatever, Adam said to himself, his heart dancing, we'll show them what it is to challenge England!

CHAPTER 5

'Not much of a river line, is it! More like a flooded ditch!
Have to see what the Sappers can do to improve things –'

Colonel Fosdike was talking half to himself and half to
Adam. It was their first tour of the battalion's forward
companies since arriving on the Dyle position during the
preceding Sunday night.

It was true that as an impediment to the German army's
advance the River Dyle was narrow and unimpressive. Adam
didn't feel that any response to the colonel was appropriate.
He was carrying the colonel's map, with company positions
neatly marked. Private Inglewood of the Intelligence Section
was also accompanying them. 'Always bring one of the section
with you,' Colonel Fosdike had said briskly, and Inglewood,
rifle slung over shoulder, respirator in its canvas container
hoisted to the chest in the 'ready' position, had joined them.
He had no particular function. Adam had every intention of
himself noting anything the CO required; and the map was
hardly a two-man load. Inglewood, a sophisticate, looked
mildly ironic.

Also accompanying them was Major Simon Brodie, Royal
Artillery, whose battery of twenty-five pounder field guns
directly supported the Westmorlands. A man of few words,
those few (Adam thought) were invariably sensible. His job
was to see that if the Westmorlands had to fight on this river
line they would at least have support from as many of the

division's guns as he could arrange; and that targets would be selected and recorded – even, in some cases, registered.

Frank Fosdike seemed in an extraordinarily bad humour. Adam had noted already the colonel's habit of muttering to himself, the frowning absorption, the sentences begun and not finished. Colonel Frank's jolly tired, Adam thought, with unwonted sympathy. He supposed that an old man in his forties like the CO must find particularly taxing the sort of journey they'd just completed. The battalion had moved from near Vevers by transport of varying types, much of it civilian and requisitioned, leaving their previous billets late on the Friday afternoon and proceeding for twenty-four hours in fits and starts, with many long hold-ups and traffic blocks. Everyone had expected that the column would be bombed but they'd been left alone. Then, during the Saturday night, they'd been ordered to debus, fall in and start marching. By then it had been dark. There'd been the usual hourly halts but no long halt for nearly fifteen miles and the men had been very, very tired. Colonel Fosdike had a small run-about vehicle known as a PU, and Adam sat in the back of it. Part of the time, however, the CO had climbed out and marched with one of the companies. Adam had approved.

After what felt like eternity they had been ordered to halt and, following a prolonged wait beside the road, cookers had appeared and food had been available, and tea. They'd travelled with haversack rations but had had nothing hot since leaving their winter billets. Then, to everyone's surprise, another column of empty transport had driven up, and they'd embussed again. And by that time – Sunday morning – the movement of their column was already being held up by the long, miserable columns of refugees.

Some refugees had cars or lorries. A good many had carts – handcarts they were pushing or carts drawn by horses, donkeys; in several cases Adam observed oxen. But the great majority were trudging along on foot, and the main impression left in Adam's mind was of the very old and the very young. Both these categories seemed to be moving back along the roads in large numbers – small children padding along with a look of utter exhaustion on their faces, a look Adam had never seen before; and old men and women – particularly women – wearing expressions of passive despair. Adam knew that he was observing faces which had witnessed total loss – homes, property, livestock, perhaps relations, almost certainly hope. And maybe not for the first time.

To the drivers of military vehicles the refugee columns were a considerable irritant. On one occasion – Adam was sitting in the small canvas-covered compartment behind Colonel Fosdike – they found that they were held up by a troop-carrying lorry which had broken down two vehicles ahead of them in the column. It was at a point on the narrow, poplar-lined road where it caused an instant obstruction, and the driver in front of Colonel Fosdike's vehicle was trying to ease his truck past the breakdown. The refugees were blocking this manoeuvre and Adam saw the truck stuck and likely to remain stuck until the tide of refugees could be diverted off the road for a few yards. He saw the driver's hand out of the window of his cab, heard him banging the outer metal of the door, and listened to the flow of abusive language he was shouting at the refugees. Colonel Fosdike muttered angrily and got out of the car, followed by Adam.

'No damned traffic control at all! Should be Military Police accompanying the columns, diverting all these civilians to other routes!'

'Excuse me, sir,' Adam had said. He had moved swiftly to the truck in front and tapped on the panel of the door. The Service Corps driver looked down at him through the open window, a weary grin on his face.

'Bloody civvies!'

Adam said curtly, 'There's no point in swearing at people in that way. It's stupid.' The man looked at him with an insubordinate scowl. Adam said, 'Now shut up, and wait.' He then moved into the refugee column. He knew that a good many would be Flemish rather than French speakers but French would get somewhere. Calling out in French, very courteously, Adam persuaded the refugees to stop about fifteen yards from the obstruction. He then waved on the truck with its driver and saw the man muttering irritably as he accelerated with unnecessary force to get going again. Adam ran back to rejoin Colonel Fosdike whose car had drawn level with the broken down vehicle. He pointed.

'Sir, it would be perfectly possible for these civilians to get past by going up to that farm and down the parallel farm road over there, back to this one further on. I want to explain it to them. I'll not be a minute.' He ran off and found, by good luck, two Belgians in a small car in the refugee column who had been nosing forward. They were young women, and they looked both troubled and sensible. Adam explained the problem. The two columns couldn't pass each other.

'*Bien!*' said the girl sitting beside the driver. Rapidly, she told her companion that she would, for a few minutes, police this diversion. When the refugee column got moving in the required direction it would carry on under its own impetus. Of course! She gave Adam a charming smile. He told her how grateful the British army was for her help and ran back to climb in behind Colonel Fosdike. What an excellent girl! She showed authority.

'It should be all right, sir!' Then they had, for a few miles, bowled along without hold-up. Then another unexplained halt. Debusment again. Fall in on the road in threes. And the march went on. The whole battalion had reached their new positions on the Dyle before dawn on the Monday and Adam never remembered feeling more tired. And I've had it cushy, he thought, driving in the CO's vehicle for much of the way! He wondered how 5 Platoon were.

With luck he'd soon discover. Fosdike, Hardrow and

Inglewood were now striding along towards the right-hand platoon of B Company, or where it should be. A dispatch rider had been sent out after breakfast to tell each company that the CO was coming round and approximately when. They were taking much longer on their tour than anticipated, Adam reflected. Not that Ben Jameson would be particularly concerned when or whether they arrived, he thought with an inward grin. He found, for a moment without reservation or embarrassment, that he was hugely looking forward to seeing Ben.

Ben was standing on the track which ran roughly parallel to the River Dyle. Defensive positions were meant to be sited to take maximum advantage of the obstacle, however inadequate, provided by that river. The Westmorlands now had to dig trenches and create those positions. The assumption given to Colonel Fosdike and relayed by him to his subordinates was that they'd got at least two weeks. They were a very long way from the German–Belgian border and the entire Belgian army was deployed between that border and the British front line. That army was meant to delay the Wehrmacht, no more; but two weeks had not seemed to the planners unduly optimistic. To the north, where German forces had invaded Holland, the entire Dutch army was arrayed parallel to the Belgian–British–French forces, and the going was notoriously difficult. There should be plenty of time. Furthermore – and it was not a matter to be discussed freely, the contingency might be remote, the Belgians were sensitive – there could, in the last resort, be withdrawal from this Dyle line to another of the rivers Colonel Fosdike had once laid out with tapes on the floor of a barn near Vevers for the edification of his officers. Belgium was seamed by defensible rivers, and each of them should enable the Allies to do what they'd failed to do in 1914 – hold forward, give depth to the defence of France.

'Morning, Ben.'

'Good morning, sir. We're getting below ground reasonably fast.'

'More important to make sure you're properly sited than be in too much of a hurry. You've got this footbridge in your sector, haven't you?'

'Yes, sir.'

'May have to destroy it one day, of course.'

'I intend to quite soon, sir.'

'Quite soon?'

'Before the Germans arrive, I mean, sir.'

'Ben,' said Colonel Fosdike patiently, 'there are at least three Belgian divisions between the Germans and that footbridge. As well as our own armoured cars.'

'Slightly fewer than that in the last hour, I think, sir.'

'What do you mean?'

Ben pointed. They all looked, and Colonel Fosdike made a huffing, puffing sound. They could, quite clearly, see a straggle of men in Belgian khaki moving towards the footbridge on the opposite bank. One or two were carrying rifles. Most were not.

Ben said, conversationally, 'They're not the first.'

'Have you reported this?'

'The real rush only started a half-hour ago, sir,' said Ben pleasantly. 'I've sent a message to battalion headquarters. I reckon we've counted over a hundred across.'

'Deserters! Good God –'

'They all say, sir, that their units are withdrawing fast and that they were ordered to get back as well and as quickly as possible. They say – of course it's probably nonsense – that the Germans are pretty close behind them.'

They stared at each other and Colonel Fosdike said, 'I expect we'll get the whole picture after this morning. I can't understand –'

'You'd like to see round the company, sir. Sergeant-Major, the CO is going round the company.'

'Yes, sir,' said Company Sergeant-Major Darwin, 'start with 5 Platoon, sir.' He smiled at Adam as he said it, saluting again. This, thought Adam, is home. But their tour was very rapid and Adam had no time for more than a brief word with Sergeant Pew, with George Garthwaite, unworthy successor to Hardrow in command of the platoon, and with Wilkins (digging a two-man slit trench with Wright) before Colonel Fosdike said sharply, 'Adam!' and intimated that he wanted to return to battalion headquarters. 'Must find out the general situation,' Frank Fosdike said, as they walked away, fast. 'Must find out how much time we've really got. It's all quite different from what we were led to believe.' And when they reached battalion headquarters, Adam found that Sergeant Cobb had a very long and very clear statement of the situation, rung through from brigade by field telephone. Belgian forces to the front had indeed 'suffered some severe setbacks' and 'in some cases retreated rapidly'. The main body of the enemy could be expected on the Dyle position at any time from this afternoon.

In the event the Germans did not bother the Westmorlands until the following day, Tuesday, 14 May. The Monday was quiet. Each forward company reported a continuing trickle of Belgian soldiers, moving to the west and shrugging shoulders to any requests for information. The hours passed.

Adam's intelligence section had set up a passable situation map in one of the rooms of the farmhouse that battalion headquarters had commandeered, and Adam, feeling extraordinarily amateurish at the business, had organized a system whereby Colonel Fosdike and Harry Venables, his adjutant, were fed information without delay. Communications within the battalion were mainly by field telephone and runner or dispatch rider, and Adam gathered that much of the higher communication network was by civil telephone. A cable had been laid to them from brigade headquarters.

It was at four o'clock in the afternoon that Harry Venables, yawning, put his head round the door of Adam's intelligence lair.

'Seen the colonel?'

'Not for the last two hours.'

'A Company have been shelled.'

'Shelled?'

'Mortars apparently, and the right forward platoon have seen a number of Germans on the far bank. They've opened fire. And there was some firing back but nobody was hit.'

'I'll tell the CO.'

So the enemy was at last quite near! Adam felt his heart beat slightly faster and despised himself for the excitement. This was nothing. They were four days into what was billed already as the decisive battle of the war in the west and until now nobody in the Westmorlands had yet seen a German. Still –

Whisky Wainwright appeared behind Harry in the doorway. During these days Adam had not been particularly aware of the second-in-command. His huge bulk periodically moved in and paused before the situation map Adam was building up. Generally he then disappeared without a word. Adam had no idea what particular duties the CO had assigned to him. He seemed to be away from their farmhouse a good deal. Now he said abruptly, 'Strong Hun patrol.'

Harry and Adam looked a question. Whisky was gazing at the battalion map.

'Tapping in. A Company. Trying it on. Twenty minutes ago. I was there. Strong patrol.' Whisky indicated exactly where Germans had been seen and where shelling had taken place.

Adam said, 'I'd better tell the CO. First contact.'

Whisky said, 'I've told him,' and Harry Venables said 'Where *is* the CO?'

'Lying down. Headache. I've been to all three forward

companies in the last two hours. Old Hun's up to the river bank. Not showing himself much.' Whisky sounded contented. Adam telephoned brigade headquarters, and while he was doing so Colonel Fosdike suddenly appeared. He looked overwrought.

'Where's the IO?'

Harry pointed at Adam, who was passing information to the brigade headquarters intelligence officer.

'Why wasn't I informed that we are being attacked?'

'Just come in, sir,' said Whisky strongly. 'Pretty well as I told you. I've put them in the picture here. A Company message only just come in – bit of delay. Line was cut. But as you know I was there myself twenty minutes ago.'

'*The line was cut!* How was the line cut?'

'No idea,' said Whisky. Lines were cut, whether in war or training. It was a hazard of military life. He said, dismissively, 'Cows, probably.'

'You're very credulous,' said Colonel Fosdike. 'It was much more likely to be saboteurs. German sympathizers! We were warned that there could be plenty of them.' He turned to Adam.

'On no account are you to delay for an instant in passing information about the enemy to me.'

'No, sir.'

Colonel Fosdike stood in front of the map. No particular illumination came from it. Whisky Wainwright said, in a casual voice, 'Will you be going to A Company, sir?'

There was a pause. Adam could feel the electricity.

'Not at the moment. I must stay here. There may be developments on other company fronts.'

'Yes, sir. I think A Company positions are OK – I gather you've not seen them yourself. And Ben's in a good place, as you know.'

The electricity was undiminished. Colonel Fosdike

nodded. He said to Harry Venables, 'Has the brigadier been on the line?'

'No, sir.'

'I think I'd better ring him.' And later they heard Colonel Fosdike's voice on the field telephone. He was telling the brigadier that they had been attacked but that everything was perfectly under control. No casualties.

'I hope we gave them a nasty shock, sir.'

And then – 'Thank you, sir!'

Replacing the handset, Colonel Fosdike said, with an appearance of nonchalance, 'Several attacks, it seems. Probing attacks, at a lot of points. May be more during the night, I wouldn't wonder.'

But the Westmorlands were undisturbed during that night, and it was not until midday the next day, Wednesday, that Harry Venables sought Adam and told him to accompany the CO to brigade headquarters for a conference due to start in thirty minutes. No time to waste. And during that conference, as Colonel Fosdike sat licking his lips and Adam scribbled notes on a pad, they learned that the 'probing attacks' made against the brigade front might or might not be resumed but were of relative unimportance. Far to the south, in the area of Sedan, the German army had crossed the Meuse and broken through the defending French army corps. There was, the brigadier told them, a 'large-scale penetration'. German mechanized forces were reported moving west – fast. Because of this it was necessary for the entire British Expeditionary Force to be withdrawn westward. Otherwise its flanks would be turned and it would be surrounded.

'I said "flanks",' said the brigadier. 'As some of you know, we've not got much on the northern flank either. The Dutch have surrendered. Totally.' There was a shattered silence as the news penetrated. The Dutch army surrendered! A complete void to the north of them and what was described as a 'large-scale penetration' to the south! The brigadier's voice was continuing, without any particular expression –

'In five days the whole of Holland will be in German hands – as soon as they can march into it.'

They were given the withdrawal plan. Each division was to withdraw, by stages and phases, to the River Escaut. Routes and timings were allotted. It sounded, rather comfortingly, a matter of routine. As they drove back to the 2nd Westmorlands battalion headquarters Colonel Fosdike said not a word.

When they arrived, and Frank Fosdike had disappeared after giving curt orders to his adjutant to convene an order group of company commanders, Adam told Harry Venables and Whisky Wainwright what was up. There had been no more shelling or mortaring, no further sign of Germans on the battalion front. As they bent, dumbfounded, over a map of Belgium and north-western France which Adam produced, Whisky said, 'They won't push here.'

'Think not, sir?'

'Of course not. Just want to keep us sufficiently busy not to slip away. Why push us back when they've got every chance of getting right round us?'

But in this, unusually, Major Wainwright was mistaken.

It was Wednesday night. At five minutes to eleven the members of battalion headquarters who were awake heard a succession of single shots followed by the rippling sound of a machine-gun burst, a faster, shorter burst than that produced by the British bren-gun. Although Adam didn't know it he was hearing for the first time the German Spandau '38, with its 7.92 calibre ammunition and its particularly high rate of fire.

Adam said, 'That might be German.' He said it with a great sense of exhilaration. Sergeant Cobb nodded. They were on duty at the command post together. A moment later the sound was repeated, and then repeated again. It came from somewhere to the front, the exact direction hard to tell.

The field telephone at battalion headquarters rang at exactly eleven o'clock. Adam lifted the handset and recognized the voice of Geoffrey Purvis, deliberate, pedantic but mercifully clear. Line to companies was cut or destroyed frequently and the battalion line parties were out most of the time and were getting tired. Company radio sets appeared unreliable, and anyway were switched off once positions were taken up, in order to conserve batteries.

Purvis's voice said,

'Adjutant?'

'IO here.'

'B Company. The forward platoons have been attacked by strong enemy forces who have got across the river. No positions have been lost. Enemy strength estimated at two companies.'

'Right, Geoffrey.'

Geoffrey Purvis sounded as if he found this intimacy inappropriate. He said, 'Is that Adam?'

'It is.'

'You've got that?'

'Clearly. And I'll try to get the gunners on to the crossing places and so forth. Please give me targets where you'd like fire.'

Major Brodie, the battery commander, was living with the Westmorlands, and his signals operator was snoring in a corner of the battalion headquarters cell. Adam reached out with a foot and kicked him awake. He pointed him to the parallel handset, and jotted down details as they came over from B Company. The Royal Artillery lance-bombardier was also jotting and nodding. Adam was still listening to Geoffrey Purvis as he heard the lance-bombardier murmur, 'Should be no problem, sir. I'll tell Major Brodie.'

It was Adam's first experience of the uncanny competence

and confidence of artillerymen, and of the extraordinary fact that their communications seemed to work when nobody else's did. He was still on the line to Geoffrey Purvis three minutes later, when the lance-bombardier reappeared and simply gave Adam a thumbs-up sign. It wouldn't have been considered appropriate protocol in the Westmorlands but it gave Adam what he wanted.

'I think they'll be firing those targets pretty soon, Geoffrey.'

'Good. I hope the gunners will be accurate.'

'I'm sure they will.'

'Things are a bit mixed up near the river. Ben's forward.'

'I'll tell the CO. Good luck, Geoffrey.'

But Colonel Fosdike had appeared during this last exchange and had heard it. The pressure lamp which illuminated the small room cast shadows, and the tall Fosdike frame threw a long dark pattern over the wall behind him. He said, 'What was all that about?'

Adam told him.

'You – *you* – have ordered defensive fire –'

'It was called for by B Company, sir,' said Adam. 'They're being attacked. I passed the message.' Something was ticking angrily in his brain, like an old-fashioned kitchen clock.

'You should – you should –'

Adam said, 'I'm sure we can cancel the fire if you wish, sir. I'll speak to Major Brodie.'

'No!'

'Then it ought to be coming down at any minute, sir. Three of the five references he gave, Captain Purvis gave, are registered targets.'

'Have you passed all this – the information – to Brigade?'

'I'm about to, sir.'

'It's urgent.'

'Of course, sir.'

'At five o'clock tomorrow morning thinning out starts from the forward companies. As you know.'

'Yes, sir.'

'They can't thin out if they're in the middle of a battle! I must know exactly what the situation is, minute by minute. I may have urgent decisions to make.'

They had been joined by Whisky Wainwright and Harry Venables, both aroused from slumber. The signals sergeant, Abel, could be heard in the tiny passage outside cross-examining another signals NCO about line. Nobody responded to Colonel Fosdike. After a long pause Whisky Wainwright said, 'Expect Ben will be all right.'

Frank Fosdike rounded on him. For some reason he appeared furious.

'Why do you expect that, Major Wainwright?'

Whisky said, imperturbably, 'Because he's that sort of chap.'

'I wish to speak to Captain Jameson. Or, rather, to Captain Purvis, since it seems Captain Jameson is not at his headquarters.'

No, thought Adam, he's away fighting somewhere! He busied himself with the field telephone. A moment later Sergeant Abel appeared and saluted.

' 'Fraid the line to A and B is cut again, sir. I've got a party out.'

'Wireless –'

'Can't get through, sir. Trying. Sets are too low-powered for these –'

But Colonel Fosdike interrupted. His eyes were gleaming almost as if something had brought him unexpected joy.

'You see!'

'Sir?'

'It's as I thought! Cut off! No communication! No way of knowing what's going on.'

Bobby Forrest tried to interject comfort. He had completed his long signals course and a week's leave, returning only two days before the storm broke on 10 May, and he was having

130

some difficulty asserting his position as signals officer in the face of a supremely competent Sergeant Abel and a commanding officer who tended to ignore him. He cleared his throat and said, 'We'll have line through within minutes, sir, I'm sure of it.'

Colonel Fosdike looked through him as if he didn't exist. He said in a low voice, 'B Company may be overrun for all we know. Then there'll be nothing between the Germans and this place. The Huns could be through us just like they've cut through the French in the south.'

Whisky spoke up. 'Well, we know B Company wasn't overrun five minutes ago because Adam here was talking to them.' And as he spoke they all heard the very distant sound of guns and, a little later and much nearer, the sound of exploding shells. From the direction of B Company.

Colonel Fosdike appeared slightly calmer. He said, 'The urgent thing is to find more about the situation in B Company. On B Company front.'

Adam stood up. 'I'd better go to find out, sir. It's a light night and it'll only take me about fifteen minutes. There ought to be line through again before then, but –'

'Yes. Yes, Adam. I think that would be best. You go. Take someone with you.'

'Of course, sir.'

'And don't forget that the crucial issue –'

'Is whether they can start to thin out on time. I understand, sir.'

Harry Venables glanced at Whisky Wainwright. Young officers didn't interrupt the CO in that way, whatever the situation, whatever the pressure. Whisky appeared not to have heard. He said, 'We'll keep on trying to get B on the line. If we get 'em no point in sending the IO –'

'No, no,' said Colonel Fosdike, 'of course he must go! We're blind here – blind! And deaf! We know nothing!' They all heard the dull thump of more shells bursting from the direction of B Company. More British shells, it might reasonably be presumed.

The way to B Company ran down a level farm track with a small coppice on one side of it. It was a bright moonlit night and Adam, accompanied by the silent and somehow comforting Inglewood, walked fast. B Company was the nearest to battalion headquarters, and the headquarters farm selected by Harry Venables was, in fact, pretty near the forward position. 'We're very exposed here,' Colonel Fosdike had said dubiously on seeing it four days earlier. He had been assured that there was no other suitable building.

Adam had estimated that he'd need fifteen minutes but in fact it only took him ten to reach the point where they'd left Ben Jameson on their first tour of the battalion on Sunday morning. B Company headquarters had been established in a single-storey cottage beside the track, with what had, in daylight, looked like some sort of allotment or smallholding round it. As he raced down the track towards it Adam heard no more shooting. He hoped Geoffrey Purvis would know enough of what was going on in his own company sector. If there was confusion it might well be that Adam would have to stay some time before being able to take back enough information to satisfy Colonel Fosdike. And the hands of his watch were ticking on towards the hour when the rear trenches of the Westmorland companies would be quietly evacuated, men slipping away, leaving the front positions to be withdrawn last, a brave show made until the end. Then the forward companies would file back through C Company, deployed very near battalion headquarters as a firm base for the movement back of the rest – would file back, unless so engaged by the enemy as to make it impossible. Adam saw the dark outline of the cottage roof before he expected it. Simultaneously he heard the sentry's challenge.

'Halt. Who's there?'

'Mr Hardrow and Private Inglewood.'

'Advance one.'

Adam went forward. There had been something familiar in the sentry's voice and to his pleasure as he closed up to the figure with levelled rifle he realized that it was Crowe.

'All right, Crowe.'

'Advance two,' said Crowe. He sounded relieved. Adam grinned in the darkness. It was delightful to find Crowe. So 5 Platoon had not been entirely destroyed! Inglewood strolled forward.

'Captain Purvis inside, Crowe?'

'Think so, sir. And Captain Jameson.'

'So Captain Jameson's back here, is he? Grand!'

'Up the path, sir.'

In the cottage kitchen Adam found Geoffrey standing with a flask in his hand and a rather elated-looking Ben Jameson, sitting on a wooden chair and smoking a cigarette. They looked up as Adam came in and saluted.

'Good God! The battalion staff! We are indeed honoured!'

'I'm meant,' said Adam, 'to find out the form, as well as I can.'

'I sent the message back,' said Geoffrey Purvis in his precise voice. 'It was you I spoke to.'

'Yes. And the gunners –'

'Have fired as requested. Most accurately as far as I could observe.' It was Ben's voice, entirely as usual.

'Oh – er – good,' said Adam, feeling already a stranger. The bonds round the little circle of B Company could be almost physically felt. They had now been in action together. He had been at battalion headquarters. He was excluded.

Ben was talking. '– didn't amount to very much. Several parties of Jerries crossed over and one of them set up shop behind 6 Platoon. Then opened up, simultaneously with two parties from the front. Gave 6 Platoon and the left section of 4 rather a nasty turn for a few minutes. They blazed away into the darkness. We've had nobody hit. When light comes we'll see if we've scored. A number of Jerries were seen by 6 scurrying back – it's fairly good visibility down there. My view is that it was a couple of strong patrols. Trying it on.'

'Captain Purvis,' said Adam, 'mentioned two companies –'

'Might be that,' said Ben carelessly, 'from the fairly wide frontage. But you can say two strong parties, or patrols.'

'And you think they've all gone back across the river?'

'The fire we called for was on the pretty obvious crossing places. As you know, it's not much more than a ditch. May have caught a few. Hope so. Yes, I reckon the area's clear; 4 and 6 are quite happy now. I've seen them both. It was all most exciting.'

'5 Platoon –' said Adam.

'Round here. A little depth. Well, what's the news from the Olympian heights of battalion headquarters?' Ben seemed in tiptop spirits and Geoffrey Purvis was smiling complacently.

Adam said, 'Not much since the CO's conference. Of course he's anxious to know whether anything's going to interrupt the withdrawal timings.'

'Of course. Of course. And I can't really answer or calm his anxieties, poor man. It depends on the Germans, you see.'

Adam smiled politely. The note of mockery in Ben's voice made him uneasy. Ben was looking at him, by the flickering light of the hurricane lamp, his smile ironic.

'Yes, it depends on the Germans. But I'm sure we'll enable our –'

Adam somehow knew that Ben was going to say something unpardonable, something to which he mustn't listen. 'Our glorious commander to get away safe'? 'Our CO's nerves to get some respite'? Something like that. He said quickly, 'Well, I'd better be getting back.'

'I expect so. Thanks for the visit. We don't see all that

much of battalion headquarters people here.' The implication was clear; Adam knew, with worried inexperience of what should and should not happen, that Colonel Fosdike had only paid the one visit to B Company in three days.

At that moment the field telephone rang and they heard Company Sergeant-Major Darwin, in a dark corner of the little room, lift the handset, say, 'B Company,' and then 'Right. Right.'

'We're through, sir.'

'I'd better,' said Ben, 'have a word myself. With whoever's there. Tell them we're all well. And that the IO's on his way back.' He smiled and nodded to Adam. As Adam trudged back up the track with Inglewood he felt a sense of dissatisfaction. The line was through again. His journey had been futile. To those who had been his closest and dearest comrades in arms until a week ago he was now the representative of an alien and unadmired superior. Loyalty was under strain. There were troubling notes being sounded in the orchestra called 2nd Battalion, Westmorlands.

'Thank you, Adam,' Colonel Fosdike remembered to say as they packed up battalion headquarters two hours later, preparatory to moving out. 'Thank you. I thought it best to send you up, as the situation might have been rather tricky and we couldn't get through. I'm afraid I'll probably have to use you as a sort of personal scout quite often.' There had been no further enemy moves.

'I like it, sir.'

The march back to the line of the Escaut river was, according to the map, about sixty-five miles, and the army was due to take up an intermediate position about half-way. As things turned out the intermediate position was somehow abandoned and the Westmorlands pushed on westward day after day, hour after hour, without remission, towards what they were told would be final and permanent positions, to be taken up by Sunday, 19 May. Adam never forgot that march. The men did most of it on foot, covering over twenty miles in one day. Then there were – as on the journey eastward to occupy their first positions, a journey that now seemed a lifetime away – the long, unexplained halts, the moves off the road into fields 'to wait for transport', the arrival of empty trucks at long last – or, on more than one occasion, a message that the trucks had been diverted to another unit. 'Fall in on the road again, sharp there.' The resentful groans of tired men led to believe in a few hours' respite from marching, and then disappointed.

Adam travelled some of the way with Colonel Fosdike in his little car, feeling guilty at so much ease. Sometimes, however, the CO allowed him to range more widely among the companies, especially after one of their visits, on which Adam invariably accompanied Colonel Fosdike. Adam would say, 'I'd like to try to visit the company commanders at the next halt, sir. Put them in the picture.'

Colonel Fosdike had taken to long silences. His usual, rather sardonic but generally friendly – almost ingratiating – manner had been entirely shed. He seemed wholly wrapped up in himself.

When they paid a visit on the fourth day to brigade headquarters, already established on the Escaut position, Frank Fosdike could hardly respond coherently to the brigadier's questions or comments.

'Sorry you had no transport yesterday, Frank.'

Colonel Fosdike mumbled something.

'Where's the head of the battalion now, d'you reckon?'

No answer. Adam piped up respectfully. He reckoned that the leading company must by now be about fifteen miles from the brigade dispersal point. Say four hours. From the river Escaut.

'Hm-m.' The brigadier pointed on the map to the frontage

he wanted the Westmorlands to defend next, as soon as possible.

Then they were told the general situation by the brigadier in commendably simple and unequivocal terms. South of the British army and the neighbouring French army there had been so complete a breakthrough of German armoured forces that there was nothing between the Germans and the English Channel. That morning the Germans had entered Péronne, far to the south-west. German columns were driving towards Amiens. There were, however, bright spots. Fresh troops had been brought from England to defend Boulogne and Calais.

'The Huns are in a sort of sack,' said the brigadier. 'It's a hell of a penetration, no doubt about it. Probably more serious, certainly more sudden and ambitious, than what happened in March and April '18. But we've got to hang on until they run out of steam. They're completely exposed. Flanks in the air.' He was a calm, sensible man, and whether or not he believed his own reassuring words his manner brought hope. The Escaut line would be held. To the north of the British Expeditionary Force were the Belgians, and beyond them the Schelde estuary and salt water. The Dutch might have surrendered but now the left flank was firm.

Colonel Fosdike only had one question. It took the form of a comment.

'I cannot see, sir, what is to prevent the Germans swinging north and entirely surrounding us. They seem to have a great mass of armoured and mobile forces. We haven't.'

He was gazing at the map spread out on a wall behind the brigadier. The conference had taken place in the *salon* of a small manor-house, hastily occupied by the brigade staff. The brigadier glanced at the map and then grinned affably.

'Well, I suppose the answer to your question, Frank, is "Not much". But obviously that's GHQ's headache, and they'll be juggling forces around to see we cover all fronts. *Our* job is to make sure our own front holds firm.' There had been talk in corners – but not from the brigadier – about further retreat, about even going back to the French frontier, to the positions they'd dug for seven months and abandoned with excited optimism of spirit only nine days ago. As Colonel Fosdike drove off with Adam he mentioned this contingency.

'Did you hear something about going back to the frontier positions, Adam? Was that mentioned by the staff?'

'I heard something, sir. Somebody said, "I suppose it's conceivable we might go back to the frontier," something like that. No more.'

'They're mad,' said Colonel Fosdike bleakly.

'Sir?'

'Mad. To talk about that as if it were a solution, a defensible position. The frontier positions have already been turned. In effect.'

'I suppose so, sir.' He sees it all perfectly clearly, Adam thought. Colonel Frank understands it all, almost too well. Adam realized, instinctively and certainly without articulating the thought with his tired mind, that it was a time for as little reflection as possible. For men in the situation of Frank Fosdike or Adam Hardrow, just as for Ben Jameson, Sergeant Pew, Private Wilkins, it was simply a time for marching, digging, facing the enemy to the front of them; and for minimum intellectual speculation.

They drove without too much difficulty by minor roads to inspect the area which the weary, tramping Westmorlands were to reach and defend, behind the Escaut river. Colonel Fosdike covered the ground, mostly on foot, with commendable speed. He was muttering to himself a little, but Adam noted that the activity of reconnoitring and planning a new battalion position, activity at which he felt competent and at home, seemed somewhat to restore Colonel Fosdike's equilibrium. Adam marked the colonel's map obediently, made a few notes and looked at his watch.

'If they've not been allotted transport, battalion ought to be about nine miles away now, sir.'

'We'll get on and meet them.'

Inevitably they had to rejoin the main east–west axis down which the Westmorlands were trying to make their way. And very soon they found themselves in one of the intractable traffic jams. Refugee traffic had impeded their original, eastward movement but it was insignificant compared to that which now mingled with the long retreating columns. It seemed as if the whole of Belgium was on the move, moving to God knew where, moving somehow to get ahead of and away from the Germans. 'Extraordinary,' Adam thought, 'I've not yet *seen* a German! Let alone shot at one or been shot at!' The traffic jam in which he and Colonel Fosdike were now trapped seemed particularly thick with refugees. Military police had managed to keep the refugees to one side of the road in order to allow military vehicles and marching columns of soldiers to take the other, all going in the same direction. Colonel Fosdike and Adam were bumping and weaving their way against the tide. Many times Adam said, 'I'll get out, sir,' and jumped from the car to try to force or wheedle a way through.

It was on that particular journey that he saw for the first time a considerable number of British soldiers moving as individuals rather than in formed bodies. A good many of them were not carrying rifles. Adam accosted one man, one of a party of three, trudging along rifleless and hatless. There was no way of telling their unit. Adam said, 'Which are you?'

'Eh?' The man looked confused, hostile and exhausted. No 'sir', no soldierly reactions of any kind. Bewilderment. Resentment. And, not far from the surface, fear.

'Your unit?'

The man mumbled something. One of his fellows chipped in.

'We got cut off.'

'Cut off? From your unit, you mean?'

'That's right.'

'Where?'

'Dunno where.'

Stragglers. Liars. Probably deserters. But, Adam thought with angry sickness at the heart, also very probably – almost certainly – let down by their superiors. Abandoned. Inadequately sheltered and consoled by the strong fabrics of discipline and comradeship and leadership and order. Military flotsam, through the fault of others beside themselves. He supposed he should take names, details. There was little hope of it. The men would probably refuse. All subordination had gone, and self-respect with it. He rejoined Colonel Fosdike. He felt shame. He had never seen British soldiers like that before.

'Who were those men, Adam?'

'I'm not sure, sir. They said they'd been cut off from their unit.'

'Deserters, more like!'

'I expect so, sir.' There seemed to be a short stretch of clear road ahead, astonishingly. The refugees trudging along with their carts, animals and perambulators were keeping like dazed automata to their side of the road and there was, for a moment, no military vehicle in sight. Adam murmured, 'Tread on it,' to the driver. He reckoned that with about two more lucky breaks like this they'd not be far from where the head of the Westmorlands might have reached. Then they could sit by the roadside and mingle with the column, and chat and recognize and feel at home again.

Colonel Fosdike heard it before Adam. Adam heard him suddenly yell to the driver, 'Stop! Get out!' And as the surprised man slammed on the brakes, Adam saw his commanding officer, followed by the driver, jump from the passenger seat and dive into the ditch beside the road. Somewhat confused, Adam saw that all along the road refugees were crouching in ditches, pulling children down beside them, while the animals, patient, uncomprehending, stood in the shafts.

The dive-bombers came straight down the line of the road. Their appalling screech, specially developed for its effect on nerves, instrument of terror, hit the cowering figures on the road a fraction of a second after the roar of the aircraft engine, as the machine flattened out and climbed away. Adam, galvanized by fear into extraordinary athleticism, had already dived head first from the back of the Fosdike car through the open door, hit the surface of the road hard and rolled, all in seconds, into the same ditch as his commanding officer. As he reached it and huddled down as deep as the ditch permitted, he found that there was clearly printed on his mind a cameo picture of the road as he had seen it before the first dive-bomber noises. There had been a very over-laden, top-heavy Belgian cart, with an old woman and two small children, probably grandchildren, walking beside it, wearing socks, their legs bare; and there had been a donkey between the cart's shafts, dragging along its difficult load. Behind the cart Adam knew that there was – unusually – a man on a motor cycle, wearing a pair of goggles. A civilian.

Adam cowered down. His shirt was soaked with the sweat of fear. As the screech of the second dive-bomber rose and rose in volume, seeming to tear the atmosphere as if it were paper, attacking the ears, inflicting instant pain, Adam realized that although these two aeroplanes had probably scattered the column and put the fear of God into every creature on the road there had, miraculously, been no bombs. The agents of death had dived and terrified; but on this occasion they had not bombed.

Then came the third Stuka.

The third Stuka pilot was flying slightly higher than his two predecessors but following the same path, along the line of the road from east to west. But the third Stuka had a bomb to release, and shortly before reaching the point where Adam was lying, he released it. The bomb exploded just off the surface of the road, on the far side of it from Adam's ditch and about twenty-five yards away. There was a deafening crash and a powerful smell of cordite. There was then, for what seemed a significant period but was probably, Adam reckoned afterwards, not more than five seconds, absolute silence. In the distance Adam could hear aircraft, presumably the Stukas, flying away.

Cautiously Adam levered himself to his feet and climbed out of the ditch. One bomb. He already felt ashamed of the abjectness of his terror. A glance showed him that Colonel Fosdike and the driver, still apparently burrowing into the ground, were perfectly all right. Adam looked down the road. The first and very pitiful sight that hit him was the donkey.

The donkey was standing in the shafts, head rather lower even than before. A bomb fragment had found an artery, clearly, and blood was pouring in a violent jet from the donkey's hindquarter, pouring and splashing on the road. The donkey was standing, very quietly, bleeding to death. It could do nothing for itself and it was clear that nobody else was going to do anything for it. There could, in any case, be nothing to do. Then Adam saw the child.

One of the Belgian children, the grandchildren of the old girl, as Adam had described them to himself, was lying on the edge of the road. Adam couldn't see whether it was a boy or a girl, but as he ran across to where the old woman was crouching beside the child he saw that instead of legs was a shapeless mess of bone and blood. The child was making no sign or sound; he or she was presumably in a state of total shock, literally struck dumb in spite of pain. Adam dropped to his knees beside the old woman. At the same moment he realized that the child was a boy; an almost man-sized cap was lying in the road. He saw the other child standing now beside the cart, gazing at the bleeding, dying donkey with huge, suffering eyes. The grandmother, if grandmother she was, was starting to wail. Adam knew that such rudimentary knowledge of first aid as he possessed would be wholly inadequate to the occasion. He remembered about tourniquets; but how did you usefully apply a tourniquet to a child who had had the bottom half of his small body smashed to pieces but was still alive? The boy's eyes, like his sister's, were large, living and dazed.

'Excuse me.'

The English was accented but confident. Adam looked up, surprised. He recognized the motor cyclist, goggles now pushed up above the peak of a cap.

'Excuse me, I had better do what I can. I am a doctor.'

'Good heavens!' Adam nodded, and the old woman started to talk volubly in what Adam recognized as Flemish. He could, he thought, make out imprecations mixed with expressions of grief and, no doubt, of terror. The Stukas would probably be back. He could now see vehicles, what looked like military vehicles, approaching from the east. The temporary lull in traffic which had followed the dive-bombers' visit was over.

'Adam!'

Adam had almost forgotten both Colonel Fosdike and his duties. He walked quickly back to where the colonel, having climbed from the ditch, was inspecting the car.

'Lucky thing, seems to be quite untouched.'

Adam thought Colonel Fosdike was trembling a little. Why not, he said to himself fiercely, I was in a blue funk, don't pretend otherwise. The driver walked quickly round his vehicle. One of the headlight glasses was broken. That was the entire extent of the damage.

'Damned lucky,' said Colonel Fosdike again. He added shakily, 'Bomb blast is a funny thing. Well, we've had an escape. Get in. We've got to get on.'

'There's one rather marvellous thing, sir. That man on the motor bike is a doctor.'

Frank Fosdike grunted and Adam added 'The child's in a bad way.' They had climbed into the car.

'What child?'

'That Belgian child.'

Colonel Fosdike nodded, and they drove on at a fair speed. Adam knew that it was inappropriate to mention the donkey. He could, in imagination, see it still – and always would.

'I want a word with this military policeman. Stop! Hey – Corporal – can you tell me –'

They had been driving for a further twenty minutes. No more Stukas. Adam had said, 'I think the battalion ought to be quite near, sir. If they're marching. And if they'd been given transport they'd have passed us.'

Colonel Fosdike had nodded and a moment later had spotted the figure on a motor cycle, red cap instantly discernible. The man had stopped, still astride his saddle.

'Corporal, can you tell me if you know where 2nd Westmorlands have got to? I'm their CO.'

The odds, thought Adam, were that the military policeman would shake his head. The traffic which had streamed past them in these last twenty minutes had been a hotchpotch, a mixture of administrative vehicles, converted civilian lorries, ambulances and troop carriers with benches roughly fixed up inside. No Westmorlands. It was unlikely that any military policeman could make much sense of this withdrawal as far as knowing the whereabouts of particular units was concerned. They had passed no marching bodies of men.

To Adam's surprise the corporal considered and then said, 'Yes, sir.' He had a broad Scots voice. 'Yes, sorr.' Then he said that he was pretty sure the Westmorlands had been caught in an air attack. He spoke precisely and without emotion. Colonel Fosdike said, 'When? When?'

'It would have been about two hours back, maybe. They were marching. I passed up the column just after. They'd been caught.'

'Casualties?' Adam's mouth was dry. Most of all he felt ashamed. Would he always be somewhere else when his friends were suffering? The corporal weighed his words, as Colonel Fosdike echoed, 'Casualties, Corporal? As far as you know?'

'I'd say very light, sir. I expect they got off the road pretty sharp. I saw one field ambulance, but it didn't look like a real bad business. They were caught, as I say, but no badly, I'm pretty sure.'

'Thank you, Corporal.'

'I hope I'm right, sir. And I'm pretty sure your battalion has just settled into a village, now let's see –' he consulted his map. 'Bekkerbeek, sir. I'm reasonably sure they're in Bekkerbeek. Resting, like.'

Adam had identified it. The turn to Bekkerbeek was only two miles ahead of them. Colonel Fosdike said, as if to himself, 'Somebody may be going to produce some transport for them,' without much confidence, and heard the astonishing Scots corporal respond.

'Aye, sorr, that may well be, that may well be. Now the distances are less there's a bit more lorry capacity, you see, sorr. There's more battalions can be lifted. Yours may have had word.' He saluted, started his machine and rode westward, stolid, well-informed, competent and reassuring. Five minutes later Adam said, 'This is the turn to Bekkerbeek, sir.'

'We'll try it.'

At the first house in the small, scattered village they saw Whisky Wainwright standing talking to the regimental sergeant-major. Both saluted as the car stopped and Colonel Fosdike climbed out. He said, 'Well, Whisky, I gather you've been dive-bombed.' As he spoke they all heard a single shot.

It seemed most unlikely that a German patrol was adventuring thus far ahead of the main body, which, by even the most pessimistic reckoning, must be many miles away. Sadly, Adam supposed that it was an accidental discharge. Such things shouldn't happen, and the Westmorlands prided themselves on their skill at arms and their discipline. But they were tired.

Whisky glanced in the direction of the shot, the centre of the village. Then Adam saw Whisky's nod. It was an expressive nod. It said, among other things, that yes, they'd been dive-bombed, yes, the battalion had behaved sensibly, there'd not been serious casualties, no, there was nothing to get too worried about, it might have been worse. Most of this was grunted out by Whisky in the following minute, somewhat expanded by the regimental sergeant-major.

'Two men in C company copped it in the legs. Nobody killed, I'm glad to say, sir.'

'We've been told,' said Whisky shortly, 'that we can stay put. The men need a rest. The other brigade's dug in four miles up the road. Covering us. We marched through them. They don't look too bad. Squadron of armoured cars beyond them, too. Perfectly all right here.'

'The brigadier wants us on the new position as soon as possible –'

'Transport's coming at 4 a.m. We've had a message. The men are whacked. We've got seven hours at least. Godsend.'

'Yes. Yes. I'd better have a conference later this evening. Company commanders. Put them in the picture. It's pretty grim, Whisky.'

'Suppose so. You don't want that conference too soon, do you, sir?'

'Why not?'

At that moment they all heard several more shots. Colonel Fosdike said 'What the hell –' and Whisky Wainwright, continuing as if he'd not been interrupted by rifle fire, said calmly, 'I think everyone's asleep. Except sentries, I hope.'

Colonel Fosdike looked irritated, as he often did at Whisky Wainwright's interjections. He started to say – 'I'm afraid the general situation –' when a sergeant whom Adam recognized as being from A Company ran up and saluted. Adam couldn't remember the sergeant's name for a moment, a measure of fatigue he supposed, since he knew the members of the sergeants' mess particularly well. Then it came to him. Sergeant Prince, Ivan Perry's platoon sergeant. Sergeant Prince was out of breath.

'Excuse me, sir. Captain Stubbs has been shot.'

'*Shot*?' said Frank Fosdike. Then he said, 'By whom?'

Sergeant Prince, despite his evident fatigue, looked gratified by the impression his words had created. 'Don't know, sir. Shot through the head.'

CHAPTER 6

Captain Roger Braid was A Company commander. A fussy, conscientious man, he found it hard to relax at the best of times. These were some of the worst of times. Colonel Fosdike, Whisky Wainwright, Adam Hardrow and the regimental sergeant-major approached him, preceded by Sergeant Prince with the air of a sheepdog who has marshalled a recalcitrant flock through a difficult gap. Roger Braid was standing in the middle of the village street and seemed to have recently shouted a series of orders. Men were moving in various directions. Roger Braid yelled, 'No. No, Sergeant Foster! Over there! Over there!'

He turned and saluted Colonel Fosdike. His face was grey with exhaustion. He said, 'It was a sniper, sir.'

'How did they –'

'You warned us about German fifth columnists, sir. There are several in this village. They shot Tom. From an upper window in the end house there.' He pointed and they saw several Westmorlands moving about near the house in question. There was a certain amount of shouting. The company sergeant-major of A Company came up, saluted Colonel Fosdike and said something to Roger Braid. Adam thought he heard, 'We've put Captain Stubbs in the front room of that house.' He listened as Roger Braid continued speaking to Colonel Fosdike. Yes, Tom had been killed instantly. No, there was no doubt the fifth columnists, German agents, had been in that house. A Company had gone into it straight away and shot them.

'*Them?* How many?'

'There were three in the house, sir.'

'And all three –'

'One had a rifle with him, sir.' The company sergeant-major was holding a rifle of antique pattern. Colonel Fosdike glanced at it and nodded. No doubt Belgian Nazi sympathizers had been told to arm themselves with whatever could be obtained or salvaged from previous wars, to wait for opportunity and then play their part. All the same, Adam reflected, it was a pretty odd part. Suicidal, really. But, of course, they were expecting the Germans any minute – it must have been an over-excited fifth columnist, a premature shot that had killed Tom. Poor old Tom. Adam's first adjutant.

'One had that rifle,' Colonel Fosdike nodded. He said, 'Discharged, I imagine?'

'Yes, sir.'

'And the other men?'

'Were with him, sir. With the one with the rifle. They were all in it, obviously. There they are.' Roger Braid indicated three bodies which had been brought from the house in question and were lying in the street.

They walked over to inspect the fifth columnists' corpses.

One was a dark-haired young man, of about Adam's age; the company sergeant-major lightly kicked the dead man's shoe with his boot and said, 'That one was the sniper.' The other two were middle-aged and nondescript. Each had been shot at close quarters, and Roger Braid said, 'They tried to get away, of course, by a window at the back. But 2 Platoon were jolly quick. Got them all.'

'Anybody else in the house?'

'No, sir.'

And indeed there were no Belgians about in that end of the village street. Bekkerbeek was one of two villages which joined each other so closely as to be almost one, and the Westmorland companies had been crowded into houses, outhouses and barns at the far end, where the unfortunate Tom Stubbs had met his end. Roger Braid explained, 'I wasn't going to put anybody as far out as this, sir, but then we were getting a bit crowded and I told Tom –'

'Quite. Quite. Point is, how many more snipers are around?'

'I've got a feeling,' said Whisky Wainwright, 'that they may lie a bit low now. Until the Germans get rather nearer.' There was a grim note in his voice. Adam glanced at him. He sensed that to Whisky a Belgian *franc-tireur*'s death was a matter of total insignificance. The *franc-tireur*'s friends' ditto. They'd all been together, all involved obviously, bloody murderers. Poor old Tom. They buried him in the small garden behind the house from which he had been shot.

They reached the Escaut, at long last, just after dawn broke on 20 May. Transport, merciful transport, had reported to Bekkerbeek only half an hour after the time announced and then, surprisingly, everything had gone right. Traffic had been heavy but they'd kept moving. The men had lain sleeping on the floors of the trucks. The guides, sent ahead in two of the battalion carriers with Adam, had led each company to its particular sector. These lightly armoured carriers formed a platoon which could, in theory, move light machine-guns – the ubiquitous 303-calibre bren light machine-gun of the British army, firing the same ammunition as the standard Lee-Enfield rifle; Czechoslovak in design, named after unpronounceable Brno, reliable, invaluable. Carriers could move brens quickly to some selected flank or point, to protect a vulnerable area or surprise the enemy. The carriers were also, in practice, useful as very slightly protected runabouts, and Adam felt ashamed of his mild feeling of relief that he and the guides were to travel back carrier-borne. They wouldn't, he knew, help much if Stukas arrived, but there was some small illusory comfort in the armoured walls.

Then breakfast. Water. Washing. Spirits began to recover, and soon picks and shovels were plying and arm muscles beginning to ache. At least, the Westmorlands shouted to each other, their bloody feet were getting a rest. This was going to be the main position, where they'd see Jerry off. So far they'd been tabbing along, attacked by bloody Stukas, never a chance to have a go at bloody Jerry. Apart from the flurry in B Company on the night of 13 May, and A Company's encounter with a Belgian traitor or two in Bekkerbeek, the men hadn't yet fired their rifles. Adam got his corner of battalion headquarters set up – they were in a small café beside the main road, vehicles parked round the outside of the building – and then obtained leave to go round companies.

'I'll tell them what I know, sir.' They were only a ten-minute drive from brigade headquarters and he had paid an early morning visit. The Germans opposite them, advancing through Belgium towards the Channel and the French frontier, were expected to attack at any time and at any place along the Escaut front. The last brigade, that which had been deployed covering the Westmorlands in Bekkerbeek, had now been withdrawn. The armoured-car squadron to their immediate front had had several brushes with German mobile columns, including tanks, and had, it was said, 'done wonders'; they were expected back over the Escaut bridges any moment – one of these bridges was in the Westmorlands' sector. But to the south the news was all bad. The brigade intelligence officer, a very articulate captain, had said, 'They've reached the sea!'

'I suppose they're pretty vulnerable? I mean, it's a very narrow front.'

The captain had sighed. A mature man, a solicitor in civil life, he was no professional soldier but his instincts were shrewd. Vulnerable the Germans might be, but the last ten days had reduced his confidence that the Allies were in any position to exploit that vulnerability. Any of the Allies. He had said, 'You're probably right,' and Adam had left him and returned to the Westmorlands' battalion headquarters without much comfort.

Adam's request to go round the battalion was acknowledged by Colonel Fosdike with something like a sigh. The colonel had not been restored, as most of them had, by breakfast, a wash and a shave. His spirits appeared beyond recovery and Adam's news did little to mend them. He said to Adam, 'Yes, off you go. I'm afraid they'd better know the worst.'

Adam started with A Company. He was told that Captain Braid was going round the platoons. The men were digging hard. A Company positions were sited in a number of orchards, bordered by thick hedges. These orchards crowned a small ridge about three hundred yards from the River Escaut itself. Adam knew that A Company had about five hundred yards of front to hold, and that the river had soggy meadows on each bank. It would be impossible to dig there, and it was anyway overlooked by a higher ridge on the east bank. Roger Braid, Adam knew, was in the right place. Presumably he'd establish some sort of listening posts down by the river, perhaps some forward patrols at night. Any Germans making their way across to the west bank (Adam had seen, on his reconnaissance with Colonel Fosdike, how narrow and shallow the stream was) could be raked with fire from the orchards on the ridge in this sector. And the valley would be covered by our own guns and the battalion's mortars. It looked a strong position, at least by day.

Adam set out along A Company frontage. He glanced from time to time across the river to the east. There was no doubt that it was stimulating, almost thrilling, to feel that at any moment field-grey uniforms might appear on that skyline. Adam hoped that the Westmorlands would have had time to get themselves properly dug in by then; but he also profoundly hoped that they wouldn't be withdrawn again before the encounter. He was still very aware that he'd not, himself, seen anything of the enemy. He'd heard shelling, experienced air attack, visited his old friends in B Company well after their brush with German attackers on the Dyle, seen the corpses of three fifth columnists (as I hope they all were, Adam said to himself with a touch of unease) and watched with pity the death throes of a donkey; but he'd not yet met the Wehrmacht. It couldn't be long now.

He found Roger Braid between two of his platoon areas, standing and talking very loudly to his company sergeant-major, who appeared to have come seeking him from company headquarters. Adam could see at once that Roger was extremely upset. A methodical, immensely conscientious man, lacking imagination but dedicated to the care of his company, Adam knew that he had felt very sharply the loss of Tom Stubbs yesterday afternoon. Roger Braid had probably blamed himself, absurdly, ever since. Should he not have taken some additional, particular measures *in case* of snipers? Of course not, anybody would tell him, but he wouldn't listen to anybody and he wouldn't believe them if he did. He was constituted to take things hard, too hard.

As Adam approached him Roger Braid said, 'Ah! You've come from battalion headquarters. You probably know something about this.' He waved a piece of paper.

Adam could see it was a message form. He said, 'I left nearly half an hour ago, as a matter of fact.'

'This has just arrived. From the CO.'

'I don't know about it. What does it say?'

Roger Braid said that the message quoted a direct order from higher authority. Not less than one third of all forward troops were to be deployed on the actual river line. Not behind it, on it. No crossings by the enemy were to be accepted, and any which took place were to be eliminated by immediate counter-attack. The message went on to emphasize CO 2nd Westmorlands' commitment to the letter of these orders, and pointed out – unnecessarily – that they implied that not less than one platoon in each forward company must man positions on the river itself.

Roger Braid looked grimly at Adam. Never in his life had he queried an order. Never before had he supposed that he would be doing so – or almost – in action and in the presence of a junior officer. Nevertheless he said, 'Do you suppose Colonel Frank knows what this would mean? On this ground?'

'He's been all along the front. Yesterday. I was with him.'

'But by day,' said Roger Braid, 'my chaps would be totally overlooked down there. I was going to have patrols down there by night, of course. But by day I can see it all from back here. And cover it with fire. I don't want to deploy men down there. And digging's impossible.'

'I'll tell Colonel Frank you're worried, shall I?'

'Please tell him that I want to –' He ran through his entirely sensible reasoning once again. Adam realized that he'd better return to battalion headquarters, and if possible find Whisky Wainwright. He asked Roger Braid if he had spoken to Colonel Fosdike on the field telephone and was told that he'd tried but that the CO was with the brigade commander. Twenty minutes later Adam returned to battalion headquarters, giving up for the moment his plan to visit other companies. He burst into the main room of the café which was doing duty as a command post and said to the first soldier he saw, 'Know where the second-in-command is?' Only Whisky could sort this out.

'Think he went to visit companies, sir.'

'Who's that who wants Major Wainwright?' Frank Fosdike's voice called sharply. Adam's heart sank.

'Me, sir.'

'What's the trouble?' The CO's voice was edgy.

'I've just come from A Company, sir.'

'Well? I told you to go to all forward companies to put them in the picture.'

'Yes, sir. I came back because Captain Braid is rather worried.'

'What about?'

'The order to deploy a platoon right on the river bank.'

'That is my personal order. It also happens to be the general's.'

'Yes, sir. I think Captain Braid would be grateful for the chance to discuss it. In his sector he reckons that a platoon down on the river would be overlooked by day, and that if the enemy try to cross they can be dealt with more effectively from where the platoons are deployed at present. Back a bit, on the ridge, sir. In the orchards.'

Frank Fosdike beckoned Adam into a quieter corner of the café. He spoke in a low, concentrated voice.

'Mr Hardrow, I sent you round the companies. Instead you return here to tell me that one of my officers is questioning my orders.'

'Yes, sir.'

'You return here, and strut in asking to see the second-in-command. Why?'

'I understood you were away, sir.'

'You will now continue your visit to the other rifle companies. I shall be seeing Captain Braid personally. Orders in this battalion are not issued as a basis of discussion.'

'No, sir.'

'And if any of my company commanders is dissatisfied with my orders it is a matter for me – *me*, do you understand? Not for my second-in-command.'

Adam said nothing to this, and a moment later Colonel Fosdike, rather alarmingly, smiled. He said, in a completely different tone, 'Well, that's that, Adam. Never mind, we all get things wrong at times. I know you meant well.' The voice was confidential, almost wheedling. It continued – 'You see, Roger Braid sees the difficulties. War is an option of difficulties – always has been. What he – and perhaps you, Adam – don't fully appreciate is that if one has an obstacle to defend, it must be defended *on* the obstacle, while the other fellow is at a disadvantage trying to get over it. Not afterwards. Otherwise one gives away the whole benefit. Now, off you go, and if you see Roger again, just tell him that I quite understand his worries but that the orders are deliberate and considered, and that they stand.'

Quarter of an hour later Adam passed exactly that message. Roger Braid said, 'I see.' Then he turned away. Adam heard him say to his runner that he wanted to see Mr Perry, immediately.

After A Company came C, in the centre of the line. Captain Jack Pettigrew was a noted battalion athlete, a cheerful extrovert, generally regarded as tough but somewhat stupid. It so happened that in his company sector the ground climbed steeply from the river. A platoon deployed 'on the river' presented no problems – it was, in effect, where Jack Pettigrew had put them already. He chuckled when Adam arrived, and waved the same message at him that had so perturbed Roger Braid.

'Battalion headquarters getting rather involved in minor tactics, aren't they?'

'I suppose,' said Adam loyally, 'that it is very much the concern of the powers-that-be, isn't it? Whether we actually hold the river line, I mean, as opposed to holding back from it.'

'Suppose so, suppose so. Anyway, no problem here, you

can tell the colonel.' When Adam explained to him the general situation as far as he'd most recently gathered it, Jack Pettigrew looked uninterested.

'Expect they'll patch something up. Frogs are probably getting a big counter-attack ready.'

'I expect so.'

'It's this front we've got to worry about. Ought to be OK here. Mortars got this bit well covered – just the ticket, steep slope down to the river. Hope the Huns try it on!'

'Quite. I'll be on my way to B.'

Ben Jameson, as Adam reached him, looked unusually taut and concentrated. Ben was lying against the forward wall of a sort of embrasure which had been scraped out of a bank. The bank ran along the east side of the farm road down which Adam had walked. The road ran roughly parallel to the river; parallel to the front. Ben's binoculars were up to his eyes. He lowered them, turned, saw Adam and nodded, and then turned his head and brought his binoculars up again. Beside Ben was lying a lieutenant in the Royal Artillery, a forward observation officer from Major Brodie's battery, a quiet, rather earnest young man whom Adam had met on several occasions at battalion headquarters. The bank against which they were lying was appreciably above the level of the River Escaut, on a gentle ridge, a continuation of the ridge manned by A company, and similarly overlooking the Escaut from slightly higher ground.

After a little, without turning his head again, Ben said quietly, 'What brings you here?'

'The CO wanted me to go round companies and tell them the general situation.'

'Which is?'

'Shall I show you on this map –'

'No. Tell me.' Ben's binoculars were still to his eyes. Adam knew that Ben was not a man who required truth to be sweetened.

'The Germans have reached the Channel at Abbeville. The BEF is cut off by the German panzers from the main mass of the French army.'

'So they're behind us. Behind our right shoulders. In strength.'

'Yes.'

'Does your superior realize how tired these men are? How absolutely whacked?'

'Certainly.'

'Well, I hope I'm not sent any more bloody silly orders, like –' Ben was gazing at the front and speaking away from Adam. He suddenly snapped to the artillery lieutenant, 'See that?'

'Got it.'

Adam had crouched beside him and had his own binoculars up. He, too, muttered. 'Ah! Got it!' Ben hadn't addressed him, he was unimportant at this moment of B Company's life but he had seen what Ben had seen and he needed, desperately, to feel involved.

The forward observation officer said, 'One, two, three separate parties.'

'That's it,' said Ben, 'and I make it two more about two hundred yards further back. The first lot of three are carrying loads –'

'Assault boats –'

'They reckon they're hidden from us by that line of poplar trees –'

'So they would be if we were lower down. Ah –'

'What?'

'Lost 'em. They're down in the corn.'

Adam had seen, with huge excitement, the three parties of helmeted figures in grey-green uniforms. Each party had seemed to comprise about twenty men. Now none were visible. On the far river bank, in this sector pretty flat country compared to their own side, there were standing crops, and the Germans had sunk into the concealing cover as if on a word of command.

Ben said, 'Wait till they come on. Wait till they start crossing. Then let 'em have it – on the valley bottom and on the far side where they'll be coming down to the river. OK?'

'Perfectly OK.' The gunner officer spoke in a gentle, precise, almost academic voice. He had turned his back to the bank and was sitting looking at his map.

Ben said, 'Presumably they're tapping in on a pretty wide front. Or will. Any news from along the line, Adam?'

'It was quiet when I left A. And C.'

'Can't be for long.'

'I suppose I'd better get back.' Adam couldn't bear to lower his binoculars, which were glued to his eyes and focused on the cornfield where those grey-green, helmeted figures, at least sixty of them, had sunk out of sight one minute ago. Ben had turned and was quietly talking into a field telephone which the ubiquitous Private Bliss had crawled across the road and placed by his left foot. Adam heard him give a succinct account of what he reckoned was in front of them. Just as he finished – Adam knew from his bantering tone that he was talking to Harry Venables – they heard the successive deep-toned bangs far to the east which meant German artillery opening up; followed by the higher-pitched and much nearer cracks which could only mean German mortars – probably the 81 mm mortar, handy, quick into action and, as it always seemed to their enemies, uncannily accurate.

'Keep down!' It was Ben's yell. The bank gave them some protection, but they weren't dug in. Adam presumed that he'd found Ben in an improvised lookout position, adopted on the spur of the moment and some little way ahead of what must be a company headquarters slit trench, or building. Ben had come forward to look, had found exactly the spot, had told Bliss to get a telephone line and handset run forward, and had stayed. Perhaps imprudently.

'Keep down!' They burrowed into the shallow ditch at the foot of the bank. Explosions – one, two, three, four, five, six – came well behind them. The next salvo fell a hundred yards further south, along the ridge. To the front, however, peering again over the bank, they saw the brown earth spurting up in the valley from German mortar fire. Mortar fire speckled the valley all along the company frontage. It went on for what seemed to Adam an hour and was actually one minute and a half. Then they heard again the whisk and sigh of artillery shells.

'Keep down, I said, Adam.' Ben's voice was quiet now. Normal. Adam had a tiny spasm of pleasure that Ben was almost accepting him again as an individual, was conscious of his presence. Then he heard Ben say, still very quietly, binoculars up now – 'Here they come!'

Along the valley, as far as the steep unpromising stretch in front of Jack Pettigrew's C Company, the grey-green parties were now running towards the river, carrying two-man loads – assault boats. Faintly, from the ridge, Adam could hear shouted orders. He could see other grey-green figures climbing into the boats. The enormous sense of urgency could be felt even from where they were watching, three hundred yards back from the river and above it. Then they saw – and no binoculars were needed – what looked like a further five, six, perhaps seven parties racing down the far bank towards the river, trampling, as they ran, the standing corn. Simultaneously the air was ripped by the sound of machine-gun fire from across the river – machine-gun fire which was being poured from the German positions on the far bank on to the west bank of the Escaut, where any British defenders of the river line itself might be found.

'Twenty-second wonder!' Ben remarked easily. 'They'll hit

their own chaps unless they cease fire about now. They've neutralized our people down by the river, or so they'll reckon.'

'Who – who have you got down by the river, Ben?'

'Don't be a bloody fool. Nobody, of course. The near bank's well covered. Your old platoon and others are safe and sound up here.' Ben's glasses were up again and he said to the gunner lieutenant, very sharply, 'Right?'

'Any time.'

'Off you go then,' said Ben happily. Moments later they heard the comforting roar of British guns and heard the brushing, sighing sound of British shells going over to seek the valley and the far bank of the Escaut. And not only the far bank – Adam watched a mass of shell-bursts send earth spouting from the meadows on the near bank also, seeking enemy soldiers who might have crossed already. Three minutes later, half incredulous, he saw some grey-green figures running away from the far bank. Running eastwards. Simultaneously he saw a number of abandoned assault boats lying forlornly on the other side, unused.

Ben said softly, 'Well, we'll have scored. I'm sure we'll have scored. There'll be a few this side, but there shouldn't be enough to trouble us.' He said to Adam, lightly and as if as an afterthought, 'Platoons are well dug in. They won't open up unless they are attacked or they see an obvious target. Don't want them to give their positions away.'

'I see. I suppose I'd better get back now.'

'If I were you I'd walk a little way west, get clear of this road and ridge. They've got its range and they can see it from several places. Hello, what's that?'

There had been a good deal of artillery and mortar fire, probably both German and British Adam supposed, from their right, from the direction of C and A companies. Particularly, thought Adam, A Company, since the noise was comparatively distant. Now they all heard the unmistakable, rather slow and deliberate rattle of British bren-guns, interspersed, it seemed, with the very short, ripping, tearing, snapping sounds of German Spandaus and Schmeisers – the deadly, short-range machine-pistol often regarded with envy by the Wehrmacht's opponents.

'It sounds,' Ben observed, 'as if Roger's having a little bit of a battle. Noise is coming from the valley.'

Adam said, 'I think he's got a platoon in the valley. Put one there a short time ago.'

'He can't have!'

'I think so. There was that order, that message –'

'God!'

'– it said at least one third, one platoon per company –'

'You don't mean you think Roger *obeyed* that? He must have got A as snug back on and behind the ridge as we are!'

'I heard him,' said Adam, 'get hold of Ivan Perry, as I left, forty minutes ago. I think it was to send him forward.'

Ben said, 'Then he's in trouble.' He grunted, no smile on his face, eyes hard. Adam asked if there was anything he could do for the company at battalion headquarters and was told no, nothing. Thanks for such an informative, encouraging visit! Ben's voice was back to normal. From the direction of A Company there came the sound of more firing. As Adam hurried away westward, to get clear of the ridge as Ben had advised, he passed some slit trenches and to his delight saw that they were manned by 5 Platoon. 'Deployed in depth,' he thought.

'Hullo, Wilkins.'

'Hullo, sir.'

Wilkins didn't smile. He's tired, Adam thought. But there was something listless, almost sullen in Wilkins's demeanour. Suddenly Adam saw Sergeant Pew walking towards the slit trench.

'Morning, Sergeant Pew!'

Sergeant Pew saluted but didn't smile. B Company were certainly down in the dumps.

Back at battalion headquarters Adam found Harry Venables glued to telephones. Colonel Fosdike and Whisky Wainwright were talking together in a corner of the room. Nobody seemed to have particularly missed him.

Sergeant Cobb said, 'Latest sitrep, sir.' and showed him a piece of paper. Adam saw that a number of towns in western France were said to have been entered by German troops. The name 'Amiens' caught the eye, with its particular echoes from only twenty-two years before. He felt detached from these happenings, enormous though their strategic significance no doubt was.

He said to Harry Venables, 'I was with B Company when the Germans tried to get across.'

'Were you indeed? We've got the picture clear, I think. Didn't amount to much, did it?'

'I think the gunners broke it up. Ben's in perfect control as usual.'

Alarmingly, Harry – a loyal, easy-going soul as Adam thought of him – muttered, 'I wish I could say something like that here.' Adam asked the news from A Company. His imagination, too vivid for a soldier in circumstances like these he supposed, held the picture of Ivan Perry near the River Escaut, adopting improvised positions overlooked by the Germans, caught in the sort of fire which Adam had watched in front of B Company. In front of B Company it had beaten the air. Had it beaten into the ground Ivan Perry and his platoon? He could see Ivan's face too clearly for comfort.

'Bit of trouble near the river. Several parties have got across.'

'I see.'

'CO's upset,' said Harry in a low voice. 'Seems the forward platoon gave up a bit early.'

'Well, they can't have been in a defensible position!'

'Maybe. Whisky's trying to calm him!'

So that was it! And what about casualties? What about Ivan? Harry didn't know. The position was confused. And Roger had said stretcher-bearers couldn't get down to where they were needed.

Adam next heard Whisky Wainwright's voice, at unexpected length. For the first time he seemed to be making no attempt to soften it, so that it boomed over the chatter of signallers sending or recording messages, even above the jarring squeak of Sergeant Cobb's coloured chinograph pencil on the talc surface of a map as he depicted, to his own sombre satisfaction, the latest German achievements.

'Only thing to do, sir! Tell Roger to get the remnants of that platoon back behind the ridge as and when he can. They may be able to get back in ones and twos.'

'How could he communicate –'

'He'll probably go down himself, sir, or something like that. Anyway, he'll help them back, he can keep the Huns' heads down with fire from the other platoons. Probably find he may not have lost as many as he thinks.'

'Ben Jameson,' said Colonel Fosdike angrily, 'held a similar attack. Exactly similar. As far as I can make out.'

Whisky said tersely, 'Ben Jameson could plaster the river with gun and mortar fire. Ben Jameson didn't have a platoon stuck like sitting ducks down on the river. Sitting ducks who'd only just arrived.'

'My orders, as you know, went out earlier –'

'Yes, sir,' said Whisky Wainwright, 'they did. But in the end poor old Roger Braid carried 'em out. And look where it's got him.' He banged out of the little café and they heard the sound of his boots ring on the pavement outside. Colonel Fosdike went through a door into a small adjoining room he was using as a private sanctum. A few minutes later he emerged with a piece of paper, thrust it at Harry Venables saying 'send that to Brigade', and disappeared. The scribble on the paper said that 2 Westmorlands had been heavily attacked. German storming parties had attempted to cross the Escaut and had been repelled at all points except in one place at the extreme right of the battalion sector where a small lodgement had been obtained. This lodgement was now sealed off. A few casualties had been suffered. Considerable losses had been inflicted on the enemy.

Adam settled down to help Harry Venables run the headquarters. There didn't seem much intelligence to handle – the news was clear and it was all bad, while on the battalion front matters had boiled up, quietened down and would no doubt boil up again before long. As far as was known they'd taken no prisoners. Adam found that Harry Venables was a bit slow at his work and a helping hand was, he knew, not unwelcome. They worked and rested turn and turn about.

'Adam.'

'Ivan? *My God! Ivan!*'

'That's it.'

'What are you doing here? I thought you were dead!'

'Most of us got back. Roger's been told to rest us, whatever that means, so the platoon's in reserve. And I've been told to hand over to Sergeant Prince for twenty-four hours and come back here. For a few hours out of it.'

'Told by who?'

'Whisky. He came up to see Roger. He was grand.'

'How did you get back? It sounded as if you were locked in with the Germans, down on the river.'

'More or less. We'd only just got there and they started to cross, and threw everything at us, shells, machine-guns, the lot. It was a case of getting people down and returning fire at anything we could see. They got behind us.'

'So?'

'Wasn't much I could do. We weren't dug in or anything

like that. I tried to go from section to section and tell them to crawl back in ones and twos. Luckily there's more cover down there than you'd suppose.'

'And you weren't hit.'

'God knows why, but I wasn't. But we lost Corporal Watson. I saw him go down. Spandau, I think. And four others, for certain. Two of the boys who got back were hit, one in the shoulder and one in the bottom. But they made it.'

Adam was stretched out on the floor in a small back room of the café, a store in normal times he guessed. It had a pervasive but not unpleasant smell. Ivan, apparently ordered to spend a short spell at battalion headquarters, had found it, found Adam and was similarly stretched out alongside. Adam had, with luck, a two-hour period off duty, agreed with Harry Venables. His watch showed him that it was just after two o'clock in the morning. The small hours. The low point in human resilience. A lamp burned on a shelf of the little store and by its light Adam could see that Ivan's face, his fair, amused, almost feminine features looked lined and old. Ivan must be totally exhausted.

'Get some sleep, Ivan.'

But Ivan wanted to talk. They were murmuring to each other, and Adam knew that Ivan needed him, needed listening ears. He fought off sleep.

'I don't think there was more I could have done.'

'I'm sure there wasn't, Ivan.'

'Except that if I'd been quicker, when we first got down there, I could have got a section into a little ditch that runs down to the river. We could have manned it and opened up from it. I didn't see it till the whole thing started.'

'I don't suppose it would have made a difference, Ivan.'

'It was slow of me.'

'I don't expect so.'

'I was damned windy, Adam.'

'Who wouldn't be!'

'Then, when we obviously had to get back, nothing else to do, I could have organized a sort of supporting fire point myself. I had one of the section bren-guns and two, no, three riflemen with me –'

Adam said nothing. Ivan had to get rid of it all.

Now Ivan said, in a voice of unnatural evenness, 'Corporal Watson was a good man!'

'I know.'

'And a very nice man, too. Very nice.'

'Very nice. I hardly knew him, of course, but –'

'Very nice. Married. Three small children.'

'Better go to sleep now, Ivan.'

'In Penrith.'

'Sleep, Ivan.' Adam reached out and took Ivan's hand and held it for a little. Ivan's eyes were open, gazing at the ceiling of the little store. He said, 'I believe the CO thinks it was all my fault.'

'Balls, Ivan.'

'Well, it was.'

'You shouldn't have been put there.'

'Well –'

'Sleep, Ivan, for a bit. I need to.'

'Do you know what the men are saying, Adam? They're saying, loudly, to each other, but in such a way that they mean one to hear, "When's old Johnnie coming back to command us?"'

Adam said he'd not heard that. A minute later, to his great relief, he heard Ivan snoring.

He was completely unaware of the German shelling which rumbled sporadically through the night. He was even unaware of the shell which blew all the front windows out of their café. When he blearily moved into the command-post front room at half-past four Sergeant Cobb, now about to rest in his turn, said, 'A bit draughty here, sir.'

'Yes, it is, isn't it!'

'Some casualties in both A and B, sir, shelling. Captain Purvis has been hit but he's not bad. And A have lost three killed and five wounded. Apart from Mr Perry's platoon, of course. They lost seven from that, all told.'

The brigadier's orders were given out at half-past six o'clock that morning, 21 May. He began by congratulating them on their performance the previous day. The brigade had, it was true, had a comparatively easy time. There'd been no particularly strong attacks –

'Unlike our next-door neighbours. The Huns have got a strongish lodgement on the west bank there –' The brigade staff officer pointed at the map.

'Unless one counts a very small bridgehead in the Westmorlands' sector –' Again the pointer, and the brigadier said, 'That right, Frank?'

'Just about, sir.'

'– we're holding firm. And I congratulate you all. We didn't face a main effort, but what we got was unpleasant. That bridgehead in your area, Frank –'

'It's negligible, sir. We're containing it.'

The brigadier went on to tell them that to their north the story was less happy. To the north throughout the previous twenty-four hours the defending battalions had been attacked from the air, in very effective close support of the German assault troops. He said, sharply, that he didn't want to hear any more grumbles about our own air forces – they were flying round the clock trying to minimize the Luftwaffe's attacks and the fact that the British didn't see the RAF's roundels in the sky above them all the time meant nothing. The fact was, however, that a sizeable penetration of the Escaut line had taken place and it was to be eliminated by a fairly major counter-attack. A brigade counter-attack; another brigade.

'Intelligence reckons that we, here, are not going to get the worst of it today or tomorrow, and I've been ordered to give up one battalion to the counter-attacking brigade's command, which will give it four battalions for the operation. I'm assured the attachment will only be for twenty-four hours. The battalion to go will be the Westmorlands. I'll talk to you about that in a minute, Frank.'

Further details on adjustments to the front for the next twenty-four hours were given out. The plan was for a French battalion to relieve the Westmorlands. When the conference dispersed the brigadier said, 'Frank.' He beckoned. Colonel Fosdike moved towards an inner room where the brigadier was standing in front of another map. Adam moved along behind him. This sounded challenging!

The brigadier said, 'Now, Frank –'

Colonel Fosdike turned. 'Wait outside, Adam.'

'Right, sir.'

Ten minutes passed, and the brigadier's head appeared at the door. He saw Adam.

'Get word that if Colonel Tansley hasn't left headquarters I want to see him.' Colonel Tansley commanded another battalion of the brigade.

'Yes, sir.' Adam trotted off. Colonel Tansley was still with the brigade major. Looking surprised he obeyed the summons and Colonel Fosdike reappeared.

'Come on, Adam.'

'Sir, I think I'd better, if I may, try to get some details about this attachment of ours, this other brigade we're going to for the counter-attack. It will help Harry. I'm sorry, I should have done it while you were with the brigadier. I apologize, sir, but I think I'd better do it before we leave.'

'No, come along. I want to get back.'

Resentful and surprised, Adam climbed into the CO's car. Colonel Fosdike looked secretive. As they drove off he pitched his voice to a note he thought could reach Adam's ear but, with luck, not carry much to his driver. His head was turned.

'I didn't let you go off just now, because as it happens we're not going to be detached for that operation after all.'

'I see, sir.'

'I had to be pretty firm, but Brigadier Andrew saw my point. I had to tell him bluntly that the battalion isn't up to an operation like that. An attack. At the moment.'

Adam could hardly believe his ears. The Westmorlands not up to doing an attack! Ben Jameson, Jack Pettigrew, Whisky Wainwright, Sergeant Pew, Wilkins, Crowe, Wright, Harry Venables! For that matter Roger Braid! For that matter Ivan Perry! Not up to doing an attack! When so far they'd had little but brushes with the enemy. They'd held the line. They'd seen the Huns off, if one excepted poor old Ivan's disaster. They were as good, as steady, as reliable a battalion as you'd find in the whole British Expeditionary Force. Colonel Fosdike was murmuring away, barely audible.

'– A Company a bit of a shambles. D inexperienced as yet. Can't feel that the battalion as a whole would justify –'

Adam felt physically sick.

'– Pembrokeshires in a stronger position –'

Colonel Tansley commanded the 1st Battalion, the Pembrokeshire Regiment.

'– brigadier quite agreed when I explained one or two things to him –'

Oh, shame! Shame!

'– keep all this quiet, Adam. Don't want the chaps to get their tails down. They needn't know we were planned to do another show.'

But they will! They will! And their commanding officer has described them as not up to it. For no reasons except such as could directly be attributed to his own inadequacy.

*

When they returned to battalion headquarters Adam told Harry Venables what the brigadier's orders contained, and passed on such news of the general situation as hadn't already been gleaned by Sergeant Cobb. Maps were marked. Boundaries adjusted. Adam didn't mention the counter-attack. Five minutes later Colonel Fosdike said that he wanted to go round all companies. Adam would accompany him.

They started with A Company. Roger Braid looked miserable. He spoke to Colonel Fosdike in a low voice, with a good many noddings of the head. Adam couldn't hear him and was sure he wasn't meant to. He had a word with one or two men in the nearest platoon. One asked if there was any news of Mr Perry. Ivan was popular.

'He's all right. I saw him last night.'

'There were some poor blokes that weren't all right, sir. They had a rare pasting, did Mr Perry's platoon.'

'I know.'

There were no smiles, and the undertone, most unusually for the Westmorlands, was surly. Colonel Fosdike was talking with animation to Roger Braid. He called out after another minute, 'Adam, make a note. I've explained to Captain Braid that I intend to relieve A Company with D Company this afternoon.'

D Company was commanded by the (very elderly) Major David Bassett, the only company commander to hold field rank, and enormously senior in the Westmorlands. It was said that he had joined long before Whisky Wainwright but that some early peccadillo had reversed their respective stations. He was, by general consent, very, very sound and very, very slow. D Company took their tone from their company commander. The company were in a reserve position about half a mile to the west of battalion headquarters.

Adam made a note on his map. It was the first he'd heard of this proposed arrangement. To get Major Bassett's company on the move forward would need longer than the norm, but it could be presumed that A Company, although only the unhappy Ivan's platoon had been seriously engaged, would profit from the rest. Colonel Fosdike was talking away to Roger Braid. His manner looked ingratiating. Adam heard Roger say, 'You'd like to see round the platoons, sir.'

'No. No, think I'd better go and see David, old David, right away. Explain things to him. All right, are they?'

'Sir?'

'The platoons. The men. All right?'

'More or less, sir.'

Roger saluted. As they walked rapidly away Adam turned and saw him still standing where they'd left him, immobile, still looking at their retreating backs.

They did not go to B Company. They did not go to C Company. From Major Bassett's company headquarters Colonel Fosdike telephoned battalion headquarters.

'Better check all's well.'

He seemed in a better humour. He learned, however, that the second-in-command had gone to visit B and C. This made his own visits somewhat redundant and Colonel Fosdike looked morose again.

'And there's a personal and confidential letter come by hand for you, sir.' It was Harry Venables talking.

'From whom?'

'From the brigadier, sir. To be opened by you personally.'

'I'll come back right away.'

They were met by Harry, who told them that there'd been no attacks on the brigade front reported so far, and on the whole it had been a quiet morning. Sergeant Cobb looked at Adam rather reproachfully. Mr Hardrow liked the gadding-about part of the job but serious information seemed to absorb him less than it should. Fancy allowing a situation to arise where the adjutant, not the intelligence officer, announced news of this kind! Harry was suggesting to

Colonel Fosdike that he should have some late breakfast. He'd left without eating anything for the brigadier's orders at six-thirty. It was now eleven o'clock.

'Yes, something, something. Where's that letter?'

Harry produced it. Adam thought afterwards that a sort of hush, inexplicable by any rational process, had instantly spread through the crowded, smoke-filled little café. Even the telephones ceased to ring. Three minutes later Harry was called. Six minutes later Harry came from the CO's sanctum and said with unusual sharpness to the nearest soldier, 'Get hold of Major Wainwright.'

'Second-in-command's out, sir; think he's still with C –'

'Then get word to him, telephone, send a runner. He's to return here immediately. Got it?'

'Yes, sir.'

Harry, face impassive, moved to the little table in front of the map which he'd made his own. Clips with messages hung on hooks from an improvised rack. As he passed Adam Harry paused, looked at him, and, relying on the other's lip-reading rather than his ears, mouthed one word: 'Sacked!'

CHAPTER 7

'My dear General,' wrote the brigadier. It was the evening of 22 May and once again his brigade was going back. Orders had been given, troops were on the move, there was nothing the brigadier could do for the moment to affect events. His own headquarters were already at the new position, extremely near the billets they had left on 10 May. Twelve astonishing days ago. Soon, moving in transport through the night on congested roads, the air thick with rumour and unease, his brigade would once more be back deployed on what all knew as 'the frontier position', yet certainly not in the circumstances for which they'd originally prepared it. By now most, if not all, knew that the Germans were threatening not only the front but the right rear of the British Expeditionary Force.

I am grateful that you acted so promptly in the matter of Frank Fosdike. As I said on the telephone, it was clear to me that his nerve had completely gone, in spite of the fact that his battalion – potentially an excellent battalion – has only been very slightly engaged so far. He allowed himself to be hypnotized by his own imagination about the dangers threatening the BEF. He was also too inclined to take orders over-literally, and to rely on receiving them in matters of detail rather than exercising his own judgement. It is a pity, because he is in many ways a competent and intelligent man, but I'm afraid that he had lost, to a large extent, the confidence of his battalion. He should be perfectly adequate – possibly better than adequate – in a staff appointment, but he should certainly not command again, in my view. And he should certainly not command in circumstances like the present. I appreciate, of course, that his removal has to be regarded as an interim measure and I will put in a formal report as soon as I can – although I'm afraid it may not be for a week or so! Wainwright will be all right for the time being.

We're moving back slowly and so far without being unduly harassed except by refugees – both in and out of uniform! We were all encouraged by your visit yesterday –

Adam afterwards remembered the 'frontier position' – re-occupied by the Westmorlands that 23 May for a brief while – for three particular things. Days and nights were now passing with such speed and confusion that his memory could only fix dates and places by some particular event or series of events. If nothing striking or bizarre had happened, he later found that a particular day or sequence had faded altogether from the mind.

On the frontier position the battalion was not directly attacked by the Germans, and, perversely, this merciful fact somehow increased the men's unease. They knew – grate-fully, because desire for battle does not burn strongly in the ordinary breast – that compared with what they heard of the fortunes of other regiments they'd got off lightly. There'd been that business on the river line, but apart from A Company's losses (for which the whole battalion, word magnified and spread like fire in corn, blamed Colonel Fosdike) the Germans had been held there, and forced back by artillery and mortar fire. Most men in the Westmorlands – a curious reflection, no doubt unbelievable by distant observers at home, Adam supposed – had not yet fired their rifles at the enemy. But, going back day after day and still not directly assaulted, the Westmorlands increasingly felt that some awful fate must be creeping up on them, round them, behind them. It wasn't natural. They were told the Germans had broken through in the south. In the north there were worrying rumours about the Belgians – deployed on the left flank of the British Expeditionary Force. And yet here they were, having a quiet time as far as Jerries coming at them from the front was concerned. What was up?

Yet the first thing Adam would later associate with the frontier position was the German shelling and the extraordinary ill luck with which it found human targets. It was not – or so he supposed – shelling of the intensity his father's generation had experienced, hurricane bombardments which were said to have drowned speech, shattered senses, burst ear-drums; but it was long-range, sporadic and unnerving. It was uncannily accurate. And one of the first shells killed Roger Braid.

The captain of A Company had been busying himself round the trenches, grumbling like all of them at the inadequacy of what they found. This stretch of the old line had not been dug by the Westmorlands and they were loudly contemptuous of the troops who, presumably, had been at work on it up to a short fortnight ago. 'Useless mob,' they muttered to each other, exhausted, muddled and uneasy about dangers the worse for being as yet unseen. Then they had set to work. One day, presumably, the bloody Jerries would actually turn up. Meanwhile dig, dig, dig! Swearing with all the energy they could, the men of A Company had worked away, good humour largely absent. Roger Braid had been round, telling them for the hundredth time that it was highly likely the enemy would be at them before morning. And, while exhorting 2 Platoon in his worried way, a German shell had found him. He had thrown himself flat on the edge of a slit trench which was being dug and which saved the lives of the two men nearest to him. Several shells burst, and then there was silence and men resumed their shovels and there was nervous laughter and blasphemy and obscenity, and life went on; but Roger Braid didn't move, and a man

176

called out, 'Hey, Mr Perry, sir. The Captain's hit,' and when Ivan Perry ran over he found Roger Braid dead – dead and apparently unmarked. 'It can happen,' the doctor said, at the battalion aid post. 'It can happen. Internal, all of it, probably.' But in fact they found a wound, a very, very small wound where a splinter of shell casing had penetrated near the armpit and killed instantly. The men of A Company felt sorry, for they'd liked him, with a certain amount of tolerant shrugging at his fussiness and anxiety. But they also felt disturbed and lonely, because Captain Stubbs, a reliable figure, had copped it from that bloody fifth-columnist sniper, Mr Perry had nearly caught one on the river, and now Captain Braid had gone. Ivan Perry took command – a popular figure with his laughter and charm, but 'Nowt but a lad,' the older ones said to each other.

Then there was George Garthwaite. Adam heard of his death with particular guilty regret, for the truth was he'd not warmed to George Garthwaite and recognized that the cause of this aversion was unworthy. Garthwaite had taken over Adam's 5 Platoon when he'd so suddenly been made Colonel Fosdike's intelligence officer. Garthwaite had appeared, a somewhat brash figure, parading a north-country accent obtrusively, as if to show his robustness, his practicality, his empathy with the men he would command; had appeared, direct from the cadet training unit, a salesman in civilian life, a man of twenty-five and thus Adam's senior in years and (he seemed to imply) in knowledge of the world. He had said 'Good lot, are they?' about 5 Platoon, affecting a no-nonsense confidence Adam knew he did not feel. That was on the frontier position long, long ago, on 7 May.

'A very good lot.' Adam's voice had been chilly. He had felt himself being unhelpful. He had known, too, that Ben Jameson would find this newcomer uncongenial, and had enjoyed the knowledge. Contemptible! He, Adam Hardrow, should help George Garthwaite.

'A very good lot.'

'Sergeant Pew OK, is he?'

'Sergeant Pew is completely reliable. He'll teach you a lot. He's certainly taught me a lot.'

'Good,' said George Garthwaite. 'They were pretty thorough with us at OCTU. Put us through it. Too much bullshit for my liking, but a lot of it was well done. Looked to me as if Pew was rather one of the old school.'

'He is. In a way.'

'As long as he can move with the times.'

Adam had turned away. Could this man understand he had joined a family? During his visits to B Company in these last ten days he had only once seen George Garthwaite, and that in the distance. He had never heard Ben Jameson mention him. He had known that his instinctive dislike of Garthwaite had been ignoble, had stemmed from resentment at Garthwaite inheriting authority over men Adam Hardrow regarded as his own. It had derived from a sense of rather snobbish exclusiveness about the Westmorlands, the regimental family, which Adam recognized as wholly inappropriate to a major war which needed the efforts of everybody competent to serve. Garthwaite had arrived, was obviously keen to do his best. Bother his rough edges. Make him welcome. Help him. Adam had known what was decent, and later despised his own reaction. And now Garthwaite was dead. A shell had killed him as he was marshalling some transport for the company, had destroyed two trucks, and severely wounded two drivers at the same time. Adam grieved and felt a little shame as well.

And Jack Pettigrew. Jack Pettigrew, battalion athlete, extrovert, physically tough, had shown recent signs of unexpected exhaustion and anxiety. He had, Adam recalled, been confident and easy on the Escaut position, when Adam had visited his trenches at the crown of the steep slope running to the river. C Company had been out of it that day, and not long afterwards had come the depressing and only half-understood march back to the frontier. But on the frontier position Jack Pettigrew had, when Adam visited C Company with Whisky Wainwright, shown a wholly uncharacteristic irritability, an unreasonable side. He'd said, 'Why the hell can't companies be told more clearly what's going on?'

'You're being told what I know,' Whisky had answered. No man took a high tone with him, but he was prepared to humour tiredness and he knew Jack was very tired.

'Well, it doesn't make sense. Look at these trenches! Look at the anti-tank ditch! How can I expect men to do their stuff when they're given no chance, plumped down in bloody awful positions like this, having nothing explained to them –'

'Jack,' Whisky said with gruff patience, 'it's up to *you* to explain. You know what I know. The army's back on the frontier. Our southern flank is protected by part of the BEF deployed down there, so we're all right. Our supplies are coming through Dunkirk, so we've got a port. Our job, yours and mine, is to see off the Huns opposite us. That's all you've got to tell 'em. I'm sorry about these positions, but your men aren't bloody fools and they know that it's in their interest and nobody else's to get cracking. All right?'

Jack Pettigrew nodded, and saluted in a resentful sort of way. Whisky Wainwright was in what the order had described as temporary command. Then, when Adam had returned to battalion headquarters after a visit to D Company, he and Whisky had been met by Harry Venables, sad-faced.

'Sir –'

Jack Pettigrew and his company sergeant-major and three other men had been killed by a salvo of shells which had fallen about ten minutes after Whisky and Adam's visit to C. 'We're certainly catching it as far as officers go,' Harry had remarked to Adam, unnecessarily. 'That's three on this bloody position. Just stray shelling.' So that Adam's first recollection of those two days on the French frontier would be the sense that the Westmorlands were losing officers in an uncanny way. Perhaps three was a negligible figure compared to the casualties of others; but it was three during a period in which the battalion was not directly attacked, was only paid this sporadic attention by German guns, was having a quiet time. And the proportion of officer casualties was bizarre. Furthermore there was sadly little British shelling in response. Artillery ammunition was in grimly short supply, as were all the army's necessaries. Major Brodie had told Whisky Wainwright about his daily ration of shells and Whisky had simply raised his eyebrows, grunted and shrugged. Nothing to bloody do about it. But it was bad.

Then there had been Sergeant Bishop. Sergeant Bishop of D Company had always struck Adam as a disagreeable man. He had the reputation of being intelligent and efficient but to Adam, who hardly knew him, there was something sneering and supercilious about Sergeant Bishop. Whenever Adam had found himself in D Company area in the past he seemed to have come across Bishop. Bishop's salute – very smart, a half-smile accompanying it, more than a touch of the sardonic in the smile – had always made Adam feel that Bishop was inwardly contemptuous. Adam had decided from early days in the battalion that Sergeant Bishop was an unpleasant man. He had wondered whether the men of D Company liked him and had had something of an answer when visiting them just after taking over as intelligence officer, before the advance, before the campaign. He had been in search of David Bassett with some new maps and had happened to ask Sergeant Bishop if he knew the company commander's whereabouts. Bishop had answered smoothly and unhelpfully. He had been standing with a small group of men, presumably from his platoon.

As Adam had walked away he heard a round of laughter. It sounded sycophantic. He looked back and saw Bishop, smiling, salute again. Bishop, Adam was sure, had said something disloyal, something humorous, something deflationary of puffed-up second-lieutenants who thought they understood intelligence. He recognized, with irritation at his own reaction, that he disliked Bishop. Bishop might be able – was, indeed, often spoken of as one of the best sergeants in the battalion, probably be commissioned one day – but he grated on Adam.

So Adam heard without sense of personal sadness and with contempt for his own indifference that Bishop had 'copped it', as the Westmorlands put it. On the frontier position. On the first morning. A shell had fallen on D Company – a stray shell, the main salvo had landed some distance away – just as they were shaking out into their new deployment; and it had found Bishop, found his stomach so that he had been taken to the aid post in great pain and had died later in the day, they learned. 'Best sergeant in the battalion,' David Bassett had said angrily to anyone listening. Adam felt, without logic, that the praise, the emphasis, reflected his own inadequacy.

Adam's next mental picture from this period was of the terrible transformation of the civilian world. Panic had engulfed much of it. The Westmorlands were some way from their positions of the winter, but the situation was certainly similar throughout the area. People were very hungry. Communications, civil transport, civil administration had broken down. Employers and civic authorities alike had in most cases fled. Wages had not been paid. Everybody who could do so had taken to the road, trying to escape the German advance, fleeing the terror rumour was reporting, fleeing the unknown. Houses were abandoned. Some villages appeared wholly deserted – a circumstance which enabled the Westmorlands to incorporate the houses into the defensive plan with easy conscience, breaking windows and loopholing walls with a will. By contrast to what they saw of the unfortunate refugees, the troops themselves were eating well. Rations had been officially cut because of the Expeditionary Force's tenuous

Dunkirk supply line, but there were a good many larders still partially stocked and abandoned, while in the fields beef cattle and milk cows were easy to appropriate. The army was living off the land, and the land, empty of its proper inhabitants, was silent and resentful beneath the brilliant blue skies. Adam wondered where Angélique had gone. Perhaps she was still in Vevers – the whole population couldn't have decamped. The thought brought Felicity to his mind for the first time in two weeks.

The third thing Adam would always associate with the frontier position was the transformation in the 2nd Battalion, the Westmorland Regiment.

Adam had accompanied Whisky Wainwright on the latter's tour of companies after their arrival – the movement from the Escaut had been mainly carried out in transport. He had everywhere found a difference in atmosphere. With the exception of poor old Jack Pettigrew, tails were up. Men, everywhere, were tired, dirty, puzzled; but they grinned. When Whisky muttered something at them they laughed, no doubt unclear of what it was he'd actually said. There was a certain alacrity in the air, despite the exhaustion. The undercurrent of suspicion and resentment of which Adam, troubled, had been very aware in these last two weeks was wholly absent.

It was the same at battalion headquarters. Harry Venables talked with a new confidence. Bobby Forrest no longer looked harassed and uncertain. The carrier platoon commander, Charles Wade, who had been largely invisible in the last fortnight, deploying his carriers to cover the withdrawals on foot or to watch a battalion flank – and releasing them, reluctantly, to act as occasional battalion runabouts – now turned up at battalion headquarters more often than not, and always helpfully. Charles, a very senior subaltern, was a moody fellow, as Adam knew well; they had never been close, and Charles had seemed often to be filled with suspicion that

his carriers were about to be misused – and that Second-
Lieutenant Adam Hardrow was a battalion intelligence officer
who was a great deal too young and inexperienced to know
his job. But now Charles Wade seemed to have warmed. The
team at battalion headquarters – Venables, Forrest, Hardrow,
often now augmented by Wade – had become happy and
close.

And it all derived from Whisky Wainwright. Scowling more
often than not, no more affable than ever, certainly under
considerable pressure, Whisky Wainwright, by his simple,
grim integrity, by being who he was, had made the Westmorlands feel right with themselves once again. It was, Adam felt
obscurely, providential that this should have happened at
exactly this moment. Their testing time could not be long
delayed now. They should meet it under a chief they could
serve with pride. It's odd, Adam said to himself, I suppose
the army's situation is worse than it ever has been. Damned
near hopeless, I expect. And yet, just here, we're all in fine
form, we feel fit for everything and anything. Poor old
Colonel Fosdike – he really has done us a wonderful turn by
getting the sack!

'Adam!'
  'Yes, sir.'
  'Come here.'
Whisky seemed almost embarrassed. He was frowning, as
often, but it looked as if he was having unwonted difficulty in
articulating what he meant.

'Adam, look here, the thing is –' Adam heard, 'Sergeant
Cobb all right, bit of an old woman but knows his stuff –.
Damned short, trouble is this PSM policy doesn't cater for a
few casualties, asking for trouble –'

There were some more obscure, disconnected sentences.
Then, incredulously, Adam realized what his acting commanding officer was trying to convey. Whisky was sacking

him as battalion intelligence officer! Whisky had decided that at battalion headquarters he was dispensable! Whisky was sending him back to B Company.

Whisky was now saying more and Adam recognized the logic. He was aware of the current brigade plan, just received. They were to leave the frontier position. There was a bad situation developing on the left. Their brigade was to move, in transport, some miles to the northern flank and, once there, would have to adopt a new position very quickly. In uncertain circumstances.

Or counter-attack, that was the latest idea. To restore some sort of stability to the left flank of the British Expeditionary Force. And the Westmorlands' rifle companies were by now, by this and that, by trickle rather than haemorrhage, damnably short of officers.

Whisky was saying, 'Sorry about it. Don't feel bad about it. Don't want you to feel you've failed.'

And Adam heard himself saying, 'I don't feel bad about it, sir. I feel very, very good.' He supposed he'd get his old platoon back. Poor old Garthwaite. It wouldn't do to look excessively happy.

Nevertheless he couldn't drive a grin from his face when he reported to Ben Jameson very early the following morning. They were moving at six, and Whisky had decreed that Adam must accompany him to brigade headquarters for a midnight conference and orders, and do all that was needful at battalion headquarters during the remainder of the night – a busy night. The battalion was due to travel some way, to the left of the front (which now described a sharp angle, with the right bent back to confront the Germans to the south and southwest) and, having arrived, to move straight from an assembly area to a place where they would form up, and attack, and drive the enemy back across a river – not their original Dyle, or Dendre or Escaut, once depicted for them as formidable barriers by a confident Colonel Fosdike. Yet another river.

The river constituted the front line for part of the front, but at the point to which the Westmorlands' brigade was directed the Germans had crossed it and got a pretty large lodgement on the west bank. Or so it appeared.

It was just after dawn when Adam reported, dawn on 26 May. Ben was standing by a truck talking in a low voice to Company Sergeant-Major Darwin. As usual he looked calm, turnout impeccable.

'Ah! Well at least you know the general picture –'

'And the company objective,' Adam nodded. A Company was to take a small village, as a firm base for the advance, astride that village, of B and D. C Company, a subaltern called Winter having taken over command from Jack Pettigrew, would be in reserve. The first phase of the attack would be to get A Company to the village. The next phase – on battalion orders – would be the advance of B and D to take a ridge just short of the river.

'Where,' said Ben softly, 'we are credibly informed the Huns were establishing themselves at last light, and were showing no signs of coming further. They'll have pushed patrols forward, presumably, but we may, we just may find the enemy holding the position which has been named as our objective. Just like on an exercise!'

Adam smiled. Ben, thank God, was the same. He even sounded merry as he pointed out on his map the company start line. The journey in transport was due to take ninety minutes; they had been assured that Military Police had by now cleared the way. The distance from the debussing point was not long and should see the whole battalion, tense and as yet untried, in the attack assembly area before eight o'clock. Whisky Wainwright had insisted on as short a time there as possible before launching A Company at the village – its name was Koreyck – which was to act as anchor for the swing forward of the attack; a village, Ben said, which the staff asserted was still in our hands – just.

'So A, in theory, won't have to fight for it.' Adam hoped very much that this was so. His heart, or such of it as he could spare from his own forebodings, was with Ivan Perry.

'That's so,' Ben said. 'In fact apparently Whisky's being regarded as over-cautious in making it a first phase to establish A in it. Or so he grunted to me. The powers that be wanted him to send you and me and dear old David Bassett straight at the ridge and the river. Whisky said no. Whisky said he wants to be sure of that village, Koreyck, first. I'm delighted. It would be a bugger if there were Huns there – we'd catch it directly we crossed the start line.' The start line for B and D companies' attack ran just forward of the village of Koreyck. Germans in Koreyck would indeed be a bugger. Ben was indicating on his map where B Company was to form up, cross a start line, and then move on its objective. He told Adam the fire plan. It didn't sound awe-inspiring.

'As you know, gun ammunition's short. Now, Adam, we ought to have time and opportunity to look at the ground from this point, about three hundred yards from the assembly area,' – he pointed to his map – 'and if you're thinking that none of this conforms to the best practice, motoring into battle, plan made off a map, no proper recce, no time for detailed briefing within platoons after looking at the ground, no this, no that, so be it.' He smiled agreeably and Adam loved him.

Ben said, softly, 'We're in a bloody awful mess, that's obvious. But never mind. We'll have to do our best. Whisky will look after us.'

'I know.'

Ben looked at his watch. They were due to move in twenty minutes.

Adam said, 'Ben –'

'Well?'

'I suppose you want me to take 5 Platoon again?'

'Ah,' said Ben, 'I'd almost forgotten!' But he hadn't, Adam

knew. 'The company,' said Ben, 'can only field two platoons. We've had a dribble of casualties, so I've divided 4 Platoon up and given Jack Brett and you a strongish platoon each. So yes, you take 5. Sergeant Pew's still in good heart. And there are some men from 6 Platoon there as well. You've got over thirty.'

A platoon at full strength was thirty-five. B Company had indeed had a dribble of casualties. And Platoon Sergeant-Major Merrow, thought Adam, has proved less than an outstanding success perhaps. With a few more brief questions he went in search of Sergeant Pew, to find, as he confidently expected, that the augmented platoon was sensibly organized. He remembered several of the newcomers from Merrow's platoon. In the remaining minutes he chatted in a low voice to Sergeant Pew about the battle they ought to be fighting in three hours' time. An attack. Their first.

The 2nd Westmorlands reached their assembly area before eight o'clock, as planned, and their move by road had also gone as planned – the first bloody thing that's gone right, Ben Jameson observed, in this whole campaign, as far as I know. But something else went right – they were not shelled in the assembly area. It was this that Whisky Wainwright had feared above all – he hated the whole business of a daylight attack with minimal supporting artillery fire, against an enemy who'd had several hours to prepare a position, but it had to be done. Of all things, however, he feared most German artillery fire while they were assembling, moving forward, forming up. In the open. Unprotected. Whisky sensed just how difficult it would be thereafter to get men going forward. 'Give us a decent start, Lord,' he'd prayed. He certainly didn't hold the petition incongruous.

But the first thing of which Adam was conscious in the assembly area was a straggle of British soldiers. British soldiers who were, it seemed, coming back from the village of Koreyck. Adam was standing near Company Sergeant-Major Darwin and heard him say, 'What the hell –'

There were about twenty men. They were indescribably dirty and few looked as if they had shaved in the last ten days. Several had slung rifles but many had no weapons at all. They had clearly not expected to find themselves among other soldiers for some time.

Ben Jameson said sharply, 'Hey!'

A man looked at him with a sour and insubordinate grin, and no other sign of recognition.

'Hey! Who are you? What unit?'

Several of the stragglers paused, listening. What would happen? The Westmorlands gazed at them as if at creatures escaped from a zoo.

The man said, 'We was cut off.' It was an expression Adam was to hear with depressing regularity.

'What do you mean, cut off? Were you in that village? Koreyck?'

'Dunno what it's called.'

'Who's in it now?'

A shrug, and Ben snapped, 'Are there Germans there?'

'Guess so. There's civvies there. Belgies. In the cellars, like.'

Another straggler joined the first and said, sullenly, 'We'd no orders. There was shooting.'

The first man said, 'Snipers.'

His mate nodded, fastening on to the word, 'That's right. Snipers.'

But not, Ben thought as he looked at them with contempt, very dangerous snipers. You were slouching away from the place without much sign of anxiety. Unseen, Whisky Wainwright had joined them from somewhere and had heard the exchange. He now said sharply, 'All you men will wait by that clump of trees. Do you hear?' He pointed.

They gazed at the clump of trees, at this major who looked

like a bull and at the clump of trees again. Whisky had immediately sent his runner, as Adam heard clearly, for Ivan Perry – 'and ask Mr Perry to double,' Adam heard. Whisky then turned again to the stragglers.

He said, in a voice of surprising gentleness, 'Now you men will be fed when my own men are fed – some time soon after our attack. You will meanwhile be looked after by this battalion and will fight with it. Those without rifles will be issued with rifles very soon. Stay together. By that clump of trees. Our regimental sergeant-major will take your names and record them.'

One of the men said, 'We didn't know –'

Another chimed in, 'There was nobody said nothing –'

'Never mind all that,' Whisky said. 'Do what I told you.' He turned to greet Ivan Perry and said, 'Ivan, it's possible Koreyck has got neither side in it. Go for it now, exactly as I told you, and ready to take on the Huns if they're in it. But I don't think they are. So go fast – really fast. One platoon on the ground, as I told you, by the first farm, and then in with the rest, flat out. With luck you'll be tight in the place in twenty minutes.'

'Right, sir.'

'Off you go.'

The men of the Westmorland companies were well dispersed, down behind banks, in ditches or covered by the scattered cottages with which the area was peppered. They remained thus for half an hour, and during that half hour Adam accompanied Ben and Jack Brett forward to a point where they could see a good deal of the ground over which they were to advance. There was a false grassy ridge which concealed what Ben worked out was their actual objective – another low ridge which would only become visible after they'd advanced some way. Crowning this false, intermediate ridge was a farm – a house and steadings surrounded by barbed-wire fences. An extensive place.

'I'll set up company headquarters there,' said Ben, point-ing, 'when we get there. It's called Droot Farm, or so it seems and so we'll call it. The objective, I reckon, is about three, perhaps four hundred yards beyond Droot, no more. You'll go to the left of Droot, Adam, and Jack to the right. Got it?'

'Right, Ben.' The country consisted of open corn land, with a few grass meadows interspersed.

'I'm keeping what amounts to a section, with three bren-guns, in my hand. At Droot, if we get there, and if we go hard – as we must – our guns ought to be hitting the objective; just before we cross the intermediate green ridge. They open up at zero plus ten, as you know.' The start line was a farm track, running north and south out of the village of Koreyck and more or less square to what they supposed would ultimately show itself clearly as the objective.

Ben said, conversationally, 'Green Ridge! It won't seem like a ridge when we get there, of course, but the Huns can't hit us with direct fire until we get to it, or thereabouts. Now let's go back to the company.' Ben looked at his watch. They were all wondering desperately how Ivan Perry was getting on. If the Germans were in Koreyck their battle would take a very different form. But five minutes after they had rejoined their waiting men a dispatch rider was seen reporting to Ben. Ivan had been forbidden to send up a success signal; his inadequate communications with Whisky Wainwright had had to suffice for the report of results, so the rest of them were in the dark. From Koreyck no shooting was heard – a good sign.

The platoon commanders had been assembled near Ben under the lee of a bank. As the dispatch rider started his machine, Ben stood up and beckoned them.

'Zero hour nine-fifteen. Twenty minutes to shake out, into the forming-up place and straight across the start line. All right?'

'All right, Ben.'

'Koreyck was empty except for a lot of dubious-looking civilian characters. A's firm there now. Off you go.'

Adam called, 'Good luck, Jack!' And Jack Brett turned, smiled, and shouted, 'Same to you.'

Until they reached the intermediate ridge, christened by Ben Jameson 'Green Ridge', Adam's platoon walked forward without the slightest interruption. No enemy fire of any kind. Every man's ears were ready for the sigh and whistle of approaching German mortar bombs but there was nothing. The sections moved towards the unknown under a very clear blue sky, in extended order, each section commander in the middle of his small group of riflemen and bren-gunners. It was extraordinarily quiet. Adam's eyes were fixed on the skyline. Green Ridge was only a hundred yards now, and already visible ground was opening out beyond it. As Ben had said, Green Ridge was a shallow false crest, no more. Soon the limit of vision would extend to the next ridge, the objective. And if Germans were on the objective then the Westmorlands would soon be visible to them too.

Far behind them Adam now heard the deep voice of British 25-pounder guns. There had been sporadic rumblings of artillery all the time but this sounded like the Westmorlands' own fire programme. Adam's heart beat fast as he turned his head and nodded to Sergeant Pew. They were about two minutes behind perfect schedule – they needed, Adam reckoned, to cover perhaps another two hundred yards before they'd be within sight of German positions; two minutes – but gunfire on the objective was due to go on for five minutes. He quickened his pace. He'd had time in the assembly area to brief the platoon – they all knew the form. And as they heard the swishing sound of shells going overhead, a sound like a giant breathing, they knew that their attack was unlikely to be a surprise to the enemy for much longer. Artillery will keep the bloody Jerries' heads down, that's the idea, Sergeant Pew had said to them in his matter-of-fact way before Mr Hardrow had rejoined them (and it was a good job he had). Keep their bloody heads down. Just keep going, and remember all you've been taught.

Although it was imperceptible, B Company had now breasted Green Ridge; the ground ran very gently downwards before them. Droot Farm was now in the centre of the company front, with 6 Platoon passing to its right and Adam to its left. Ben Jameson and his little company reserve would pause at Droot Farm. The advance was going like clockwork. Five hundred yards away must be the river. And this side of the river, holding a shallow bridgehead, B Company had been told, was Jerry. Every man in 5 Platoon was afraid, but they tramped on steadily. Bloody Jerries might have buggered off. Ahead of them came the sharp crack of British shells exploding somewhere near the objective.

The first shock was at one remove. The first shock struck 6 Platoon, to their right; Jack Brett's platoon. It took the form of light machine-gun fire, and as far as Adam could see it hit 6 Platoon from two different directions. From the front – Adam reckoned it was from the front – came the rasping, rapid sound of a Spandau; two, three, perhaps four Spandaus, all cutting into 6 Platoon. Adam could see 6 Platoon very clearly – Jack Brett's inner section was only about four hundred yards from Adam's right-hand man. Adam saw men drop, whether as casualties or to get down and perhaps return fire was uncertain. At the same time, and much nearer, Adam became aware of more Spandau fire – at least another two machine-guns – from Droot Farm. Droot Farm now lay just behind Jack Brett's left, just behind Adam's right. Germans in Droot Farm had held their fire, withstood the temptation to open up to their front – held their fire until B Company platoons were past and then caught them in the rear.

Caught Jack Brett's platoon, that was. Nothing had yet hit

Adam's men but in the seconds in which he realized what was happening, realized where the enemy was, Adam decided three things, came to three conclusions so rapidly that the process would have been impossible to time. First, he reckoned that his own platoon must be about to get the same treatment as Jack Brett's – fire from both flank and front. Second, he decided that it would be impossible to press an attack to the front until this menace from Droot Farm was cleared up. Somebody would have to clear it up, and it took priority; to press forward with one platoon (he never questioned in his own mind, although afterwards he supposed the conclusion had been hasty, that Jack Brett's platoon, suffering concentric fire, was pretty well pinned to the ground they were lying on and was almost certainly incapable of any offensive movement whatsoever – and in this he was right) would be a disaster in the circumstances. And it was highly unlikely that he'd be able to, anyway.

Thirdly, Adam was vividly aware that somewhere away to his right rear Ben Jameson was advancing towards Droot Farm. Ben would have heard the Spandaus. Ben would have instantly appreciated what was happening. But Ben, with a section of men, was unlikely to be able to drive the Germans from Droot Farm on his own. And Ben couldn't in time, get orders to him, Adam. Droot Farm was in the way.

Adam's reactions were instantaneous. He later thanked Providence that he'd had no time to think, confident then as afterwards that the instinctive response in such circumstances is generally the best. A thoughtful weighing of pros and cons might have led him into every kind of difficulty – were his orders not simply to advance to the front, to the objective? Suppose the rest of B Company was also about to concentrate on Droot Farm, would there not be chaos, with Westmorlands shooting Westmorlands? What about the artillery programme? Its benefits would be squandered if the advancing troops failed to keep up. And so on.

Adam had time to consider none of this. He yelled, 'Sergeant Pew', and at that moment two German machine-guns opened up from the front, and Adam heard the dreaded hiss and thud of German mortar bombs, saw the earth shoot and the stones leap in the air, and realized that a cluster had fallen just behind 5 Platoon. The rear section, Corporal Barney's section, were down but Adam couldn't see if anybody was hit. Sergeant Pew tore up to him.

'Back here, Sergeant Pew.'

Adam was aware of a low bank which they had passed thirty yards back, a raised grassy edge to a farm track, no more. It gave pitiful cover, probably none; but it could provide the illusion of a place of shelter and deliberation. Adam saw that each of the section commanders had got his men down on the ground, and that they seemed to be crawling towards the left flank. Prone, they were probably invisible from the front and anyway, as far as he could judge, the German machine-guns had fired high. Adam threw himself behind the bank, Sergeant Pew alongside.

'We've got to go for Droot Farm. Tell Corporal Barney to get into fire positions somewhere where he is now – there's no cover but the ground's uneven. In –' Adam looked at his watch '– four minutes I'll have gathered up the other two sections and I'm going straight for the place. Maximum fire from Corporal Barney's section. Got it?'

'Yes, sir. The captain –'

'Will join me there, I expect. You stay with Corporal Barney. Off you go.'

Doubled up, Sergeant Pew ran towards the rear section. From the front, the original company objective, Adam heard the continuing crack of British shells. The Germans, on what was assumed to be their main position, had not started firing again. Adam supposed they were suffering a certain distraction from our artillery fire, as intended; probably, too, they could see little of 5 Platoon, lying, crawling and, with luck, mostly on the safe side of the crown of a convex slope.

Adam covered the distance to the nearest section commander, the original left-section commander, in forty-five seconds, bent double and weaving. He didn't know whether, if he stood upright, he'd be visible to the Germans and he didn't intend to discover. What was certain was that all of 5 Platoon could, without much difficulty (although, as he'd said to Sergeant Pew, the ground was uneven) be seen from Droot Farm. Adam had acquired a rifle, a spare from company stores. Officers' personal weapons were .38 revolvers, but Whisky Wainwright had issued an order that platoon commanders were to carry rifles and a bandolier of ammunition each – it would make them less conspicuous and it would come in useful. Whisky had grunted, 'Bloody revolver useless except when you're about hugging a Jerry anyway. Different if it was a long-barrelled Luger.' But it was typical of the British Army, Whisky had muttered, 'to skimp money even on officers' pistols and give them something near-useless'. So Adam as he raced across the field held a rifle.

The nearest section commander was Corporal Egan, he who had once failed Jack Brett in the matter of counting his men out of a defensive position on training. Corporal Egan had not forgotten it. Night withdrawals! Stunts! A hot drink when it was all over! Christ, this was bloody different, bloody different! Corporal Egan found to his unconcern that he had pissed inside his trouser leg. He looked at Adam with no attempt to disguise fear.

'It was best to get them down, sir –'

They'd got themselves down, Adam knew, and without any command from Corporal Egan. They'd got themselves down at the first bark of the Spandaus, the first hiss and crack of mortar shells. In some circumstances the right thing, the only thing, would have been to get them up, roar commands, march out in front, drive the movement forward somehow,

somehow. Some circumstances but not these ones. These were different.

'Corporal Egan, we're going straight for Droot Farm. You right, Corporal Travers left. With me. Flat out. Watch me. Got it?'

'The bren groups, sir –'

'Bring the whole lot, brens firing from the hips when we hit them. Got it?'

No time for more. Across to Corporal Travers. Another fifty seconds. Still no firing from the front, but a constant chatter of machine-guns from Droot Farm directed away from them, directed on Jack Brett's men. And perhaps directed on Ben Jameson, for Ben must be nearing the place and was probably under fire as well, from the rear of the buildings. They couldn't, Adam panted to himself, fire in all directions with equal effect from Droot Farm. The whole bloody Wehrmacht couldn't be in Droot Farm. And at least if the Huns reckoned they were holding Droot Farm they wouldn't shell it themselves. Or would they?

About two hundred yards to Droot Farm. Pretty level. One cattle-wire fence. Grass underfoot as far as the outbuildings. God knew what they'd find there. No time to think about that – no time for anything but Corporal Travers left, Corporal Egan right. Thirty seconds. Then the crackle of Corporal Barney's bren-gun. Good old Sergeant Pew – he'd see they didn't shoot up the rest of the platoon while it covered the distance!

'Right – 5 Platoon – GO!'

The first German Adam Hardrow saw at close quarters in the war that began in September 1939 wasn't trying to kill him or anybody else. He was weighed down with three belts of machine-gun cartridges hung round his neck and he was carrying in each hand a tin box of ammunition. He'd obviously just collected these from the nearest outhouse to the flank from which 5 Platoon were racing towards Droot Farm, and, equally obviously, he was astonished. There must, Adam had reckoned, be a sentry and no doubt another Spandau looking out in this direction, but by some miracle he hadn't opened up as they crossed the field, flat out. Two hundred yards, flat out. One cattle-wire fence, and Adam neither then nor later remembered getting across it. It had seemed to disappear. Then the nearest outbuilding of Droot Farm, red brick, large barn door to the right, a blank brick wall on this side. A gap into what must be the farmyard. No firing. And then a grey-green helmeted figure, hung with ammunition, back turned, head turning.

Adam shot him, a quick, accurate shot from the shoulder which dropped the German. Whether it killed him was unimportant. Adam had a fleeting impression of an amazed, terrified face, and then he heard the tearing, ripping sound of Spandau bursts from the far side of the outbuilding, well to his left, firing (it must be) into Corporal Travers's section. Again there was the split-second reactions of the brain, logic lagging behind, only articulated later. German sentry on this flank had failed to see the centre and right of 5 Platoon's two-hundred-yard dash. Could only see the left – Corporal Travers. Vision of the rest masked by the outbuilding – inadequate sentry position siting, inadequate cover of all possible lines of assault, they must be short of men. Most men still looking at Jack Brett – and, perhaps, Ben Jameson, to the farm's rear flank. Anyway, game's up now, they're shooting at Travers, he looked as if he was lagging behind a bit. But at that moment Adam heard the unmistakable sound of a British bren-gun. From the left – Corporal Travers's section. And to his right he saw, hardly daring to believe, that Corporal Egan's men were moving – cautiously now, very cautiously – round the outbuilding at whose door he, Adam Hardrow, had just shot a German carrying ammunition. He saw a British helmet and head at the far end of the outbuilding wall. It was Wilkins! Wilkins was looking almost fierce. Adam raced towards him, his own runner, Crace, trotting behind in an agonizing mix of excitement and fear.

'Corporal Egan –'

Wilkins jerked his thumb to his right and Adam saw Corporal Egan and what looked like most of his section. God knew how Droot Farm was laid out, but 5 Platoon was now in it, and it had to be a matter of fighting through it and keeping some sort of control as they inched forward and explored and killed, explored and killed. Meanwhile –

'Very Light, Crace!'

Crace carried a Very Light pistol. With trembling fingers and clumsily he stuffed in a cartridge, raised it to the heavens and fired. A green light, gentle and almost beautiful, hung for a moment over Droot Farm. That, with luck, would bring Sergeant Pew, Corporal Barney and the rest to join him. And, with more luck they'd do so without opposition – Corporal Egan had been unmolested during his section's one-minute sprint.

'Go firm just here, Corporal Egan!' Adam was shouting now. 'Corporal Egan!'

'Right, sir.'

'And they'll come at you now, from any direction! Look sharp!'

'Right, sir!'

Incredibly, there was as yet no German reaction to 5 Platoon's arrival in Droot Farm, except for the chatter of that Spandau at Corporal Travers; and that seemed to have been silenced by the answering bren. Adam realized with a bit of his mind that they'd still only been in the place for less than a minute. He yelled again to Corporal Egan. Corporal Egan was crouching by an enormous heap of manure.

'And when Sergeant Pew and the rest arrive tell him I want a platoon firm base right where you are!'

'Right, sir.'

It was probably a hopeless plan but it was the best he could do. Now, what was happening to Corporal Travers? Adam ran to his left, round another outbuilding. Corporal Travers must be somewhere here. There seemed to be a small yard, not the main farmyard surely? With an opening on the far side which might connect to the main farmyard, and a huge stone trough in the middle. No sign of Corporal Travers.

'Corporal Travers!'

There seemed no way out of the little yard, except forward, the opening gap between what looked like two barns. The shooting had been somewhere to the left. Droot Farm was a big place, bigger than it had seemed from the north, the direction from which Adam had appeared. The Germans must be on the south and south-eastern side. How many Spandaus had fired originally? Two? Three? And another (or one of the three?) at Corporal Travers. What was here? A platoon, or its German equivalent? A company? But no sentry had been posted on the north-west side –

'Corporal Travers!'

Adam stopped and turned his head. Conceivably Corporal Travers hadn't reached the farm, was frozen with his section in some fold of ground in the grassland they'd raced across ninety seconds ago. Conceivably he was crawling forward – or, damnably, not even crawling forward but lying prone, inactive, terrified, and his section with him. Or bolting back, abject, mindless, running to get away from that bloody Spandau! Running away! But the Spandau hadn't fired again. And a bren had! And then silence.

Corporal Travers was a large, slow-spoken Cumberland man. It was never easy to get him moving or acting rapidly. He was what soldiers called steady, and he chewed over orders thoughtfully before making the appropriate response. It was predictable that in the dash to Droot Farm he had, with his men, lagged a little behind; but less easy to accept that he had turned or faltered. Yet Corporal Travers was human, capable of fear and failure like all of them.

'Corporal Travers!' Adam saw that on the northern side of the little yard, on the side from which Corporal Travers would have approached (if approached he had) there was a large cattle gate. He could look from it, look over the fields crossed by Corporal Travers. He could see whether –

'Corporal Travers!'

'Sir!'

It was Crace, a sort of scream. Adam swung round.

There were three of them moving through the gap between the two barns, the gap which Adam had surmised might connect this yard to a larger farmyard, a principal centre of Droot Farm perhaps. All three were steel-helmeted and had Schmeiser machine-pistols slung across the body, barrels lowered and pointing forward. Adam threw himself to the ground behind the stone horse trough as the bursts of fire crackled deafeningly, and the bullets spattered against the barn wall to his right and ricocheted wildly round behind him.

Adam was aware of Crace's body, prone on the yard floor round the corner of the right-hand barn wall, aware of the strap of the Very light pistol bunched by the back of Crace's head. He was unsure whether he, Adam, was hit. He might, perhaps, be dead? A half second returned him to reason and realization of life. The massive horse trough had protected him. But to get his rifle up would involve exposing himself, impossibly. They must be moving forward now, must have got him covered. God knew how they'd missed! They'd been twenty yards away, no more.

Well, they might have a better target if he brought his rifle up but, Christ, one couldn't lie here and wait for the buggers to close in and shoot one like a cornered animal! Adam, hardly knowing what he was doing or how he was doing it, inched his way towards the corner of the horse trough, solid to its base as it mercifully was. He moved his rifle muzzle cautiously forward, still keeping his body wholly crouched behind the horse trough. At least he could have a shot at one as they moved forward; and they'd have to move forward, they couldn't get him where he was unless one of them moved.

But they could get him with a grenade! A stick grenade, perhaps, lobbed over the horse trough while they got down where they were until after the explosion, and then came forward to identify the pieces and exult over them. A grenade would do it all right.

Ten seconds gone. Death very near now. Charge them, shooting his rifle from the hip? Hopeless of course – what could he do, working the bolt of a Lee-Enfield against three Schmeisers! Still, he'd be in the open, on level terms with the buggers! They might fire wildly, miss him as he charged? Then what? Brain's bursting –

The noise was deafening. Schmeisers firing rapidly in the short, controlled bursts which characterized this useful weapon – but different from the last bursts, a different sound. Why? *Firing in a different direction! Firing away from him!* Then – unmistakably, incredibly – the sound of a British bren-gun's long, deliberate bursts. British soldiers were trained, Adam's mind incongruously flashed, to squeeze the trigger for a four-or five-round burst, no more. More tended to be wasteful and inaccurate. Well, this bren-gunner was giving them a longer burst than that, much longer. And Adam risked his life and peered round the corner of the horse trough to see the helmeted grey-green figures drop, one, two. The third figure seemed to turn, stagger, turn again, bring his Schmeiser up (but not pointed towards Adam, pointed to Adam's left, to somewhere beyond that gap between two barns where Adam's eyes couldn't reach). Bring his Schmeiser up and then, in turn, drop, Schmeiser sling round the neck, weapon clattering as he, like his mates, hit the irregular round stones of the farmyard floor.

'Right, sir,' said Corporal Travers. 'Right. We lost Sharrow, sir, old Sharrow copped it from the Spandau, bullet through the head, and Brimstow's arm's hit but he'll be all right. That was coming across the open, see? And I got the old bren going and we reckon we got one on 'em, not sure though. The ones with the Spandau legged it, see? Then we found those three Jerries, but they weren't looking in our direction, see? We got in pretty well, into the garden like, just beyond this barn. Worked round here, got Crowe with the bren down by the corner, saw these three Jerries, thought "Here we go!" and they wasn't looking our way, see? So Crowe, he did well, did Crowe, he got 'em, point-blank like – they wasn't looking our way at all!' Corporal Travers sounded positively complacent.

Adam realized for the first time exactly what a gifted man Travers was. He had the trick of appearing leisurely, almost lethargic at times, but he was always in exactly the right place at the right time; he was unhurried, appeared unworried, completely objective in his assessment of what a situation required – all these thoughts came to Adam later rather than at once, and showed him how easy it was to underestimate a man like Travers. Travers, although it was unlikely he would have thought it of himself, was a born soldier. There weren't many like Travers.

Travers was nodding his head and saying again, 'No, they wasn't looking our way at all!'

'No,' said Adam, 'they were looking my way.'

Adam didn't dissect his own reactions until later. He knew that his principal and no doubt inglorious emotion was of relief at personal survival. Second – shamingly second – had been relief at finding that Crace was completely unhurt. He got Corporal Travers into a reasonable fire position covering what seemed to be the opening to the main farmyard. He told him that he proposed to pick up the rest of the platoon, line them up and shoot their way forward through the rest of Droot Farm. Corporal Travers was to act as pivot for this, to shoot anything he saw moving as long as it wasn't in the Westmorlands. The shape of the farm was still hard to discern, it was a big place, there might be several connecting yards. The only sure thing was that somewhere on the outer perimeter of the farm complex were at least two Spandau nests. And somewhere, too, was an unknown number of German soldiers. Armed with Schmeisers, no doubt. Armed with more Spandaus, possibly. And almost certainly armed with stick grenades.

Adam ran back with Crace to rejoin Corporal Egan and found him, mercifully, with Sergeant Pew. Sergeant Pew had Corporal Barney's section down facing the way they'd come. All-round defence. Sergeant Pew had no idea what Mr Hardrow wanted.

'There was a lot of firing just over there, sir. On that side of the farm. Schmeisers, and a bren certainly.'

'Yes, that's Corporal Travers. He's all right.'

'Are you all right, sir?' For the first time Adam was aware of blood pouring down his face. He put his hand up. A cut forehead. A ricochet, probably. Nothing.

'Fine. Now, Sergeant Pew –' Adam explained his plan. Corporal Travers was in position; if things went wrong they'd got him firm at least. The rest of them, two sections, would line up and move through the farm, covering each other, group covering group, taking it methodically. Shoot their way through. When the Spandaus opened up, '*as they will*,' Adam said, 'there's two, maybe three of them, the ones we heard at the start – throw everything at them, everything!' There couldn't be many Jerries in the farm in all, Adam said, their look-outs had been minimal, and so far he'd seen the three killed by Corporal Travers and another he'd dropped himself on first arrival. They were thin on the ground. Right, spread out, get cracking. Adam pointed Corporals Barney and Egan towards their first immediate objectives and saw their sections move forward in reasonably workmanlike fashion. They'd never practised this sort of thing but commonsense was dictating tactics and doing so effectively.

Adam glanced at his watch as he picked his own way through the farm buildings, yards and small cattle enclosures void of cattle, his field of vision never more than twenty yards. Unbelievable! It was only seven minutes since he'd first arrived. Since he'd meant to look and see if that Jerry laden with ammunition was dead or only hard hit. Poor devil, a tiny part of his mind whispered, but it was a very tiny part.

They worked forward, Adam feeling a certain confidence returning to his nervous system as he realized that 5 Platoon were doing their work well, moving sensibly; and were, more or less, under his control. He was no longer a terrified individual crouching ignominiously behind a horse trough and deprived of any power to command anything or anybody. He was again Second-Lieutenant Hardrow and NCOs were glancing towards him again, making sure their moves and actions were as he wanted.

No Germans. No sign of Germans.

They reached, astonishingly, the far edge of the Droot Farm complex, the southern edge, still with no sign of Germans. Adam yelled at the two section commanders to get their men down facing south and east, and to Sergeant Pew to take a patrol thoroughly through the buildings to make sure they really were deserted.

They were. The enemy, the Spandau teams, the whole detachment holding Droot Farm, had obviously decided to withdraw. They'd done their bit, they'd broken up the momentum of a British advance, they'd probably been given discretion to get back when that was accomplished.

Adam looked at his watch again. Remarkably, only twenty-five minutes had passed since the Germans had first opened up from Droot Farm at Jack Brett's platoon. And now, where *was* Jack Brett, and his platoon? When last seen they'd been in the open, three or four hundred yards from Adam and under fire from several directions. Where were they now? And, come to that, where was his company commander, Ben Jameson? And what was the next thing to do? He, Adam, had decided to switch from the objective given him; had taken, with his platoon, a farm which he'd thought had been holding up their advance; had found it deserted, after an initial clash in which he'd lost one man and killed four: and was now out of touch with everybody, including the enemy. He supposed that, with Droot Farm now in British hands, he should pick up the platoon and advance again towards the original objective – the battalion, after all, had been ordered to drive the Germans back across the river and so far he, Adam Hardrow, hadn't contributed very greatly to that object. It was perfectly possible that at any moment Ben Jameson would appear and in his easy, deadly way inquire what the hell he thought he was doing, and was his little private battle sufficiently concluded for him to rejoin the British army and the war? Adam could imagine.

'Right, Sergeant Pew –' They were standing in the main farmyard, men showing some signs of relaxing, signs which Adam instinctively recognized as potentially dangerous. But at that moment things happened. Sergeant Pew, in a perfectly normal low voice, sounding exactly as if he was in barracks, said, 'The company commander, sir,' and Adam, looking up, saw Ben Jameson walking across the farmyard towards him. And, simultaneously, the Germans started to shell Droot Farm very heavily.

CHAPTER 8

They found themselves crouched in one of the farm outbuildings. Adam never remembered consciously selecting it or moving to it, but suddenly he, Ben Jameson, Sergeant Pew and Private Bliss were huddled together in a corner, grateful for the brick walls and all very aware that the slate roof was flimsy and that its construction looked ramshackle. Whine, thump, crack, pain in ear-drums, drifting smoky smell of explosive, here comes another, whine, thump, crack, and another, whine, thump, crack. A shower of brick dust and flaking mortar. Whine, thump, crack.

Then – 'Keep down, there's nothing you can do till this is over.' It was Ben's shouting voice to Adam. 'Christ!' Several, following each other in continuous sequence, whine, crack, whine, crack. Smoke and dust everywhere, swelling through the open doorway into their constricted, illusory sanctuary. Now another sound, separable from the shell bursts. A crackling. Fire! Then more whine, crack, whine, crack, whine, crack. Some shouts and what sounded like a series of screams. Whine, crack, whine, crack, crack, crack.

Then Ben's voice – 'Over for a little, perhaps,' and Adam darting through the door to discover what, if anything, of 5 Platoon had survived. His company commander's future intentions and plans, rebukes or commendations, could wait. How many were hit, and how hard?

*

They had, all of them, got under cover of some sort and casualties were small. Two of the men who had once been in Sergeant-Major Merrow's platoon were wounded, one severely as far as Adam could see; he was already grey in the face and had a hand to the stomach. It was, Adam thought, probably he who had uttered the screams of pain which had cut the air a minute ago, but now he was silent, face drawn, eyes open and resigned. Sergeant Pew, following Adam faithfully, disappeared for a half minute and returned with two of the company stretcher-bearers. Ben Jameson, bringing up his little tail of spare bren-gunners, had stretcher-bearer teams under his own hand, and one of them was now with the wounded man, morphine at the ready. Adam, to his shame, couldn't immediately recall the man's name but Sergeant Pew said, 'Griffiths,' adding without expression, 'Doesn't look as if he'll last long.' The other wounded man, unlike Griffiths, had blood pouring down his face, but was cut only superficially, as was obvious. He was surrounded by several friends, uttering facetious remarks about his gory appearance – this was a characteristic of the Westmorlands which Adam noted often. They treated injury as a subject for mirth, unless it was clearly fatal, and the mirth – involving a certain release from the immediate fear of death – was often loudest when uttered by the sufferer's closest intimates.

Only Wright was dead. Wright had been in the open when the first shell had fallen in the middle of the farm's main yard and the blast had thrown him back against the yard's wall, where he lay crumpled, on his back, one leg drawn up. There a splinter of casing had found his throat and caught the jugular with a violence which at first sight seemed almost to have decapitated him. There was nothing at all to be done for Wright. Adam was becoming inured to the sights of death and injury but Wright's poor body still had power to shock. Adam knew that in the mind of Sergeant Pew, as in his own, the first thought was that Wilkins, if Wilkins was alive, would take this hard, would need looking after. Meanwhile there was work to be done. There'd been crackling. Where was the fire?

Providentially, the roof of a byre which had caught and was burning merrily was near the largest water trough on the farm, and Corporal Egan had already organized several men with buckets who appeared to be slowly winning their battle against the flames. Sergeant Pew had again disappeared, and when he returned he thought Adam was looking unusually distraught. Mr Hardrow's always got himself in hand, Sergeant Pew had often observed to himself, he always knows what he's on, does Mr Hardrow. On this occasion Mr Hardrow had not got himself in hand. He'd appreciated, with a sense of criminal folly at not doing so earlier, that the shelling of Droot Farm would almost certainly be quickly followed by a German counter-attack. And while he'd been standing, smug, pleased with himself at having got into the place, and had then been diving, bent only on self-preservation, into a cowshed for a scrap of cover, the Germans were probably already doubling across the fields between farm and river, about to follow up this bloody shelling, steel helmets bobbing and weaving, Schmeisers and Spandaus levelled, stick grenades at the ready! And what the hell was he doing? As far as he knew he'd not even got sentries looking out.

'Sergeant Pew!' A shout, a peremptory gesture, and Adam ran towards the east side of the farm, the side occupied a few minutes ago by Corporal Travers and his section. There, not for the last time, he discovered that others beside himself could think and react. Could even, sometimes, be trusted. Could show that it wasn't only the nominal commander who had the best ideas. It wasn't only the bloody officers who had minds! Corporal Travers was moving, slowly and deliberately, from man to man, from bren-gunners to riflemen. They were spread out, on corners of buildings and behind walls. He grinned at Adam as he saluted.

'Reckoned after that little lot Jerry might have a go at us, sir. I've got the lads down, there's Bennett can see as far as the clump of trees there from where he is –'

'Corporal Travers, have you had anyone hit?'

'No, sir, it was all farther over, near the yard. Nothing within thirty yards of here. Made a hell of a row, some of 'em thought their last hour had come!' Corporal Travers was still grinning. He was anxious to show Adam the skill of his dispositions.

'There's Crowe up that little stone stair, sir, he can see over to the right, like, to where Mr Brett's platoon was –'

Where Mr Brett's platoon was! Where was Jack Brett now? Where was the rest of B Company? And what was the immediate purpose of 5 Platoon? To defend Droot Farm against counter-attack? To resume (God forbid) the advance to the original objective? To – what? For the first time in five minutes Adam remembered that his company commander was also in Droot Farm. Saying, 'Well done, Corporal Travers,' aware that his bacon had been saved by his subordinates, he ran back towards where he had very recently been cowering, expecting death each second. He called to Sergeant Pew to see that the other two sections were in fire positions facing, roughly, north and south on the farm's perimeter; and to indicate that he was about to report to the company commander, he'd come on round in two minutes. And he uttered a fervent prayer that those two minutes would pass free from further shelling.

Ben Jameson was standing by the shed in which they'd recently huddled. He had lit a cigarette and was chatting to Company Sergeant-Major Darwin of whom Adam had been unaware until that moment, but who had been following Ben, with Ben's signaller, stretcher-bearers and spare bren-gunners firmly under his own hand. Ben looked as if he hadn't a care in the world. Adam saluted. He was out of breath.

'Corporal Travers's section is covering the east flank, sir.

If they come from that direction we'll get several minutes' warning.'

'I'm sure we will. I'm sure we will.' Ben looked as if he naturally expected his subordinates to do what was required, and sensibly. He gave an impression of being unconcerned by events, and Adam felt a fleeting sense of anticlimax. Weren't they in the middle of a battle?

'I didn't continue the advance, sir,' he said, 'because I saw that they were in the farm here, and that Jack's platoon was catching it. So I reckoned we'd have to clear them out of it, and I turned to do that, or try to –'

'And succeeded. Adam, I'd seen exactly that at the same time. I told battalion headquarters that B Company couldn't advance till we'd cleared Droot Farm, and that I intended to do just that. You were the only platoon who could do so. Poor old 6 Platoon were very cut up. They're mostly back now, the ones who'll get back. I'm afraid a good many are lying out there, wounded. We've got – how many have we got back, Sergeant-Major?'

'Thirteen, sir.'

Ben said, without emphasis, that the thirteen were 'a bit shaken' but were all right, back at the company base he'd established before moving forward.

'So B Company has got those thirteen, my little reserve here, and your lot. Who've you lost, Adam?'

'Three. All from the shelling. We got across the open without losing anyone.'

'Is that cut all right?' Ben nodded towards Adam's forehead.

'Perfectly all right.'

'Now we'll go round the farm together, Adam. Sergeant-Major, you hang on here, with the stretcher-bearers. Company headquarters, in fact.' Adam saw the aerial of Ben's man-packed wireless set – as far as Adam knew these wireless sets had only been issued to a limited number of battalions.

The Westmorlands were lucky, although there was a good deal of scepticism about their effectiveness; from Ben's account of having told battalion headquarters of the situation, however, it sounded as if the wireless had actually worked, at least recently.

As they walked fast towards Corporal Barney's section, Ben, his tone conversational, said, 'Well, as you see, you anticipated my orders, my dear boy! You cleared the Huns out of this place! Well done!'

Adam felt a glow. He reckoned that he'd been lucky – very lucky. The platoon had done well, the NCOs had acted sensibly. He'd been in control sometimes, not always. He'd been uncertain as to whether his decision to break off the advance, turn and fight a little battle of his own had been right – now Ben said that it had indeed been right, it had been what Ben was himself proposing, somehow, to do. And then he'd allowed personal fear to distract him from his duty of being ready for a German counter-attack; but, a tiny voice whispered, I suppose Ben's personal fear was distracting him too! A remarkable thought! Was occasional inadequacy not confined to Adam Hardrow?

He said, 'Is Jack all right?'

'Jack was killed.'

'Oh!'

Jack Brett. Jack whom he'd perhaps bullied a little when he'd first joined the company, Jack who'd needed from Adam a demonstration of what were and were not the responsibilities of an officer, Jack who'd been shown the seniority and superior knowledge of Second-Lieutenant Hardrow, and no mistake. Jack who had not hesitated to join the army before his time came, who was full of good will and decency and sense of duty. Unselfconfident Jack, now gone.

Ben was saying, 'He did perfectly well, poor old Jack, it was my fault for not insisting that we took this farm as a first phase of the attack. Entirely my fault.' His voice was calm but

Adam glanced at him and thought he saw a new and different Ben Jameson. Ben was accusing himself. Ben reckoned he'd lost Jack Brett and twenty men. Ben was in hell.

Adam said, 'I suppose they're bound to attack. The Jerries.'

'Not necessarily. What you don't know is that our own attack, the brigade attack, is off.'

'But it's hardly started.'

'Quite. New orders. We're withdrawing. The whole division, I mean.'

'So –'

'In fact, the whole army. Those who haven't withdrawn already – some of them rather faster than the powers-that-be intended. We – the battalion – have got to break off this business and get back behind Koreyck. Ivan will hold Koreyck with A Company until everyone else is back. Then he'll get out. Some armoured cars are going to see Ivan safely out. That's the idea.'

'So we, here –'

'Go back. But we can't do that very easily if the Huns are actually at our throats! I want to go back by stages to Koreyck itself, where Ivan's not been attacked, as far as I can see. Then on back to where I've got what's left of 6 Platoon. Then march back, together, to where we reckon there ought to be transport. Whisky's in Koreyck, he's set up battalion headquarters there.' Ben, his composure restored, spoke briefly and decisively about how they'd go back to Koreyck, who first, who following, who covering at each stage. Provided the Germans didn't first attack Droot Farm. Then he said, 'The reason they *might* not attack us is that, as far as I can make out, the Huns are almost round us already, and might want to keep us here rather than pushing us back. They're attacking all along the southern flank, the right flank, you see – as far as the Channel; attacking northward. And now the news from the left is also bad, I gather.'

'The Belgians –'

'The Belgians,' said Ben, 'have packed it in. Or are about to. That's the rumour.'

And then he told Adam that the British Expeditionary Force was to move back to a series of positions covering Dunkirk. Dunkirk was the only port of resupply or reinforcement. Dunkirk was the only port which might be used for escape. And back to the next of these positions, on a canal line of which Adam had never heard, the Westmorlands (having extricated themselves from the nasty situation to which they'd recently been committed) were next to withdraw.

Then Adam had a sensation of Ben Jameson taking over control so intimately that events didn't thereafter stick in his mind as vividly as the course of the morning until now would always do. He remembered afterwards Ben saying, 'Right, we'll divide this lot, all of them, into two parties. I'll keep Sergeant Pew, Corporal Travers and Corporal Barney with their sections and my spare gunners, that gives us something to hit with. You, the sergeant-major, Corporal Egan, the wounded will go back first. You'll go to that belt of trees –' he pointed. The belt of trees was just over half-way back to Koreyck, about six hundred yards, 'and you'll get in position there and stay there till I bring this lot through you. Then I'll leave a few men behind to thicken the position at the tree belt –' He made it all clear, simple, commonsensical.

'When shall I go?'

'Whisky wants B Company back as soon as we can make it.'

'So – ?'

'Let's have a look round. If the Huns are attacking you'll have to stay. God knows who does what then, but you'll have to stay. I'm not having you caught in the open. If they come in I'm going to meet them from here, and chuck everything we can at them.'

'Ben,' said Adam, feeling suddenly so close to him that any

213

other address would have jarred, 'Ben, what about the gunners? What about some defensive fire in front of the farm? Is that –' It wasn't his job, it was the company commander's job, the battalion commander's job, their supporting artillery commander's job to think like that, but Adam felt that they were all naked. It had to be said. Ben observed in a matter-of-fact voice, 'Quite so. When I last spoke to Whisky it was made abundantly clear to me that the gun ammunition will only run to priority tasks. And that defending Droot Farm against counter-attack is not a priority task.'

'I see.'

'Nor, incidentally, would taking it have been a priority task. There's only one priority task now. To get away.'

Droot Farm was not immediately attacked again. Guns were rumbling both to north and south all the time but not particularly near. The Westmorlands were lucky – or perhaps, Adam reflected, Ben's speculation was right and they were unmolested to the front because they were about to be surrounded. Whatever the reason, Adam got his part of the residue of B Company back without incident as far as the belt of trees, got them down in fire positions, waited there until Ben and Sergeant Pew and Corporal Travers and Corporal Barney and the rest came back, moving in small groups, moving without particular haste as far as appeared. And at the line of trees Adam heard Ben rap out the next order in his quiet, incisive voice. Everybody but two bren-gun teams, one pair of stretcher-bearers and Private Bliss to go back to Koreyck with Mr Hardrow and the sergeant-major.

Bliss to remain. That meant Ben had decided not to go back through Adam's position but to remain himself. Perhaps one thousand yards of a narrow dirt track looked as if it ran straight to the nearest house of Koreyck. From Droot Farm, six hundred yards away, no sound.

'Right, Adam, and you, Sergeant-Major. Off you go.'

'I thought that you –'

'Did you hear me, Mr Hardrow?'

Adam said, 'Yes, sir.' Ben's face wore the familiar half-smile which sometimes accompanied his sudden bleak demonstrations of authority; a half-smile which could soften rebuke, or sometimes intensify the sting.

Now Ben said, 'I'll come back fast once you're out of range of the farm but I want to be able to sharpen 'em up if they come forward while you're moving. Anyway at first.'

'Is there any sign of them being in Droot? I've seen nothing.'

Ben said briefly, 'They must be.' Adam quickly and quietly organized the move back to Koreyck. He brought up the rear, accompanying Corporal Travers's section, keeping Ben's wireless set and signaller with him.

'Are we through to battalion, Rogers?'

'Yes, sir.' And at that moment Adam heard what was certainly Bobby Forrest's voice give B Company call sign and ask how they were getting on. 'Answer,' he said to Rogers as they trudged along, 'that most of the company will be back in ten minutes.'

A minute later he heard Rogers acknowledging and asking control to wait.

'It's the second-in-command, sir. He wants to speak to the company commander.'

'I'll take it.' Using the obscure codewords and soubriquets which passed for secure speech, Adam said that the company commander was still in position covering the withdrawal of part of the company, a part which was now only about five hundred yards from Koreyck. He heard Whisky Wainwright's voice, careless of correct wireless procedure, say 'Right. Right,' in a thoughtful sort of way. Whisky's voice heartened Adam none the less.

He had covered another hundred yards when he heard the

unmistakable sighing sound of approaching shells followed by five or six equally unmistakable cracks behind them. Looking round Adam saw earth leaping from the line of trees he'd just left, the line of trees where Ben, presumably, was still in position. At the same time came the sound of distant machine-gun fire. It sounded as if it were from Droot Farm. Then came another two or three bursts, ripping the air with the peculiar urgency of Spandau fire. Corporal Travers yelled, 'Down!'

'No, Corporal Travers, get 'em up! Up and double! Double everyone! Double!' The company sergeant-major took up the shout. He was leading Adam's party, was nearest Koreyck.

'Double everybody! Flat out!'

By now they were a thousand yards from Droot Farm and, wherever the Germans were firing from, Adam reckoned that they were probably out of Spandau range. Nevertheless the sooner they got back to Koreyck now the better. If this was running away it might as well be as fast as possible.

'Double everyone! Come on Rogers!' Rogers, the heavy wireless set on his back, was straining and sobbing with the exertion. He needed no encouragement – Rogers was no hero and the Spandaus behind had sounded to his ears with particular menace; but the set was strapped to him and it was heavy. There was no time, however, for faint hearts or bodies.

'Get a move on, Rogers!'

Adam doubled steadily behind the others. He heard now, they all heard, the drumming sound of British bren-gun fire from the line of trees they'd just abandoned. Ben was keeping up near-continuous fire. Droot Farm's at extreme range from Ben, Adam thought as he pounded along. Six more shells fell somewhere behind him.

Droot Farm's at extreme range from the line of trees. Maybe the Jerries are advancing from Droot, coming straight on, realize there's next to nothing in front of them? That last Spandau certainly sounded nearer than Droot! Adam paused, and realized what an appalling stitch he had. He turned his head.

Six more shells – four, five, six spurts of earth. On the line of poplar trees. They'd got the range. And then one, two, three, four, five bursts from Spandaus – two, three Spandaus? Sounding not much further than the line of trees itself. Closing on Ben Jameson's position, which was being held long enough to enable Adam and the rest of them to get clear out of it.

'Get a move on, Corporal Travers, get 'em all going! Only two hundred yards to cover! Then through the houses and collect up –'

Sergeant Pew had paused. Sergeant Pew had remained with Ben at Droot Farm, but had then been ordered on by Ben. As ever, thank God for him!

'Are you all right, sir?'

Adam was doubled up with his stitch. His face was still blood-streaked from the morning's cut, was covered with dirt and was anyway dark from the long days beneath the unusually hot Flanders sun. Only his ancient scar still showed white against the blood, the tan, the grime. Sergeant Pew's face, bronzed, with its small, invariably neat moustache, and rather hooked nose, showed a measure of quiet concern. Mr Hardrow was only a lad, after all, it was easy to forget it. Very easy.

'All right, sir?'

'Of course I'm all right. The sergeant-major's going to collect 'em all up somewhere in Koreyck – I don't know where –'

Adam was gasping. Bloody stitch! The incongruity of it in the middle of battle infuriated him.

'Double on, Sergeant Pew. I'll see you there.'

Rogers, emitting little moaning sounds, was shambling forward with his wireless set. Another three bursts of Spandau fire sounded behind them – no nearer, Adam thought.

This time it was answered by only one bren-gun. So Ben's still there. Ben's still holding that line of trees. Adam stopped and turned. The relief was immense, and he reckoned that for a moment he'd prefer to risk death from a German Spandau than run another yard. They'd only a hundred yards to cover now. Men were melting into Koreyck in front of him. Behind him the line of trees was, he knew, nine hundred yards away. It looked nearer.

No more firing. No more shells.

Adam, ignoring his own orders, walked slowly back towards Koreyck. The road had been running between fields of high, standing corn, and beside the road was a deep ditch, with only a trickle of water in it. He could, he thought without shame, leap into it if the whine of a German shell sounded uncomfortably close – Adam had already concluded that self-preservation was a duty in war, provided that it didn't conflict with other duties, of course. Ears cocked, he stepped out. Then he turned again and brought his binoculars up.

To his joy he saw the unmistakable shapes of several men, soldiers from Ben Jameson's party, perhaps Ben himself, walking back down the road. So they'd left the line of trees, they'd not been overrun! Ben had answered the German fire from Droot Farm, had perhaps checked the German advance from Droot Farm, had made the enemy pause, had probably contrived to give an impression of more strength than he had. And had then slipped away. Adam focused his binoculars again. Yes, there was no doubt, some of them were now running! And thank God for it! They were only about five, six hundred yards behind him and they were running! He stood watching them, hating the fact that he could do nothing to help them. He himself was now only a hundred yards or so, a half minute at most, from the friendly houses of Koreyck where Ivan Perry's men of A Company must be watching, in fire positions, ready to take on any Germans who pushed forward from the line of trees.

If they'd reached the line of trees.

Adam brought up his binoculars again. The B Company men were still running. He tried to count. As far as he could guess most of them were there. Ben would have left one bren-gun team to the last, probably fired off a magazine to show an illusory strength to the Jerries and then out! And now they were doubling back, all together, to rejoin Adam's party and the residue of B Company. Not forgetting the 'shaken' thirteen from poor Jack Brett's platoon, who'd been resting somewhere behind Koreyck. Soon they'd all be together again. And at that moment Adam instinctively dropped to the ground as a burst of Spandau fire sounded, unmistakably, from the line of trees itself, and dust spurted from the track on which he'd been standing, down which Ben Jameson's party had been running. Half in the ditch Adam cautiously raised his head and again brought his binoculars up. Of the Westmorlands, of the B Company men doubling along behind him he could now see no sign.

The first man Adam saw in Koreyck was Whisky Wainwright.

Whisky was standing in the middle of the main street.

Koreyck, like many small towns or large villages in Flanders, consisted of a long single street of modern houses off which ran short culs-de-sac, and which broadened into a small *place* at the town's centre. The street ran east and west, and B Company's withdrawal took the men along this main street, from the east towards the *place*. The houses on the edge of town were occupied by A Company's men and were mostly undistinguished single-storey buildings. Adam remembered that in a similar village poor Jack Brett had said, 'Pretty ugly, aren't they! Modern and characterless, these Flemish villages hereabouts,' and Adam, perhaps priggishly, had said that it was unsurprising, they'd been utterly destroyed only twenty-five years ago. And only recently rebuilt by the poor devils now cowering in them or fleeing from them once again.

Whisky was standing in the central artery of Koreyck about one hundred yards from the first house on the east side. He looked more than ever like a bull or buffalo, hirsute, massive and immovable; and possibly dangerous if roused. His first words to Adam were, 'Where's Ben?'

Adam saluted. Whisky looked at him thoughtfully. He saw a strong, confident young man; probably more confident as well as stronger than he himself understood. Whisky had seen a number of failures in the last week and he liked, as he had always liked, the impression made by Adam Hardrow. In spite of the blood on his face he was obviously all right. You could tell his nerve was sound from the way he walked and the expression in his eyes as he saluted. And, by God, a few like this were needed! The battalion was very, very short.

'Where's Ben?'

Adam told him. Ben had ordered back pretty well everybody, staying at a belt of trees about nine hundred yards to the east with a party of bren-gunners until sure that the Germans weren't in hot pursuit.

'He wanted to give us a good start back, sir. Then I saw him – I saw a party, I presume Captain Jameson was in it – start back from the belt of trees. I was nearly here by that time and well out of range of Germans in Droot Farm.'

'See anything else?'

'A Spandau started up then, sir. I think it was from the belt or near it. Firing down the road we'd come down, the road Captain Jameson was on. And there was some shelling. I think they must have dropped into the ditch – there was a good ditch beside the road.'

Whisky established that Ben's covering party must have been about four hundred yards from Koreyck when they came under fire.

'They'll make what distance they can,' Whisky said, 'in

220

between stonks. They'll crawl up the ditch. It's a long time before dark, and –'

He grunted. Adam supposed he'd been about to say that the battalion had to get back, give up Koreyck, withdraw to another position, long before then. No question of hanging about for a small detachment from B Company. No question of waiting for Ben Jameson.

'I'm sure they'll make it, sir. The odds are that even if they run straight down the road they'd get away with it.'

'Probably,' Whisky said gruffly. 'Probably.' He was at that moment joined by Ivan Perry. Adam's eyes caught Ivan's and Ivan smiled with a look which conveyed what Adam was to find one of the most enduring impressions of war – the enormous joy brought by unexpected encounter with a friend. He smiled back at Ivan. For a moment both were radiant. Ivan was reporting to Whisky that his look-outs covering the east flank, watching the direction from which B Company had withdrawn, could see no signs of a German advance but there was, of course, high corn obscuring vision from about two hundred yards out. The latest Spandau firing seemed, as Adam had presumed, to have come from the belt of trees recently manned by Ben Jameson and his stalwarts. No grey-green uniforms had been seen this side of the trees since. But Ivan's man had seen what Adam had seen – the small party of Westmorlands, individuals unidentifiable, running; and then the Spandaus and the German artillery had opened up and there was no movement thereafter.

Whisky said, 'They'll turn up.' Then he said, 'You'll be collecting all of B Company here. I'll see you again, say in half an hour, Adam. Let me know exactly what B Company consists of, and then I'll go through the timings with you. The others know them. The withdrawal timings.' He turned away and moved towards the *place*, his orderly trotting at his heels. Ivan told Adam that Whisky's headquarters were in the town hall.

'The *mairie*. Well, I'd better track down the others of B Company.'

'They don't call it "*mairie*",' said Ivan. He seemed his old self. 'They don't like speaking French. Very Flemish.'

'I see.' Adam saw, with relief, Company Sergeant-Major Darwin hovering near by. Darwin approached and saluted. He said that he'd got all of B Company except the nine men with Captain Jameson, in a warehouse just off the *place*.

'And then there's the rest of Mr Brett's platoon, isn't there, Sergeant-Major?'

'No, they're here too, sir. Second-in-command ordered them up early this afternoon. Wanted everyone up here. Reckoned Jerries might have a go at this place, apparently. Wanted to strengthen A Company.'

'Well, I suppose they still might.'

'Yes, sir. And we might have gone before.'

'Sergeant-Major,' Adam said, 'we've still to get Captain Jameson.'

'Yes, sir.' There was something in Adam's voice which decided Sergeant-Major Darwin to say no more for the moment about the imminent evacuation of Koreyck. He told Adam that the residue of 6 Platoon were more or less all right. A bit jumpy, like. And then there were the stragglers from other units whom Whisky had rounded up in the assembly area, before the advance. The sergeant-major grinned.

'Major Wainwright had them up too, sir. The lot. They're in B Company now.'

'They looked useless.'

'No, they're not bad, sir,' said Sergeant-Major Darwin unexpectedly. 'Not bad, most of them. We've sorted 'em out. They've had some scoff off the company cooker. Sergeant Phipps has got their names.' Phipps had been Jack's platoon sergeant. A survivor.

'No discipline, that's the trouble, sir,' said Darwin.

'I dare say.'

'Go to pieces if there's no discipline. Stands to reason.'

'Yes.'

'I've had a word with them. Quite a chance they'll be all right now, sir. Or not too bad anyway. They just needed sense talking to them. Firm but friendly.'

'Good,' said Adam. He suddenly felt immensely tired. And at that moment Sergeant-Major Darwin, looking across the street beyond Adam said, under his breath, 'For crying out loud –'

Adam spun round.

'Good God! *Bliss!*'

Bliss was covered in mud from head to foot, unrecognizable. He was walking slowly and with what looked like a sort of dazed exhaustion. Behind him were four or five other Westmorlands. All, Adam saw at once, from B Company. Ben's party. Ben's bren-gunners. Ben's stretcher-bearers.

'Bliss!'

Bliss looked as if he could hear little and understand less. Sergeant-Major Darwin knew instinctively that it was a moment for quietness, for gentle handling.

'All here, Bliss? Any lads hurt?'

Bliss, talking with a lot of hesitation, stuttering a good deal in a way Adam could not recall him ever doing before, said that Wickens and Smith had copped it when the first shells fell, when they were about half-way. Half-way from the trees to this place. We all jumped into the ditch, said Bliss, and Wickens and Dusty Smith copped it. One shell seemed to – to –

Bliss shook his head, looking miserable. Adam felt sure that the shell had blown Smith and Wickens into small pieces and that Bliss had not been far away. Smith and Wickens were the stretcher-bearers. Sergeant-Major Darwin said softly,

'And the captain, Bliss?' Seeing the talk going on the other men had slumped down on the pavement, backs against the walls of houses, cigarettes handed round. They weren't talking.

Bliss said, 'The Spandau got Captain Jameson. In the leg. Left leg it were. He dropped into the ditch beside me. He told me to get on, to stick with the others, he'd be all right.'

'How badly was he hit?'

'It were his leg, sir. I couldn't say how bad. But he couldn't walk, nor stand. Nor crawl, neither. The rest of us were crawling. If we stood up to walk the f—ing Spandaus –'

'Quite. So Captain Jameson's wounded in the ditch.'

'Yes, sir.'

'And you couldn't carry him.'

It was painfully clear that this thought was plaguing Bliss, and had been plaguing him throughout his agonizing crawl back up the ditch to Koreyck, and all the time since emerging from it. Bliss was very attached to Ben Jameson. He avoided Adam's eye and said, 'The captain told me to get on out, see?' There was no 'sir', no subordination. He was angry, miserable and quite unnecessarily ashamed. Adam turned away. He heard Sergeant-Major Darwin quietly collecting the men, cracking a joke here, imparting a bit of news there. He was telling them about the collecting point in the warehouse by the *place*. There'd be tea.

Adam found Ivan suddenly by his side. It seemed providential. Ivan was exactly the man he needed.

'Ivan, did you hear any of that?'

'Any of what?'

'Ben's wounded in the ditch by the lane running from here eastward. The one I've just doubled back along. He's not far away, perhaps three hundred yards. He can't walk.'

'I see.'

'Ivan, I'm going out for him. Ben's quite light, although he's tall.'

'You can't go alone, Adam. And it's not your job. Frankly.'

'I'm going, and I'm going alone.'

Ivan stared at him. He said 'And B Company? You're their only surviving officer, I seem to recall.'

Adam had thought of this. He said, 'I know. And Whisky's bound to merge them with another company. And there's the company sergeant-major still, and Sergeants Pew and Phipps. B Company's all right. Anyway, I'm going. I'm going up the ditch. And I can lug Ben back all right, after giving him a splint or something. Stretcher-bearers could only use the road, and the road's murder. They've got Spandaus firing down it. And there's not much time. The Jerries are bound to come at us here soon.'

'There's a troop of armoured cars due to cover us out of here –'

'Well, they're not here yet, are they? Ivan, I'm due to report to Whisky in,' he glanced at his watch, 'twenty minutes. He's going to give me the withdrawal timings.'

'We're all going to be clear by five o'clock, I can tell you that. No doubt Whisky will elaborate.'

It was already half-past three in the afternoon. The day had fled.

'Ivan, please do two things for me.'

'Well?'

'First, send a man to find Sergeant-Major Darwin, and ask him from me to report B Company state to the second-in-command at three forty-five; to explain I'm –'

'Otherwise engaged.'

'– or something. And take the orders.'

'What you want,' Ivan Perry observed, 'is really to send a message to your sergeant-major to take command of B Company, because you've decided to lay down your responsibilities and indulge in some personal heroics instead. OK, what's the second thing?'

'Keep a strong look-out, fire positions and so forth, straight down that road. And if the Jerries come up it while I'm in the ditch –'

'Try to frighten them off. My dear Adam, I think it would be our job to engage them anyway, wouldn't it? Regardless of two gallant friends cavorting in a ditch in no man's land! Or has my tactical flair, never very pronounced, deserted me once again?' But yes, Ivan said, of course they'd cover him as well as they possibly could. He squeezed Adam's upper arm and they parted. One day he'd get the father and mother of a rocket from Whisky Wainwright for conniving in this enterprise.

The first two hundred yards were the worst. The ditch then became very deep, the banks high, and it was possible to stand, stooping. But the first stage had involved continuous crawling, and often Adam had said to himself that the Germans couldn't be alert all the time on a warm afternoon, the belt of trees was anyway at extreme Spandau range, why the hell not get up out of the ditch on to the road and run? But something in his mind whispered that perhaps, perhaps, the Germans were nearer, had advanced from the line of trees by now. Towards Koreyck. There'd been no fire from Koreyck to indicate grounds for this suspicion but it was hard for the defenders of Koreyck to see, the standing corn made concealment easy. Anyway, A Company wouldn't open up until the Germans were within range, would they? Which, Adam supposed as he moved slowly along the ditch, must be somewhere near where I am now. He reckoned he'd covered three hundred yards from Ivan Perry's most easterly positions.

Then, hearing before seeing, there came a voice. From the ditch in front. Faint. Clear. Familiar.

'Who's that?'

'Ben,' said Adam in his normal speaking voice. 'It's me. Adam.'

'What the hell are you doing here?'

'I've come to help you back, Ben. Everything's fine. Everybody's got back to Koreyck. And the battalion's clearing out of it in one hour from now. Covered by some armoured cars.'

Ben was breathing very heavily. Adam, stooping, came up to him. Ben was sitting in the ditch at an angle, his back against the bank on the road side, his body twisted. Adam could see the dark blood staining his left battledress trouser. The leg was extended straight forward and looked as if it were detached from the rest of Ben. Ben's face was very pale beneath the sunburn, Adam could see that clearly. He said, 'I've got a morphine squirt, Ben.' He'd taken it from Bliss who, by Ben's order and in addition to the stretcher-bearers, was always so equipped. Not waiting for Ben's nod, he crawled up until his body was close to Ben's and applied the morphine. Ben's sleeve was open, his flesh pale and unresistant.

'Ben, you obviously can't walk –'

'Nor stand, I'm afraid,' said Ben softly. They were both looking at the leg. Adam had spoken earlier of a possible splint but in the haste to get back to Ben he'd not brought anything that would do. It would, anyway, be a job likely to be beyond his rudimentary first-aid capability, a likelihood confirmed by Ben observing in a calm voice, 'They got me pretty high up. Thigh. And lower down as well. Leg's smashed. The buggers.'

'I can carry you, Ben, but it'll have to be up the ditch. We'd be sitting ducks on the road.'

'How do you propose to carry my dead weight up a ditch?'

'That'll be all right,' said Adam. He felt no confidence at all, but Ben was a slightly built man, light for his inches. And Adam was strong.

'It'll be all right. I can get you over my shoulder for the first bit – the ditch's pretty deep. But the last bit's rather

227

shallow. The last two hundred yards. I had to crawl. What we'll do is this. We'll –'

'Adam,' said Ben softly, 'I think it's hopeless.'

'No it's not. Are you still bleeding?'

'Doubt it.' The morphine was taking effect and Ben's voice had less edge. 'Doubt it,' he said. 'Can't really feel much now. Leg doesn't do what I tell it.'

'Of course not. Now listen, Ben. When we have to crawl I'm going to put these under your shoulders –' Adam had taken off two webbing straps from his equipment. Pouches would have to be abandoned.

'– and tie them round my body. And then I can crawl and carry you along. And keep both of us down and out of sight. It won't be far. The alternative will be to get you out of the ditch and hump you down the road –'

'Through the corn, what about that?' Ben muttered.

'No, there's no corn, no cover on the last stretch. It's completely open, it's a crawl or nothing.'

'Adam –'

'Yes?'

'You'd better leave me. I'll be all right. Jerries will look after me.'

'Damned if I do. Come on.'

The first hundred and fifty yards were as exhausting as any physical effort Adam ever remembered. Ben's body was heavier than he'd anticipated. Adam got him over the shoulder in a fireman's lift, and although Ben yelped with pain despite the morphine, Adam managed to move along the ditch, bent almost double, for about seventy yards.

'Ben, I'm going to put you down. I've got to straighten and rest.'

Ben seemed not to have heard. As gently as he could, Adam eased him to the bottom of the ditch and cautiously straightened his aching limbs. The ditch was about four feet below the level of the road and by stooping Adam could still remain concealed. He didn't want to waste a minute, but he thought it prudent to push his head and shoulders up a little, to the point where he could just squint between tufts of grass on the road's edge, on the ditch's border.

He saw he was very near the edge of the corn – in a few more yards the road ran towards Koreyck through open meadows. Then he squinted back down the road and his heart seemed to stop.

Moving up the road, in single file each side of it, were German soldiers. They were moving without effort at concealment, slowly but confidently. Adam's binoculars had been left with Ivan Perry but there was no mistaking those helmets. They were, he judged, about half-way between the belt of trees once defiantly held by Ben Jameson and the point where he, Adam Hardrow, now crouched in a ditch with Ben Jameson's smashed body. Say two hundred yards. At most. Perhaps three minutes.

Unless they came under fire. When, oh when would they come under fire? When, oh when would the bren-gunners and riflemen of A Company open up on these arrogant Huns, strutting down the open road as if they hardly recognized the necessity of caution in the face of so trivial a foe?

He knew the answer, of course. Ivan – and it was more than possible that Whisky was with him, watching – would open fire when the enemy was nicely within range, not before. Ivan, Whisky, would appreciate that at any moment the Germans would themselves bring down artillery fire on Koreyck, but possibly not until satisfied it was occupied by their opponents. A Company would try to produce devastating fire at as close range as possible. They would not, they would certainly not, open at extreme range, driving the Germans into concealment in the corn, bringing artillery retaliation upon themselves and failing to score the small tactical victory which might come from catching a German company, at short range, in the open.

But Adam, with a queasiness he recognized angrily as funk, knew that whatever Ivan's or Whisky Wainwright's judgement of range shellfire couldn't be long delayed. The British army might be desperately short of artillery ammunition but there must be at least some for defensive fire in front of a battalion main position. And surely Koreyck was that? In which case, at any moment now, there would be the comforting whistle and sigh and crump of British shells bursting among these Huns as they strolled so confidently towards the Westmorlands. But the comfort was undoubtedly diminished by the fact that Adam Hardrow and Ben Jameson were in a ditch somewhere about where the British artillery target ought to be. One minute, Adam thought, and the Jerries will be all around us. Probably jumping into this ditch with us when our own shelling starts. Oh God! Oh God!

'Ben!'

It was unclear whether Ben had fainted. His eyes were closed. Adam settled the webbing straps under Ben's shoulders and tied them round himself with trembling fingers. Ben's eyes now opened.

'Ben, the Jerries are coming, they must be about to attack Koreyck. Any minute now they'll be all around us here, and our own fire is bound to open up. There's nothing to do but crawl. Off we go!'

Ben's mouth was open as if to expostulate, but all he managed was a small cry of pain as Adam heaved himself forward, crawling on hands and knees, taking the weight of Ben's body dragging beneath him, lifting himself, driving his own limbs forward, dragging Ben forward. Yard by yard. Sweat poured down his face and dropped on to Ben's. Adam stopped every few yards, heart pounding, muscles agony. Ben's eyes were closed again and he moaned slightly but softly as they moved forward as if joined in a grotesque embrace. The ditch was only three foot deep at this point,

Adam knew. And now, surely, there were German grey-green uniforms within yards of them? Moving the same way? Moving, perhaps, more cautiously now; wondering whether this small Belgian place in front was occupied – or deserted, as so many had been on the Wehrmacht's triumphant advance.

But after a fight at Droot Farm, Adam's mind painfully told him, and after a bit of a fire fight at the belt of trees they can't, they simply can't, think Koreyck isn't held. So why aren't they shelling it? Suddenly he realized two things and was ashamed of both of them. The first was that he didn't care a damn about German shelling of Koreyck – his fear, his dominant fear, was of British shelling of Adam Hardrow and Ben Jameson.

And Adam's second realization was that he was too exhausted to go on. He couldn't drag Ben any further. He felt utterly sick – sick at heart with the sense of failure and sickened in the stomach by the frightful and unnatural exhaustion. He had, he reckoned, dragged Ben nearly a hundred yards. Ben seemed unconscious now.

Adam knew that he must make a decision. Both their lives were probably forfeit already, but the decision might, just might, affect that. The decision had to be his. He loosened the straps which held Ben's body to him and once again cautiously levered his head and shoulders up from the ditch. He fully expected to see a pair of jackboots level with his eyes, although he could hear nothing indicative of troops moving about near him. What he saw astonished him.

The Germans had vanished.

Very carefully he looked back down the road, and then turned his head towards Koreyck. Towards Koreyck he saw that he was, as far as he could judge, only two hundred yards from where he knew Ivan Perry's nearest positions were sited. Back down the road the line of standing corn was a hundred yards away, no more. And of grey-green uniforms and helmets there was no sign whatsoever.

Adam understood. They'd slipped into the corn. They were formed up in the corn for an attack on Koreyck. They knew it was occupied, of course they did, how not? And they'd marched as near as they could, unmolested, and then deployed for assault in the concealing corn. And any moment now their artillery would start crashing down on A Company, and the grey-green uniforms would come doubling forward. And a Schmeiser burst into a ditch would dispose of two khaki uniforms which had somehow got left in the wrong place and were in the way.

He couldn't, he knew, crawl and drag any further. The body wouldn't do it. The decision – and Adam had recognized it as already forced upon him a minute before – must be between surrender, and hoisting Ben over his shoulder once again for an exhausted two-hundred-yard run down the road towards his friends.

Surrender? Practically under Whisky Wainwright's eyes? Adam almost grinned to himself. One couldn't! And although, in theory, he might leave Ben – there was no reason to suppose the Germans would behave other than correctly towards a wounded British officer – and run for it himself he knew that that was impossible. Somehow, somehow, he must try to get Ben back.

So it came back to a run for it, but a run for it with a company commander over his shoulder, down a road covered by Spandaus, and under the eyes of a German company – or more – lined up, alert, waiting to attack, weapons at the ready.

'Ben,' said Adam aloud. He didn't think Ben could hear or understand but he felt an obscure need to speak before dragging him up for what was almost certain to be their last journey on earth.

'Ben, the Jerries are about to attack. They're lined up in

the corn, less than two hundred yards away. I'm going to climb out of the ditch, carry you and run for it. Sorry about the leg –' for as Adam heaved Ben's shoulders up Ben seemed to wake to consciousness and gave something of a scream. Then Adam, expecting a bullet each second that passed, stood upright in the ditch and dragged Ben's body up from the ditch's bottom, up until Ben's torso lay along the ditch's border, only his smashed leg now to lever up. Then Adam would face the moment of standing upright on the road, of heaving Ben's body across his shoulder in a fireman's lift and starting the run. Ben's body would at certain points protect his own, he realized. Well, that diminished the heroic element, certainly! Adam said to himself, 'Here we go!', and at that exact moment he heard the swish of shells in the air, of what sounded like a very large number of shells in the air. And two seconds later he heard the crumps of British twenty-five-pounder shells bursting near the line of corn one hundred yards away. Swish, crack! Swish, crack! A shell burst thirty yards from Adam, and he felt a stinging sensation and smelt the cordite.

'Up we go, Ben!' Adam was shouting now, one arm holding Ben's arm, his other arm between Ben's legs, Ben's body like a carcass round his shoulder. Adam started to run.

Swish, crack! Swish, crack! A bit of Adam's mind worked. They must, the Jerries must, have some sort of timed programme. With luck they won't come forward earlier. Until they do it's possible, just possible, that for a minute they'll concentrate on keeping their own heads down rather than shoot towards Koreyck ahead of their assault time.

Swish, crack! Swish, crack! It was already a little way behind him. Fifty yards to go, and still no direct German fire down the road. No direct fire from A Company in Koreyck, either. The Jerries must still be in the corn; they couldn't be coming forward yet.

The Spandau opened up when Adam was fifteen yards

from the nearest house in Koreyck. He had noted that Ivan had a section down in slit trenches in the garden, with another in the house itself. It was, Adam remembered, a solid, comfortable-looking bungalow, a dwelling-place of a Koreyck citizen of some substance. It was built of a reddish-purple brick, with stone facing. In fact eighteen years old, it looked very new. Adam, hardly knowing how he did it, body utterly exhausted, mind near vacant, ran towards it. He heard the singing of Spandau bullets in the air, to his right and high, mercifully high. Five yards to go. He saw the men in the nearest slit trench ready in their fire positions, ready to take on the Jerries who must emerge at any moment now from that corn three hundred yards away. Adam passed them, walking now, knowing that the house wall was protecting him from the front and then stopped in the little garden behind the house and carefully, carefully, lowered Ben's body from his shoulders. He laid Ben on the ground. He saw the blood-soaked trouser, the smashed leg; it seemed to accuse him, Adam Hardrow, of lack of skill, lack of consideration. Ben's eyes were closed. Perhaps, Adam thought, without feeling anything very much, he's dead. But at least we're in Koreyck! Soon, within seconds, people would arrive, stretcher-bearers would be organized to take Captain Jameson to the regimental aid post and Adam would make his way somehow to B Company, wherever B Company now was. Soon, any minute, perhaps while Captain Jameson was being carried to the regimental aid post, German artillery would open up on Koreyck. It might well catch the stretcher party *en route*, mightn't it? And soon the Jerries would attack, and would or would not prevent the Westmorlands from slipping away from Koreyck as ordered. Covered by armoured cars. And where the hell were the armoured cars? Meanwhile, Adam supposed, Koreyck had to be defended and he'd better be off to play his part. Unless Whisky Wainwright put him in arrest for gross dereliction of duty in abandoning his company.

Adam suddenly felt an overpowering desire to sleep. He arranged Ben on the ground as comfortably as he could. Looking up he saw, without particular emotion, Ivan and his sergeant-major running towards him. So the word had got round.

Prone, Ben suddenly moved. His eyes were open; they were not only open, they were fixed on Adam and there was a smile in them. Ben was saying something but so softly that Adam could hardly distinguish words. He bent, and said, 'We'll get you to the RAP quickly now, Ben. We're safe back with A Company.' He didn't say that the Westmorlands were, as far as anybody could predict, about to be attacked by the German army.

Ben opened his eyes wide. Then he said, 'Adam –'

'Yes, Ben?'

'Well done, Adam.' It was a whisper, but not without expression. Adam gave a nod. Exhaustion rose in him once again. He wondered whether an officer could sleep upright, like a horse.

'Dear Adam –' There was no doubt about it now. Ben was smiling.

Adam bent down towards him again. Ben said, almost inaudibly but very slowly and clearly, 'As a matter of interest, did you roger Felicity when you had dinner with her that time?'

'Felicity will be told about you, of course, Ben,' Adam said encouragingly, 'and I'm sure you'll soon be right as rain.' He decided that he simply hadn't heard Ben's remarkable inquiry. Just at the moment there were too many things to think about.

CHAPTER 9

It was 29 May. The Westmorlands had withdrawn without disaster from Koreyck. The German attack had, miraculously, melted away under shell fire and the men of A Company had seen the grey-green uniforms and inverted coal-scuttle helmets moving back towards the line of trees from which they'd emerged. Soon thereafter the promised troop of armoured cars had appeared and had taken up positions among A Company's men. Ivan Perry told Adam afterwards of his conversation with the armoured car troop leader. A young man of roughly their own age, Ivan said, he had been cutting about some of the scenes he had witnessed at other parts of the front, and between the front and the coast.

'He said,' Ivan reported, 'that it was a rare mercy to find himself among troops who weren't simply streaming away towards Dunkirk like a lot of disorderly and often drunken hikers!'

'He must have been exaggerating, Ivan.'

'Perhaps. Yes, on reflection I'm sure he was. I think the worst impressions are generally the most profound, don't you?'

Adam nodded. It was intensely distasteful to think of any part, even a small part, of the British army meriting that sort of description. It must be, he told himself, the sort of rag, tag and bobtail which any army produces in the rear areas. It was a well-known fact that the further away from the enemy the more liable units and individuals were to panic. Adam remembered that even Colonel Fosdike (an unlikely oracle, it had to be admitted) had warned them of this phenomenon. But, Ivan said, the armoured-car troop leader had spoken of 'companies'. Infantry! Throwing away weapons! Bolting! It had to be largely nonsense – largely but not, perhaps, entirely. The stragglers shuffling back from Koreyck hadn't been rear area troops. They'd once been infantry. And Adam recalled Sergeant-Major Darwin's quiet, emphatic tones: 'No discipline,' Darwin had said. 'Firm but friendly, that's all they'd needed.'

There had been a few blessed hours' respite after leaving Koreyck and before starting work on the next new position. They had moved in trucks in darkness, not thinking or caring much about whither. Then they'd been decanted in the very early morning, told to dig personal slit trenches for protection against air attack; orders would be given shortly. 'Shortly' had turned into three hours, and after the protection had been dug men had rested and eaten and laughed and slept. And Adam had wandered a few hundred yards to find Ivan. Each now commanded his company. And Ivan had told him about A Company's final withdrawal from Koreyck (in which B Company had played the simple and unheroic part of marching back first, unmolested, to the embussing area two miles west of the village). Some north-country guardian angel had looked after the Westmorlands so far, in that after the first withdrawal days they hadn't been directly attacked by the Luftwaffe. Koreyck might have been a prime target; but Koreyck had been spared.

Then came the orders. It was 29 May. Whisky Wainwright gave them out to company commanders sitting in the kitchen of a small house by the roadside. There was a strong smell of cheese, and periodically the owner of the house could be seen peering at them from a doorway. The man looked utterly wretched. He sensed, without difficulty, that he was looking at reasonably friendly soldiers for the last time.

Adam had not seen Whisky since before the rescue of Ben Jameson. He knew that he ought to be in grave trouble, but Ben was safe, should be all right, would otherwise be in Hun hands. And B Company had been all right, too. The company sergeant-major had had them all well in hand, rested, tea brewed, some local Koreyck supplies gathered in without difficulty (and with a good deal of zest) from abandoned and almost-abandoned houses. B Company's morale had mounted. Sergeant-Major Darwin had simply observed to a very exhausted Second-Lieutenant Hardrow, now his company commander, 'Major Wainwright wanted to know where the hell you were, sir. As he put it.'

Darwin had been loyal. Darwin had said that Mr Hardrow was urgently looking into the whereabouts of Captain Jameson and had ordered him, Sergeant-Major Darwin, to attend for the withdrawal orders. Whisky had said nothing more.

Now, about to issue orders for the occupation of yet another position, Whisky was face to face with Adam for the first time. He took no notice of him whatsoever. He gave out his orders in his usual way, briefly, gruffly, without adornment, but entirely clearly. He also told them what he knew of the general situation.

The whole army was withdrawing to Dunkirk. The whole army was to sail to England. Dunkirk was to be the port of embarkation, and would be protected by a series of defensive positions which the Expeditionary Force would man on successive days. They, the 2nd Westmorlands, were about to man part of the first such position. Whisky didn't know for how long, but long enough to enable the close perimeter of Dunkirk itself to be prepared or improved. Then, when ordered, they'd go back again, either to the Dunkirk perimeter or direct to Dunkirk to take ship for home.

Whisky was no strategist, but he made other things clear

and as his hearers shifted uneasily on their bottoms they knew that Whisky had no illusions, didn't fool himself, realized what bloody awful straits they were in. But they also knew that he'd look after the battalion. He wouldn't accept an idiotic order, but where it made sense to try Whisky would try. And so would they. The position they were about to take up ran through one large village which they'd hold as long as possible. Through the village, north and south, ran a canal and the canal produced something of a ditch which would be incorporated into the Westmorlands defensive front, north and south of the village as well as in it. The battalion front was one and a half miles; and they were very, very short of men. Whisky gave out details. It all looked pitifully thin.

Whisky talked about the flanks. On the left of B Company – the Westmorlands' left-hand company, to take post on the canal north of the village – was a battalion of another brigade. It would be necessary to liaise with them, direct, and Whisky wanted B Company commander, Mr Hardrow, to do so. He was also sending Major Bassett to try to find the neighbouring battalion commander. B Company commander was simply to contact the nearest front-line company and co-ordinate. But not yet, Whisky said, not until I give the word. The brigadier's told me they've been ordered to liaise with us, not the other way round, so let's wait and give them a chance to do so, or you'll spend the whole bloody morning chasing each others' tails. And I'll send a carrier to take B Company commander over, when I give the word, said Whisky. He indicated where the neighbouring company of their neighbour battalion should be.

There ought to be a bit of time before the Huns attacked, said Whisky. Once again, there was to be a squadron of armoured cars in front, but the armoured cars weren't meant to get seriously involved, so if the Huns attacked in any strength on this front they'd be up against the battalion pretty quick. No time to waste, therefore, but at least some warning.

He told them the artillery targets he'd agreed. There was mighty little ammunition, but if they were attacked, really attacked, it should be possible to put down at least some fire, the gunners said. Particularly on the canal and the eastern approaches to it. He gave them the map coordinates.

'Further to the left,' Whisky grimaced – there was, however, to be no softening of the blow – 'the Belgians have packed it in.'

There had been rumours of this but it was the first definite news they'd had of the Belgian capitulation two days earlier. Some British troops had been moved to the British left, to help fill what seemed an open gap. The British army could, it appeared, be rolled up from left to right, from north to south. And pretty quickly too. Unless everyone held, and held firm.

And, Whisky added in his matter-of-fact, no-nonsense way, from right to left, from south to north too, of course. The Germans had reached the Channel a week ago. The mass of their armoured divisions were ranged along the southern flank of the British Expeditionary Force. Up to now they'd been held.

'Sure they will be, too,' Whisky said. 'Difficult country that. Ditches. Dykes. We'll be all right.' He stood up. That was all.

So far the Westmorlands had seen no German tanks. Rumours abounded of massed panzers on all sides but their adversaries hitherto had been infantry, behaving in a skilled but orthodox manner. In fact, as Ivan had told Adam as they gossiped an hour earlier, the Wehrmacht might dispose of a lot of tanks but much of the German army was traditionally organized and equipped in a style abandoned by the British a short while before.

'From Koreyck,' Ivan told Adam, 'I could actually see some of their artillery moving up. Beyond the old river line we were meant to drive them back across.'

'Really?'

'With those excellent binoculars. And the gun teams were horsed – all the guns were horse-drawn.'

On this front at least, if the British army was being driven back, it was not by the unmatched forces of mechanization and modernity. True, Adam reflected, they'd not so far seen any British tanks either. There were German panzers in huge numbers south of them, and probably north of them as well, menacing, terrible, creatures from another world. Even if they'd not attacked the Westmorlands, their presence was felt, unnerving, a little incomprehensible. There seemed to be no British equivalents. They'd always been told that the French had huge numbers of tanks, but nobody was counting on the French any more.

Orders over, they all moved out of the kitchen to hurry back to their companies.

'Mr Hardrow! Just a moment.'

Here it comes, Adam thought, I know I did what I shouldn't but to hell with it. He faced the acting commanding officer. All Whisky said was, 'B Company all right?'

'Yes, sir. Not very numerous, as you know, but perfectly all right.'

'You all right?'

'Yes, sir.'

'Good! Well done.' Nothing more.

The dive-bombers came in from the north-east, fast and low, when B Company's trenches were about half dug. First there was a low murmurous roar, a sound not necessarily approaching and not necessarily hostile. Then a yell from a number of voices, Adam's among them. Adam recognized that particular note, a note he'd last heard on a certain refugee-packed Flanders road. Adam was standing with Company Sergeant-Major Darwin near the platoon commanded by Sergeant Pew – the company had been reorganized into two small platoons

241

and one of them was Pew's. Sergeant Pew himself took up the shout – 'Stukas! Down, the lot of you!'

Shovels, picks and everything else were dropped as the men leapt into their half-excavated slit trenches and burrowed into the damp earth, straining and elbowing, driven by fear, burrowing like animals to get some protection from the frightful birds of prey moving in on them with that indescribable siren-scream of the dive-bomber. The bombs and their explosions followed a second later, as the German aircraft lifted and tore away westward. Adam raised his head. He'd been sharing the tenuous protection of two feet of trench with Sergeant-Major Darwin, a large man.

'Keep down! They're coming round!'

The Stukas' second run was from south to north. B Company needed no bidding to keep down. As far as Adam could see, the first bombs had fallen slightly to the east of where the company was digging – very slightly, but perhaps enough to have saved bodies from bomb fragments. They mightn't be so lucky this time.

'Down! Down!' Adam saw one man's head raised looking curiously, indifferently, towards the dark shapes of the Luftwaffe's hawks as they raced in, down and in, fractionally ahead of the ear-splitting noise which accompanied them. He saw that the head was Crowe's. Crowe had been an excellent soldier throughout these last two extraordinary weeks – throughout the last six months in fact. He'd not applied to speak to Adam or anyone else about his private affairs and Adam had hoped they were not entangled. Once, in winter quarters, Adam had said to Sergeant Pew, 'Is Crowe hearing from his wife, do you happen to know?' Mail had been regular when on the so-called Gort Line, before the advance into Belgium. Before the campaign, if one could call it that.

'He's heard, I know that,' Sergeant Pew had observed noncommittally. Not, perhaps, very encouraging but not presaging disaster. Sergeant Pew disapproved of soldiers' wives who made trouble, whose effect was distraction.

Now Crowe's head was up, almost as if he cared little for danger. Was he, Adam thought for a fleeting, blinding second, actually courting death?

'Down, Crowe.'

Crowe's head dropped, without hurry, and the aircraft came at them, steeply, terrifyingly, the black crosses visible on the underwings, several of the bombs themselves, small, black, almost insignificant-looking, clearly discernible in the air as they fell. Nearer now. One damned near. Adam pushed his head and shoulders down, on to the ample hindquarters of Sergeant-Major Darwin. The crash almost split his ear-drums and the air was full of smoke, dust and clods of earth darkening the sky. The sour smell of explosive was every-where. Through it all, stunned, Adam made out that he was still alive. He also heard, very definitely, the sound of Stuka engines, Stuka birds of prey, not wheeling this time but moving away, moving away northwards. Respite.

'Right, get on with it!' Sergeant-Major Darwin was on his feet now. Adam climbed up, feeling a little shamefaced that Darwin's recovery from abject cowering had been slightly quicker than his own. He would have been surprised to know that Darwin, at that moment, was thanking his stars for personal survival but was also inwardly muttering that thank Christ they've not yet hit young Hardrow anyway, we need him, we need him a hell of a lot, there's nobody else. Adam grinned at him.

'I don't enjoy that much, do you, Sergeant-Major?'

'No, sir! All right, get on with it!' The sergeant-major's voice was potent. 'Anybody hit?' he roared. There was somebody hit, somebody very near. A voice said, 'Over here, sir,' not shouting, just conveying the information quietly, conversationally. The same voice – Adam couldn't see who the man was – said, 'Sergeant Pew, sir.'

Sergeant Pew's head had been smashed to pieces by a bomb fragment which had caught him from very close quarters. Adam walked quickly over – Sergeant Pew had been in a slit trench about twenty-five yards from his own. The bomb fragment had found its target with terrible accuracy. Pew had been below the surface of the ground, had turned his head it seemed, and somehow met the bomb fragment face on and fatally. Adam remembered, and had never thought of it in those terms before, that Sergeant Pew had been a strikingly good-looking man. His face had been so essentially soldierly, his expression so generally stern and disciplined that one didn't think of him as either plain or handsome; now, in retrospect, Adam realized that Pew's features had been noble. At the same instant it was borne in on Adam for the first time that Pew was young. He had, in the way of senior NCOs, seemed ageless, but he was young, young and fair of face. A sculptor would have relished Pew.

Not now. The bomb fragment, cutting like a razor, had taken off the front of Pew's head, his forehead, face, nose, eyes, lips, leaving a messy, scarlet sponge without identifiable shapes in it.

Darwin said, 'Oh Christ!'

Adam spoke softly, 'We'll bury him right away.' There was no point in stretcher-bearers, medical officer, regimental aid post or palaver. It would be good to have the chaplain, but the battalion's own chaplain, a charming man, had been evacuated with pleurisy just before the advance into Belgium and, unsurprisingly, the authorities had not yet posted in a replacement. Officers all held the field-service prayer-book with its abbreviated text of services, including the burial service. It would be for Adam to read the last words over Sergeant Pew.

He felt, as he was often to feel, numb rather than sorrowful. He knew that, one day, he would be overtaken by grief – for many perhaps but very particularly for Sergeant Pew. Sergeant Pew had been stalwart, utterly loyal, a conveyor of strength, unobtrusively wise, the man on whom Adam had relied, nominally his subordinate but actually, he said to himself, his mentor. Adam had never met Sergeant Pew's wife, but something assured him that she was in the mould of Pew, north-country, rough-edged, robust, inwardly tender, wholly good at heart. And brave, probably. He would write when he could, and prayed he'd find some sort of words to convey truth. He couldn't articulate feelings now. There wasn't time.

Meanwhile Sergeant-Major Darwin was saying something and Adam heard himself answering, 'Quite right, of course, Sergeant-Major.' Darwin had observed that burials had better wait until this position was finished.

'Quite right, Sergeant-Major.' A groundsheet was drawn over Pew's hideous remains, and men took up shovels and set to again with fervour.

Two of the battalion carriers drove up just as Adam completed his first full tour of inspection of B Company trenches, alleged by the remaining NCOs of the company to be complete. The line was depressingly thin – about twenty slit trenches, with about a third of their number staggered back in some sort of depth and the whole company frontage nearly half a mile. Adam had divided the company once again into two; previous platoon and section organization had largely disappeared as a result of the drip of casualties and disorganization following the abortive advance past Droot Farm, the massacre of Jack Brett's command, the retaking of Droot and the subsequent withdrawal. To say nothing of the Stukas and the irremediable loss of Sergeant Pew. Adam had the impression that B Company was now the weakest of the battalion in men but he wasn't sure. Every company probably felt like that, felt particularly vulnerable and overdone. One just had to keep going.

It was a wretched position, too, Adam had remarked gloomily; flat and featureless, with the canal in front easily crossable anywhere by determined Germans equipped with assault boats and paddles. Beyond the canal was deployed a squadron of armoured cars, but half an hour after the Stuka attack some of these had appeared on B Company's left, on the near side of the canal. These were the lightly armoured Morris vehicles, generally reported by Adam's acquaintances in the cavalry as thin-skinned and not up to the job, but on this occasion extraordinarily comforting. It seemed they had been ordered to cross westward and blow the bridges. One bridge was in the Westmorlands' centre, in A Company sector, and one was outside the battalion area, away to Adam's left. It was by this last that the armoured car troop which now materialized north of B Company had crossed. The sergeant in charge motored across and contacted Adam. Adam was impressed – a sharp-eyed, smiling little man, who looked tired but alert – and by no means gloomy.

'So you're off,' Adam said. He supposed a loud rumbling explosion heard ten minutes earlier had been a bridge blown. Soon, no doubt, the other, in Ivan's sector, would go the same way.

'That's right, sir. Sappers did a good job.'

'Did you see anything of the battalion on our left? I've to go over and see them soon if they don't contact me, and they haven't yet. They're meant to extend to that farm, beyond the next road over there.' He pointed. The sergeant looked at him wryly.

'Someone there when I came by ten minutes ago, sir. But if you want to see them you'd best move fast.'

'Why? They're not pulling out, surely?'

The armoured-car sergeant said, 'They looked a bit dicey to me!' and Adam gathered that he had been less than impressed by what he'd seen of the neighbouring battalion.

Adam said, 'Well, I hope you're staying to cover our left yourselves,' but the sergeant said that he'd been told to withdraw, if he had no more orders, at eleven o'clock. In about forty minutes. Meanwhile they'd have a brew-up, and yes, they'd be watching out northward. Exactly half an hour later the two Westmorland carriers appeared.

The corporal in charge of the leading carrier jumped down and approached Adam, saluting in a somewhat perfunctory way.

'CO wants you to jump on and go over to liaise as ordered, sir.'

Adam shouted for Sergeant-Major Darwin. Darwin nodded as he heard that Mr Hardrow was off into the blue to find who, if anybody, was on their left, they'd seen nothing and nobody, but that little cavalry chap was still a few hundred yards over to the left, cool as a cucumber. He'd said he'd be off any minute though.

'Right, sir,' said Darwin. Then he said, hesitantly, 'Sergeant Pew, sir.'

'When I come back. Dig –'

'Yes, sir.' Darwin knew how much Pew had meant to young Hardrow. The tie between platoon commander and platoon sergeant was a very special one, Darwin reflected, when they were as good as each of those two. Darwin was not a religious man, having been brought up like most soldiers to regard church as a matter of preliminary and unwelcome polishing and regimentation, followed by uncomprehending boredom; but he knew that Mr Hardrow wanted to read the words over Sergeant Pew and he knew that this was right.

Adam climbed into the carrier, and the small square vehicle jolted away on its caterpillar tracks, with its distinctive see-saw movement, and passed the left-hand B Company trench. Adam held his glasses to the east, the front. Nothing. Several clumps of trees. Flat meadows. Frequent clusters of farm buildings. The canal marked in many places by parallel rows of poplars but itself invisible. Of the enemy, nothing. Adam swung his binoculars round to the direction in which they were travelling. Between the left of B Company – a number of slit trenches in a hedge, about two hundred yards back from the canal bank – and the farm which he'd been told was held by the neighbouring battalion's right-hand company lay a distance of some five hundred yards, up a very slight slope. As the two carriers pounded up it, Adam scanned the buildings ahead. He could see no sign of movement or occupation, but the troops were, he said to himself, presumably well concealed. Anyway, they were probably forward of the farm, nearer the canal. Whisky had been vague.

Adam leant down to shout at the driver, 'Up to the near corner of the barn!'

Adam decided he'd dismount once the farm was reached. He didn't want some trigger-happy member of the neighbours to mistake him for an intrusive panzer and try out the anti-tank rifle, no doubt for the first time in the campaign. What was the word the armoured-car sergeant had used about this battalion's atmosphere? Dicey!

The carriers stopped, closed up and with the wall of a massive barn between them and the east, the enemy.

'Come with me, Corporal Staines.'

Corporal Staines was a carrier corporal, a character well-known throughout the battalion. He was a massive Lake District man with a very rough tongue. No respecter of persons, he was said to hold nobody in awe and remarkably few even in respect. One of the few was Whisky Wainwright. In Corporal Staines's table of assessments second-lieutenants came nowhere, and he made little attempt to conceal the fact. Now he paused for a moment to give two necessary instructions about the carriers to the two drivers, climbed down, looked around him as if deliberating what to do next, and then, struck by an impulse as it were, ambled over to where Adam waited. Adam moved off round the farm building, knowing that Corporal Staines, having demonstrated independence, would slowly conform.

At the corner of the farm nearest the front Adam stopped. He had found B Company's flank neighbours.

Moving back towards the farm from the direction of the canal came a straggle of men. They were walking fast but without order, and they were talking loudly among themselves. Adam could hear the sound of swearing, shouting and laughter when they were still a hundred yards off. He couldn't imagine what they were supposed to be doing. Had they just been relieved by some other platoon or company, and been ordered to withdraw to reserve? If so, why on earth were they moving like this? They could be in full view of the enemy, or almost so. He said, 'Come on, Corporal Staines,' and moved out into the middle of the small track up which the men were making their way towards him.

Corporal Staines said, 'Got no bloody rifles, most of 'em.'

Adam saw that this was true. He felt sick and angry. This resembled the first stage of the advance near Koreyck, but this was worse.

As the men approached they saw Adam, and came on but more slowly and in silence. When they were twenty yards away Adam said, 'Hang on there!' Very sharply. He then walked towards them. Corporal Staines stayed where he was, watching. Adam's voice was uneven from rage, but he knew that self-control was essential.

'What's going on?'

'Going back!' said one of the men. They were all filthy, mostly hatless and the majority were unarmed. This, thought Adam, can't be a battalion, a British battalion!'

'Going back where?'

There was a confusion of voices. Adam heard various words, phrases and sounds.

'Dunkirk.' 'Everyone for his fucking self ain't it!' 'No fucking good hanging about waiting for Jerry!' And, from nearer the back, 'Get out of the fucking way.'

'Now listen to me,' Adam said as steadily as he could, 'it's not every man for himself. This is a defensive position. This battalion is on the left of my battalion, and there is no question of withdrawal until ordered. Which is not yet. If you straggle away like this you will be overtaken by the enemy and you won't have a chance. Where is your company commander?'

'Buggered off, 'aint 'e?' said a voice, followed by a sour chorus of assent. Adam said, 'Now wait here. I'm going to find what your orders are. Wait here for me.' It was, he knew, pretty futile. They didn't want orders. They wanted escape. The men with rifles were probably capable of shooting him if their wretched and cowardly impulses were frustrated, but he had to try to win time, he had to find out what the situation really was. If this knot of miserable and mutinous deserters represented the spirit of this whole battalion there was an open gap on the left flank of 2nd Westmorlands and it wasn't going to take the Wehrmacht long to discover it and fill it. The lives of his men, his friends, his comrades, every one of them, probably depended on some sort of sense and spirit being driven into this gutless bunch. In a tone of confidence he certainly didn't feel Adam said, again, 'Wait here for me.' Trying not to register surprise he noted that several sat down. Perhaps they were, secretly, a little relieved to be told to do something, and something not particularly dangerous. Adam turned and said, very sharply, 'Corporal Staines!'

Corporal Staines reacted admirably, and Adam was proud of him and of the Westmorlands who'd bred him. He said 'Yes, sir!' and stamped to attention with a promptitude and vigour which at once brought to mind the parade-ground at Aldershot and which nobody had ever observed in Corporal Staines before.

'Corporal Staines, cover this track with the two carriers. I'm going to have a look around.'

'Right, sir,' said Corporal Staines.

Adam had no clear idea of what he was going to do next

but he wanted to create a breathing space. These miserable men would know that on each carrier was mounted a bren-gun. The words 'cover the track' – although Adam had deliberately spelled out no threat – meant that bren-guns would, very soon, be trained down the track which these would-be-evaders of battle had intended to use for flight. They looked, Adam noted, thoughtful. Reinforcing the impression, and almost encouragingly, he said once again, 'Stay here! I'll be right back.' Then he quickly moved round the next corner of the building and out of sight. He had to think, if only for half a minute; and to think clear of the instant pressures of what he knew was the most testing moment of his life so far. He heard the carrier engines start up.

Once past the corner of the barn Adam saw another building – the principal farmhouse, red, shuttered, four square. In front of it was a white domestic fence with a gate in it. From the gate a five-yard path ran up to the main door of the farmhouse. And in front of the gate, on the farm roadway which presumably connected with the nearest public road somewhere to the west, was standing a small car. With Belgian registration plates. Adam moved towards it, without any particular purpose in mind. Then he saw that the car had two occupants.

He moved closer.

The occupants were two British officers.

One wore on his shoulders the crown of a major and the other the three stars of a captain. Both had very red faces. One was sitting in the driver's seat, the other, for a reason Adam never discovered, was sitting in the back. It was a four-seater car. As Adam approached he saw that the front window on the side nearest to him was open.

The captain – sitting in the driver's seat, furthest from Adam – looked at him and said, as Adam came up to the car, 'Who are you?' His speech was slurred and Adam sniffed the powerful cloud of alcohol. The man, he saw, was pretty drunk. A menace at the wheel, certainly, but even more of a menace from what he was doing. Or not doing.

Adam said crisply, 'Second Westmorlands. On your right flank. I've been sent to liaise.'

The major in the back seat then spoke. His face was mottled and crimson. It was clear that he, too, had drunk plenty. He said, thickly, 'Bugger off.'

Adam looked at him. He saw a man of about forty with a short neck, a bristly moustache, a slack mouth and bloodshot eyes. He said very quietly, 'Where are you going in this car?'

The captain answered. He said, 'You don't seem to have heard the news, boy. There's a general retreat. To Dunkirk. Every man for himself.' Oddly, he seemed now slightly more sober.

'There is not,' said Adam so softly that he could only just hear his own voice, 'a general retreat. There are positions to be held. Your company is meant to be holding this one, on 2nd Westmorlands' left. Your men are running away. I've got a dozen of them sitting on the ground twenty yards from here, covered by our carriers.'

The major belched. He said again, loudly and angrily, 'Bugger off! Who do you think you're talking to?' It was this last obscene attempt to invoke the authority of rank by one who by his actions was discarding all claim to it which snapped something inside Adam. He slung his rifle, drew his pistol, laid the barrel on the ledge of the car's open window and said, 'Get out of the car!'

The major said, 'How dare you! Andy, for Christ's sake get going!' The captain pulled the self-starter. Nothing happened. Again, Adam said, 'Get out. Both of you. Back to your men.'

'Start up, Andy! And you –'

'Get out,' said Adam, 'Or I shall shoot you.'

There was a silence, an absolute silence, broken by the

futile whirring of the starter motor as the captain again and fruitlessly pulled the self-starter knob.

'I shall shoot you, too,' said Adam to the captain, 'if you touch that starter again. Now,' to the crimson occupant of the back seat, 'for the last time, get out and take control of your men.'

'Bugger off, you little whipper-snapper!'

'You have six seconds. I shall count. One –'

'Start her up, or swing her, damn you!' yelled the major to Andy. Andy sat completely still.

'– three, four –'

'I suppose you want a seat in the car, you bloody little twerp –'

'– five –'

'Put that thing away,' screamed the major. When Adam had counted 'six' aloud, he levelled his pistol and shot the major dead, through the centre of the forehead. He was conscious of the terrified incredulity in the bloodshot eyes for a split second, then it was done, the upholstery of the car a sickening mess, the hole in the forehead unforgettable.

'Now, you,' Adam said to the captain.

'Listen, I had to obey orders –'

'Get out, and back to your men. Some of them haven't got rifles but I'm sure they know where they threw them away.'

'I'm from a different company –'

'Back to your men. Now.'

The voice which came back at him was still slurred. It muttered, 'Know you think you're doing the right thing, don't blame you or anything, but things were difficult, things –'

Adam led 'Andy' back to the little group squatting beneath the eyes of Corporal Staines, his mates and their carriers, posted a short distance away. He said loudly, 'Right, your major has had an accident, but the captain here knows what you're meant to be on.' To the captain he said, softly, 'Hold this farm. I'll get word back that you've got it, and I promise,

I truly promise, that when the withdrawal orders come you'll not be left behind. My CO will see to that. You'll be much safer going back in company. Specially in company with us.' Adam couldn't entirely decipher the dazed expression on 'Andy's' face as he left him two minutes later, but noted that the men were responding to some sort of rudiments of organization. He had himself indicated to the captain exactly where, at the farm, positions should be adopted. No judgement, no decision, was required of 'Andy' – just a minimum of self-control and sense of duty. 'Andy' had some armoured cars protecting his right for a few minutes more. Beyond them he had Westmorlands. He had defensible farm buildings. There was, at present, no sign of the enemy to the front. For the short while necessary until withdrawal was ordered, 'Andy' could surely cope.

Adam rejoined the carriers and told Corporal Staines to get him back to B Company as fast as possible. Corporal Staines glanced at him. He'd heard a shot from somewhere among those farm buildings, that was sure. Now here was young Hardrow, second-lieutenant, a grub the officers called them, looking mighty grim. Mighty grim. Could be forty, Corporal Staines said to himself, funny look on his face. Different to half an hour ago.

Adam turned his mind back to B Company. He supposed the car was the farmer's, but regretted nothing else.

Adam had a few men near the canal, eyes and ears intended to be alert to the sound of Germans approaching the bank, the sound of paddle boats being softly slipped into the water. It was, Adam reckoned, unlikely that this would happen: the Germans seemed undisposed to be surreptitious and probably found little motive for subtlety. It was more likely, Adam thought grimly, that when the Huns decided to push at this point – if they did – it would be a well-orchestrated attack, assault troops racing down to the canal on a wide front accompanied by a bombardment from German guns and mortars; probably accompanied by a return of the Stukas. Adam's positions, too few and too isolated, but the best he could devise, were sited well back from the canal, not immediately discernible from the front – or so he hoped. With luck he'd get warning, and with warning and good shooting he ought to be able to do some damage. As to protection from bombardment, the slit trenches were now in decent shape.

During the early afternoon a dispatch rider appeared with a written order from battalion headquarters. Communications within the battalion were now entirely by motor cycle or field telephone, the wireless sets having failed dismally throughout the last forty-eight hours and being by now mistrusted. B Company's set would, Adam had already decided, soon have to be jettisoned. The written message was clear. The battalion would hold present positions until last light. Thinning out would then take place on a timed programme and the march back to an assembly area would be complete by one o'clock the following morning, 30 May. Thereafter, God knew.

Adam encouraged men to get out of the slit trenches, to walk about. A strict watch was kept, and he knew that at the first distant roar of dive-bomber engines or rumble of German artillery in this direction (it was surprising how recognizable this had come to be, how easily distinguishable from the more distant, general grumble of guns which went on most of the time) men would leap into the weapon pits, probably cracking jokes as they did so. Spirits had recovered from the down point of the morning when they'd dived for cover from the Stukas, when they'd lost Sergeant Pew. It was a beautiful warm afternoon. From time to time Adam focused his binoculars on the farm on the rise away to their left. Immediately after rejoining B Company he had identified one particular position by the corner of a barn, a position he had impressed on 'Andy' as being essential to man strongly because the arc covered by it interlocked with B Company's own left. This was hardly true – but Adam had known he would be able to detect through glasses whether it remained manned.

So far he could still see men in that position. A section perhaps – anyway a small group. So far so good. He'd asked 'Andy' if he wanted any bren-guns loaned – the mutinous stragglers seemed to have nothing but a few rifles. Sulkily 'Andy' had answered no, they'd got some brens in the farm buildings, the men had –

'Buggered off' Adam inelegantly expected. Still, if there were light machine-guns at the farm and enough men to fire them, the place might, just might, hold. Or at least give warning of a collapse on the Westmorlands' left. Adam wondered whether he should try to get hold of a carrier and send Sergeant-Major Darwin across to the left 'to liaise again' but decided against. On return he'd sent a written message back by Corporal Staines to the effect that the next position on B Company's left, at the farm previously noted, was occupied but that the morale of the defenders was poor. He was trying to keep the place under observation and had done something to stiffen their spirits. That was all. Adam scrawled the message, informally phrased, in a note to the adjutant. He wondered when Whisky would be coming round.

Whisky turned up soon after the dispatch rider. As usual, he appeared, an orderly trotting behind him, without warning or visible means of locomotion. B Company had just had some food and men were mostly wandering about with something like relaxation.

'Afternoon, Adam.'

'Good afternoon, sir.'

'Happy about the evening? Timings and so forth?'

'Yes, sir. Where are we going?'

'Perimeter. Dunkirk perimeter. Suburbs really.'

'Do we know for how long?' Adam ventured.

'No. Are those chaps on your left going to run away?'

'Sooner or later, yes, sir,' Adam answered. 'In fact they were doing so as I arrived. I think I've stopped it for a bit, but I expect only a bit.'

'What do they need?'

'Officers.'

'Were there any?'

'I left,' said Adam, 'a captain. Whom I found. I saw no subalterns – certainly nobody wearing rank badges. And I saw nobody dressed as a NCO.' They might, he had told himself, all have been killed or wounded; but somehow he didn't think so.

Whisky nodded and said, 'Well, try to keep an eye on them. If they bolt we'll just have to –'

But at that moment, his eyes and bull-like expression fixed on Adam, Whisky snapped out, 'Bloody hell!' and they both simultaneously heard Spandau fire; Spandau fire not east but west of B Company's position. Spandau fire from behind them. And at the same time they heard the familiar singing and whining of Spandau bullets – burst after burst coming over their heads. Too high. Extreme range. But from Jerries who'd established themselves somewhere behind the Westmorlands' front.

Adam never remembered how he'd reached the slit trench, nor exactly how Whisky Wainwright had fitted into it as well. All he recalled afterwards was the gasp and chuckle of Private Bliss. Adam had inherited Bliss as company commander's orderly after Ben Jameson's wounding, and had come to value Bliss's slowness and stolidity. Now Bliss, Wainwright and Hardrow were sharing one slit trench. Everywhere men were now below ground, weapons at the ready. The laughter and chaffing of thirty seconds ago were absent. Moods changed very swiftly in war.

Whisky said, 'The bastards have got through. Infiltrated.'

'I'm sure that here, sir, they've not –'

'Doesn't matter where. May be through your chums on the left, may be between you and D. They're behind. Now you'll get an attack in front. Bound to.' Whisky was thinking fast. Very quietly, and in a much gentler voice than Adam had ever heard him use before, a voice wholly without gruffness or menace, Whisky said, 'Listen, Adam. If they're behind you, and possibly going for D, I want you out of here. Otherwise I'll never get you back.' They were talking at very close quarters in the slit trench and every movement of Whisky's prodded Adam painfully in the ribs. Now Whisky pulled his map from his pocket – Whisky disliked map cases. There continued to be distant bursts of Spandau fire but not, as far as Adam could judge, in this direction. He'd yelled to Sergeant-Major Darwin to check that the sentries were keeping a wide-eyed watch to the front, but so far there'd been no alarm sounded. Germans were in position behind them, but so far none were visible to B Company.

'Look here, Adam. This village,' Whisky stubbed it with his finger, 'is a mile and a half away over your right shoulder, south-west. Right?'

'Right, sir.'

'From the sound of it those Jerries are north-west of us. I'm going to move A into the place, what's it called –'

'Possel, sir.'

'Possel. Ivan's reserve company, I'm taking him into Possel. Then I want you to go back – go south along the canal line and then turn west – make for Possel. All right?'

'Yes, sir. When?'

'When I tell you. We're still through to you on line, and if it's cut I'll get a runner to you. Somehow. You see, I've nothing to counter-attack them with, I'd have the battalion running all over the place if I tried, cut up in bits and pieces. Got to concentrate it.' Whisky was thinking aloud. He might be wrong but he was making up his mind. 'D and C haven't far to go, they'll move back first. But I want to get the whole battalion out of this during the next two hours. Then we'll concentrate in these farms' – again he stubbed the map – 'round Possel. And defend there until night, until it's time to go back. But we can't stay on the canal.'

Adam said, 'Our neighbours to the north –'

'I'll get a message to Brigade. They'll have to sort that out. And Brigade will have to lump the fact that I've got to get you out early or not at all. The brigadier will understand.'

'– I must tell them what's happening, sir,' said Adam, 'I promised. I promised we'd not go back without them.'

Whisky said nothing to this and jumped up to level ground, leaving Adam to plan the next half hour as best he could.

'Sergeant-Major, we may get the word to go back at any time after the next half hour. Major Wainwright is getting A Company into the village of Possel, and as soon as possible moving C and D back from the canal to the same area. Followed by us.'

They were sharing Adam's trench. So far there had been only sporadic fire from the Spandaus to the rear. Adam supposed from the sound and the erratic nature of this fire that those particular Germans might be six or seven hundred yards away, and attending, for the moment, to other targets.

'It'll take a bit of time, sir.'

'He may start us off before the others are back. Once he's got A Company firm in Possel he may bring us all back pretty quickly.' It had been impossible in the available minute to clarify much with Whisky, but Adam had certainly supposed this. Reference to 'D and C moving back first' surely hadn't meant that B must wait on the canal until their sister companies had completed withdrawal? That would, indeed, take a bit of time, in Darwin's words. The sergeant-major observed, 'I'd say so, sir. If Major Wainwright talked about getting the whole battalion back in two hours you'll get the message in half an hour, bound to. I'll just have a look –' But before Sergeant-Major Darwin could finish his remark there came a yell from a slit trench thirty yards to the east, and at the same moment the sound of a bren-gun firing, from the same quarter as the yell –

'They're over! They're coming over the canal!'

And now once again, the distant Spandaus began firing from the rear. And once again the bursts came high, but unmistakably in B Company's direction now. And the same yell, as if frustrated at the scant reaction shown –

'Jerries! They're coming over the canal!'

Adam supposed afterwards that the man in B Company's foremost observation post had been less than very alert. The canal bank was in shadow much of the afternoon and to watch it and watch the flat country immediately beyond it demanded vigilance. Everyone was tired with the ceaseless digging and marching of those days and to stay wide-eyed and observant demanded a lot of will-power. The fact remained that the Germans had moved with skill. They had assembled a number of small parties under some sort of cover – clumps of trees, houses, in one case the bank of a disused canal – about a hundred yards from the far bank, with a sufficient number of inflatable rubber boats. Then each party had moved very rapidly to a crossing place, obviously selected with care and after reconnaissance. At each crossing place one or more boats were launched, and in an extremely short time one and then several squads of helmeted figures in grey-green uniforms were across. Once across they moved like well-fashioned automata – fast, accurately, each piece meshing with the next. They used the shelter provided in many places by the west bank itself; they spawned what seemed an astonishing number of Spandau teams west of the canal almost as soon as the cry was taken up throughout B Company – 'Jerries! they're coming over.'

260

And soon bullets were singing through the air over the heads of B Company from attackers on the canal bank, who had again, and infuriatingly, made themselves invisible.

From his own slit trench Adam could reach a number of the company's positions with his voice, and he had established Darwin within earshot – Darwin, who could command with his immense lungs even further to the left of the position. To the right was Corporal Barney, and what had once been Sergeant Pew's platoon. Beyond Sergeant-Major Darwin was Corporal Travers and another series of slit trenches. Adam grabbed the field telephone from Bliss – the metal container was sitting on the edge of their trench. By good fortune the line was uncut and he heard Bobby Forrest's voice at the other end. Briefly Adam described what he knew. Germans across the canal in B Company sector. They'd not yet assaulted, they must be in the canal area. And more, far more, must still be on the east-bank approaches.

'Can we have every shell possible on the canal and the east bank? We'll deal with the Jerries this side.'

'Anything else?'

'They're behind us, too. Whisky knows where. But further away. The immediate thing is these brutes on the canal.'

'Right. Good luck.' Bobby sounded unperturbed and matter of fact. Things would turn out all right. Bound to. It was his old company. Adam started shouting, and the orders were relayed from trench to trench. All eyes and weapons towards the canal, but Corporal Barney and Corporal Travers to keep one man watching to the rear at all times. They'll probably try to rush us, Adam yelled, brens and grenades, brens and grenades. Got plenty of magazines?

'Plenty, sir.' One thing had been insisted on since the beginning – bren-gun magazines were removed from casualties, and bren-guns now constituted a high proportion of B Company's armament. B Company would not be over-whelmed from lack of ammunition.

'Some of them will probably start crawling forwards,' Adam yelled, 'trying to get through and behind.' Close infiltration – already they all knew German skill at that game. 'Try to spot them without exposing yourselves, and use riflemen on them.' He swung his binoculars northward for a quick look at the farm where 'Andy' might now be about to protect the Westmorlands' left, his finest hour. There was absolutely no sign. I expect they've gone, Adam thought without surprise or particular concern, I imagine my left flank is wide open. Well, at least I won't have to fulfil my promise and keep him informed when we go back! If we ever do go back. It seems pretty likely that we'll die here. Oh God, oh God, he prayed, let our guns start firing soon. He glanced at his watch and saw to his astonishment that only three minutes had elapsed since the first shout, the first intimation that the Jerries were over the canal.

The suspense almost choked Adam. When were the Jerries coming? When? Bursts of fire were still coming from the direction of the canal, demonstrative rather than concentrated, designed, surely to harass rather than destroy. Adam tried to clear his mind, to think calmly. Something was missing – what? Then he realized that this German attack had not been preceded by any sort of bombardment. The Germans had slipped down to the canal, embarked, crossed, were now forming up under the bank's lea. They'd first infiltrated troops – a company? a battalion? – to a point which must be nearly a thousand yards behind their objective sector, and these infiltrating troops had opened up on B Company from the rear, from extreme range – and probably on the Westmorlands' depth positions; but they'd not shelled the canal line themselves, they'd not shelled the British front. They hoped to achieve complete surprise, Adam thought. They reckoned that shelling meant warning, and that without warning they might slip over without too much difficulty. But once they come at us and we take them on, what then?

German shells? Mortars? By then they'll hope to have their own assault troops on the objective. Here. So perhaps they won't shell. His mouth was dry. Then he heard Company Sergeant-Major Darwin give an enormous cheer, and Bliss simultaneously gasp, 'Bluidy 'ell.'

Adam's first instinct had been right. The Germans were rushing them. Very few minutes had been needed for what they'd reckoned was the necessary number of storming parties to form up, creep forward a short distance from the canal bank and then rise from the ground and come racing forward, weaving and bending, most apparently firing on the move, firing Schmeiser machine-pistols slung across the body and here or there stopping to take a shot with a carbine. Every bren-gun in B Company was now firing. The noise was deafening. From the Germans Adam was vaguely conscious of incessant shouting, and much blowing of whistles. When he recalled those wild moments later he tried to compute how many of the Wehrmacht had actually stormed B Company sector and admitted to himself, with some dismay, that it was probably not more than about forty. At the time he had the sensation of being charged by the entire German army.

Adam brought his rifle up. Sixty yards away a German soldier stopped and bent his body back gracefully like a javelin thrower. Adam saw the stick grenade in his hand, destined for one of the foremost of Corporal Barney's slit trenches – there had, in those desperate seconds, been a good many of the sharp, lethal cracks of grenade explosions, both German and British. Adam took a quick shot and saw, with satisfaction, the man fall. Then he took aim at another soldier, a man shouting, perhaps a NCO, a leader, but as he watched the man threw up his arms and crumpled, and as he fell Adam saw that the German's entire head had been taken off by a burst of bren fire from very close range. And it was then that Adam heard the sound for which he'd been longing, the sound, far to the west, of British twenty-five-pounder guns. And a few seconds later there came the crashing sound of exploding shells on and about the line of the canal.

Bliss, no hero, was keeping very near the bottom of the trench. Bliss was trembling in a way Adam had never seen him tremble before. Bliss had the telephone set in his hand and held the instrument out to Adam, wordlessly.

It was Whisky.

'Don't want to bother you, Adam –'

'It's all right. We're holding them. Gunners have just done their stuff.'

'I know. Any good?'

'I should think so. We're dealing with them here. I think we can continue to do so if it doesn't go on too long. They're all among us now. Nearest is about –'

A burst of bren-gun fire came from the next slit trench. It was directed, Adam saw out of the corner of his eye, at a small party of Germans, perhaps three or four, who had dropped, risen and hurled grenades, then dropped again. And then risen again and were now hosepiping sub-machine-gun fire towards the group of trenches from which Adam had been trying to command B Company. Adam heard and felt the swish of bullets stinging the air. He ducked his head, but not before seeing the small group of helmets go down again; and at least one, perhaps two, had done so involuntarily. He held his rifle in his left hand, ready to bring it up again, and in the right resumed the field telephone.

'Hullo.'

'Adam?'

The crash of artillery shells sounded again from the general line of the canal. For the moment no Germans were visible. They seemed to have gone to ground, but gone to ground, presumably, within fifty yards of B Company trenches. For the most part.

'Adam?'

'Yes, sir. We've held them so far. The gunners sound as if they're pasting the next lot. The follow-up. If that's worked, we ought to be able to cope. Just.'

'Adam, Possel –'

'Yes?'

'Forget what I said about orders. Get your chaps back there, as and how you can, by whatever route you choose, whenever you can. You obviously can't just now.'

'No, sir.'

'But pick your own moment. If you can let me know, do so. If you can't, don't bother. I'll know what you're trying to do.'

'Right, sir.'

'Good luck, Adam. I don't think I can do any more for you just at the moment. The gunners will do their best. Good luck.'

Adam threw the handset at Bliss and peered over the edge of the slit trench. For the half minute during which he'd talked to Whisky there'd been no rifle or machine-gun firing. A sighing in the air followed by yet more crashes from two hundred yards in front of them demonstrated that the Royal Artillery, though short of ammunition, had not yet entirely run out.

'Mr Hardrow!'

It was Sergeant-Major Darwin's voice. The first German assault, by Adam's watch, had taken place only fifteen minutes ago!

'Mr Hardrow, I reckon they've cleared off.'

Adam got shouted reports from the furthest left to furthest right. It did indeed seem that, for the time being, the Germans had withdrawn. They won't have gone back far, Adam thought. They won't go back into our artillery fire, they know that the nearer they can stick to our positions the safer they are. But they've not been able to take our positions, and the follow-up echelon's been broken by our guns. Thank God for the gunners!

Adam decided to leave his slit trench. It might be foolhardy but he felt tolerably sure that the German assault wave would by now be sheltering back under the lea of the western canal bank. They wouldn't lie out in the open – except for the wounded and the dead.

'Sergeant-Major, I'm coming over!'

As Adam ran as fast as he could across the intervening space between his slit trench and Darwin's, he was aware of a number of grey-green bodies lying very still. Ten? Fifteen? B Company had surely given a decent account of itself. Ben Jameson would be proud of B Company. And nobody had lost a trench, or given an inch.

Sharing a slit trench with the sergeant-major, Adam began to assemble information about their own casualties. These, considering the hubbub, the explosions, the lead flying, had been astoundingly light. Two men had been hit by grenade fragments, one in the shoulder, one in the neck. Field dressings were being applied and both could walk. And one man had been shot clean through the head by a Schmeiser bullet.

'Who?'

It was Crowe, Sergeant-Major Darwin said. Crowe had bought it. Decent man. Good soldier, too.

They talked hurriedly. There had recently been no sound from the Spandau parties who had infiltrated so far to their west, and it might be presumed that they were now involved in a wider plan, having made a demonstration to assist their comrades who had crossed the canal and assaulted frontally – and unsuccessfully. The Jerries would come on again when reinforcements crossed, but reinforcements had suffered from British artillery, although to an unknown extent. The next main effort might be made in five minutes or five hours. Or something between the two.

'Sergeant-Major, Major Wainwright spoke to me just as the Jerry attack started. We're to go back to Possel in our own time.'

Darwin nodded. The sooner the better, the nod implied.

Adam agreed a quick plan with him. Darwin and about half of each of Corporal Barney's and Corporal Travers's detachments would go back now. Darwin would shout to each trench and gather them up at a point they identified four hundred yards to the south-west, well clear of the canal, well clear of their present positions. Five minutes later, having held themselves ready to open up with maximum fire if attacked during those five minutes, Adam would bring the remainder back. Fast. Then B Company would move as rapidly as they could to the area of Possel where, providence consenting, the rest of the 2nd Battalion, Westmorland Regiment, would be established. It wasn't glorious, it wasn't how these things were done in the text books, Adam recalled. It was thin out and then scuttle. But they'd killed a number of Jerries, they'd held their positions as ordered and they'd had few men killed. Including, however, Sergeant Pew. Including Crowe.

CHAPTER 10

Ivan Perry announced that he must be gaining a reputation for skill in defence of towns and villages. To his tired but ever-whimsical mind it seemed that whenever orders were given out for yet another defensive position there was, somewhere, the sentence – 'and A Company will hold the village itself'. Koreyck. Possel. Others whose names he was too exhausted at present to remember. And now Boskapelle.

Whisky had divided the battalion into two detachments, combining A, B and D Companies into one force under David Bassett, a force about one hundred and twenty strong; the rest of the battalion – C Company, and every man who could be squeezed from battalion headquarters, the transport, the carrier platoon – were combined in another strong detachment, of about the same size, under Lieutenant Charles Wade, the carrier platoon commander. Adam had never known Wade really well – a very senior subaltern, Wade was notoriously taciturn and had the reputation of being humourless and a little grim, although he had become noticeably easier after Colonel Fosdike's departure. In the last two weeks orders had, again and again, referred to some withdrawal or movement 'covered by the carrier platoon', or to some position with 'carrier platoon to watch the right flank, and send one section to cover the left flank'; the platoon had also provided occasional minimally protected runabout vehicles at the commanding officer's behest for such forays as that made by Adam to his left-hand neighbours on the canal position, recently abandoned, and was often used by Whisky himself for getting round companies. Throughout, these small, noisy vehicles had defied traffic conditions, mud, steep banks, water-logged meadows, and had stayed running. Adam knew that Charles Wade had only lost one vehicle (for the want of a spare part which nobody could produce) since the campaign started. Wade habitually said little at Whisky's orders, but when a carrier section or individual vehicle had to report to one of the companies he would tap the recipient on the shoulder before they all dispersed.

'It'll be corporal so-and-so. Please make sure he's properly looked after.'

'Of course.'

Charles Wade would nod, unsmiling.

It seemed wholly right that he should now be in command of one wing of the battalion. Orders had been given out on the previous day, 29 May, that all vehicles, including carriers, were to be put out of action and abandoned when the Westmorlands withdrew from this, their last defensive position before reaching the coast. The beaches of Dunkirk were only five miles from their backs.

Charles Wade had said, 'Right. They'll be immobilized. We'll probably burn them as a matter of fact. But before then you might, sir, find it useful to have one or two still available.'

'I might, Charles. But the orders are quite clear. On leaving this place, all, I repeat all, vehicles are to be immobilized. Got it?'

Charles Wade had said nothing. Everybody knew that he would go his own way and that if the assembled company ever got away from France the Westmorlands' carriers would be ablaze at the water line – not much before.

Whisky had then told them that the other wing of the battalion, under Major Bassett, would hold Boskapelle itself. He was giving his orders to all, or nearly all, the surviving officers of the battalion, regardless of the chain of command. He was treating both Adam and Ivan as company commanders, only grunting that Major Bassett would coordinate A, B and D. Effectively, Adam thought, Ivan and I are again platoon commanders, under David Bassett. And it makes sense. He was sitting on a flimsy church chair next to Ivan and this made them both happy.

Ivan thought, I wonder how Adam got on in that last place – he had one hell of a time as far as one can make out, he was attacked by the Jerries, and strafed from the air and the people on his left ran away, or that's the story that's going round; he looks very tired and very grim. They had not had the chance of a talk in the last twenty-four hours of somewhat confused withdrawal from the canal, first to and then from the village of Possel. And now here they were, only a few miles from the sea. Next stop England.

'– Boskapelle itself,' Whisky was saying. They were to take advantage of the cellars where cellars existed, to protect men resting or men wounded from shelling and from air attack; but they were to make utterly sure that nobody started skulking in cellars whose business was shooting Germans in Boskapelle's streets. The place was bound to be attacked pretty shortly. From Dunkirk itself, and from the beaches, evacuation was proceeding, Whisky said. Covered, at the moment, by us. Somebody asked how embarkation was being managed if they were meant to go to beaches rather than a port, and Whisky said briefly that they'd find out when they got there. If they got there.

They dispersed. Orders had been given out in the new-looking red-brick church in the main square of Boskapelle and as they left to return to their men, already slumbering in the ground-floor rooms of some of Boskapelle's houses, Ivan took Adam's arm.

'Yet another built-up area! I think I prefer them, on the whole, to the hedges and ditches.'

Adam said, without answering Ivan's smile, 'They eat up men, though.'

'Of course.' David Bassett, with unusual briskness, had allocated to each of them specific parts of the town to defend, an allocation based on where their men now found themselves. There had not been time for elaborate planning. A good many streets, houses, gardens to each. Hard to cover. Hard to coordinate fire and action.

'I'm sorry about Sergeant Pew, Adam.' Ivan had heard.

'Thanks.'

'Adam, do you think we're going to get away?'

'Might, I suppose. Depends a bit on how hard the Jerries push.'

'It must depend at least as much on whether there are any boats to take us.'

Adam said, with a slight return to an easier humour, 'Poor old Charles. Leaving his carriers. Burning his carriers!'

'Poor old Charles, indeed. Adam, the roads running away east and north-east from this place in my area are completely blocked with abandoned vehicles. As far as the eye can see.'

'I know. And in mine. The whole country's like some enormous scrap-yard.'

'And the fields each side of the roads –'

'Exactly. Not difficult for the Jerries to get cover from view as they advance! When they advance!'

They knew that they must hurry back to their responsibilities. They knew that they hated leaving each other.

'Well, good luck, Ivan.'

'And to you, Adam. See you on the boat deck, unless the bar's open.'

Adam didn't smile. He said, 'Ivan –'

'We'd better be going.'

Adam had wanted to say, 'I had to shoot a British officer, a senior officer. He was running away. I want to talk about it. I've not had the chance to report it to the CO yet. It –'

271

Instead he nodded and walked fast down a Boskapelle street. Company Sergeant-Major Darwin had been organizing food.

Darwin said, 'I'd leave them, sir. To hell with them.' He had just reported to Adam that in three of the cellars in B Company's sector he had found a number of British soldiers, helplessly drunk, unarmed and apparently mindless.

'They didn't know their units, sir. Or pretended not to. Deserters, that's all they are. Should be shot.'

'Sergeant-Major, tell them that if they form up now, we'll arm them, and they've a chance to –'

'No good, sir. They're past it. Not making sense, you might say. Doubt if many can stand.'

'Well, tell them that they can stay in the cellars, and if the houses burn after shelling or air attack they'll probably burn to death. We're not going to help them out.'

'Right, sir.' This was congenial to Darwin. The look on his face was one of disgust. Adam knew that Darwin would prefer to shoot the deserters, but burning alive would do. Adam, however, remembered a flushed, drunken face in the back seat of Belgian car. Who knew to what extent these men had been abandoned by those whose duty was to lead them, care for them, exert decent authority? He hadn't long for such gloomy speculations, however. Private Bliss, still alive, still nervous, still faithful, called out 'Major Bassett, sir,' and Adam saluted the rubicund, amiable face of David Bassett, now his immediate superior in the defence of Boskapelle.

David Bassett, walking rapidly for him, had approached from the direction of the main square. B Company's sector of responsibility was the south-east quarter of the place, a network of narrow streets with an enormous builder's yard marking the periphery of town. For this task Adam now had thirty-seven men. Between them, however, they numbered seven bren light machine-guns. It was, Adam thought, eyes of which he was short, not bullets. And now there was nothing in front of them, no friendly armoured cars, no carriers, no observation posts. Just flat, poplar-lined fields, largely covered by the abandoned carcasses of much of the transport, close packed, of the British army.

David Bassett, 'slow but sure' as his reputation ran, was unkindly nicknamed 'Lightning' within the Westmorlands, a nickname of which he was aware, without resentment. He said, 'The CO's just on his way round. You all right here, Adam?'

'I think I can just cover every street. But only just.'

Then David Bassett, voice unhurried, unchanged, said, 'Here they come. Pretty punctual.' They both moved sharply into the lee of a doorway. The Heinkels came over fairly high and there was no doubt that Boskapelle was their target. The shriek of bombs descending, the crash of the explosions, a few scattered shouts, drifting smoke – it was all familiar by now, and Adam wondered whether he was the only officer in the British Expeditionary Force who found it more, not less, disagreeable each time; who found, with shame, that his heart was beating faster and his body sweating more freely than when the Westmorlands had first received the Luftwaffe's attentions over a week ago. I suppose, he thought, one imagines that the odds shorten each time. That's what makes one windier! He wondered if what he thought of as his cowardice showed. It was, or seemed to be, in sharp contrast to David Bassett's reactions. As the bombs burst – one, two, three, four, five, six, seven, eight – then a brief pause – then nine, ten – David Bassett was actually laughing.

'Bloody shits!'

As far as Adam could guess from the sound of the attack the bombs had fallen in the centre and north, near battalion headquarters and in the sector held by Charles Wade and the left half of the battalion. He hoped Whisky was all right – one of the ear-splitting crashes seemed to come from very near the church where Whisky had given out orders, very near battalion headquarters. But three minutes later, when he and David Bassett had straightened themselves and moved away from the cover of the doorway, he saw Whisky Wainwright walking rapidly down the street towards them. They had already observed several columns of black smoke climbing skyward.

Whisky grunted, 'Two houses set alight. Some of battalion headquarters.'

They looked question marks at him and he said, 'Bobby's in a poor way, and Venning.'

Venning was a signaller, a mainstay of headquarters. Whisky told them that a bomb had brought the roof down, that those two had been hit hard by falling masonry and that a large lump had come down slap bang on Bobby Forrest's head. 'Think he'll be all right, tomorrow,' Whisky said briefly. He added that the upper floors had started burning and they'd had difficulty getting the casualties out. But had succeeded. It had all happened very quickly.

Whisky didn't know about bomb casualties in the rest of the battalion, he'd been about to go round and was now doing so. David Bassett said in his deliberate way that it sounded as if the attack had mostly fallen on 'Charles and his boys'. He nodded towards the other half of Boskapelle, and Whisky said, 'Well, I'd better be off and have a look. You all right here?'

'I think so.'

Whisky said that after 'a talk with old Charles' he'd come back this way and have more of a look round, he didn't want to hang about now. The signallers were trying to run line out, meanwhile they knew where headquarters were, he'd be back, good luck. And half an hour later, during which nothing had happened, Whisky turned up again in Adam's sector. David Bassett was with him. Both their faces were grave. Whisky said that Charles Wade's detachment 'had caught it pretty badly'.

'Damned unlucky bomb. Bloody awful luck.'

It appeared that Charles Wade had been giving out orders to his two remaining officers and to three NCOs. A bomb had hit the actual house – a detached bungalow – where they were lying on the floor, and a second bomb had found a house three doors up the same road, which several men were converting to a defensive point. Total casualties were five killed and eleven wounded; including most of the remaining junior commanders in the northern half of the battalion. It was miserable luck. Charles Wade himself had, miraculously, escaped. A large piece of roof had smashed down inches from where he'd lain on the floor, and the flying glass from a shattered window had skimmed just above his head. He was now reorganizing his remaining men.

Whisky said, 'I'm not going to send anyone up from this bit of town. We've only got to hang on for about twenty-four hours, and it'll be best to leave people where they are, rather than –'

Rather than muck them about, Adam thought. He was sure Whisky was right. The Westmorlands' dispositions, numbers reduced by casualties, might be imperfect but it was almost certainly best to hang on wherever they now found themselves, and shoot it out if the Jerries attacked.

Whisky had just mentioned twenty-four hours and Adam ventured the question, 'Where do we go in twenty-four hours, sir?'

'Unless things change, we march back to the coast. Down the road which runs north-westward from the main square.'

'Covered –'

Whisky seemed disposed to talk. He said, 'Twenty-four hours takes us to – well to tomorrow afternoon. Might have to wait until evening. Then we pull out to the beach, covered by ourselves. Company by company.'

'And at the beach –'

'There'll be people in position, obviously. Covering us off, covering the actual embarkation.'

It sounded extraordinary. It also sounded as if twenty-four hours might well be thirty-six. What could possibly delay for long a determined German push to the sea in this area, a push which would enable the Wehrmacht to sweep beaches, port, sand-dunes, everything, with direct fire? Whisky said, 'Doubt if they'll want to mix it, hand-to-hand. They'll hope to shell us to hell and bomb us to hell. They'll think they've got us in the bag. Why waste men on us?'

Adam nodded. It was reassurance of a sort. A pretty odd sort. And it didn't exactly tie up with Whisky's earlier remark that the Germans were bound to attack Boskapelle soon.

'You all right, yourself, Adam?'

'Yes, sir.'

'Sorry about your platoon sergeant. Pew.'

'Thank you, sir.'

'Good chap, Pew.'

Adam suddenly felt the moment was ripe for more. He said, 'I ought to report one thing that happened on the canal line, sir. I've not told anyone of it until now.'

'Well, hurry up.'

'I had to shoot an officer. A major. He was in a car, going to bolt, leave his men. They were bolting too.' Adam described it, very accurately.

Whisky said, 'Hmm.' Then he said, 'I heard something of this. Or guessed it, anyway.'

Corporal Staines, perhaps.

'Who knows about this? So far?'

'I suppose the captain who was there. I was prepared to shoot him too. Then he seemed to pull himself together and sober up. They – the men of that battalion – were still there for a while. I watched them, from that position. I think the other chap, the captain, must have done all right. I'm glad I didn't shoot him.'

'Not sure I am. Well, that's all right, Adam. You did the right thing.' Whisky Wainwright plodded off in the direction of Ivan Perry's sector.

For some reason the series of single shots which snapped the air of Boskapelle at seven o'clock next morning struck Adam's ear as more sinister, more menacing than the other sounds for which all ears had been nervously ready throughout the previous day and night. There had been no return of German bombers, no whistle and whine of black, descending bombs, no crashes and cracks as smoke rose and flames caught. There had been no German shelling of the town itself, although they could all hear, all the time, the rumble and thud of the Wehrmacht's artillery pounding the country, and presumably the roads, east and west of them. One apparently purposeless strafe from German mortars had hit the southern rim of the town in the early evening, mortar shells distributed over a wide frontage on and near the houses on the outer perimeter. It had done no harm to the Westmorlands, but Adam had supposed it presaged an infantry attack and they all stood ready. Nothing happened. Another intensive hail of mortar bombs had fallen on the same places exactly two hours later, and again they stood ready and again nothing happened. The night was astoundingly quiet, although the shellfire on targets somewhere behind them, between them and the coast, seemed to intensify. Was Whisky right in his assertion that the Germans were probably so confident of having the British army trapped that they didn't propose to spend men and effort on further assaults?

Then dawn. Stand-to. Brew-up and breakfasts. Washing. Cleaning up. In every man's mind there was now only one thought – England. Would they get away? Would Jerry attack, and would that attack spoil their chances, spoil them probably for ever? And by now 'chances' meant, very simply, 'chances of survival'.

And then that series of single shots. Adam was drinking a mug of tea with Sergeant-Major Darwin and they looked at each other. Darwin voiced both their thoughts.

'Pretty near. A Company sector, I'd say.'

The shots had sounded not from the periphery but from the interior of the little town. A minute later Adam saw Private Amey racing down the street. Amey was David Bassett's runner. He reached them, very out of breath.

'Major Bassett – orders – every available man –' Amey was gasping and pointing. Adam heard, 'In between – post office and –'

Darwin was quick. Amey needed prompting.

'That's all right, Amey. Post office' (David Bassett's head-quarters were in the post office) '– and the canal, is that it?'

Amey, still gasping and stuttering, nodded. Darwin snapped out 'Jerries?' And Amey went on nodding. He was coughing now, completely incapable of articulate speech. Darwin turned to Adam.

'Jerries seem to have got in somehow, sir.' There was a long strip of tree-lined open ground, a sort of park, along the edge of the canal which ran through Boskapelle. Near the post office. Very near David Bassett. About three hundred yards away.

Adam said, 'Sergeant-Major, leave one look-out in each section, one pair of bren-gunners. Every other man here, at the double.' Darwin moved off sharply, picking up two or three men as he moved and dispatching them in several directions. Four minutes later Adam found himself with some twenty-five Westmorlands of various ranks. Aware that he was probably contravening every principle of infantry tactics, and especially of infantry tactics recommended for built-up areas, Adam snapped, 'After me, each side of the street,' and ran towards the direction of the canal. Thirty yards short of the point where their street debouched on to the open space by the canal bank he held up his arm, gestured to the men behind him to get down, and made for the end of the street. Very cautiously, he put his head round the corner of the end building. And then jerked it back.

The message had been accurate. The canal bank park, as Adam thought of it, was filled with Germans. They were sauntering about, apparently without a care. Did they not *know* that they were in the middle of a defensive position of 2nd Battalion, Westmorland Regiment? Did they think the British army was beaten already? That nothing lay between them and the Channel beaches?

Presumably. Nor were these Germans behaving as if they supposed they were at any risk. Adam saw what looked like an officer, with a map, pointing. Another man approached him and snapped to attention. It all looked very formal, very efficient, very much a matter of routine. Adam absorbed this remarkable picture in about five seconds. He backed round the end building in the street and grabbed Sergeant-Major Darwin's arm. This situation couldn't last. Soon the Germans would have set up machine-gun nests and strong points in the canal park. Were they already established in another sector of the town, or were those individual shots he'd heard seven minutes earlier the work of snipers, stealthily infiltrated and picking off the defenders from the rear, while their comrades walked in through the front door, bold as brass? It didn't matter. Here and now there was only one thing to do. The Jerries in this bit of Boskapelle had got to be cleaned up, and very, very quickly. Adam hissed at Darwin's ear.

'You – two bren-guns – end of street –' He pointed. Darwin nodded.

'I'm taking the rest – parallel street –' again he pointed. A short parallel street ran straight to the canal park. Another, even shorter, street connected this with where they were standing.

'In one minute – open up – for one minute – then I'll go in.' Again Darwin nodded. With luck they'd get off four magazines. Over a hundred rounds. A hundred rounds at very, very close quarters.

Adam gestured to the men behind him. His face was contorted with urgency and excitement, and it infected them, tired, dispirited, avid for safety and escape to England though they were. He muttered, and the word was passed on – 'Bayonets on!'

Men fixed bayonets as they ran, the long sword-like bayonet of the British army. As they reached what Adam had called 'parallel street' he turned and, with an expressive gesture, threw the men into single line behind him and across the roadway itself. The roadway, with its pavements, was wide. They formed a twenty-yard front. Simultaneously, they heard Sergeant-Major Darwin's bren-guns open up, a deafening sound – fractionally early a tiny bit of Adam's mind suggested. It didn't matter. Probably they'd been spotted and Darwin wasn't going to miss the chance of getting the first shots in.

The bren-guns clattered, and almost louder came the yells of orders, and here and there the shriek of a wounded or dying man from the open space ahead of them, now only about twenty-five yards away. Astonishingly, no German was looking down their street, looking towards them. Adam swung his arm, palm downwards.

'Down!'

Several men edged their rifles forward, ready to shoot down the street if Jerry turned in their direction. Christ, what a do! Lying down in a road, in broad daylight, under twenty yards from Jerry, and Sergeant-Major bloody Darwin brassing them up with bren-guns! Christ knew what Hardrow thought he was on –

The bren-guns stopped. The yelling from ahead of them intensified and now Adam heard the high, ripping note of several Schmeisers.

'AFTER ME!'

Adam tore towards the canal park, yelling now. And he was afterwards assured, by several witnesses, that they'd followed him. They'd all followed him. He supposed later that it was lunacy, that as much or more might have been achieved by selecting and occupying fire positions overlooking the canal. He only knew at the time that the Jerries must, absolutely must, be driven out of Boskapelle. They mustn't be allowed to establish themselves in the town, mustn't force the Westmorlands to mount some sort of deliberate attack for which men and resources and time were all in short supply. There had been only one thing to do – go for them, flat out, and hope that they weren't in too large numbers. And that, shocked by the surprise, they'd bolt.

They weren't in too large numbers. They were shocked by surprise. They bolted.

Five minutes later David Bassett, attempting a somewhat similar manoeuvre with men from D Company, joined Adam on the canal bank. The Germans, firing as they moved, had withdrawn under orders. It looked as if they'd withdrawn beyond the far rim of the village, and David Bassett was pushing a section of men towards that far rim, shouting at them to move with caution, get into those houses over there. There was no firing now.

'Well done, Adam,' David Bassett said, without any sign of particular emotion. 'Well done. I got a nasty shock when I saw the buggers, pretty well just outside my window! You were the nearest chaps I had, and you seem to have sorted them out!'

Adam remained uncertain exactly what had happened. Certainly no bayonets had been bloodied, he discovered, although the exploit swiftly became magnified in the recollections of the Westmorland survivors. In one or two, realism persisted. 'I saw one bastard's face as I got round the corner,' Adam heard Corporal Travers recount, long after the event, 'and buggered if he wasn't as f—ing scared as I was! It fair boosted me f—ing spirits!'

As to the earlier single shots Adam had heard, there had, indeed, been snipers infiltrated into the town and two men of A Company had been shot dead by them. Accurately or not, the word had got round that these snipers were civilians, or German soldiers in civilian clothes, and Adam learned afterwards what had happened then. A small party from A Company, led by Ivan, had identified the house whence the lethal shots had been fired, had broken into it and been instantly menaced by a man in civilian clothes with a rifle. They had shot him dead, and then, hearing a hubbub of other voices in a sort of storeroom at the back had assumed that these were more supporters of the sniper.

'The whole house,' Ivan told Adam next day, 'was packed with them. Jerries, I'm sure. In disguise.'

'Armed?'

'We didn't wait to see. I pulled the pin of a grenade and tossed it in among them. Through the door and down some steps. Shut the door and got clear. It went off all right. There were no windows.'

Ivan's rather soft, very youthful face wore no expression as he described the incident. Adam nodded. At least he understood. War wasn't exactly what people at home supposed. He said, 'I expect they were all in it together. Fifth columnists, German agents, whatever they were.'

'I'm sure of it. Good riddance.'

'Good riddance.' He knew that Ivan and he were dogged by the same doubts and probably always would be. Ivan said quietly, 'They got Bowes and Sharpson. I don't expect you remember Bowes. The men always called him Stringer. He had a marvellous smile. His whole face smiled. He cheered everyone up, always.'

'No, I don't remember him.'

It was 1 June. They were lying behind a sand-hill, one of the range of dunes bordering the Dunkirk beaches. They had marched, company by company, out of Boskapelle, and Whisky had varied the orders – and gone well beyond his own – by decreeing that the remnants of the carrier platoon would constitute a rearguard, withdraw last and only destroy their vehicles when that had been done. Charles Wade had simply nodded, and said that when his detachment of the battalion was clear of the town he'd return to the carriers and see them out. Whisky had not demurred.

Then every company, once Boskapelle was behind them, had closed up in threes and marched down the road towards the beach, marching past Whisky Wainwright. They'd marched well, every man turning head and eyes on the command and looking Whisky Wainwright full in the face. No man in the Westmorland ranks was without a weapon. Adam felt Whisky's eyes on every one of them – there was still a little evening light in the sky; the last company marched out at ten o'clock. Adam heard Whisky's voice just after he'd passed.

'Mr Hardrow!'

It was the usual bellow. He left his position and ran back to report to the CO. Whisky said, 'Do you know how many men in your detachment don't belong to the regiment?'

'Five, sir. We picked them up on the day we had the fight at Droot Farm.'

'Are they all right?'

'They've done well, sir. They want to stay with us now.' Whisky nodded, and said something might be fixed, you never knew. In England, if they ever reached it. Adam doubled off to resume his place at the head of the rump of B Company. Although the remnants of three companies had been combined under David Bassett's command in Boskapelle, they'd marched out as the old companies of the 2nd

Battalion. Adam had B in step behind him and wished for nothing else.

It was dark when they reached the beaches. They could make out the enormous masses of men, forming what seemed huge, shapeless columns with their heads near the lapping waters of the Channel and stretching back into the dunes themselves. The men had dug slit trenches everywhere – on the beach, among the sand-hills. There was a low murmur coming from that great, vulnerable assembly, a sort of corporate sigh for rescue, for hope; above all, perhaps, for orders and organization. Whisky Wainwright, again flouting his own earlier instructions, had ridden to the beach in one of the last of Charles Wade's carriers, its last passenger before immolation. He had moved quietly from group to group of Westmorlands in the darkness, his voice clear, unfussed, grumpy as usual and conveying like electricity its own brief impulse of confidence.

'Dig in here in the dunes. Bombers bound to be over at first light. Jerry guns will soon get range of the beach, too. Soft sand, they won't do you much harm as long as you dig in now. Doesn't matter where.'

Then, to each company commander as he passed, 'Don't know how they'll get aboard, but there'll be boats plying when it's light and the tide's in. Don't try to organize 'em, just get the men to queue up, do what the rest are doing, take their chance. We'll all get on somehow. Chaps have got to look after themselves now, I'm afraid.'

To Adam, Whisky also said, to Adam's surprise and sadness, 'Brigadier was killed last night.'

'I'm sorry, sir.'

'Shell. Great loss. Good friend to the battalion.' That certainly was the brigadier's reputation. Whisky stumped on.

At daybreak they could all see the considerable array of ships of various kinds and sizes lying off the coast. They looked a long way away. Would it be possible to swim it,

Adam wondered? He was not a strong swimmer. Few of the men could swim at all – they'd be dependent on small boats getting in and ferrying men out. Meanwhile what about the Luftwaffe? Great queues of men had re-formed as light came, waiting, hoping, eyes fixed on the ships. A few small boats were visible, moving cautiously towards shore. Adam tried not to think of how many thousands of men were waiting to be taken off. Large numbers had now removed boots and rolled up trousers, and were paddling in the nearest waves, willing some boat or other to come within reach, fearful, hoping.

Adam always had one eye cocked on the sky. The queues to the water's edge were orderly but massive and he had decided that there was no point yet in edging towards possible rescue. Most of the Westmorlands were together, and could support and comfort each other. In the eyes of most was resignation. All still had rifles or bren-guns in hand. He lay behind the sand-hill, dozed a little, talked to Ivan.

At nine o'clock in the morning came the first diversion.

The sound of the Junker bombers was by now familiar to most of the men on the beach, and as they came in, wave of four following wave of four, swiftly succeeded by a second and then a third echelon, there was an unnecessary, spontaneous yell of 'Here they come!', and then most men were down, huddling into slit trenches scooped from the sand or simply lying on the beach shielding their heads with hands clasped behind necks in the instinctive, useless gesture of the frightened. But the Junkers' target was not the men standing in their anxious, patient queues but the ships which might conceivably take them to safety. Adam heard a terrible, heart-tearing moan suddenly go up from the pack of men cowering nearest to him.

'Ah-h-h-h!'

It was a destroyer, struck amidships and now burning. A destroyer which might, within the hour, have crowded hundreds of men somehow on to her decks. Then came another shocked, shattered gasp, the gasp of hope frustrated, of hope slipping away. A small tugboat, of the sort familiar in estuaries, had suffered a direct hit. They could see bodies round her, and a few fortunate ones still alive and leaping into the water.

But then a great cheer went up. A large flat-bottomed barge had survived, and had apparently shipped a small motor boat which could be seen with three, if not four, rowing-boats roped and in tow; and this little caravan was, unmistakably, heading towards shore. Furthermore, Adam could see a number of other similar exercises going on up and down the beach. Men were on their feet now, and there was movement in the queues and towards the queues. The whole beach was suddenly alive, as on some bizarre bank holiday. Adam had already told them to make their own way, take the best chance each individual could see, swim to a boat if there was a boat within the swimming distance of a man's capability. Small knots of men were now making off towards the water's edge.

'Hopeless!' Adam heard an officer of another regiment say, as he trudged past through the soft sand, a small gaggle of men behind him. 'Absolutely hopeless! They'll never get these numbers off. Must be thousands! Never get more than a handful of boats in, and the Junkers will soon be back.'

'Well?'

'Best march along the beach to Dunkirk. There's a proper evacuation going on at Dunkirk. Ships alongside, that sort of thing.'

'He may be right,' said Ivan.

'He may be. But I think there's a decent chance of getting a good few off here when the tide's higher.' There seemed, now, to be even larger numbers of craft lying offshore.

'You may be right, too,' Ivan said, his usual rather languid manner again in evidence. 'You may both be right. I rather feel that each individual has to decide such a matter for himself. I'm sure they're all – our excellent Westmorlands – at least as competent to decide it as I am. I feel the character of the decisive leader rather missing in me at the moment.'

'And in me,' said Adam, but Ivan knew he didn't mean it. He looked at his friend Adam Hardrow with intense, troubling affection and wondered whether they'd ever have dinner together in England again.

'I'll just see whether any of A Company have decided to swim or something like that. I don't want to be the first away. Or rather I don't want to look as if I'm the first away.'

'All right,' Adam said. 'I'll stay here. I won't start swimming till you get back.' He was half in earnest. Beyond the waterline, a hundred yards distant, a rather smart motor cruiser was bobbing on the waves. No small craft seemed to be plying from or to it at the moment. How far was it? Six hundred yards? Surely not more, and that must be comfortably possible if one stripped. If weapons couldn't be carried off, Whisky had said, they must be made useless, rifle bolts and bren spare parts jettisoned and so forth. Well, that was all right. If one stripped, then even though rather a feeble swimmer that must surely be –

Six hundred yards? Adam recognized with one of those stabs of truth to which he was liable, that the motor cruiser was probably in fact a thousand yards off shore. And showing no signs of moving nearer. Still, if the shore was shallow one could probably walk out quite a way, which would reduce swimming distance. There were a good many men now in the water, up to their armpits, even up to their necks in some cases. They hadn't, Adam had to confess, yet got very far towards England. Still –

The Messerschmitts came in low and fast from the east, and the spurts of sand which went up as their bullets struck the beach hit Adam's senses just before he was aware of the roar of the aircraft engines and the rattle of their machine-guns. Everywhere men were dropping with the familiar reflexes of self-preservation. Rat-a-tat-a-tat-a-tat! Rat-a-tat-a-tat-a-tat-a-tat! Adam, prone, was glad to see that a lot of men were firing up at the Messerschmitts with rifles and brens. Not everyone, he thought, is cowering, like I am! Still, my pistol's not much good and my rifle went to arm one of the reformed deserters from another regiment.

Rat-a-tat-a-tat-a-tat-a-tat! They were away, they were showing no signs of turning, relief rippled like a sighing wind through that enormous multitude. Adam levered himself to his feet. He saw a sergeant he knew by sight moving heavily through the sand towards him. The man called out, 'Mr Hardrow, sir!'

And then moved nearer, panting with the exertion. Everywhere men were standing up, rejoining queues, moving again towards the water, talking excitedly. There were gestures towards the skyline near Dunkirk, beyond which the Messerschmitts had withdrawn. Adam expected that several claims were already germinating.

'Got him with a whole magazine, I'll swear it!'

'Yeah, he's probably down beyond the tower there –'

He said to the sergeant, 'Yes?' It was, he recognized, one of A Company's senior NCOs.

'Mr Hardrow, sir, it's Mr Perry. Messerschmitt, sir.'

Adam looked a question, but he knew what the answer would be. It was extraordinary, and merciful, that the machine-gunning of a crowded beach had apparently caused so few casualties, but for Adam the mercy had now run out. He cared nothing for the German shelling, which had hitherto been sporadic, but started in earnest soon after the Messerschmitt's run. Now the Wehrmacht's guns had ranged on the beaches.

CHAPTER 11

It was a time for letters. Few of the Expeditionary Force evacuated from Dunkirk could be spared for leave, to see their families, to relax. Dispatched from Dover and other ports by train to hastily appointed destinations, regiments, battalions and brigades reassembled in various parts of the country, were issued with new equipment as far as it existed, and with very old equipment or no equipment at all where it did not; and were swept into the feverish plans now being made to defend England against invasion.

Such was the immediate fate of 2nd Westmorlands. The unthinkable had happened. Britain, for so long able to regard war as something to be conducted on someone else's territory, something in which one could decide to play a larger or a smaller part dependent on taste and circumstances, Britain had now to face the ultimate reality to which Continental nations had always been exposed. 'I don't even know how to feel,' Bobby Forrest remarked obscurely to Adam. 'I suppose Frenchmen grow up knowing this sort of thing in their bones. We don't!' Adam agreed. Astonishingly, war was now something which immediately threatened home, family, loyalties, the entire framework of existence. And if the war were lost –

But nobody seriously thought that the war would be lost. Despite newspaper articles (censored and for the most part optimistic) on the balance of forces now in the field, despite the alarming stories of men recently evacuated from the fields of Flanders, despite the size and menace of the Luftwaffe, now apparently poised to obliterate much of England in preparation for the Wehrmacht's invasion – despite all this everybody expected that in the end the British would win. Nobody knew how. An attempt to open another front in France by shipping more troops to Brittany had quickly fizzled out. From beyond the Channel came news of German divisions across the Somme, reaching the Seine; of a front which seemed permeable everywhere and a French government with little stomach for the fight. Then came news of a peace, negotiated by France with the conqueror: of German troops marching down the Champs Élysées in Paris. Britain was alone. And still everybody refused to believe in ultimate disaster. And everybody, in whatever time was available from his or her particular duty in facing the expected German onslaught on Britain, the German invasion of Britain – everybody tried to recover human contacts, which for many had been severed by the chaotic events in France and Flanders since 10 May. It was a time of telephoning, for those who had access to a telephone, though the exchanges were desperately overworked. But above all it was a time for letters.

Dear Mama,
I'm glad I managed to get through on the telephone at last. Sorry my only letter was just a scribble to let you know I'm alive and really very well. But, as you can imagine, since getting back we've been busy every hour of every day, sorting the battalion out and issuing new equipment and so forth – not to speak of getting ready for another job – the most important one in history, perhaps. But there seems to be a lull for a day or two, getting a second wind so to speak. And so I'm writing. I'm sure weekend leave will start *if* – well, *if* you-know-what is delayed for a bit or doesn't happen. Just at present there's

no hope of days off. And of course I hate thinking about air raids – you may soon be much more in the war than I am, darling Mama! And I think about you all the time.

I eventually got away from the Dunkirk beaches in a small motor boat with nine others. We reached what seemed like a sort of tramp steamer, quite big and smoke coming out of the funnel, and they yelled, 'How many?' We said, 'Ten'! All sorts of swearing and a voice shouted that they'd no room at all, they could just cram in two or three – and I'm bound to say that they were so packed on her deck, one could see that, that I saw what they meant. But we yelled back, 'Thanks. They're little ones,' or some such nonsense, and helped two or three up a rope ladder and on to her deck, and when they got there one of our people was persuasive and said that two of the men in the boat were badly wounded (which was half true, they were wounded but not too bad, they could walk) and by that time we were helping the wounded ones up and just hoping for the best. And somehow we all clambered up after that and just collapsed over the whatever-sailors-call-the-wall-round-the-deck, and found about the last square feet of deck and lay like sacks of potatoes, pretty well on top of each other.

Then two Dorniers came over and we thought that was the end. But – and I'm ashamed how grateful I felt – they bombed a wretched cross-channel ferry about three hundred yards from us, and got it. And we got off scot-free because by then we were under way. The ferry was hit and we saw her sinking and a lot of poor chaps in the water but I think most of them were picked up somehow, there were a number of small craft about which had been plying to and from the shore and they helped with the rescue as far as I could see. But although I had a corporal's boots in my face I just *slept*, when we were clear

291

of France, slept like a log. And England looked unbelievably lovely. No bombing on the way over.

In fact I was incredibly lucky – a lot of chaps had ghastly adventures, hours in the water, that sort of thing. And of course we – the battalion – lost quite a few, apart from the men we lost in the campaign itself. But, by and large, I suppose the losses weren't enormous, compared to the last war, anyway; and the battalion is beginning to look like its old self again. We all arrived in dribs and drabs and are only beginning to discover who's here and who isn't.

We were – and are – commanded by the second-in-command as was, Whisky Wainwright. And there isn't a man who wouldn't die for him if he asked them, which he wouldn't (if you know what I mean). I hope you meet him one day. He's not exactly a ladies' man but he's grand, really grand –

Adam wrote that he would write to Nicky and Saskia when he had a moment. Re-reading his letter he thought it pretty colourless. The journey from Dunkirk to Dover was something which wouldn't quit the mind, perhaps ever; yet he had surely described it in particularly unmemorable language. Better so, he thought. Natasha had excitement enough with the bloody Luftwaffe showing signs of turning its attentions to the capital.

'My dear Brigadier,' wrote Frank Fosdike,

Thank you for your letter. Many congratulations on your promotion. It was sad about your predecessor. I'm not going to be a hypocrite and pretend that we always got on because it's common knowledge that that wasn't so. As you probably heard I was pushed out because I declined to support a hare-brained idea for an absolutely disastrous operation which my battalion was called on to do. I'm

afraid I had to speak out and it wasn't popular. No matter
– these things happen, as you and I know well, and
personally I always found him charming and sincerely
regret his loss.

In your letter you refer to a report which has reached
you on young Hardrow and you ask for my unofficial and
private opinion. I much appreciate the confidence your
request shows. It is certainly an extraordinary story – an
officer in my regiment alleged to be, in effect, a murderer!
Of course, as most of us remember from the last show,
fairly desperate measures have sometimes to be taken
when troops get jumpy; but, even so, the murder of an
officer, in cold blood (as you tell the story) is surely
impossible to justify.

You ask whether, from my experience of Adam
Hardrow's character, it seems credible, and I got the
impression from your letter that you haven't yet decided
what line to take. Naturally I can't help hoping that things
won't go too hard for the young man and that extenuating
circumstances exist – I know the Hardrow family quite
well, it's a Westmorland Regiment family; and of course
any publicity would be intensely disagreeable. As I know
you realize. The incident in question must have happened
(if it did) some time after I, myself, gave up command.

But as to the young man's character – I would hate to
think this story true, but I'm afraid I must, in honesty, admit
that I sometimes found him headstrong, even impetuous.
He was certainly efficient and I believe he was popular. But I
was not always one hundred per cent confident of his loyalty.
He had a streak of temper which sometimes let him down.
He had a certain reputation for playing around with women.
None of this is necessarily damning but it makes me hesitate
to give him an unqualified good name, in so far as 'stability'
is concerned –

The brigadier sighed. A report had been referred to him for urgent inquiry. It had taken some time moving up and down official channels. And its contents were troublesome. There was now a folder on his desk containing all matter relevant to Lieutenant Adam Hardrow. He read with irritation another document copied on the file. The brigadier liked issues to be clear-cut and solutions to suggest themselves without excessive difficulty.

– throughout this time Second-Lieutenant Hardrow (now promoted to Lieutenant Hardrow) showed exceptional powers of leadership and resourcefulness of mind, as well as exhibiting great courage. Four instances must be given.

First, Lieutenant Hardrow, during an attack by this battalion, found a German strongpoint unexpectedly established at a farm, Droot Farm, dominating the axis of advance. He immediately and successfully led his platoon in a counter-attack, dislodging the enemy.

Second, when his company commander, Captain Jameson, was wounded in the same action, Lieutenant Hardrow personally and very skilfully moved into no man's land and rescued him. Captain Jameson is recovering well; without Lieutenant Hardrow's performance he would be dead or a prisoner.

Third, in command of his company on what was known as 'the Canal Line', Lieutenant Hardrow's conduct was beyond praise. He, personally, intervened in the sector of a neighbouring unit and persuaded troops who were shaken and to a large extent leaderless to remain firm. He then repulsed a determined German attack across the canal and ultimately withdrew his company without serious loss.

Fourth, he led a counter-attack in the town of Boskapelle, part of the Dunkirk perimeter defences. A German party had infiltrated into the place, and snipers were active in one quarter of the town. Lieutenant Hardrow gathered all available men and routed the infiltrating troops at bayonet point.

I submit that any one of these actions would have merited the award in paragraph three above, for which I now very strongly recommend Lieutenant Hardrow.

The army form had been signed 'George Wainwright, Major, Commanding 2nd Battalion, Westmorland Regiment'; the brigadier also had before him a personal letter which had accompanied the form and its citation. His staff captain had pointed out to him that such unofficial additional representations were irregular, and the brigadier heartily agreed. Meanwhile the letter remained on the file.

My dear Brigadier,
I haven't spelled it out in the citation because I don't want to cause trouble and some things are best forgotten, but in fact Adam Hardrow rallied both officers and men of that battalion (my 'third instance') who were running away. He did a fine job, which he fully and confidentially explained to me afterwards and which I highly commended. But unless you want me to write the details, which I suggest would be a pity, my wording can stand, understatement though it is!
Yours sincerely,
George Wainwright

All that had been four weeks ago. The staff captain had discussed all these citations with him, marking the Hardrow file 'outstanding'; and had drafted for him a glowing supportive paragraph which he'd signed for onward transmission to divisional headquarters. He'd since heard from the divisional commander that all but three of his recommendations had gone through and were about to be gazetted. With the army nursing its wounds and England under instant threat the authorities had evidently decided that morale demanded a more rapid process than was usual in these matters.

And now, in the face of his previous encomium – ('known to be an outstanding young officer – deserving in every way of recognition' and so forth) there came this damnable, awkward report. And all the staff captain had done was to minute on the folder, 'You will presumably consider an initial investigation and report from Acting Commanding Officer, 2 Westmorlands. But may we speak?'

From George Wainwright! And that was another source of irritation. The brigadier had decided even before arriving to take over the job that Wainwright was unsuitable to command a battalion in an army – and particularly in this brigade – which now had to look forward, develop new ideas, match the Germans in modernity. The brigadier had only met Wainwright once in earlier times and had been unimpressed. He was slow. He was uneducated. He looked like a game-keeper. He could hardly string two sentences together. It was obvious that his surprisingly articulate letters and reports were written by his adjutant. His appointment as CO was still only 'acting', since Frank Fosdike's departure in May (about which the brigade major's account was somewhat different from Fosdike's story, but the brigadier was content to let that pass, water under the bridge), and had not been confirmed. The brigadier had written strongly on the subject immediately he assumed command – a new CO was required, urgently, for 2nd Westmorlands. Yet nobody had been appointed. The general had even said to him, 'You may not be right about Whisky Wainwright.'

'He's a good fellow, sir. But nothing more. No new ideas. Slow.'

'They say he did damn well in France and Belgium.'

Just that. Just that, with its implied, though surely uninten-tional suggestion that he, the brigadier, had been at home in England, at Northern Command, throughout the campaign. Through absolutely no fault of his own, he said to himself (and others) frequently. But at home. Joined by Frank Fosdike, an old friend.

Whereas Wainwright –

The brigadier's dislike of Wainwright had been exacer-bated by an astonishing scene which had been played out at the end of the previous week. The brigadier had decided to address all officers. In the period since Dunkirk the brigade had reassembled, shaken itself out, absorbed reinforcements. Then the days had been absolutely dominated by counter-invasion plans and preparations. Defensive areas. Strong points. Coastal mining and wiring. Anti-tank obstacles. Removal of signposts, town signs, village signs. Additional air-raid precautions and liaison with the civil agencies; the police, the fire-fighting services. Study days, training, training, training. Changes of plan. Changes of role. More orders. More paper. And, overarching all this, the question mark. When would *they* come? When would the preparations be put to the test?

And so, with climax sometimes threatened by anticlimax, tension in danger of being succeeded by relaxation, the brigadier had decided to address all officers. He intended the affair as an exhortation. The sense of imminent peril was on the wane, a certain routine overtaking it. The brigadier reckoned that there were things which needed saying and he proposed to say them.

He did so well. He told them, very frankly, that they all knew he, personally, had not experienced the recent campaign. 'And had I done so neither I nor you have any idea whether I would have behaved with distinction or the reverse, or, indeed, survived.' But this fact did not absolve him from making one or two comments. If, among his audience, the cap fitted here and there, so be it. He had no desire to point the finger; but he wished it to be absolutely clear that from now on certain behaviour would never, he repeated never, be tolerated.

'If a position is to be held, it will be held. If the defenders of a position can't remain in it alive they will remain there dead. That principle, gentlemen, was by no means universally observed in Flanders recently. Some, perhaps unkindly, would say that the prevailing principle in certain quarters was "We'll remain here until things get too hot, then we'll pull out." I am not absolutely convinced that what I have said has no applicability to this brigade. I know of at least one instance in this brigade where withdrawal took place very significantly before the time given by my headquarters. And why? Because the situation looked dangerous. Because there had been infiltration. Because the enemy was through our lines somewhere. Gentlemen, in future that sort of excuse will never be accepted for premature abandonment of a position.

'In future, our country depends on a very, very different spirit. In future –'

And so on. The brigadier made many points, all with conviction, and had the impression that his talk went well. He was, however, astonished on leaving the small market-town cinema where they had assembled (the brigade was concentrated in east Yorkshire) to find between himself and his car the burly form of Major George Wainwright, acting commanding officer of 2nd Battalion, the Westmorland Regiment.

'May I have a word with you, sir?'

'Yes, of course.' Inadequate Wainwright might be, but he was one of the brigadier's commanding officers and he could hardly be denied audience.

Whisky looked at his brigade commander as if he was a bull about to charge. His voice was low and grim.

'When you spoke about withdrawals before the time laid down, I want to ask whether you were referring to my battalion on the Canal Line?'

The brigadier looked and felt astounded. Really! He tried to make his voice frigid and dismissive. He couldn't entirely recall the incidents he'd read from the account of his brigade's recent exploits which had given rise to that part of his address, but he had no intention of being heckled on the matter by an acting commanding officer, about, God willing, to be superseded.

'I don't think, Major Wainwright, that there's anything to be gained by going further into details.'

'Well I do,' said Whisky bluntly. 'If what you said applied to us it as good as means that the Westmorlands baled out before they needed to!'

Impertinent lout, thought the brigadier, he has no idea how to behave. He knew, nevertheless, that Whisky Wainwright had 'done well' in Flanders, within his limited capabilities of course. There was no point in picking a quarrel with 2nd Westmorlands. He smiled at Whisky and said, 'You're being over-sensitive!'

Whisky gave one of his grunts. It was rather an offensive sound but the brigadier let that pass. He continued to smile.

'Let's leave it like this. I have heard nothing and intended to say nothing to imply that 2nd Westmorlands behaved at any time other than as I would expect from so distinguished a battalion. Will that do?'

Whisky nodded. He felt, dimly, that in fact it wouldn't really do, but he was unsure why. The brigadier held out his hand to shake Whisky's as a gesture of friendly reconciliation, but Whisky's right hand was at his cap in a very formal and smart salute and the encounter had ended in mild confusion.

That had been last week. And now the brigadier found himself sharply regretting that he had been led to endorse with such enthusiasm the Wainwright commendation of Adam Hardrow. Wainwright had done his best to pre-empt the whole issue. Or make it more difficult, anyway. Damnably so. The brigadier decided that he needed a more helpful minute of advice from his staff captain.

Adam!
I just want to say that I now know what you did for Ben, that we owe his life to you. And he knows it too.

299

Bless you, dearest Adam. I can't write much, my heart is too full, but I think of you often. Very, very gratefully.

Ben's getting on fine and is due for sick leave next week. He should be walking perfectly well in three months the doctors say.

Love,
Felicity.

Dear Adam,
I was glad to hear from someone, I forget who, that you'd got back all right, and I hope you're well. If, one day, you get a weekend off and come to London to see your mother perhaps I'll see you. My driving is pretty demanding but it's quite an amusing job as jobs go. Life is hectic and sometimes a bit emotionally trying, but at least every day's different! And so far I prefer being in London to some God-forsaken corner of the country. I am still living at home, and let's hope the wretched Germans keep their bombing attention on the coast and on aerodromes rather than on us! Probably a bit selfish, but I expect most of us feel the same! Anyway we seem to be beating them, don't we?

Daddy's fairly well, although he was naturally very upset at what he calls 'paying the price of honesty, the penalty for telling the truth'. You're bound to know more about that than I do, but he does seem (at least to his daughter) to have been pretty unfairly treated. However, he says 'in wartime one must simply serve where one's sent' and he's been given a new job – again in the War Office but a different bit of it – which he's told me will be fascinating, though of course he can't say exactly what he does! He's been in York, and will be glad to come back to London, the work up there was a bit boring I gather although, of course, he was only there a few weeks. I also rather gather – because I can generally tell with Daddy – that the new job may well lead to promotion. Of course he'd obviously prefer being back with all of you, but there it is –

Love,

Caroline.

Darling Adam,

I do hope that you manage to get a weekend soon. It was lovely talking on the telephone, do try to ring up again when you can; but I long to see you, my darling son. I relished your long 'Dunkirk' letter, and indeed all your letters, but there's so much I want to ask you.

Nick is enormously excited – he starts his flying training on 1 August, very soon now. It just wasn't possible to talk him into further delay, and of course it's difficult, with all this air fighting, to say that he can't be needed yet, there's plenty of time. I gather (not from him) that the whole process is likely to take *at least a year*, and I pray that's true. These times are hard for all of us, but especially for mothers, I can't help feeling, in my usual self-pitying way!

Well, I suppose the Germans *are* going to invade us, and that you're all going to drive them into the sea, and 'fight on the beaches' as Churchill says. I can't really see *why* Hitler wants to come here, or why anyone should want to keep this war going at all! The French have been more or less beaten, and seem to have patched up something not too bad with the Germans. Why can't people start talking instead of fighting? All these brave young airmen – it makes me weep!

Of course one gets no news from France, and I suppose one won't until this wretched war is over so I don't know how Uncle Alex and his family are. Just one more worry! And the Germans in Paris!

By the way, darling, I never told you but I ran into F.F., once your commanding officer, the other day. He was walking down Knightsbridge, smart in his uniform, and I was shopping or trying to. We chatted for a minute or two, and I *quite see what you mean*! I won't say more. Something a little creepy about him, it suddenly hit me –

Natasha's letter contained more personal news. Saskia, of all people, was getting restive at school and 'thought she should be doing something in the war'. An old cousin of Natasha's was lodging in Elm Park Gardens, which at least was company. Adam sighed over his mother's scepticism about the necessity of the war. She was incorrigible, and there it was. He'd been promised a weekend in September or October, if there was no significant change in the situation.

There was one unexpected letter.

Dear Adam,
I was glad to hear that you have returned safely from Dunkirk. An officer called here about some sort of training and billeting they may be about to impose on the village (perfectly rightly) and I discovered he was in a Westmorland territorial battalion – the 5th, I think. His name was Jenkinson, he didn't know you, but he knew your name and that you are home and unharmed.

This letter is simply to say that the news gave me much pleasure. Your mother must be greatly relieved. I suppose she is still in London and no doubt you worry about her as much as she recently worried about you.

It is difficult to see what course the war will now take. I do not believe the Germans will invade England. It is too difficult – even an ignorant woman like me can see that. Nor do I believe that they really wish to, in spite of Hitler's noisy rhetoric. It is unclear, indeed, what they – the Germans – *do* want, just at present. They have got almost everything in Europe, and most of the world is applauding them, as the world always applauds winners. I shed no tears for the French – they were vindictive in victory themselves and they seem to me to have got off comparatively lightly.

But the world is more than continental Europe and where it will all end none can say. Remember me to your mother – we know each other only slightly and share no memories and, I imagine, few interests. But she has sons and I feel for her – sympathy a little, but mostly envy.

      Your loving cousin,
        Beatrice.

Adam replied with a long, rambling and carefully edited account of the 2nd Westmorlands' adventures in France and Belgium. He composed it at leisure, his instinct telling him that with Cousin Beatrice time was not particularly important. It was odd, he thought, how his memory of one boyhood visit to her house in a northern valley had created a picture which the word 'home' evoked more vividly than it did any image of Elm Park Gardens – odd, he thought, because home must really be about people rather than places, and he hardly knew Cousin Beatrice Hardrow. Her house was called Stonehead, and the village Crossfoot, and he wrote the address with curious pleasure. Perhaps the old girl would like a line from time to time.

The brigadier had not warmed to his staff captain, but had to acknowledge that Captain Walter Price knew his job. It was true that Price gave advice and spoke his mind without fear or favour. He was now standing in front of the brigadier's desk. Headquarters was in a large villa on the outskirts of the small Yorkshire town where they'd assembled immediately after evacuation from Dunkirk, two months ago. The brigadier's own office was in what had been the villa's dining-room, on the ground floor. The brigadier had asked where the owners of the villa now were, but did not remember the answer. Furniture had remained in position, with a few exceptions, and he had a large, ugly but adequate desk. As billets went this was a good one.

'You've seen the Hardrow file, sir.'

'I have. As far as I can see you advise I take absolutely no action. Say I've gone into it and recommend the matter be regarded as closed.'

'The difficulty is, sir, that the next step would be a court of inquiry into the officer's conduct. Calling evidence, on oath I imagine. As I put in my minute, sir, the Special Investigation Branch have seen the papers in the case and don't wish to pursue it further unless they receive directions to do so.'

'From me.'

'From the general, sir. On your recommendation. The SIB say – or imply – that they don't think a criminal investigation likely to be appropriate to what they call 'the confused conditions of the battlefield'. So they could be told, by higher authority, to get on with it regardless. Or a court of inquiry could be convened as a next step. Or we do nothing.'

'A court of inquiry –'

'Might establish sufficient facts to justify the matter going to court martial. Yes, sir.'

'Or it might not.'

'Exactly, sir.'

'Can't we have the court of inquiry and then – depending on what it finds, of course – I would simply deal with Hardrow myself?'

'I very much doubt it, sir. If there were a charge to be made against him I can't see that it would be other than a very serious one. Certainly one requiring court martial.'

The brigadier frowned at the file. He did not relish the prospect of a serious charge being laid against Lieutenant Hardrow, endorsed by his brigadier – a charge arising from an incident about which the same brigadier had just written of the same Lieutenant Hardrow in positively effusive terms. Indeed the brigadier, anxious to make his mark and secure recognition for his officers and men, had actually 'had a word' with the general. He recalled it now. He had said, 'of course I wasn't there, sir, but you may have read of young Hardrow's performance – I went into it pretty thoroughly, and there's no doubt it was a particularly fine show, on the Canal Line'. He had, he reflected, been let down. He'd been put in a false position. A very false position.

The staff captain seemed untroubled about the perplexities into which his commander had been allowed to wander. He now said, 'Division tell me the awards will be notified tomorrow. Including a Military Cross for Hardrow. So nobody higher up has put the various strands together to stop it, or anything like that.'

'Hmm. I know that all makes it difficult, Walter –'

'In a way, sir.'

'Embarrassing, even.'

'I think so, sir.'

'But we mustn't let the possibility of embarrassment stop us doing the right thing.'

'Certainly not, sir.'

'There's such a thing as justice, Walter.'

'Yes, sir. And as hanging. For murder.'

The brigadier stared at him. After a long, silent minute, he said quietly, 'You're in no doubt, yourself, as to my right course of action to take in this matter?'

'No doubt, sir,' said Walter Price, 'I think you should see Major Wainwright tomorrow, to tell him privately what's happened. And as for division, sir, I have a suggested letter for your signature here.' He produced it and the brigadier read it, frowning. The letter said that the brigadier had made exhaustive inquiries into the allegation in the paper under reference, had concluded that no possible purpose could be served by further action in the matter and had decided that none should be taken.

' "Decided" Walter? Shouldn't I "recommend"?'

'The general won't overrule you, sir. I've had a word. This will put the matter to bed.'

The brigadier took up his fountain-pen. He did not see that his staff captain, signed letter in his hand, was waylaid by the brigade major in the passage outside his door, nor did he see the thumbs-up sign made by Walter Price.

Whisky Wainwright plumped himself down in the next chair to Adam's in the mess ante-room. The Westmorlands were inhabiting a cheerless hutted camp surrounded by the bare coastal fields of this part of Yorkshire and the officers' mess was in a large hut, with one half serving as dining-room and the other half fitted out with an inadequate number of easy chairs. They were working too hard for comfort to have much significance, and the lack of chairs was largely unnoticed. Most of the time most of the officers were out on some sort of duty. In addition to the hard, indeed feverish, training programme set in hand by Whisky there were operational duties on the coast where observation posts had to be manned at all times and where duty platoons took turns at readiness. Invasion scares were a regular feature of life, and the exhausting routine was regularly laced with excitement. It was generally supposed – although the authorities preached otherwise lest complacency set in – that invasion would come in the south or possibly in East Anglia, but everywhere there might be raids at the least, everywhere there must be readiness; and everywhere there could come the call to move to a threatened area in the chartered civilian buses which generally transported the troops – to move and counter-attack when the Germans came.

And surely they must come before the winter? It was already the beginning of September.

It was mid-morning and Adam had come off night duty with the beach emergency platoon after breakfast. He was clear of duties now until lunchtime and the men of the platoon were already snoring in their hut. Adam felt sleepy. The ante-room was deserted. And then, surprisingly, the CO came in and parked himself in the next chair. Adam struggled to his feet.

'Sit down, Adam.'

Adam became a little more wakeful. A little warier, too. It was clear that this was no accident and that Whisky Wainwright wanted to talk. And talk here, rather than send for Adam in his office. There was a long silence. Adam wondered whether he should say something. Probably not.

Whisky cleared his throat. Then, haltingly, he said that he'd meant to say this months ago, never got round to it somehow. Particularly sorry about Ivan Perry, knew what friends he and Adam had been, rotten luck. Adam knew beyond doubt that the reason Whisky hadn't spoken like this earlier was because he couldn't have trusted his self-control. Or Adam's. As it was Adam found his own voice hard to master.

'Thank you, sir. Yes, Ivan's a loss. Like all of them, I suppose.'

Whisky seemed to have something else to say.

'Expect you've heard I'm going.'

They had all been wondering, furiously and incredulously. It seemed astounding that Whisky's appointment as their leader, their inspiration, had still not been confirmed. Nor had his services in the campaign received the smallest recognition. Adam looked at him as he sat massively hunched in his chair, staring straight ahead.

Whisky said softly, 'Bound to come. Not senior enough. Not qualified, really.' This was more and more absurd. There could, however, be nothing, absolutely nothing, to say.

'Might get another battalion later on, they tell me.' Still nothing to say. How could a subaltern respond to developments such as these? And why was Whisky confiding them, so informally, and to such an insignificant as Adam Hardrow? Even though it was now Lieutenant Hardrow, MC?

Whisky said abruptly –

'Had to catch you, anyway, and not to talk about myself. That business of yours on the Canal Line, the business you told me about –'

'Yes, sir.'

'There was a report, you know.'

Adam nodded. He had always presumed this likely, with what outcome for himself could only be guessed.

'It's been killed. The subject. Brigadier told me. Took a bit of time but it's final now.'

Adam looked at him. He was sure that, somehow, this large, grumpy, primitive man, with his fierce loyalties and simple principles had contributed to the killing. He said nothing.

'Killed. No more trouble.'

They sat silent. After a little, however, Whisky said, 'There's another thing, though.' He didn't sound comfortable. Adam recognized that he should play some responsive part in the conversation, make things easier. It couldn't be any official issue or misdemeanour. Whisky was a stickler for the proprieties and would no more have administered a rebuke in the mess than attempted to play the violin.

'To do with me, sir?'

'Yes. Rather embarrassing. Don't want to go into it in the orderly room.'

Adam's mind flashed straight to Felicity Jameson. He'd answered Felicity's letter, thanked her for it, said the usual things, he'd done nothing, Ben had been unbelievably brave, he was so glad Ben was getting on all right. They were all missing him and praying he'd not be sent to another battalion, love, Adam. That was all. Was it possible that some rumour had reached Whisky? If so the embarrassment of Whisky, no ladies' man, was comprehensible! But surely –

Adam said, 'I'm sorry to hear that, sir. That it's embarrassing, whatever it is.' He looked at Whisky in a guarded sort of way.

'It's about your mother.'

'Has something happened to my mother?' Adam spoke fast and sat up very straight in his chair. Air raids on London itself had now started and everybody was expecting them to intensify. Like many others Adam felt ashamed that he, a soldier under arms, was probably at very much less risk than his own mother; and likely to remain so.

'Is my mother all right, sir? What is it?'

Whisky spoke hesitantly, and at first obscurely. There was much reference to 'probably misunderstood', to 'bloody censors probably getting the wrong end of the stick', but the ultimate message was clear. It had been brought to the notice of the authorities that Mrs Hardrow was talking, and on occasions writing, in a defeatist way. She was showing signs of lacking in support for the war. Under the Defence of the Realm Acts such attitudes could be prosecuted as criminal.

'My mother has her own views, sir –'

'Quite. She's Russian, isn't she?'

'Russian-born. Of course she has British nationality. It's perfectly true that, like many women I expect, she hates the losses and the suffering war is likely to bring. Has already brought.'

'Nothing wrong with that.'

Adam continued, 'And this leads my mother, sometimes, to wonder whether it couldn't be patched up, peace negotiated, something like that. She sees things very differently from, well, from me for instance. But she's not in the least political. Or, in my view, realistic. She's just unhappy about war, about people getting killed, and she talks and writes a bit, well perhaps a bit foolishly as a result.'

'Think you could have a word with her, Adam?'

'Yes, sir. She knows I disagree.'

309

'Not what I mean. Have a word to warn her off. Could be in serious trouble. That sort of thing.'

'You don't really suppose, do you, sir, that my mother could actually be prosecuted?'

'Yes, I do. It's been passed to me because you're one of my officers. So your own – well, your own reputation so to speak – could be, you know –'

'Could be affected by my mother's words and opinions.'

'Exactly. But that's not the reason to talk to her – the reason is to stop her getting herself into a jam.'

'I'm going on a weekend at the end of the month, sir, 30 September. Unless the balloon goes up. I hope that'll be early enough. It's not a thing I'd want to put in a letter.'

'Of course not. But you're not going on a weekend at the end of the month. You're going on a week's leave a bit earlier than that – 18 September in fact.'

'A week's leave!'

'Yes,' said Whisky. 'That's the other, the last thing I wanted a word about before you're told officially. It's embarkation leave. You see, you're being posted.'

Letters. Wartime letters.

Darling Mama,
I'm coming down to London on next Wednesday fortnight, and I've got a whole week's leave, a week and a bit in fact. The reason is that I'm being sent away from the battalion.

As I know you'll understand I'm absolutely wretched about it. This battalion is my home and it's like my family. I lost some good friends at and before Dunkirk but there are plenty left, and I simply hate leaving them.

And it's not only leaving my friends. It's leaving them just before what must be the crucial battle of the war. If the Germans come – and I know no more than you, and

310

obviously couldn't say even if I did – everyone expects it before the end of October. The papers are guessing all the time but they must be right about that, I imagine. Tides, weather – everything points to it being earlier rather than later. So in the next few weeks the crisis is going to come. And for the last three months we've been preparing for it. All of us. All my friends.

And at exactly that juncture *I'm going to leave them*! I know one goes where one's sent in wartime (and any other time for that matter) but it really makes me feel utterly miserable. I feel a skunk. I can't bear to look my platoon in the face! I was going to get the carrier platoon in this battalion, too, which would have been a change and great fun. But now it's goodbye! 'Goodbye all, I hope the battle goes well!' Imagine!

And then there's you, darling Mama! While here I'd have got the odd weekend, letters have been regular and we've sometimes talked on the telephone. Now I've got to leave you, worrying all the time about you if and when the invasion comes or the Germans intensify their bombing. Because, Mama, I'm not only being posted away from this battalion, I'm being sent to the 1st Battalion. The 1st Battalion! *In Egypt*! Can you beat it? Egypt! Where absolutely nothing's happening, or is likely to happen, and where the only enemy are the Italians. We pulled out of Somaliland and handed them that on a plate and now they're sitting in Libya and we're sitting in Egypt, and both sides are likely to spend the war doing exactly that. While here the real war is about to be fought! And so off I go, to what people call 'the fleshpots of the Nile' and here you stay, darling Mama, in blacked-out, rationed, bombed, about-to-be-invaded England! I'll miss you terribly and I hate the idea like hell, but there it is. I've now had my grumble and I promise not to indulge myself like that again!

It was only after posting his letter that Adam realized he, too, could be in trouble with the censoring, the security authorities. He had no business to write that the 1st Westmorlands were in Egypt. Well, he said to himself, unworried, to hell with them! Let them charge me if they want! The 1st Westmorlands had been in Egypt, written up and photographed there, since 1938!

Adam was as good as his word and didn't indulge in self-pitying grumbles again. This was not only the last time his mother would see him but the first time they'd talked and kissed and talked again since return from Dunkirk's beaches, over three months ago. It would be mere selfishness to make his week's leave a time of complaint. He told himself that his letter to Natasha had been rather contemptible. With the country facing as great a menace as ever in history it certainly wasn't a moment to allow personal, selfish considerations to count. Furthermore there might, there just might be a chance that he was wrong. As the weeks passed, as one invasion scare succeeded another, Adam heard many a reasonably intelligent observer remark that possibly, just possibly, the Germans wouldn't try it on. They were getting a real pasting in the air.

He reported himself officially to Whisky Wainwright before departure. Adam knew that Whisky himself was due to leave them three days later. His successor, Colonel Freddie Barton, had at last been nominated. Adam didn't know him or of him – he came from another regiment, the final, crowning insult, the Westmorlands said to each other bitterly. Adam was glad that his own time with the 2nd Battalion was to culminate under the command of Whisky Wainwright, the old warrior. The men were quiet, a few saying in a matter-of-fact sort of way, 'It won't seem the same without Major Wainwright, will it, sir?'

Whisky said little to Adam across the regulation army table which separated them, a grey army blanket draped over it.

'Battalion sorry to see you go, of course, but you'll enjoy the 1st Battalion.'

'I hope so, sir.'

'Probably get a company before too long, the way things are going.'

What things? The 1st Battalion was hardly incurring casualties, sitting in the Nile Delta! Adam gave a polite half-smile, saluted and marched out. He'd been given to understand, it was true, that his new battalion was short of officers (and NCOs and men – Adam was to take out a sizeable draft from the regiment as part of a large army and air-force contingent bound for Egypt, travelling by troopship round the Cape). Still, it seemed an odd moment to send troops away from England.

At Elm Park Gardens Natasha seized him hungrily.

'Oh darling! Darling!'

It was extraordinary to think that to his mother this was his homecoming. The events of May seemed far away, but Natasha, torn between gratitude for his safety and misery at his imminent departure wanted to talk about them – or to hear him talk about them. In this she was shrewd. Her own interest in that or any other campaign was minimal but she had a strong feeling that it would be best for Adam to talk, if he could.

He had written, of course, but generally in a restrained, stilted way when describing actual events. She had written as she talked – voluble, careless of logic, indiscreet, instinctual, affectionate. She had communicated her pride on learning of his Military Cross. And she had shared with him her worries about the twins – she had written to him almost as if he were the twins' father. But at his own reactions to the recent fighting she could only guess. Even his letter covering the actual quitting of Dunkirk had been crowded with understatement.

'Darling, I know you had some friends killed who you really loved.'

'Yes, I did.'

'Tell me about them. Tell me all about them. I want to feel I knew them too. Describe them. I know it hurts but try.'

Describe Sergeant Pew? Describe Tom Stubbs? Describe Ivan? Already it seemed an age long ago. Adam said, 'Well, my particular friend was Ivan Perry.'

'You often wrote of him. He sounded charming.'

'Yes, he was certainly charming.' Natasha knew well that Adam was finding it hard now to keep his voice steady. It would be excellent for him to sob, if necessary for hours, but despite Russian blood she knew that was not and would never be Adam's way. He tried to talk about Ivan, and as he struggled for words he found Ivan's face, Ivan's voice, almost present in the room, and gradually his words came more easily.

'He pretended to be very unmilitary, to take everything as a bit of a joke. Really he was efficient when he tried, though he hid it. And he was certainly brave. He had a marvellous sense of humour, a lovely way with words. He –'

'What did he look like?'

'A very – well, I suppose it was a very *young* face, he often looked about fifteen. Fair. Rather pink and white, I suppose you'd say. Rather tall.'

He talked on a little about Ivan. 'His mother called him Ivan because she had a thing about Tolstoy's Prince Andrew.'

There was plenty more, which would remain in the locked safe of his memory. There was a flushed-faced major with a hole in his forehead and the back of his head spattering the upholstery of a Belgian car. There was a donkey, too, unsupported, pitiful, bleeding to death in the shafts. And much else.

'Then there was the one whose life you saved – your company commander, the one who was wounded.'

'Ben Jameson. Mama, why do you say I saved his life? I never said that.'

'No, he did.'

'What on earth do you mean, Mama? You don't know him.'

'He rang up. He said, "You don't know me, Mrs Hardrow, but your son saved my life".'

'When? When did he ring up?'

'This morning.'

'*This morning!* But, Mama, to say what? To –'

'He wanted you, of course. He's going to ring again this evening.'

'How wonderful! He's on sick leave, I think.' At seven o'clock the telephone rang. Adam answered it and heard Ben's voice, sounding the same but very slightly more formal than usual, as if his wounding, his absence from the later battles and his stay in hospital had erected some kind of small barrier between him and his former comrades; or, anyway, this former comrade.

'How are you, Adam?'

Adam said he was well. Had Ben heard that he was off to Egypt? On Sunday? Ben had – and had also heard that Adam was sick as mud. Very foolishly – nobody but an ass would stay in today's England if an alternative offered. Egypt seemed far more agreeable. How had Ben heard about him? From Whisky Wainwright.

'I talked to Whisky yesterday. He's got a few days off between jobs and he's going to spend two of them in London. I said I'd come up to have a talk and a drink. How is he?'

Adam said forcibly that Whisky was probably miserable. The whole battalion thought it outrageous that he wasn't confirmed in command.

'He did wonderfully, Ben, after you –'

'Dropped out. So I heard. Without surprise.'

315

'Now we've got an outsider.'

'Not a bad chap, I gather. Still –'

'Everybody's furious. And Whisky must be wretched. He's without any personal ambition as far as anyone can see but he looks – looked – after the battalion like a mother.' Natasha, from the other end of the little drawing-room heard and blew him a kiss, pleased.

'We'll have to cheer him up,' Ben said. 'I doubt if he's got many bright spirits to rouse him, nor pretty lasses to set upon his knee. Quotation, though I can't remember where from. So I've asked him to have a drink at a little club I belong to. It's rather entertaining and it'll be a complete change for him. All sorts belong. Both sexes and neither.'

'It doesn't sound Whisky's form, Ben.'

'Nothing is Whisky's form. It will take his mind off things. Shock therapy. Friday evening, tomorrow week, want you to come too. You're not off till Sunday, you say, so it'll give you Saturday with a hangover and Mum.'

'Ben –'

'At eight o'clock. Then we'll take Whisky out on the town. I've got a room at my other club, the respectable one. I suggest you come there at about seven, then I'll take you on to the Crowning Mercy –'

'The where?'

'The Crowning Mercy. That's what it's called, it's in Soho. And I've given Whisky the address and told him to meet us there and not to be late. You and I can have a talk first.'

Later that evening Adam, with an uneasy feeling in the stomach, telephoned the number of the Fosdike house. A female voice answered. Not Caroline.

'It's Adam Hardrow. Could I speak to Caroline?'

'I'm afraid she's out. This is Mary Benson, I live here too.'

'I'll try Caroline another time.'

'She's having dinner with Billy, you see. It's the last day of his leave, and of course they're both – well, you know. Poor darlings.'

'Billy.'

'Yes, oh dear, perhaps I shouldn't have said. I thought as you were a friend – I thought everyone knew. Billy Strode.'

'Yes, of course.' Adam rang off.

Adam said, in an obvious and he hoped blasé sort of way, 'Hullo – siren!' It was his second evening at Elm Park Gardens. The air-raid sirens were rare disturbances in the Westmorlands' sector of Yorkshire so far – most of the Luftwaffe's attacks had been directed well south of them, although they had been surprised by several forays to the north, presumed to be diversionary.

Natasha nodded and looked up from her sewing thoughtfully.

'We've not had a heavy raid for several days. But people seem to think they'll concentrate increasingly on London. It was on the wireless. The man said it showed the Germans are despairing, though I can't remember why.'

'I think it's because we reckon they've been trying to knock out the RAF, Mama. And have failed. Attacking London is going to be beastly – *is* beastly – but it won't win them the war or even do much to help the invasion. You're still determined to stay here?' The Cumberland farmhouse had been let for several years and, reasonably, the ageing tenants wished to remain.

'Absolutely, darling. And Cousin May has nowhere else to go. We keep each other company and she's really helpful.' Cousin May was seventy-three, spry and affectionate. Natasha had turned a bedroom into a bed-sitting-room for her, so that when she wanted to have the place to herself, Cousin May could be tactful and self-effacing in a somewhat un-Russian way. Most of the time, however, she sat with Natasha, and exchanged gossip, and worked away at her sewing, and was delighted to have news of the family. She had welcomed Adam like a grandson though he hardly knew her. Saskia's room was still available for Saskia, and the fourth bedroom in the house was Adam's, and would house Nicky too when he came to London. Natasha said she would be miserable away from her own home. And where would she go? Neither she nor Cousin May appeared to show the slightest alarm at air raids.

Natasha cocked an ear.

'So far the bombs have mostly dropped down the river. The East End, poor things.'

'The docks.'

'There's not been much near here, just the odd crash. And we hear the guns all the time – it's rather exciting actually! There they go!' And the hollow-sounding clatter of the nearest anti-aircraft artillery made the windows rattle as she spoke. It was not a very protracted raid and soon they heard the 'all clear' sound, its long, sustained note bringing to Adam a certain relief of which he felt ashamed. How brave the women were compared to him the warrior! Natasha had said, 'The cellar's quite good, we had the man here advising us on the work, you know. May and I went down there last Monday when there were a few rather close bangs. The first real raid. We felt very silly. Most of the time we just sit here.'

'And there's a big shelter at the end of the street you told me. Communal.'

'Yes – but, darling, it would take a lot to get me down there!'

'Don't let it take too much, Mama, darling! I want to find you here when I get back from Egypt.' He and Natasha were able to talk together about death, its chances, its avoidance, without any strained sense of the unmentionable. Just as she cried with rage at the waste and grief of war, so she took death as it came – infuriating if it removed a loved one, enraging for its premature harvesting of the young in battle, but essentially natural, not a subject to be avoided.

'No, my darling, I know, and I'll do my best to stay alive and look after things, I promise!' She smiled at him and added, 'Anyway, Nicky needs me even more than you do.'

'And Saskia.'

'And Saskia, of course.'

'Mama, I want to talk about something quite different.' Adam spoke sensibly and gently about Natasha's attitudes to the war, her often virulently expressed opinions. He said that of course she had a right to her views but at present, with England feeling so threatened and with stories of fifth-columnists and defeatists having undermined the French – and probably the Belgians, and the Dutch – it was understandable that a pretty hard line was being taken. He had heard –

'How, Adam?'

'It doesn't matter, Mama.'

'People spy on me, do you mean?'

'Mama, we'll probably have an enemy army actually here, in England, soon. Anybody suspected of not being one hundred per cent behind our resistance to that enemy is going to be in real trouble. That's what I'm saying. So please just be tactful. Don't talk, and above all don't write, in a way which could be misunderstood.'

Natasha was staring at him. Adam wondered if she was going to make some sort of scene. She must vividly resent a homily from her son, and was seldom one to disguise resentment. But Natasha sighed. Then, to Adam's relief, she said, simply and softly, 'All right, darling. I understand what you're trying to say.'

'Good, Mama.' He felt touched.

'It's a funny world, isn't it, Adam?'

'I suppose so.'

Soon after that the siren's threatening note, rising and falling, sounded yet again.

Ben was limping as he moved across the crowded bar of his club to greet Adam, but he looked well – thinner, yet well. Adam had seldom felt so glad to see a human being.

Ben gave him a drink, and said, 'I don't feel I've ever said anything to show gratitude, dear boy. I've not had the chance. But, believe me, I felt it!'

'No need.'

'Felicity told me she wrote a line.'

'Yes, she did. Quite unnecessary.' Adam couldn't avoid the small, embarrassed jump of his heart at Felicity's name. Did Ben remember the question he'd once gasped up at Adam in that Flanders village? Mercifully, however, Ben wanted to talk about the battalion, about B Company (now commanded by an agreeable, slightly colourless stranger to both of them, recently an instructor at an officer cadet training unit, who had transferred to the Westmorlands just before the war) and about almost every surviving man in B Company.

'Company Sergeant-Major Darwin's gone to OCTU. He'll be commissioned soon.'

'I knew he would. Too good to keep, I fear.'

Ben was anxious to hear about Whisky. Was it known to what job he was being dispatched? No, Adam didn't know. Whisky had muttered about 'kicking his heels for a bit'.

'He's reporting somewhere or other. He told me he'd got a few days off, no more.'

'Well, I expect we'll soon learn,' Adam replied. He felt contented and mature, a truly accepted brother officer, intimate of seniors. He said, 'Whisky did us marvellously. One felt him just behind one whenever one was in trouble. I think every man felt the same. He was grand.'

'I'm sure he was. I've never felt happier than when I heard he'd replaced that shit Fosdike!'

Strong words! Adam smiled and Ben smiled back and thought, my God he's changed, he's a different human being from the charming, serious boy who joined my company a year and a half ago. The charm's still there, and the seriousness has actually deepened, but now he's masterful, mature, knows where he's going, is confident that he understands – what? Himself? Perhaps. His doubts? Even those maybe. And has he doubts? How not – he's intelligent and sensitive and modest, so how could he be a creature of brash certainties?

Ben congratulated Adam on his MC, using words Adam felt he meant, a rare note of seriousness in his voice.

'They were a bit too good for us, Adam, weren't they! The Huns.'

'They knew what they were doing. And there were plenty of them.'

'Plenty. And more skilful.'

'Well,' said Adam, remembering the canal, remembering Boskapelle, 'I think we saw them off on occasions. But I agree that they – well, their reactions were pretty quick. And they moved in a way our men have never been taught. Their NCOs must be very, very good.'

'I don't doubt it. And enthusiasts for their beastly cause.'

'I suppose so.'

'Goodish equipment. Tanks and the like.'

'Although we didn't see much of that.'

'But they were there. Looking back on it, talking to various rather shaken friends, I get the feeling of a village cricket side taking on a Test Team.'

'Not as bad as that, Ben.'

'Almost, and I still find people who positively glory in our amateur status.'

'But a village cricket side, Ben –'

'Say a minor county second eleven.'

'Why, Ben?'

'You know the answers as well as me. Too many bits of the army with feeble discipline, officers who don't know their job, poor training – that applies to most of us, but at least our people do what they're told. Clapped-out commanders. Or too many clapped-out commanders.'

Ben looked at his watch. Adam made no comment. There was a colder, harder note in Ben's voice than he'd ever heard, which was saying something.

'It won't take us long to walk to the Crowning Mercy.' At that moment the air-raid siren sounded and Ben said, 'Bloody thing!' The barman looked up, unperturbed. He grinned at them.

'It'll probably be the docks again!'

But it was not only the docks again. When they had emerged from Ben's club and walked some way they heard the unmistakable sound of bomb explosions near at hand, saw the light of fires and were aware of shouts from close by. 'Take cover! Everyone take cover!'

'Had we better –'

'Yes, Adam, I think we had!'

They dived down steps into the nearest temporary shelter. Its entrance was several hundred yards from where they'd been standing and as they reached it Ben was saying, 'Probably get the "all clear" in a minute. Short and sharp.'

'Probably.' But the crashes were near now, and twice as they descended – slowly, for Ben's limp was noticeably impeding him – Adam heard the shriek of a large bomb coming down in the vicinity. It was a shriek like that of a tube train approaching an Underground station.

The shelter was crowded. One man was talking loudly, an expert on raids, an expert of a kind liable to surface in any of life's predicaments. He seemed now to be describing events with a knowledge worthy of one directing the Luftwaffe's operations himself.

'First wave over. Second likely to go in further down river.' People listened, wanting to believe.

'Guns got one of them, I'd say. Saw the explosion just as I came down. Not a big raid – maybe twenty, twenty-five. Docks got it worst, on Monday.'

'That's right,' another voice chimed in, obsequious to the expert. Ben, not particularly lowering his voice, said to Adam, 'Let us hope, indeed, that the second wave go in further down river. Much further down river.'

Adam nodded. Heads turned towards them and there was a moment of silence, not altogether friendly. Ben lit a cigarette and the atmosphere warmed a little as he offered his case to the two or three nearest to him, including the knowledgeable one. Another bomb fell, sounding extraordinarily near. The guns rattled away with their sound as of thousands of tin cans collapsing simultaneously on to concrete. Ben sighed.

'My worry is that Whisky will think we've forgotten him. I know he'd have arrived early.'

'He'll realize what's up. Presumably he's below ground himself.'

'I hope he is. The Crowning Mercy is in a cellar. Quite a deep one.'

'So people just stay there in a raid, I suppose?'

'Few could do otherwise. But it's a small cellar – there are seldom more than a dozen members congregated. Very select in its own remarkable way. I fear Whisky may find his companions puzzling.'

'"All clear" shouldn't be long now,' said the knowledgeable man. There had not been a bomb explosion for about three minutes. And as he spoke the familiar soaring, welcome cry of the siren drowned all speech, holding its sustained, even note, announcing that for the moment, perhaps even for that night, the Luftwaffe had withdrawn. Ben moved up the shelter steps with remarkable agility.

323

'It's not far, Adam.'

Ben knew the way well and as he limped along Adam admired his old company commander's impeccable finding of direction through the narrow Soho streets as much as the determination with which he was making best speed, despite what was probably still a good deal of pain. The raid had not lasted at all long. It was not yet half-past eight. Adam realized that Ben would be utterly miserable if he found that Whisky Wainwright had decided they'd forgotten him, and had moved on. It was Whisky's first night away from his beloved Westmorlands. Ben Jameson was determined to make it as joyful as could be managed, above all to make it an occasion warmed by familiar friends. It was intolerable to think of Whisky being lonely. Ben said, 'Not far now.'

There was commotion ahead. Ben said again, 'Not far.' Then he said quietly, 'Thought one of them must be quite near this. This way, Adam.'

He moved quickly to his right, to the opening of a small street, almost an alleyway. It was still light but an evening light now intensified by fires, fires illuminating the surroundings harshly, their crackle and splutter dominant. Torches were moving here and there, spots of ineffectual light on pavements shadowed by dust and smoke. There was a good deal of shouting, and the sound of vehicles manoeuvring.

'This way, Adam.'

'Road's closed, sir,' said a voice out of the smoke and firelight. Adam saw blue uniforms.

'Can I go a short way up, officer? I'm on my way to no. 31. It's only a hundred yards on the right.'

'Just a moment, sir.'

A few moments of colloquy ahead of them. Intensified shouting now, men running, other men guiding heavy plant forward. A vehicle backing towards them amid cries of 'Hold it, hold it!' The roar and hiss of water from pressure hoses.

A barrier run across the road ten yards from where they stood. Yells of 'Easy now! Easy!'

'Officer –'

The police officer they'd spoken to before had returned and seemed to recognize Ben in the light of flames. He peered at him.

'Was you the gentleman asking about no. 31?'

'I was.'

'No. 31's had it.'

'They'd have been in the cellar. My friends.'

'Nothing left of it. Nothing at all. Direct hit. Might find some buried of course but it looks unlikely. Very unlikely.'

Ben said, 'I see.'

'Got to leave it to the heavy rescue mob now. After the fire services have got the area under control.'

'I understand.'

'Mind you, sometimes there's someone protected by a fallen beam, that sort of thing. You can never be sure for a bit, but it looks a real goner, does no. 31.'

'Quite.'

'Family, was it?'

'Yes,' said Ben, 'yes, it was. In a way.'

'Sorry about that.'

As he walked slowly away in the darkness with Ben, Adam said, 'He might not have arrived, of course. He might well have gone into a shelter on the way. Or been delayed.'

Ben didn't answer.

'Do you know where he was staying? We could find out if –'

'He had a club,' said Ben, his voice drained of expression; 'he was probably staying there. He didn't know London well but he had a club. I expect he was staying in it. I know the name – it'll come back to me. I'll ring them up. But I know perfectly well that it's pointless. He would have kept the date

325

with us, and he would have been early. He was in the Crowning Mercy, I'm sure of it. Sometimes one knows these things.'

And, as they later discovered, Ben was perfectly right.

Adam thought of Sunday. He thought with indifference of a troopship, a sandy horizon, Egypt as he supposed it to be, remote from embattled England. Leisured, secure. Here, with the almost certain passing of Whisky Wainwright, a landmark had disappeared. This war seemed likely to maim or destroy much that was loved and familiar and reassuring – such, inevitably, was any war, as Natasha so often reiterated. And in that destruction, Adam already knew, many would go who could least be spared, many whose voices, nevertheless, would echo down whatever time was left, whose remembered character would continue to sustain. The days since 10 May had been scarred by many such losses, and the war had only just started, the future was dark and unknown. Friendship, love's cousin, seemed inseparable from both joy and pain. It was unlikely to be otherwise on a distant shore.

FOR THE BEST IN PAPERBACKS, LOOK FOR THE

In every corner of the world, on every subject under the sun, Penguin represents quality and variety – the very best in publishing today.

For complete information about books available from Penguin – including Puffins, Penguin Classics and Arkana – and how to order them, write to us at the appropriate address below. Please note that for copyright reasons the selection of books varies from country to country.

In the United Kingdom: Please write to *Dept E.P., Penguin Books Ltd, Harmondsworth, Middlesex, UB7 0DA.*

If you have any difficulty in obtaining a title, please send your order with the correct money, plus ten per cent for postage and packaging, to *PO Box No 11, West Drayton, Middlesex*

In the United States: Please write to *Dept BA, Penguin, 299 Murray Hill Parkway, East Rutherford, New Jersey 07073*

In Canada: Please write to *Penguin Books Canada Ltd, 2801 John Street, Markham, Ontario L3R 1B4*

In Australia: Please write to the *Marketing Department, Penguin Books Australia Ltd, P.O. Box 257, Ringwood, Victoria 3134*

In New Zealand: Please write to the *Marketing Department, Penguin Books (NZ) Ltd, Private Bag, Takapuna, Auckland 9*

In India: Please write to *Penguin Overseas Ltd, 706 Eros Apartments, 56 Nehru Place, New Delhi, 110019*

In the Netherlands: Please write to *Penguin Books Netherlands B.V., Postbus 195, NL–1380AD Weesp*

In West Germany: Please write to *Penguin Books Ltd, Friedrichstrasse 10–12, D–6000 Frankfurt Main 1*

In Spain: Please write to *Longman Penguin España, Calle San Nicolas 15, E–28013 Madrid*

In Italy: Please write to *Penguin Italia s.r.l., Via Como 4, I-20096 Pioltello (Milano)*

In France: Please write to *Penguin Books Ltd, 39 Rue de Montmorency, F-75003 Paris*

In Japan: Please write to *Longman Penguin Japan Co Ltd, Yamaguchi Building, 2–12–9 Kanda Jimbocho, Chiyoda-Ku, Tokyo 101*

A CHOICE OF PENGUIN FICTION

The Swimming Pool Library Alan Hollinghurst

'Shimmers somewhere between pastoral romance and sulphurous confession ... surely the best book about gay life yet written by an English author' – Edmund White. 'In more senses than one a historic novel and a historic début' – *Guardian*

The Pigeon Patrick Süskind

A novella by the author of the internationally acclaimed bestseller *Perfume*. 'Süskind's macabre talent knocks normality in a quaint and chilling tragi-comedy' – *Mail on Sunday*

Mother London Michael Moorcock

'A masterpiece ... it is London as we know it, confused, vast, convoluted, absurd' – *Independent*. 'A vast, uncorseted, sentimental, comic, elegiac salmagundi of a novel ... His is the grand messy flux itself, in all its heroic vulgarity, its unquenchable optimism' – Angela Carter

The Mysteries of Algiers Robert Irwin

Algiers, 1959, city of intrigue and disguises. The French settlers make their last stand against the FLN liberation army. Survival means knowing the mind of the enemy. But who is the enemy? How to find him? 'Irwin's ingeniously mixed-up picaresque is both political thriller and satire ... entertaining and very nasty' – *Listener*

Rainforest Jenny Diski

Why should a research trip to the Borneo rainforest threaten Mo's cool view of the world? She is only there to observe, after all ... 'A tough exploration of solitude and sexual need ... When I put the book down I needed air' – *New Statesman*

FOR THE BEST IN PAPERBACKS, LOOK FOR THE 🐧

A CHOICE OF PENGUIN FICTION

Money Martin Amis

Savage, audacious and demonically witty – a story of urban excess. 'Terribly, terminally funny: laughter in the dark, if ever I heard it' – *Guardian*

Out of this World Graham Swift

'A family saga, a love story, a moral enquiry, an examination of the twentieth century ... It appeals to the emotions, the intellect and the imagination, and its elegance is as durable as Greek art' – *Scotsman*. 'Deserves to be ranked at the forefront of contemporary literature' – *The New York Times Book Review*

Story of My Life Jay McInerney

'The first year I was in New York I didn't do anything but guys and blow...' 'Fast and sharp, like a newly synthesised stimulant, racing with vernacular speed ... a very good novel indeed' – *Observer*. 'The leader of the pack' – *Time Out*

Glitz Elmore Leonard

Underneath the Boardwalk, a lot of insects creep. But the creepiest of all was Teddy. 'After finishing *Glitz*, I went out to the bookstore and bought everything else of Elmore Leonard's I could find' – Stephen King

Trust Mary Flanagan

Charles was a worthy man – a trustworthy man – a thing rare and old-fashioned in Eleanor's experience. 'A rare and sensitive début ... there is something much more powerful than a moral in this novel – there is acute observation. It stands up to scrutiny. It rings true' – *Fiction Magazine*

A CHOICE OF PENGUIN FICTION

The Radiant Way Margaret Drabble

To Liz, Alix and Esther, fresh from Cambridge in the 1950s and among the most brilliant of their generation, the world offered its riches…'Shows a Dickensian desire to encompass the whole of contemporary British life … Humane, intelligent, engrossing' – *Independent*

Summer's Lease John Mortimer

'It's high summer, high comedy too, when Molly drags her amiably bickering family to a rented Tuscan villa for the hols … With a cosy fluency of wit, Mortimer charms us into his urbane tangle of clues…' – *Mail on Sunday*. 'Superb' – Ruth Rendell

Nice Work David Lodge

'The campus novel meets the industrial novel … compulsive reading' – David Profumo in the *Daily Telegraph*. 'A work of immense intelligence, informative, disturbing and diverting … one of the best novelists of his generation' – Anthony Burgess in the *Observer*

S. John Updike

'John Updike's very funny satire not only pierces the occluded hocus-pocus of Lego religion which exploits the gullible and self-deluded … but probes more deeply and seriously the inadequacies on which superstitious skulduggery battens' – *The Times*

The Counterlife Philip Roth

'Roth has now surpassed himself' – *Washington Post*. 'A breathtaking *tour de force* of wit, wisdom, ingenuity and sharply-honed malice' – *The Times*

A SELECTION OF FICTION AND NON-FICTION

Perfume   Patrick Süskind

It was after his first murder that Grenouille knew he was a genius. He was to become the greatest perfumer of all time, for he possessed the power to distil the very essence of love itself. 'Witty, stylish and ferociously absorbing' – *Observer*

A Confederacy of Dunces   John Kennedy Toole

In this Pulitzer Prize-winning novel, in the bulky figure of Ignatius J. Reilly, an immortal comic character is born. 'I succumbed, stunned and seduced ... a masterwork of comedy' – *The New York Times*

In the Land of Oz   Howard Jacobson

'The most successful attempt I know to grip the great dreaming Australian enigma by the throat and make it gargle' – *Evening Standard*. 'Sharp characterization, crunching dialogue and self-parody ... brilliantly funny' – *Literary Review*

Falconer   John Cheever

Ezekiel Farragut, fratricide with a heroin habit, comes to Falconer Correctional Facility. His freedom is enclosed, his view curtailed by iron bars. But he is a man, none the less, and the vice, misery and degradation of prison change a man...

The Memory of War and Children in Exile: Poems 1968–83   James Fenton

'James Fenton is a poet I find myself again and again wanting to praise' – *Listener*. 'His assemblages bring with them tragedy, comedy, love of the world's variety, and the sadness of its moral blight' – *Observer*

The Bloody Chamber   Angela Carter

In tales that glitter and haunt – strange nuggets from a writer whose wayward pen spills forth stylish, erotic, nightmarish jewels of prose – the old fairy stories live and breathe again, subtly altered, subtly changed.